TONY PARSONS
Return to the High Country

Penguin Books

Penguin Books Australia Ltd
487 Maroondah Highway, PO Box 257
Ringwood, Victoria 3134, Australia
Penguin Books Ltd
Harmondsworth, Middlesex, England
Penguin Putnam Inc.
375 Hudson Street, New York, New York 10014, USA
Penguin Books Canada Limited
10 Alcorn Avenue, Toronto, Ontario, Canada M4V 3B2
Penguin Books (NZ) Ltd
Cnr Rosedale and Airborne Roads, Albany, Auckland, New Zealand
Penguin Books (South Africa) (Pty) Ltd
5 Watkins Street, Denver Ext. 4, 2094, South Africa
Penguin Books India (P) Ltd
11, Community Centre, Panchsheel Park, New Delhi 110 017, India

First published by Penguin Books Australia Ltd 2001

1 3 5 7 9 10 8 6 4 2

Design by Debra Billson, Penguin Design Studio
Cover photography courtesy of Getty Images
Typeset in 12/14pt Garamond by Midland Typesetters, Maryborough, Victoria
Printed and bound in Australia by McPherson's Printing Group, Maryborough,
Victoria

National Library of Australia
Cataloguing-in-Publication data:

Parsons, A. D. (Anthony David), 1931–.
Return to the high country.

ISBN 0 14 029173 3.

I. Title.

A823.3

www.penguin.com.au

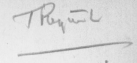

PENGUIN BOOKS

Return to the High Country

A.D. 'Tony' Parsons has worked as a professional sheep and wool classer, an agricultural journalist, a news editor and rural commentator on radio, a consultant to major agricultural companies, and an award-winning stud breeder of many animals. He owned his first kelpie dog in 1944, and in 1950 he established Karrawarra, one of the top kelpie studs in Australia, and bred the first of his many trial winners in 1954. In 1992 he was awarded the Order of Australia Medal for his contribution to the propagation of the Australian kelpie sheepdog.

Since 1947 he has published hundreds of articles, many in international publications, as well as several technical books, including three on the working kelpie. He is also a short-story writer and columnist. *The Call of the High Country*, his first novel, was published in 1999. *Return to the High Country* is the long-awaited sequel.

Tony lives with his wife, Gloria, in Queensland, where he still breeds and shows merino stud sheep and maintains a stud of kelpies.

For Gloria

Author's Note

I was completely blown away by the reception of my first novel, *The Call of the High Country*. It wasn't so much the number of books sold but the comments made by readers that was the most gratifying. A novel may be read twice – it needs to be something special to be read more times than that. Many people told me that they had read my book three times and one Tasmanian sheepman said he had read it half-a-dozen times.

On many occasions as a guest speaker I sought to discover what it was about *The Call of the High Country* that elicited such a response. I found that the reason the book touched so many hearts was because it evoked memories of past years on farm and station. This could be summed up by the comment of one female reader who wrote, 'This is the first book I have read that takes me back to my days on the property. I can see myself in the situations you have created.'

This was heady stuff for a writer, and was compounded by innumerable requests for another 'High Country' book. So here is the sequel to *The Call of the High Country*. In my humble opinion this is perhaps a more significant book than the first one because the young David MacLeod has grown up and moved on, and is faced with the kind of problems known only too well by many of today's farmers and graziers.

I cannot overstate my admiration for the many rural women who left comfortable homes to live in isolated places where they reared admirable families and contributed in countless ways to support their menfolk on the land. They did not walk away when things got tough. Some of these women are the inspiration for the women in this book.

I am indebted to my wife Gloria who, when I was furiously busy with other matters, sketched out some ideas for this book. Through good times and bad she has always been there for me and this book is dedicated to her. At times she made all the difference to getting through.

I owe special thanks to my American friend of nearly forty years, Doctor Jack Woolsey of Santa Rosa, California – distinguished veterinarian and thoroughbred authority and the most significant US importer and breeder of kelpies in my lifetime. Jack was good enough to supply me with some ideas plucked from his extensive casebook of equine problems. I am especially grateful to Jack Woolsey for his support and friendship over many years.

It would be remiss of me not to mention the great support I have received from the wonderful staff at Penguin. It has been a joy to work with Clare Forster, Rachel Scully and Debra Billson. I shall not soon forget the great present they organised for my 70th birthday . . . very special people.

Finally, I am so very grateful for all the letters, faxes and phonecalls that followed publication of *The Call of the High Country*. I answered each and every one. I sincerely hope you like *Return to the High Country* just as much.

Tony Parsons, OAM
East Greenmount, Queensland

Prologue

A pall of gloom enveloped High Peaks in the immediate aftermath of Andrew MacLeod's death. Naturally, the MacLeod family were the most affected, but messages of condolence came to High Peaks from all over the country. The letter from Andrew's old shearing contractor touched the family deeply:

> *For my money, Andy MacLeod was the best shearer I ever saw. He was also the straightest man I ever met. Gil Henderson.*

Even people who had always thought of Andrew MacLeod as 'a hard old bastard' acknowledged that he had been a man among men. The Australian reverence for physical toughness – manifested in Andrew MacLeod's case by his achievements at High Peaks, by the fact that he was the best and fastest shearer in the district and by his scrapping ability – found expression

1

in the battler trying to make something of a hill-country property.

Upon Andrew MacLeod's death his neighbour, Angus Campbell of Inverlochy, donated a substantial sum to the Merriwa Show Society for the purpose of naming their Open sheepdog trial the Andrew MacLeod Memorial Trial, in honour of the great man. This generous gesture was deeply appreciated by the MacLeod family, although they were in too much shock to focus on much beyond the basic day-to-day tasks of running their properties.

In the beginning there had been only High Peaks, a hill-country property nestled in the Liverpool Range, which is part of the Great Dividing Range that runs from Victoria in the south to north Queensland. Locally, it's known simply as 'the range'. The highest peak of the Liverpool Range is Mount Oxley, and while at 4500 feet it doesn't come close in grandeur to the highest peaks of the Monaro country, it's rugged and spectacular and awesome in its beauty. Merriwa, a bustling little town full of historic charm, is the closest town to High Peaks. Over the range lies the village of Willow Tree on the New England Highway, just a few miles on the Sydney side of Quirindi. Forty miles north of Quirindi is the city of Tamworth.

Andrew MacLeod had been raised on High Peaks single-handedly by his mother, a strong, high-principled woman who had been left there when her husband joined the Second AIF to fight in the Middle East, and was subsequently away for years. Andrew grew up to be a tall, powerfully built man who could swing an axe all day, shear a sheep with the best in the business, and break in the wildest of horses. He was also admired far and wide for his skill in breeding and training kelpie sheepdogs.

Good dogs and good horses are essential requirements to anyone grazing animals in the range country. The High Peaks property was close to 4000 acres and its highest country ran up to a peak called Yellow Rock, which dominated the property, and named because of the many split and shattered rocks that littered its slopes. Yellow Rock had an equivalent peak on the adjoining property, Poitrel.

The hill country isn't a place for slackers. It's too steep for farming, and requires a lot of ringbarking for grass to be grown. So for young Andrew MacLeod there was green timber to be rung and fencing to maintain. There was also shearing and crutching and, under the tutelage of his mother's old manager, Paddy Covers, Andrew soon learnt how to handle all these jobs on his own. To earn extra money, he also shore and crutched at other properties in the district. He broke in horses for people and sold started or partly trained dogs. Nobody could work harder or longer than Andrew MacLeod.

A descendant of the MacLeods of western Scotland, Andrew had a great love of land. His dream was to acquire more land for the children he hoped to have one day when he found the right woman to become his wife. Andrew found her in Anne Gilmour, a spirited schoolteacher who came to Merriwa from Sydney and fell in love with the high country as well as with Andrew MacLeod. But together they had only one child, David. The boy was cast very much in his father's mould, with a passion for the land and a love of dogs and horses. Like his father, he became an expert handler of both animals.

The first step towards achieving Andrew's dreams for property expansion occurred because of the generosity of a neighbour, Wilf White, who allowed the MacLeods to purchase his property, Poitrel, on very good terms. Wilf, a thoroughbred breeder and fanatic, knew that Andrew MacLeod would continue to look after his horses. Andrew's word was his bond. He shore Wilf's sheep and didn't ask for payment until the wool was sold. Wilf also had a tremendous regard for Andrew's son, David, and as a parting gift presented him with his great young race mare, Ajana.

With the purchase of Poitrel, the MacLeods formed the High Peaks Pastoral Company. But the acquisition of Poitrel ultimately came at a great cost. All the available funds earned by High Peaks were needed to pay off the bank. Andrew went back to shearing in Queensland to earn extra money where, true to his nature, he tried to 'ring' every shed. This led, eventually, to his first stroke.

The second step in the expansion of the High Peaks empire came when Andrew's longtime mate Tim Sparkes willed his Queensland cattle property, Aberfeldy, and a quarter of a million dollars, to David. Now a young man eager to carve his own place in the world, this acquisition guaranteed David's future and gave him such equity that no bank would fail to back him. Just as importantly, his improved status made a substantial difference to the way he was regarded by Angus and Jane Campbell, whose daughter, Catriona, David proposed to wed.

The purchase of another property, Glen Morrison, not long before Andrew MacLeod's death would have given him a lot of satisfaction. Advantageously situated across the road from Poitrel, Glen Morrison was to become the jewel in the string of properties owned by the High Peaks Pastoral Company.

Although Andrew MacLeod lived to see his son's marriage to Catriona Campbell, his death occurred while David and Catriona were away on their honeymoon. When the newlyweds arrived home and Anne broke the tragic news of Andrew's death to their son, David was deeply affected. Anne said later that if David had not had Catriona, he would have retreated into a shell of gloom.

Anne kept a close eye on her son following her husband's death. She realised, even more than Catriona, what his father had meant to David, and was determined to prevent David from slipping into depression. She would find David sitting on Nap's log kennel, staring out into the distance. The big red-and-tan dog would be lying with head on crossed paws watching David's every move. Across at another kennel, the famous National Trial winner, Clancy, another red-and-tan, also lay watching the silent man. In earlier times David might have been watching the eagles soaring above Yellow Rock but, if they were there now, he gave them no thought. While Andrew MacLeod lay buried on their knoll, it seemed that all of High Peaks was in mourning.

It took time for David to shake off the emptiness that filled his soul as he tried to come to terms with the fact that his father – his inspiration for so many years – was gone, and that he would never speak with him again. He realised that it had been work that had hastened his father's death. For all of his life his father had worked his guts out to pay off the debt on High Peaks, and then to purchase Poitrel. His father had worked so hard for David, so that he, David, would have a future free of the spectre of debt that had hung over High Peaks for so many years. Andrew MacLeod had left his son a legacy that David now had to protect and, indeed, improve upon. The MacLeods could no longer be regarded as battlers by people like Angus and Jane Campbell. For with High Peaks, Poitrel, Glen Morrison and Aberfeldy to their name, the MacLeods were among the more substantial landowners in the high country.

Chapter One

For the first month or so after his father's death, David rarely smiled. His young bride, Catriona, meanwhile, walked on eggshells. Then, one morning, David looked across the breakfast table at Catriona and smiled weakly. 'I'm sorry, sweetheart. I must have been miserable company since the funeral. I'll try and make it up to you, Cat.'

'You don't have to apologise about anything, darling. I know what your father meant to you. I'm just glad I could be here for you. There are going to be many rough patches we'll have to face together, but we'll weather them,' Catriona said.

'I didn't imagine we'd have something like this to cope with so soon, Cat. It's not the sort of thing a young bride needs,' David said, as he reached across and took her hand.

'As long as I'm with you it doesn't matter, David. It's been tougher on Anne than on me. She's lost her husband and lifelong mate. I've watched how she's tried to help you. God, your mother is strong. Of all the women I've ever met, it's Anne I admire the most. She's never changed from the first time I can remember her, she's always been so kind to me,' Catriona said.

'Mum had an ulterior motive, Cat. She had her eye on you for me. I always knew that. Dad used to tell her to wake up to herself, that your father would never allow you to marry me,' David teased, with a glimmer in his eye.

'I was in awe of your father, darling, I really was. He was so big and strong, and kind of overpowering. When I went over the ledge that day so long ago and Andrew came down to get me I knew I would be all right. I knew that the mountain couldn't defeat Andrew MacLeod. He would touch me on the head sometimes and, when he did, I thought he might like me just a little and not think me a nuisance like his son did,' Catriona said, and smiled.

'Yes, I did think you were a nuisance, Cat. Actually, I told Mum you were a little pest. But I still liked you in an odd kind of way. I didn't think much of girls at the time, but you were the pick of the bunch. Later, I came to like you a lot more. I knew I'd have a battle with your folks to win you and that I'd have to let things simmer for a while. It was poor old Tim Sparkes who made the difference. If I hadn't inherited Aberfeldy I would have had a tougher battle with your people. I had to dress Angus down very severely, Cat. I hope he's forgiven me, because I might have to do it again

8

from time to time,' David said, and laughed, albeit weakly.

To hear her husband laugh again warmed Catriona's heart. 'Oh, I think Daddy has forgiven you. You're a man of substance now, as well as his son-in-law. David, But I think you should go and see Anne and tell her that you're all right. She's been very worried about you and you seem to have forgotten that Anne is grieving too. She has kept her own grief hidden while trying to help you. Tell her that you'll be all right. You will, won't you, darling?'

'Yes, I'll be all right, Cat. I've got you, haven't I? Life has to go on. There's also Mum, Kate and Jean to think of. Dad wouldn't want it any other way. He wouldn't want me to mope about and feel sorry for myself. Dad didn't bust himself so I could let him down. Well I won't, Cat. We'll build an empire of properties and we'll breed some of the best sheep and cattle in the country – not to mention the dogs and horses. And we'll need children, Cat; children who want to stay in the bush and run properties and live decent lives,' David said.

'Are you thinking of doing something about that right now?' Catriona asked, and blushed slightly.

'Not right now, Cat. Look, I'm sorry if I haven't been as loving as I should have been. I'll make it up to you. I want us to have some time to ourselves before there are children. I'll go and see Mum and after lunch we'll go over to Glen Morrison and then call in on Jean. There's so much to do, Cat.'

Catriona was immensely relieved to see David's old spirit re-emerging. Anne had told her he would come right and it now seemed that he had. David had been so loving and wonderful on their honeymoon that it had been something of a letdown to have him so depressed since they arrived back at High Peaks. If Catriona hadn't known of the special relationship that existed between David and his father, she would have been even more concerned about her husband's behaviour. Now, as she watched David walk up through the dog yards to the old High Peaks homestead, she felt that everything was going to be all right. It had taken a little while to absorb that she was David's wife, which had been her dream since she was a small girl. What she also realised, even before her marriage, was that she would need to demonstrate the same kind of strength that made Anne such a very worthwhile person. David would expect no less from her.

David and Catriona's new house on the High Peaks property had been completed before their wedding, to Catriona's specifications. Her plans grew from the three-bedroom dwelling David had in mind to a five-bedroom family home with a big kitchen and large windows overlooking the picturesque range country of High Peaks. The front verandah was gauzed in – a place where she and David could relax over the years; the fireplace in the lounge room was of Mudgee stone and the large playroom had a mural of animals and bush fairies across one wall. This new house stood about 200 metres from the original High Peaks homestead where Anne lived, separated by the old orchard and the dog yards.

Anne heard her son's boots on the front steps and detected an urgency that had been missing since Andrew's funeral. Her heart beat fractionally faster and then her spirits lifted as she heard David call out loudly, 'Mum, are you in?'

'I'm not deaf, David,' she answered. 'Is something wrong?'

'Nothing's wrong. I've just realised how selfish and inconsiderate I've been towards you. I've been feeling sorry for myself and not taking into account how you must be feeling.'

'I've always known how much Andy has meant to you, David, but he meant just as much to me, only more. Andy was the only man I ever wanted, the only man I ever loved . . . It's always hard to come to terms with the loss of a loved one but life has to go on, David. You've lost your old mate but you're married now, and you must not neglect your wife. Especially such a new wife as Catriona. She has been very worried about you.'

David picked up his mother and kissed her. 'Yes, Dad was my mate but you're the rock my life has been built on. No matter what happened, or how I felt, you've always been there for me. If it had been you that had passed away, I would have been just as devastated as I have been since Dad died. But Dad wouldn't have wanted me to grieve for him; he would have wanted me to get on with the job. And that's what I'm going to do. We're heading over to Glen Morrison after lunch and calling in at Poitrel on the way back. Will you come with us, Mum?'

'I think you should check with Catriona before you ask me to accompany you anywhere – at least for a while. Some new brides object to that sort of thing, David.'

'Catriona suggested it, Mum. She said it would be nice to get you out of the house for a while. Catriona is your greatest fan . . . after me,' he said with a smile.

Thank goodness he can smile again, Anne thought. 'That's very kind of her. Please thank her for me. Shall I make up some smoko? Kate is usually too busy to spend much time cooking.'

The Glen Morrison property had been acquired not long before Andrew MacLeod's death. It was on the other side of the road from Poitrel and its front paddocks faced the road from Inverlochy to Poitrel and Strath Fillan. It was a sweeping property of over 4000 acres which ranged from a fairly steep back end through undulating hills to flatter and heavier black-soil country. David had cut off 220 acres of the steepest country for sale to his friend Sergeant Lew Hooper so that the policeman could indulge his life-long dream of breeding thoroughbreds. Lew Hooper was a disciple of Wilf White who had bred some great thoroughbreds on Poitrel before he sold the property to the MacLeods. The lower, heavier country of Glen Morrison was unsuitable for horse breeding because it spread hoofs, but the upper section was almost ideal for the purpose. Hooper planned to build a house and horse buildings not far up from the main road. David reckoned it was a good investment having Lew Hooper there as he was the right man to keep an eye on both Poitrel and Glen Morrison.

The acquisition of this property was regarded by David as a very important step in his plans to build a group of properties for the family he hoped to have. Glen Morrison was to be the main base of the Hereford and merino studs he planned for the future. It would also be used for topping off drafts of his Queensland cattle. Oats grew well on the flatter country and he would put down a fair area of lucerne. David had approached Kate Gilmour, his aunt, to manage the property. Anne's sister Kate had been a theatre sister before she came to live at High Peaks and proved herself an asset on the property, spirited and hard-working.

The Glen Morrison homestead was a charming old home with a wide verandah on the front of the house and down one side. David had had it repainted and made some alterations when Kate had said she proposed to live there. The rooms were large and the ceilings high, and the house was always scented with the flowers Kate had picked.

'I thought you'd want to keep on living with Jean at Poitrel. Won't she be lonely on her own? Won't you?' David quizzed Kate when he put the proposition to her.

'I shall be too busy to be lonely, David. The truth

is that I think I am a wee bit superfluous at Poitrel.'

'What on earth do you mean?' David asked.

'I'm getting in the road, David. Jean has a suitor,' Kate said, and winked.

'I thought she hated men – that she went to Poitrel to get away from men. Jean told me she had had enough the first time,' David said.

Kate sighed. 'That's all very fine until next time. Women might say they hate men but there's always a man they don't hate. Women are supreme optimists, David. They want to be loved and always believe the next man will be *the* one. Jean is a very sweet person. She is one of the sweetest-natured women you will ever find. I reckon I'll just give her a bit of elbow room. It's not that I'll be far away, and you're there quite often.'

As David, Catriona and Anne drove up to the Glen Morrison gate they saw Sergeant Hooper hard at work digging post-holes for the entrance to his new property. The big man was sweating freely as he shovelled out earth from one of the large holes. Two massive gateposts and their strainers were lying close by. The back of the Sergeant's Holden utility was full of assorted gear, including a new Stihl chainsaw.

'My day off,' he said, as the High Peaks trio got out of their utility and walked over to him. 'Reckoned I'd better make a start. I'll try and do a bit every chance I get. Do some internal fencing next so I can kick off with a mare or two. How's things, anyway?'

'Life's been a bit bleak since the funeral, Sergeant,' David answered. 'We're only just getting back into the swing of things. We're going to see Kate, and then Jean.'

Hooper screwed up his eyes and pointed towards the Glen Morrison homestead. 'Kate told me she had a shed to clean out. Reckoned it hadn't been cleaned out for God knows how long. She's a goer, that Kate. She tells me you've given her the job of managing Glen Morrison.'

David nodded. 'I have big plans for Glen Morrison. Look, Sergeant, I'll talk to Wilf White and see if he'd be agreeable to you taking over some of those brood mares he left with us. He'd know which ones would suit you best. It would save you a fair bit of money, Sergeant.'

'That's damned decent of you, David. Can't you use them?'

'We've mated them to stockhorse sires but there are quite a number of them, some now getting old. I wouldn't let them go without Wilf's say-so, because it was a condition of our purchase of Poitrel that the horses remain with us while they lived. But I should think Wilf might be pleased to know some of the mares were going to be used for breeding thoroughbreds.'

Hooper scratched the back of his neck and reddened slightly. 'Well, er, that would be a big help. You've already helped so much I feel damned embarrassed to accept any more. I'm afraid I can't do anything in return.'

'Don't feel you have to, Sergeant. There's more to life than money. One day we may need your help. Kate, being a neighbour, could need it any old time. Personally, I wish you were living here right now. I'll be very relieved to have you here,' David said.

'The missus and I thought we might put a caravan out here and stay overnight now and again. By the way, I wish you'd all call me Lew,' Hooper said.

'Be pleased to, Lew. What does Mrs Hooper think of all this?' David asked, and pointed up the slope.

'Paula is pleased as punch. She was a rider too, David. Not had much chance with me being moved around. We always talked about having a small place and some horses. Paula used to come with me when I went out to Wilf's. The old bugger used to load us up with vegetables and cream. Er . . . excuse me, ladies.'

'That's all right, Lew. I've heard the word before,' Anne said, and smiled.

'And I've heard my father use far worse, Lew,' Catriona added.

Hooper looked embarrassed again. The MacLeods were so damned decent. A lot of people had no time for coppers, often regarded as a necessary evil. He reckoned David MacLeod had the makings of a great man. Sure, he'd proven himself to be a great dog and horse man already, but he was going to do bigger things one day. And wasn't Catriona a great-looking young woman.

'If there is any way I can help you, just ask,' Hooper said.

'We might just do that,' David said. 'But for now we'll leave you to your post-holes, Lew. I'll talk to Wilf about the mares and get back to you.'

They climbed into the utility and drove back to the gate of Glen Morrison. 'I don't think Sergeant Hooper can believe his luck,' Anne said. 'I doubt anyone has ever given him much in his career as a police officer. He's such an intimidating man people would find it hard to get close to him.'

'You are probably right, Mum. I think he's a good man. He'll make a very good neighbour.'

They found Kate where Hooper had said she would be – in the middle of a large multi-purpose shed, her clothes covered in dust. There were piles of assorted rubbish outside the shed and, inside, other piles which suggested some degree of usefulness. The shed's interior looked as if it hadn't been cleaned out since Adam was a boy. Kate's background as a theatre sister meant that she detested mess and disorder, but this was a herculean task.

Kate straightened up and supported her back as the High Peaks trio came into the shed. 'Whew, this is some job,' she said.

'Kate, you don't have to do this. It's too big a job for you,' David told her.

'If I don't do it, who will? Besides, I've discovered some really useful things here. There's rolls of wire, drench guns, and even an electric motor. I'll toss out all the useless stuff and put everything else in some kind of order. There are tools galore and a big box of nails – not to mention the countless horseshoes. It's too good a shed to be cluttered up like it is. How are you, Catriona?' she added.

'Very well, thank you, Kate,' Catriona answered with a smile. She had once been rather intimidated by Kate.

'You certainly look very well,' Kate said, and Catriona blushed slightly. 'Which is more than I do right now. I suppose you'd like some arvo tea?'

'We've brought it with us, Kate,' Anne said.

'Thank goodness. I haven't done much cooking since I moved in. Gee, I hate mess. What's the point of having things you can't find?'

'I'll come over tomorrow and give you a hand, Kate,' David said. 'There are some improvements I want to talk over with you. I also want to have a look at the paddocks.'

Glen Morrison had been destocked for some time. David could have purchased the sheep and cattle that had been running on the place when he took it over, but declined the offer. The property had been grassing up for some months and David reckoned the spell would have done the country a power of good. What he wanted to do now was see Angus Campbell and find out if he would sell him some Hereford cattle to kick off the stud David planned. He also wanted to purchase a stud ewe flock, as soon as he could locate the right sheep, to be pastured on Glen Morrison with the Herefords.

Poitrel was about seven miles' drive from High Peaks. As it adjoined High Peaks, most of Poitrel was similar country except for one great valley, which was like a massive amphitheatre. This was where Wilf White had grazed his brood mares and, in his younger years, where he had grown lucerne. The valley had been resown to lucerne very soon after the MacLeods acquired the property.

The Poitrel homestead was a large, rambling timber construction with a galvanised iron roof that was painted green, while the rest of the house was painted white. It was surrounded on three sides by large verandahs – one at the front and back, and the third verandah facing the vegie patch. There was a large meat room under an old, massive fig tree. Fig trees were atypical of the area but this particular tree had grown to heroic proportions and provided coolness on even the hottest of days. The meat room was equipped with a large wooden chopping block of apple gum. It was here, too, that the milk was separated.

The homestead was surrounded on three sides by lawn and shrubs, all enclosed by a six-foot fence erected to keep out grazing animals and the multifarious species of poultry that ranged the property. A second six-foot fence enclosed the extensive vegie patch, which you could walk straight into from the verandah. Wilf White had devised an ingenious system of watering sweet corn and vine crops by diverting water from a stream, blocked by a single sheet of galvanised iron. When the iron was removed the water spread out over the vine patch and provided a solid watering.

Beyond the homestead were the stables, feed sheds and then, a little further away, the sheep yards and an old shearing shed, which was seldom used these days. The sheep yards were new and had replaced the old yards that had been there when the MacLeods purchased Poitrel. As Kate said, the stables laughed at the wool shed and yards, which clearly indicated where Wilf White's preference lay.

Poitrel was a merino wether property, although it also ran some Hereford breeders. When the MacLeods bought Poitrel, Wilf White tossed the cattle into the bargain. These were a very mixed lot, which David gradually culled out, but initially they had been thankful to have the cattle because anything that turned in money wasn't to be sneezed at.

The front gate into Poitrel very nearly faced the front gate into Glen Morrison on the other side of the road. Its closeness to Poitrel had been a major factor in the MacLeods' decision to acquire it. While not as spectacular as High Peaks or Poitrel, Glen Morrison was a much better property because, except for the 200-odd acres David had cut off for Lew Hooper's thoroughbred stud, it was virtually all bottom or cultivable land.

They drove from Glen Morrison to Poitrel, to find Jean, bucket in hand, feeding the large poultry population. Despite the inroads made by foxes, the poultry numbers never seemed to suffer. Hens sat in peculiar places and brought out large clutches of chickens.

Like Kate, Jean Courteney was a nursing sister. Jean had come to live at Poitrel with Kate after she divorced her husband. Anne found her a singularly tranquil woman, nothing seemed to bother her. Jean and Kate had trained together in Sydney and got on extremely well. Jean had married, while Kate's one attempt at romance had been a total failure. Jean's marriage foundered on alcohol and abuse, while Kate had journeyed hither and thither in Australia and overseas before deciding that High Peaks might give her what she was seeking. If Anne had not married Andrew MacLeod, Kate would have snapped him up quick sticks.

Jean's husband had been a presentable fellow when not drinking but eventually Jean decided she could take no more of his criticism and abuse. She left Sydney for the nursing position in Merriwa and for years didn't look at another man, though she had the highest respect for Andrew and David MacLeod. Jean simply loved to potter about the animals and poultry. As soon as she arrived home from being on duty at the hospital, she would change from her uniform to jeans or shorts and poke off to feed and water calves or lambs or chickens or turkeys or whatever there was that needed attention. Any unusual noise would send her outside and armed with a .410 searching for snake or goanna.

Years later, as he looked back at the way things

had developed, David knew that he could not have had two more devoted or diligent people, male or female, to watch over Poitrel and Glen Morrison. Jean was also a very capable cook and David had never gone short of a feed any time he called at Poitrel. Kate was more rough and ready in the food line. She would come in a few minutes before lunch, throw a few ingredients together, and then be gone again. Jean made lovely cakes and biscuits and enjoyed it when David praised her cooking. The two women were a complete contrast, too, when it came to gardening. Kate would dig a bed for some vegetable or other and then leave it to Jean to plant and minister to the plants. Both women, though, were terrific when it came to looking after sick animals. Once, one of Wilf's old mares ripped herself on wire, making a real mess of one side and shoulder. Kate, with her training as a theatre sister, really came into her own. With Jean as her assistant, she stitched and stitched and stitched until she had all the rips attended to. Then she dusted the wounds with antibiotic powder, gave the mare a feed of chaff and oats, washed her hands and was ready for the next job. No wonder David came to love his aunt. He actually loved both Kate and Jean, but he regarded Kate as a kind of second mother.

'What's this I hear about you having a new Mr Wonderful?' David asked.

Jean was a mite too old to blush, and in fact she took David's question in her stride.

'I don't know that Julian is any Mr Wonderful, but I think he is a very nice man, and I would like to build a life with him. His name is Julian Miller. He hasn't moved here because I felt he shouldn't until I talked to you. I know very well what kind of principles you live by and that you might be affronted by me living with a man out of wedlock. It's not that I am against marrying Julian, but I had such a bad run last time that I want to be sure this time. I could go and live with Julian but I love it here. Poitrel has been the best home I've ever had, with you people and the animals. I don't want to leave, and Julian thinks enough of me to live here with me. I'd still help out if you needed me to at any time.'

David looked at his mother and his wife, and Anne instinctively knew that he wanted her to answer for them. 'I'm sure that Julian is a very nice man. You must continue to think of Poitrel as your home, Jean.'

'Thank you, Anne. I wasn't sure how you would regard such an arrangement. I would like the opportunity to live in partnership with a good man before I pass on.'

'You've been holding out on us, Jean,' David said severely.

'Not really, David. I was going to say something months ago but there was all the excitement of the National and then the wedding and Andy's death. I know what Andy meant to you all and I couldn't worry you while you felt so down,' Jean said apologetically.

'David is only pulling your leg, Jean. We appreciate why you didn't mention the matter. I must say I am dying to hear how you met this lovely man,' Anne said.

'Julian was painting landscapes around Mudgee and he had an accident on the way to Merriwa. I nursed him at the hospital. That's how it began. Julian came here and he loves this place as much as I do, but he told me he wouldn't come to live with me here unless you agreed. I told him you were seven-feet high, as wide as a barn and ate artists for breakfast,' Jean said, and winked at Catriona.

'Has Kate met this chap?' David asked.

'She has. Kate thinks he's a good man. Not, she told me, that you can judge a man on a couple of meetings. Kate has chosen to live at Glen Morrison to give us more space,' Jean informed them.

'Imagine that,' David said, and tried to keep a straight face.

'Kate didn't say anything?' Jean asked with raised eyebrows.

'Kate was covered in dust and cleaning out a big shed filled with fifty years of everything,' David answered. 'Kate hasn't got some fellow hidden away, has she?'

'David!' Anne remonstrated.

'Well, for a confirmed man-hater you've surprised me, Jean. But women keep surprising me, so why shouldn't you? Time to go, ladies. One shock for the day is enough for me.'

'Can I kiss him, Catriona?' Jean asked.

'I'm sure David would love that. I've found that he likes to be kissed. Of course, it doesn't go with his image; the big tough bushman and all that.'

'Ha, Tim Sparkes was a big tough bushman and he told me not to let you go, Cat,' David laughed.

Anne and Catriona looked at each other. They hadn't seen David this happy since Andrew was alive.

Jean took his face between her hands and kissed him. 'If I had had a son I would have wanted him to be exactly like you, David,' Jean said.

'Now you've done it, Jean,' Anne said. 'David will have a swollen head for weeks.'

'It can't be helped, Anne. I've been wanting to say it for years.'

'I take it we will be invited to meet this paragon of manhood when he moves here?' David asked.

'Of course you will,' Jean said.

'Very well, Sister Courteney. We'll leave you. I am in a state of shock and will need a lot of wifely ministrations to get over it,' David said.

'Which I'm sure you will receive,' Jean said quickly.

'Well, I must say it's been a surprising afternoon,' David said, as they drove up the road towards the Inverlochy–High Peaks turn-off. 'Imagine Jean, of all people, with a secret admirer.'

'And why shouldn't she have a secret admirer?' Anne asked.

'Jean has always said she came to Poitrel to get

25

away from men. She said she had had enough of men,' he said.

'That's only until the right man comes along, David. Jean is looking for companionship now. I'm very pleased for her. I would prefer her to marry this Julian fellow but things are different now. Maybe in Jean's case it's once bitten, twice shy. It's a lot easier to get into marriage than out of it,' Anne said.

Later, Anne would say that the day Jean Courteney informed them of her Julian was the day that David climbed out of the depression caused by his father's death. From that day on David MacLeod never took a backward step.

Chapter Two

It could be said that David MacLeod's life was actually divided into two parts. The first part concluded when he won the National Trial with Clancy. Up till then his whole life had been consumed by kelpies and his desire to win the National for his father. After he had won the trial he married Catriona and, shortly afterwards, lost his father. Once David's grief subsided, he then concentrated most of his efforts on acquiring more properties and building up prominent studs of sheep and cattle for the children he hoped to have. His vision was to create a great pastoral family that would be recognised throughout the land because of the quality of its livestock. He would build the foundations so that by the time his children were old enough to take an interest in showing sheep and cattle, the standard of the family's livestock would be high enough to allow them to compete anywhere.

Two days after visiting Glen Morrison, David laid

out his grand design to Catriona. It was the first time he had really opened his heart to her about his plans for their future since his father's funeral. David was back in full flight again.

'The first thing I want is some Hereford breeders from Angus,' he told Catriona. 'They can be older cows, but they must be good. Then I'll buy a good bull to put over them and keep the pick of the heifers.'

'You can ask Daddy for the Herefords on Saturday evening, darling. We've been invited for dinner. We would have been invited sooner except that you have been so down in the dumps I asked them to delay the invitation,' Catriona told him.

'Sorry, sweetheart. I realise I've been a bit of a wet blanket since the funeral. Hardly the ideal husband for a new bride,' he said, and kissed her several times.

'There's nothing to make up, darling. Losing a parent is never easy, let alone a father who meant as much to you as Andy did. Don't forget that I know you almost as well as Anne does. Andy was my main competition for your time and love. His passing is a big loss. I would have been very surprised if you had reacted otherwise,' Catriona said.

'What a girl,' he said.

'It took you a long while to realise that, darling,' she replied, and rubbed her hair against his face.

'That's ancient history, Cat. All I will say on the matter is that I am damned glad you stood up to your parents and didn't marry one of those swanky fellows they had their eyes on for you,' David said firmly.

'Oh, I was never going to do that, darling.'

Catriona was secretly pleased to hear that David was going to breed stud sheep and cattle because that meant trips away to shows and sales. She was determined that her husband was not going to kill himself with work as his father had done. Of course, David would never have to slave at shearing in oven-hot sheds to pay off a mortgage. But he was a tiger to work and she knew she would have to see that he didn't overdo things. She was also determined that before she began having babies she would persuade David to join her on an overseas trip. She wanted him to see the sheepdog trials in Scotland and meet her Campbell relations, and come back via the United States to look at stud cattle there. She realised that once there were children it would be more difficult to get away.

Inverlochy was one of the first properties to be cut off the famous Collaroy holding, which was one of the two original properties in the Merriwa district established by white colonial settlers. With very little hill country at all, it was high-class land conducive to breeding sheep and cattle. The sandstone homestead stood on a slight rise and presented a grand appearance as one turned in off the road. Wide, gauzed verandahs enclosed the house on three sides. The front steps were sandstone and two large stone lions sat majestically on stone platforms at the base of the steps, guarding the house and its owners. The front door led into a wide hallway, off which branched numerous large rooms distinguished by very high ceilings. The large kitchen was at the rear of the house. Like some other sections of the house, it had been renovated, and now featured a cork floor, which was unique in the district. The lounge room was large and magnificent with a cathedral ceiling and a grand piano in an alcove at one end. On cold nights a huge open fire in the lounge room would blaze. There were seven bedrooms, an office, and a flat for the housekeeper. Below the side verandah two terraces, a portico and a splendid rose garden led down to the tennis court. Beside the main house a huge jacaranda gave summer shade to a variety of garden furniture. Lawns surrounded the homestead and sprinklers kept them green. It was here that Anne MacLeod had met Angus and Jane Campbell, when she had been invited to Inverlochy for a tennis party when she first arrived at Merriwa so many years ago.

Catriona had called her father ahead and told him that David wanted to purchase some stud cows from him, and to ask him if he could see his way clear to letting David have them. So Angus was ready when David made the request.

'All right. How many do you want, David?' Angus answered calmly.

'As many as you can spare, Angus,' David said quickly.

'When do you want them?'

'As soon as I can get them. Glen Morrison has been well spelled and is grassed-up. You tell me when you'll have some ready to go and I'll do the rest. I'd like some from different families if you can manage it,' David added.

Angus nodded. What David knew about livestock continually surprised him. 'So you want to start a stud of Herefords? Merinos too?'

'That's right, Angus. What I thought we might do was pool resources to buy an even better bull. I realise you've always bought good bulls but I mean a real top bull. We could both benefit from him then. By the time our children are old enough, I want to have a top herd and cattle they can show.'

For all his arrogance and high opinion of his place in the community Angus was no fool. He realised he had once seriously underestimated David MacLeod when he had discounted him as a suitor for Catriona. David was now a man of real substance with four properties and he was going places. Nobody could deny that. What he had to do now was support David and Catriona in any way he could, because their children would be his grandchildren. Moreover, with an ancestry of canny forebears, Angus knew a good deal when he saw one.

'What have you got in mind, David?'

'Well, I reckon that if we bought a Sydney winner that ought to focus a lot of attention on what we're doing. If we bought him between us, it might only mean another five or ten thousand more than you're paying for your bulls now.'

Angus saw the wisdom of what David said, and also what the purchase of such a bull would do for his own reputation. Angus Campbell was a very proud man, especially where his livestock were concerned.·

'Let's see what comes up, David. If we see the right bull, we could have a go at him,' Angus said.

'I'm pleased you agree, Cat will be pleased too.' David then dropped his own surprise. 'If you still want to breed a foal from Ajana, we'll send her to a thoroughbred next time, Angus, to return the favour.'

Angus was temporarily taken aback. He thought he had made a couple of significant concessions to his new son-in-law, but the young fellow had come straight back at him with something that was dear to his heart. Angus had bred some fair thoroughbreds, but never a champion racehorse. One of his great ambitions was to breed and race a champion horse. Ajana had won in Sydney – one in race record time – and that old fool Wilfred White had given the mare to David, who had bred her to stockhorse stallions. In Angus's opinion it amounted to heresy to waste such a mare, but the MacLeods were not thoroughbred-minded. Angus realised that Ajana represented probably the best hope he would ever have of breeding a horse that could win a classic race.

'That's damned generous of you, David.'

'Oh, I don't know. You're letting me have some good cows, hopefully some in calf,' (he added that for good measure), 'so it's not much to let you have the use of a mare to breed a foal. I'll rear the foal and hand it over to you when it's ready to go, as Wilf wouldn't want me to let Ajana leave the property. You got any particular stallion in mind?

'There's a son of Star Kingdom I've bred mares to and he's produced a couple of winners for me. Nothing brilliant, but my mares aren't up to Ajana. She had a lot of speed and there's plenty of that in the Star Kingdom line.'

David nodded. 'Righto. We'll do it. Maybe after you've got your foal I'll mate Ajana to the same sire again. Catriona seems very keen to race a horse, if only for the picnic races. I can't have her getting bored with me and my animals.'

'I doubt there's any danger of that, David,' Angus chuckled.

'Is it going well, dear?' Jane Campbell asked her daughter. The women were talking alone in the lounge room while Angus and David were in the study.

'Very well, Mother. David was very upset for a while after the funeral but he's firing on all fours now. He has very big plans for the future, and of course children feature strongly.'

Jane had not wanted Catriona to marry David MacLeod. Not, that is, until she realised that her daughter would marry him whether she and Angus agreed or not. Jane was from a well-to-do family and placed a lot of emphasis on breeding and social standing; the idea of her only daughter married to a shearer's son was repugnant. She admitted that David was a nice boy and a wonderful-looking fellow, but he had no social standing and had not attended a GPS school. Three times David had rescued Catriona from dangerous situations, but even that was not enough to make him a suitable son-in-law in Jane Campbell's eyes.

It was when Catriona accompanied David to the National Trials that Jane realised the cause was lost and that they had better make the best of the situation or risk losing their daughter's affection. In David MacLeod's favour was the fact that he was probably worth more than she and Angus. He was also the best-looking and most impressively built man in the district. David and Catriona were a splendid couple; they looked made for each other. And Jane thought highly of David's mother, Anne, even if she was not from one of the better families. Anne had been an excellent teacher and could have aimed for a more prosperous match than Andrew MacLeod. Jane knew that for a fact, and remembered the stir Anne had created among possible suitors when she first came to Merriwa to teach. She conceded, though, that Andrew was a very formidable man.

So Angus and Jane Campbell came to accept David MacLeod as their son-in-law and were doing everything they could to enhance David's position in the district. Andrew MacLeod would have been highly amused at this about-face by Angus and Jane. Although Angus had been a good neighbour, both he and Jane clearly looked down on the MacLeods. Angus was the product of inherited wealth; he didn't have to shear or break in horses to help pay off a property and Andrew had never been invited to join Angus for a drink, especially when he was entertaining other graziers. Now, the difference in the Campbells' attitude to David was palpable.

When sheep classing time came around, Angus invited David to come and watch his great sheep classer, Hugh Pfeffer, in action. David came and watched and asked a lot of questions. The great man, one of the finest classers of his time, liked David's enthusiasm and showed him a lot. David learnt the importance of structure, and skin thickness. Years later some of what David had learnt that day would be utilised when he himself judged shows and taught his children. But for now he was looking to add to what he already knew about classing sheep, so that when he bought foundation ewes for his merino stud they would be as good as he could procure.

The improved relationship between the MacLeod and Campbell families meant that Catriona's brother, Stuart, and David got on very well. Despite his schooling and the fact that he was what many would consider a ra-ra man, Stuart was rather in awe of David MacLeod. While David had never been into sport he could ride the pants off just about anyone, and nobody could get near him as a dog handler. Stuart had a secret ambition to be an expert dog handler but neither he nor his father was instinctively a natural stockman. Neither man had a keen eye for a dog and, when they worked a dog on a few sheep, the dogs were always fractionally slow to respond.

A few months after the wedding, Angus took his pride in his hands and asked David how he could improve his dogs and his own handling. It was the largest concession to anyone Angus Campbell had ever made. What Angus wanted almost as much as a classic race winner was a dog or two he could win trials with at the local show. Now he had a son-in-law who was a master handler and master breeder, even though he was only a young man. Angus recognised he'd be a fool not to take advantage of the situation.

'Do you really want my opinion, Angus?' David asked. He was very surprised that Angus had humbled himself so much as to ask for his help.

'That's exactly what I want, David,' Angus replied.

'Well, your dogs aren't really good enough, Angus. They've got too much of the wrong sort of eye and they're always a fraction late in moving. A lot of border collies in Australia have got kelpie in them. What we've got now is a kind of Australian border collie. Bill Marshall used kelpie twice in his borders and he bred some pretty good dogs – dogs that were good sheepdogs, not just trial dogs. I reckon what you should do is mate one of your bitches to one of my sires and keep all the pups. Maybe mate a bitch of that mating back to a good border collie and see how they shape. You should get better cover and quicker reactions. You'd get away from these heavier-coated dogs you've been importing.'

Angus was silent as he considered all David said carefully.

David continued, 'To win good trials you've got to devote a fair bit of time to training a dog. I doubt that you've ever done that. If you're prepared to put in more time I'll show you how I break in my dogs, and what you need to do to develop a top trial dog. I won't have the time to devote to dogs in future, so I'll probably just concentrate on one dog at a time.'

'All right, I'll mate one of my bitches to one of your dogs and see how we go,' Angus said. This was a significant concession for Angus to make, as years ago he had rejected Andrew MacLeod's suggestion that the Campbell dogs 'needed a bit o' kelpie in them'.

Angus was agreeably surprised with the quality of his litter sired by Nap. The pups had a lot of natural ability, with good cover and footwork. They were noticeably shorter in coat and a couple had one or both ears erect like their sire. These dogs had a great willingness to work and proved to be excellent all-round sheepdogs. Stuart took a fancy to one of the bitches and prevailed upon David to show him the finer points of training. Stuart was quicker to learn than Angus, and when he won an Encourage Trial with Nellie, his face was wreathed in smiles.

'Mate Nellie or Nan or both with a good border dog and I think you'll find they'll be a bit easier for you to handle, Angus,' David advised. The Nap progeny were terrific sheepdogs and were in high demand, but they were a shade too strong for Angus to handle. What he needed was a pliable, easy-to-handle dog with a lot of natural ability. It took some years to produce this dog, but in the intervening period Stuart won an Improver and then a Maiden Trial.

'It's wonderful that you and Angus are getting on so well, David,' Anne said to her son one morning. He had brought her some meat and was sitting with her for a few minutes on his way to town.

'I suppose so, but Angus is a pain in the neck at times. He's too full of himself and sometimes I'm tempted to tell him so. I'm doing my best for Catriona's sake. And Angus has his good points,' David said.

'Of course he has. Old Angus was a great help to Andy. The Campbells are good people even though they're snobby. That's just the way they were brought up, though Stuart and Catriona are not like that. Is Catriona well?'

'She's very well, Mum. Why do you ask?'

'No particular reason, dear.'

'We go everywhere together. I'm breaking in another horse for her – a nice big bay horse. Cat doesn't know it's for her.'

'That's nice, dear. But you should try and get away a bit, David. Catriona is from a family used to going places. Girls like to meet up with old school friends and talk about babies and men and trips and clothes. You should remember that.'

'We're going to Sydney Royal, Mum. Angus and I might buy a bull in partnership,' David said.

'That is something,' Anne said, and smiled. 'But Sydney Royal is a fair way off.'

'Well, we're going up to Aberfeldy next month and we'll have a day or two at Yeppoon. Would you like to come with us?' he asked.

'Not this time, dear. Maybe next time. That house has lovely memories for me,' Anne said.

'Me too,' David said, and smiled. Both Anne and David had gone to Aberfeldy after idyllic honeymoons on the Queensland coast.

'Being young and in love is the best time of one's life. At least until the first baby comes. That is lovely too, but different. I am sure you and Catriona will have wonderful children. I am so looking forward to my grandchildren.'

'All in good time, Mum. Cat and I want some time together before we start a family.' And then David dropped his bombshell: 'Besides, we are going overseas next year.'

'David, you're not?'

'Too right we are. We're going to Scotland to see dog trials and also some of Cat's relations and I'm going to look at Hereford studs. Then we're going on to the United States and I'm going to look at more Hereford studs. But of course, Cat wants to see more than dog trials and her relations,' David said with a smile.

'But how wonderful, David.'

'After that, we'll come home and start our family. I agreed with Cat's suggestion that if we were going to take a trip we should do it before the children arrive on the scene. Cat is already planning for the trip. So you see, Mother dear, I'm not neglecting my beautiful wife. Greg will be a very competent fellow by then, and Shaun Covers has asked me for a job.'

'Shaun Covers. Is he back?'

Shaun Covers had worked for the MacLeods from time to time before he left for Queensland and the

Northern Territory. Shaun, a son of Andrew MacLeod's old mentor, Paddy Covers, had been with Anne on the never-to-be-forgotten day when the creek came down and she had fallen, which had brought on David's birth. Shaun was a campdrafter of some note but he was also a top stockman and could turn his hand to anything.

'Been back a month or so, Mum.'

'Are you going to employ him?'

'I'm thinking about it. I've a good mind to send him up to Aberfeldy. There's a lot to do there to get the place into shape. I want to sow grasses and do something about improving the cattle. It would be a good idea to have a chap who could take over there, should anything happen to Don Morgan. Then there's always the possibility that Don might be offered a bigger position although he seems happy enough now he's married and has the house on the coast to go to now and then.'

'I do like Shaun, dear. I hope you can find a position for him,' Anne said.

'I'm thinking seriously about it. Is Greg Robertson keeping the wood up to you?' he asked.

'Greg is a very nice young man, David. He has dinner with me some nights and we have talked quite a lot about the land. Greg is very keen and wants to learn. He worships the ground you walk on and thinks Catriona is the bee's knees. Are you happy with him?'

'Very happy, Mum. I think Greg is going to be all right,' David said. This conservative answer indicated that Greg Robertson must indeed be going all right because David was never lavish in his praise for anyone or anything.

Greg Robertson was the third son of a couple who had a property a few miles out of Merriwa. There were a couple of older sisters who were married and lived in Sydney. David had noticed Greg at a couple of camp-drafts and been quite impressed with his ability and eagerness. Although he was only eighteen years old, Greg was a good rider. When David heard on the grapevine that Greg was looking for a job he rang and asked Greg to come and see him.

'Crikey, David MacLeod wants me to go and see him, Pa, I think he wants to offer me a job,' Greg said excitedly.

'If you can stand up to what he throws at you, it could be the making of you,' Danny Robertson said.

'What do you mean, Pa?' Greg asked.

'The MacLeods are hard men. Andrew was the toughest man in the district and made a success of High Peaks against all odds. I hear that David is just as tough. He'd have to be to get where he is now,' Danny observed.

'But he got left a big place up in Queensland, didn't he?'

'Yeah, he got left a big cattle place and that made a difference but they had two places before that, High Peaks and Poitrel. Now they've got four properties and David is the boss. He's the best dog and horse man in these parts, and you'd learn a helluva lot from him. But David will expect a lot from you, Greg. Don't go there

41

expecting it will be any holiday,' Danny advised.

'I wouldn't expect it, Pa. But I reckon working for the MacLeods could be the best opportunity I'll ever have. I don't mind work as long as MacLeod is fair,' Greg said.

'I think you'll find that he's fair enough. Andrew was the same. Don't give him any back answers as he's big enough to eat you,' Danny said.

'What do you want to do with your life, Greg?' David asked him. They were sitting on hay bales in the feed shed below the High Peaks homestead.

Greg hadn't thought a great deal about his future. He was enjoying himself competing at campdrafts but he realised that this was a sport and a hobby, and he would need a job. There were two brothers ahead of him on the farm so he would have to make his own way. The younger of the two brothers went away shearing and although Greg could shear, he didn't fancy spending his life sweating over struggling sheep.

'I'd like to become a top stockman and maybe a manager one day,' Greg answered. 'I'm pretty keen on campdrafting but it's only a sport, Mr MacLeod. I'd like to go on competing if I could.'

David nodded. 'Nothing wrong with that, Greg. We can give you a job and if you're made of the right stuff, I'll make a top stockman of you. If you prove yourself, there could be a manager's job down the track. To begin with I'll expect you to do just about anything, which will include chopping wood for my mother and me.

'We'll build you a small cottage next to the home-stead here and you'll have to look after yourself. I'll provide the feed for your horse and I'll see you have a decent dog to work, as I don't want any other dogs here. If you have to work weekends I'll make it up to you. If I ask you to do something I'll expect you to do it – no ifs, buts or maybes. If you have a gripe, see me about it. If I go away, I'll expect you to look after everything. I'll also expect you to work in with Kate Gilmour, whom I think you know. You got any problem with any of this?' David asked.

'None at all, Mr MacLeod,' Greg answered quickly.

'Okay, you've got the job, Greg. There's a spare bedroom at the back of the house where you can stay until we get your cottage built.'

'Thanks, Mr MacLeod. And thanks for the job.'

So Greg had come to High Peaks and he had been with the MacLeod family during the fire and at Andrew MacLeod's funeral, where he had cried for one of the only times in his life. In the period up to Andrew's death, the big man had taught Greg things that were to stay with him for the rest of his days. He often worked long hours but David had made it up to him as he had promised. He gave him Fridays off to attend shows that featured campdrafts, so Greg didn't have a worry in the world.

In the period following Andrew MacLeod's death, Greg was an enormous help. He rode the hills, looked after the stock and chopped big stacks of wood at both houses. He spent some time working on a horse David had said he could use. There were also horses to shoe and Greg was a very capable farrier.

Some nights Anne invited him to have dinner with her. Anne considered Greg a very nice young man and an asset to the High Peaks Pastoral Company. Kate also liked him and they worked well together. So far Greg hadn't shown any interest in girls as horses were his greatest love. But Catriona MacLeod dazzled him: she was the finest-looking woman he had ever laid eyes on, and had the best seat on a horse of any female rider he had seen. He had watched Catriona win Champion Lady Rider at Merriwa, among other places, so knew she had the edge on any other woman in the horse business in the district.

In short, Greg Robertson felt right at home with the MacLeods. He believed that his future lay with this family. David was tough and he had been stern with Greg a couple of times but those incidents had been Greg's own fault. And as Greg's father had said, David was very fair.

For his part, David was very satisfied with Greg Robertson. The young fellow had come on a treat and he reckoned Greg was going to play a valuable role in his plans for the future. Later, he would ask his mother to introduce Greg to the delights of station book-keeping. Anne was still looking after this aspect of the company's business, but David was determined to ease her responsibilities.

When Shaun Covers came to see him, David realised that he had to go forward and that he could not afford to let this good stockman go to some other place.

'How would you feel about going up to Aberfeldy for a while, Shaun?' he asked.

'What have you got in mind, David?' He had been calling the big man David since MacLeod was a small boy.

'The place needs a lot of upgrading, Shaun. Pastures and cattle. Oh, and fencing too. There's a good man there but he was never allowed to do more than routine stuff. The cattle are very yakky but we'll fix that. I want to sow a lot of grasses and build up the nutrition. My idea is to bring selected drafts down to Glen Morrison and top them off there. Think you could look after the pasture job?'

'It could be interesting. Will I get on all right with the manager?'

'Don't see why not. He's got enough to do with three thousand head of cattle. There's a separate cottage I've had renovated. I'll go up ahead of you and look at the whole situation,' David said. 'When you've finished there I might have something for you here. Well, Glen Morrison really. Kate is over there now but there are things that need to be done. It might only be casual work for a while but I'd like to have you with me, Shaun. That's if you've got the travelling itch out of your blood.'

Covers grinned. 'And you wanting me to go to Queensland? Okay, I'll give it a go, David. You tell me when you want me and how I find the place and I'll mooch on up there.'

David put out his hand. 'Good to have you with us, Shaun.'

'I'll go and see your mother, David. After Mum your mother is about my favourite lady.'

David watched Covers as he walked up to the old homestead. The ringer was a man of medium height and he walked with the peculiar gait of a man who had spent most of his life on a horse.

Greg Robertson and Shaun Covers were to be valuable employees for David MacLeod and his pastoral empire.

Chapter Three

David found that his mother's advice about not neglecting Catriona could hardly be justified. If he was not accompanying her to a dinner or afternoon tea at one or other of her friends' places, they were entertaining at High Peaks. David passed up on tennis functions as he had never been interested in sport. There had always been too much of interest at High Peaks to worry about sport.

Susan Cartwright was Catriona's best girlfriend, now married to Michael Hunter, a grazier at Coolah. Susan was the first of Catriona's friends to visit her in her new home, and of course David and Catriona were obliged to return the visit. David noticed that Susan's eyes followed him a lot, and he was aware of more tenderness in her kisses than was perhaps appropriate. He confided this information to his mother, who could always be relied upon to come up with good advice.

'You know that Susan was very keen on you, David.

She would have married you with or without her parents' consent. Susan thought she had a chance with you when you put Catriona off for so long. She is quite a nice girl but was unlucky to have such a lovely girl as Catriona always just that much ahead of her in everything. Catriona is prettier, a better rider, and got the man she wanted who was the best-looking young man in the district – you, David. Girls don't always get the best of things, dear. They don't always marry for love, but sometimes settle upon a husband for convenience. I suspect that is what happened in Susan's case. Maybe Susan is still fond of you, David. You haven't said anything to Catriona?'

'Certainly not. Cat and Susan are still very close friends. Susan was the first of her friends to visit us.'

'Susan hasn't chosen to have a baby yet, but that doesn't mean anything. She is still only a young woman. Do you get on all right with her husband?' Anne asked.

'Michael is a lot friendlier than he used to be. I used to think he was very off-handed, but he's unbent a lot. He's pretty keen on cattle.'

'I should think that owning four properties and being married to Catriona would make a difference to your social standing, David,' Anne said dryly.

'I'm still the same person I always was, Mum. Having money and property shouldn't make a difference to the way people treat you,' David said.

'I'm afraid it does where some people are concerned, dear.'

David knew that one of his mother's cherished

dreams had always been to have a beautiful garden – with walkways and pergolas and a rockery. Not long after he recovered from the loss of his father he determined to provide such a garden for his mother. It would get her mind off Andrew and she could spend as much time as she wanted tending the garden of her dreams. He put the proposition to her.

'Mum, I know you've always wanted a nice garden. I want you to draw me a sketch of what you have imagined for so long so that I can employ a landscape gardener to lay it down just the way you want it. Will you do that?'

'David, I don't expect you to do that for me. I will just expand the garden we have a little myself and that will be enough,' Anne said.

'You'll do no such thing, Mum. You're worth a hundred gardens, so just give me the sketch. In the meantime, I'll get Greg to start collecting rocks so they'll be here when the gardener arrives,' David said firmly.

Anne knew that David meant business. He desperately wanted her to have the garden and he wouldn't rest until it was laid down. Of course, she was excited by the prospect but she didn't want him spending his money on a garden for her, not now he was married.

'Very well, dear. And thank you,' Anne said meekly.

In what seemed a relatively short space of time the old High Peaks homestead had been transformed by the new garden. The vegetable patch and the old orchard, where Anne's fowls loved to scratch and fluff themselves, were retained, but the new garden included terraces, Australian natives, a rockery with variegated grasses and a pergola covered in wisteria. The tall wire fence that enclosed the old homestead was removed from the front and sides and replaced later by a smarter-looking fence that didn't detract from the newly landscaped garden. Of course, the new garden would need a lot of attention, which was one of the major reasons why David was determined to have it done. His mother could potter about in it all day long if she so desired.

'It is beautiful, dear,' she said, as she held his arm under the big pergola. 'It's exactly as I'd hoped to have my dream garden.'

'You've earnt it, Mother dear,' David said.

'A lovely garden and some grandchildren, that's what I've always wanted,' Anne said.

'All in good time, Mum.'

Catriona took a great interest in the planning and laying down of Anne's garden. When it was finished David saw her looking at it rather wistfully.

'I suppose you want a garden now around the new homestead?' he asked.

'It would be lovely, darling. It is rather bare around the house. I'd like a different kind of garden. It would be nice for the children to have a big lawn to play on. And I'd like lots of hakeas and bottlebrushes. They smell so lovely, and bring the birds,' Catriona said.

David was aware that some of the top graziers had impressive gardens to complement their gracious home-steads, and that these gardens were always one of the major topics of conversation when friends gathered.

'All right, Cat. Put down on paper what you have in mind and we'll get his nibs to come back and landscape your garden.'

'Thank you, darling. I'd be happy to pay for it myself but I didn't want to worry you so soon.' David knew that his wife meant after the death of his father. He was also aware that Catriona had sizable funds to her name that had come to her after she turned twenty-one. She was also paid a share of the profits from Inverlochy.

'No need for you to do that,' David said.

So Catriona got her garden, which included a large front lawn and a massive side garden of hakeas, grevilleas and bottlebrushes, all beautiful natives that the birds of the range country loved.

Shortly after Catriona's garden was established an abundance of birds flocked to the home – magpies warbled continuously, kookaburras cackled in the mornings and wild ducks made the sheoak-lined creeks a stopping place. But it was the honeyeaters and wrens that Catriona was most fond of.

During the next few years David concentrated on learning as much as he could about breeding stud sheep and cattle. Under Angus Campbell's tutelage, combined with his own natural ability, he developed an extraordinary knowledge of merino sheep and Hereford cattle. He attended sales and shows and watched and learnt from the different judges and their techniques.

He would pick up a well-bred cow at one sale or a heifer at another, but acquiring good sheep was a harder matter. It wasn't until the reserve price for wool was discontinued that he was able to purchase the kind of sheep he wanted.

During this period, while he was learning from Angus Campbell, David was also coaching both Angus and Stuart in how to work trial dogs. During the long hot summers he would go to Inverlochy late in the evenings and they would run dogs until darkness took over. Angus, at David's suggestion, fenced in his training ground and surrounded it with small trapdoors at different places. The dogs were cast outside the ground and, depending on their age and progress, a different trapdoor would be opened so that they could run onto the ground. This method had been used by one of the great kelpie trainers to develop wider-casting dogs, and it made a big difference to the Inverlochy dogs. Sometimes he and Catriona would stay and have dinner with Angus and Jane. In the winter months David and Catriona would go to Inverlochy on Sundays, because during the cooler weather dogs could be worked at any time of the day.

When Shaun Covers returned after a sojourn of more than six months on Aberfeldy, David gave him a list of things he wanted done on Glen Morrison. There was lucerne to be planted so they would be self-sufficient in hay and chaff, a cattle preparation shed to be built and a covered set of pens or mini-feedlot where David proposed to feed steers. It was important to

David to know just how his cattle were performing. Later, he wanted his children to show steers.

Anne cautioned her son against putting too many hopes in his children.

'They may hate animals, David. You shouldn't expect that they will automatically be in your mould. You will be very disappointed if they don't like animals or even the land.'

David looked at her aghast. 'Not like animals or the land? How could they not, with Dad and me behind them?'

'There are other forebears, David. My people weren't on the land. They are artistic and musical,' Anne said.

'Ha, I'll bet any child of mine is land-minded. The Campbells have been landowners for hundreds of years,' he said.

'That's not quite the same thing, dear. From what I can gather about the Campbell family they were also magistrates, soldiers and government officials. You are expecting any children you and Catriona might have to be cast in your own mould. I'm simply cautioning you against setting your hopes too high and being rigid in your expectations.'

But David had no doubt that *his* children would be land-minded, and based his dreams and future planning on that assumption.

One evening shortly after the two gardens had been completed, he came home to find a smiling Catriona waiting for him. 'Guess what, darling?'

'You're pregnant and we're not going overseas,' he suggested.

'Don't be a wet blanket, darling. I'm not going to fall pregnant until we come back from overseas. No, we've been invited to Poitrel to meet Jean's mystery man. He's moved in.'

'Good heavens. When are we to go?' he asked.

'Sunday, for lunch. It's a kind of buffet lunch. Evidently Julian is quite an accomplished chef. Well, not really a chef in the true sense of the word, but . . .'

'You mean he can cook a bit?' David suggested.

'Yes, I believe he is quite famous in culinary circles. He wanted Jean to go and live with him but she wouldn't leave Poitrel, so Julian has come to Poitrel.'

'Is Mum invited?'

'Oh, yes. And Kate. Of course, Kate has already made Julian's acquaintance,' she said.

Julian Miller was a man of medium height with a thick chest, which suggested some degree of physical strength. His face was strong, or seemed strong because most of it was covered in beard. His eyes were blue and friendly. His hair was worn longish and was more grey than fair as it must have once been. The artist was tidily dressed in blue slacks and a brightly coloured shirt. David liked his handshake, which was firm and strong.

David was also agreeably surprised by the variety of food set out for their buffet lunch. He wasn't vocal about it but Anne certainly was. And Catriona, who had sampled high-quality foods at many social functions, was extremely appreciative of Miller's efforts. Julian, who had been apprehensive about his reception from Poitrel's owners, where he was to reside, suddenly seemed to relax.

Jean, who had also been nervous about the get-together, looked a little bit like the cat who had licked the cream. David had been her major concern; David, and what he would think of Julian.

'I don't want you to think I came here to take advantage of the generosity shown to me by Jean and you people,' Julian said. 'I wanted Jean to come and live with me, but she loves this place so much she didn't want to leave. I'd be very happy to contribute to the bills. I'd also be happy to help out at times if you need an extra hand. I can pen up sheep and I can weld. Do a fair bit of welding at times.'

David looked at him with some interest. He wasn't worried about being paid for electricity or even the phone unless the bill turned out to be exorbitant, but he was impressed that Miller had offered to pay. It was also interesting that the fellow could weld, which was bound to be useful.

Julian displayed some of his paintings to the guests from High Peaks; several of them had been painted in the Mudgee district and were intended for a coming exhibition. Of those he saw, the one that appealed to David most had been painted in the old gold village of Hill End. David looked at this painting for a few moments and nodded.

'I like this one,' he said. 'But I hasten to add that I know nothing about art.'

'You've got a good eye, David,' Miller said. 'This painting will sell for a fair bit of money.'

'Then you *can* contribute to the electricity and phone,' David said, and grinned.

Miller laughed. 'I fell into that.'

'Julian, if Jean thinks you're all right – which she evidently does, her being a manhater all these years – you must be a special sort of bloke. We all think a lot of Jean – she has been a part of our family for some time now. We treat people as we find them, Julian. You do the right thing by us and you'll always be welcome here.'

That was David, full on and to the point. No messing about, no prevarication.

'I understand you, David,' Miller said.

Later, as they were leaving, Jean kissed David on the cheek. 'Thank you, David. Julian was a wee bit apprehensive about how he would be received. He is a very nice man,' Jean said.

'You deserve no less, Jean,' David said.

Later, as he was sitting with Catriona in their lounge room, David looked up at her and grinned.

'What is it, darling?' Catriona asked.

'Would you like to be kissed by a fellow with a beard?' he asked.

'What a very odd question. I've never given the matter any thought,' she answered.

'I shouldn't think it would be a very enjoyable

experience. You'd think Jean would ask Julian to shave it off,' David suggested.

'Julian might see his beard as part of his artistic persona, darling. But to answer your question, no, I don't think I'd like to be kissed by a bearded man. On the mouth or anywhere else.'

'That's what I thought you'd say,' David said.

Catriona looked at him for some time and then dropped her eyes. 'Poor woman,' she said. 'Jean was very anxious that you approve of Julian, darling. It means a lot to her. I think she has big hopes for this relationship.'

'Well, Julian seems all right, but time will tell. He offered to help out and maybe I'll take him up on his offer some time,' David said, and went back to reading his paper.

David was finding that Catriona had added a new dimension to his life. Quite apart from the physical aspect of their relationship, which was very enjoyable, Catriona had so quickly become a part of all he did that he could not conceive how he would manage without her. For a person who had lived in the shadow of a tough, hard bushman and who had little time for girls generally, this was a considerable about-face.

To her credit, Catriona realised that David had scant time for socialising and for females who flitted from one social function to another. What Catriona had always wanted more than anything else in life was David MacLeod. She had been prepared to defy her parents to marry him and, at one stage, had even been prepared to fall pregnant to him out of wedlock. David had been so disturbed by that suggestion that never again did she offer that avenue to him.

Catriona wanted to be with David every hour of the day, to be part of everything he did. She realised that these early years of their marriage would be crucial in establishing the kind of partnership she hoped would endure for the rest of their lives. Pregnancy and children would all too soon prevent her from being totally involved with David's activities. She realised she would have to manage things very carefully when the children came on the scene. There was always the possibility she could employ a nanny so that she could spend more time with David. It was too early to broach the subject, but she was determined not to be tied to the house. It was not that she proposed to neglect their children, but was concerned not to let motherhood infringe on her time with her husband. These were early ruminations but they were underpinned by her love for David, and by the fact that she was certain he was going to be a great man in the pastoral scheme of things. She wanted to be at his side as much as she possibly could be.

One project Catriona had taken on was planning the itinerary for their overseas trip. When it was well in hand, Angus suggested that if she and David were agreeable, he and Jane would like to accompany them, for there were many things he could show

David. Catriona was dumbstruck but could hardly reject the proposition out of hand. She had a very good idea that her father wanted David to select a border collie for him. Angus had been after a top border collie all his life and who better to select it than David MacLeod? Yet the proposition had its pluses. A few years back Angus would not have considered accompanying David anywhere. Was this her father's absolute acceptance of David? It seemed to be. He would be introducing David to members of the Campbell family in Scotland, and this had to be real approval of his son-in-law.

When Catriona told David of her father's offer to accompany them overseas there was silence for a while, as David considered all angles. Angus had been very fair to him since the wedding. He had set him up with some very good Hereford cows and he had introduced him to his sheep classer, Hugh Pfeffer, who had been very helpful. If they knocked back this proposition Angus would realise it had been him and not Catriona who had made the decision.

In fact, Catriona was less than thrilled with her father's idea. She knew very well that her mother would decline to tramp through heather up hill and down dale while David and Angus inspected dogs and cattle. Jane Campbell would want to visit shops and art galleries and craft outlets and she would expect her daughter to accompany her. This was not at all what Catriona had in mind. She wanted to take David to Glencoe and Skye and stay at small out-of-the-way lodges and hotels and maybe, just maybe, take in a sheepdog trial. But she could not very well refuse her father's offer.

Significantly, it was his mother whom David thought of first. 'If your parents are to come with us, we'd have to ask Mum too,' he said.

'I agree, darling. Well, what am I to tell Daddy?' Catriona asked.

'If you have no objection I dare say Angus would be some help,' David said.

'I have been overseas, darling,' Catriona reminded him.

'I'm well aware of that, Cat. The point is that Angus has been very fair to me since the wedding and I wouldn't like to do anything to offend him. I'd prefer it was you and I but I'm not going to make an issue of it. If they want to come with us, let them come.'

When invited to join the overseas party Anne declined the offer. 'Thanks for the offer but I saw the UK when I was young and much fitter than I am now. I'd prefer to stay to look after my garden. And I'll talk to Nap and Clancy every day, David.'

David had told her in confidence that he didn't really want to make the trip but Catriona wanted them to have it before they started a family. He didn't like leaving the properties, and Nap, especially, would miss him. Anne thought that no other young man in Australia would think of his dog when he had the opportunity to travel overseas with a lovely young wife like Catriona. But that was her son.

David grinned sheepishly. 'Nap is such a knowing old cuss that he will worry if I don't talk to him every day,' he said.

'Nap survived for three years without you so he'll survive a few weeks. I'll take him titbits every day.'

Before the overseas trip there was one very big event that both families, including Kate and Jean and even young Greg Robertson, had to attend. This was the Australian premiere of the film *The Call of the High Country*, based on the story of David's life. The story began when David was a very small boy and concluded the day he won the National sheepdog trials with his brilliant dog Clancy. Of course, it was also a love story because it involved the young Catriona and her rescue from Yellow Rock and her eventual marriage to David.

The MacLeod and Campbell party travelled to the bright lights of Sydney for the premiere. It was a night and an occasion they would all long remember. They had arrived at the theatre in limousines but the foyer of the building was set up much like the interior of a shearing shed. There were bales of High Peaks wool and a couple of fleeces on a wool-rolling table. But perhaps the pièce de résistance was the presence of David's two great red-and-tan kelpies, Nap and Clancy, watched over by Greg Robertson in genuine ringer's clobber. Greg was enjoying every minute of the great occasion, the more so because he had been a witness to, and part of, one of the most dramatic scenes in the film. There was a solid phalanx of people around Greg and the dogs because apart from the actors who played the lead roles, the kelpies were the real stars of the film. David had been reluctant to allow his dogs to go to Sydney but he was assured they would be protected by security officers for the whole time they were away. And when Greg Robertson went inside to join the MacLeod family in the theatre, a husky security officer took over care of Nap and Clancy.

David, sitting between his wife and mother, and with Kate beside her sister and the Campbell family next to her, felt his heart beat faster as the lights faded. The huge screen was suddenly filled with Yellow Rock. It was a mind-blowing entree to the film and had particular significance because of what was to come. There was the small Catriona on her grey pony riding up the mountain to meet David and to display her riding prowess, only to meet with disaster. And then there was the young David riding for dear life to bring help to the injured girl. By her side was the first kelpie to appear in the film. David felt his mother grip his arm as the Andrew on-screen went down on the rope to rescue Catriona. This was one of many very moving scenes throughout the film. Another was when David tied a message to Nap's collar and sent him back to High Peaks so that Anne could organise help for Kate who had broken her leg on Wallaby Rocks. This feat brought media teams to the property and made Nap the most celebrated dog in the country.

Another arresting scene depicted the bushfire started by the two Missen boys, made more compelling by the fact that the fire scenes were totally genuine. They had been shot by a camera crew at the scene of the fire. David felt his hand gripped by Catriona as the fire came up the hill and then enveloped the ridge in smoke and flame. David was on the ridge trying to save Poitrel sheep and they had thought him gone. Catriona had been screaming hysterically and Andrew had thrown a mug of water in her face. And then they had ridden through the still-burning logs and smoke and found David, Nap and Clancy in the big cave. Nap had taken sheep there at David's direction. But Clancy's pads had been badly burnt. The story focused on the battle to get Clancy right for the National sheepdog trials and of how they had had to put a boot on one foot.

Clancy had gone on to record a perfect score of 100 in the final, which clinched for him the great trial. But what the MacLeod family were thinking of was not the trial but the man who lay buried on a knoll above the High Peaks homestead. Andrew MacLeod was very close to them that night. He had set the standards of his kelpies so high that it was possible for David to win the trial he had set his heart on, and thus repay his father for all he had done to build a future for his son. The family were all in tears after the scenes of the National Trial in Canberra.

The film came to a close with another spectacular scene of Yellow Rock with the eagles floating above it and David and Catriona riding down its face, two red-and-tan kelpies running behind them.

'Crikey,' Greg Robertson exclaimed as the lights came up. 'What a mighty picture.' Greg reckoned that the day David MacLeod employed him had been the luckiest day of his life.

'It was lovely, David,' Kate said as she wiped her eyes with a handkerchief.

'It wasn't bad,' David admitted. Some of the film had been over-played in his opinion, but the bush part of it had been dead right.

After the film they were taken by the limousines to the after party laid on for the cast and crew. Everyone seemed to be on a high about the film, and it was thought to have the makings of an international success. The following day, after all the celebrations were over, the Merriwa party went back to their respective properties and life settled back into more or less normal routines. Catriona pasted the newspaper and magazine stories about the film into her scrapbook and then concentrated on preparing for their overseas trip.

Stuart Campbell drove David and Catriona, Angus and Jane down to Sydney and brought the car back. He would be there to meet them on their return. Stuart, married now, was very much in his father's mould – he would never set the world alight but would always be dependable and a careful manager for Inverlochy.

The long-awaited trip was almost all that Catriona had hoped it would be. There were times when she had to compromise and stay with her mother while David and Angus shot off to look at dogs and cattle but there was time, too, for her and David to go off together and explore wild and lonely places. For David one of the most memorable places they visited was Glencoe.

'It gives you the shivers to think that maybe some of your ancestors could have been involved in the murder of the MacDonalds right here,' David said, after Catriona had explained the circumstances of the massacre.

'Whew, I wouldn't like to be here in winter.'

They met many Campbells, picnicked by the shore of Loch Ness and at almost the exact spot on Culloden Moor where Bonnie Prince Charlie had watched the English slaughter his clansmen and his hopes so many centuries ago. That was before he had fled with a huge price on his head and, after weeks of moving and hiding, was ultimately taken off by ship for France. Despite the reward, not a person had betrayed him.

Then it was over the sea to the stark beauty of the Isle of Skye before coming back to look at border collies. A chance meeting with a shepherd in a Pitlochry pub sent David and Angus off to nearby Loch Tummel. On a small farm owned by a keen but as yet relatively small-time breeder and handler, David found not a male dog but a bitch, Nell, that he reckoned was just what Angus needed. Angus had wanted a male dog but David convinced him to take the bitch – there was a lot about this dog that David liked and he felt that with a bit of kelpie blood, her progeny would quite likely suit Australian conditions. Her owner wasn't really keen to sell the bitch and so he put a high price on her. He knew that American breeders would pay that kind of money but he wasn't sure about Australians – all he knew about Australians was that they had a huge lot of sheep, they were keen on cricket and were 'bonny fighters', according to his father, who had fought in the war with them. Angus paid the asking price for Nell and they took her back to London and arranged for her to be flown to Australia where she would have to remain in quarantine for three months. That done, they forayed out into the counties of England and looked at picturesque villages and Hereford cattle and more picturesque villages and more Hereford cattle, followed by the English Royal Show.

The big cities of England and Scotland left no lasting impression on David – it was the smaller towns and villages, even tiny hamlets, that really appealed to him. The country people were more genuine and although they spoke in unfamiliar accents, they were still concerned with weather and crops and the price of livestock. But what interested David the most was the country of his forebears, the MacLeods. He reckoned that his ancestors must have been tough people to have survived in the western Highlands and the islands of the Inner and Outer

Hebrides. It was spectacular country, but brutal in winter. If people could survive in those winters, it was no wonder they made a success of farming in other countries.

The trip was finished with a stop in the United States where they inspected more Hereford cattle. David and Angus were particularly keen to see the size and length American breeders were getting into their cattle, which had previously been small and 'dolly'.

In between visits to cattle studs Catriona had sandwiched trips to New York, Los Angeles, Yellowstone National Park, Monument Valley and Kentucky. They also took in a couple of sheepdog trials that were closer in character to the trials in the United Kingdom than those in Australia. David was delighted to find that the kelpie was carving a place for itself in the United States. Increasing labour costs were driving stockholders to utilise stock dogs more and more and the kelpie, with its passion for work, was now to be seen in virtually every stockraising state of the United States. Some had sold for several thousand dollars. The kelpie had not displaced the border collie as the premier stock dog but the breed was gaining ground.

It had all been very interesting and gave David much food for thought. For a young man raised in the hill country of Australia whose longest trips away from home had been to Canberra for the National sheepdog trials, and to Yeppoon for his honeymoon, this excursion had been a ground-breaking experience. He had learnt things that would profit him in the years ahead and he had made contacts that would be valuable, too – as well as friends for life. But while America had its wonders and Britain had its antiquity and history, they weren't home. Voices, customs and the scenery were all unfamiliar. Much of the terrain they had seen was spectacular, but there were no gum-trees, no Australian native birds, nothing to remind them of home, of Australia, of their beloved range country.

Eventually, they all made their way home – home to High Peaks and Anne and Kate and Greg and Shaun and home to the kelpies that were so much part of David's life. David's first thoughts turned to his dogs. On arrival he went down to the dog yard where he sat on Nap's log and talked to him while Clancy and Belle, in particular, listened with ears cocked. David reckoned people would think him peculiar if they heard him talking to Nap, but he figured that if you had a dog that knew virtually everything you said to him, why wouldn't you talk to him? So he told the old dog that he wouldn't be going away again and that he would see him every day. Later, he let the dogs off and they raced around him in sheer exuberance and pleasure that he was with them again. Not that they had been neglected for a single day. Anne fed them and talked to them and Greg took them for their daily gallop. Greg worked Needle, which had been one of the three dogs David had worked at Canberra. He also worked another younger dog, a son of Nap called Bruce. David considered Greg a fairly good hand with a dog now, though he hadn't known much when he first came to work for the MacLeods. Greg had been horse-mad, but you couldn't work sheep in hill country unless you had good dogs and Greg soon woke up to that fact. A horse couldn't go where a dog could travel and when it came to winkling out straggler wethers on Yellow Rock, you had to rely on your dog. Here, in the high country of the Liverpool Ranges, a good sheepdog was a priceless asset.

After seeing Anne and the dogs, it was back to their own homestead and the garden Anne had watched over assiduously in their absence. 'Oh, David, everything seems to have grown so much, and yet we have only been away for six weeks,' Catriona exclaimed. 'I must get something to repay Anne for looking after everything so well.'

'Mum wouldn't expect anything but yes, we must give her something,' David agreed. They had purchased gifts at various places and Catriona had a length of Scottish tartan cloth that she fancied might appeal to Anne.

'Well, I must say it is nice to be home again,' David said. 'Let's sit down and have a drink o' tea and a piece of Mum's cake. After that I might take a run over to Glen Morrison and Poitrel to say hello to Kate and Jean. Want to come?'

'Try and stop me,' Catriona said.

David picked her up and kissed her. 'Thank you for all the organising of the trip, sweetheart. It went off very well and I learnt a tremendous amount. You are a treasure, a veritable treasure.'

'Thank you, darling. And having my folks along didn't work out too badly, did it?'

'It actually worked out very well. Angus smoothed the way for us in a lot of places. I've got to hand it to your father, Cat, he's got a presence. Maybe he inherited it from having ancestors in authority and owning property.'

'It's nice to know that you've become so matey, darling,' Catriona said, and rested her face against his cheek.

'Huh, Angus wants me to take his bitch and handle her for a while,' David said.

'And will you?'

David sighed. 'I suppose so. Can't very well refuse, can I? Angus offered me a top cow to do it.'

Catriona laughed. 'Poor Daddy. He does so much want to win a good trial. Is Nell talented enough to win a trial?'

'I think she's plenty good enough once she gets used to merino sheep. The big question is whether your father can handle her well enough, Cat. I've been coaching him but he isn't naturally a skilled stockman.'

'I suppose he hasn't had to be with good stockmen working for him. But Daddy is a fine judge of stock. He's well known for that,' Catriona said.

'That's a different matter altogether. The best judge of merino sheep in the country might not be able to work a dog to save his life. On the trial ground you need to think ahead and to be ready to respond instantly to what sheep do because a point or two docked from you could lose you the trial. Now, I'm for that cup of tea,' he said.

Chapter Four

David and Catriona were soon back into the routine of life in the high country. David complimented Greg on the way he had looked after High Peaks and Poitrel in their absence. At Glen Morrison Shaun Covers had superintended the construction of a stud cattle shed and a covered feedlot. The latter was designed to handle a dozen or so steers at a time so that David could evaluate their meat qualities. The first calves bred from the Inverlochy stud cows were still on their mothers, as were other calves bred from additional cows David had purchased. However, before long the first young bulls and steers would be ready to evaluate.

A draft of Aberfeldy steers had arrived in their absence and were being topped off on Glen Morrison. Kate and Shaun had the property looking first-rate. The sheds had all been cleaned out, and concrete flooring was laid down for the grain silos David was installing. He wanted to lay in large quantities of feed oats which, along with lucerne hay and chaff, was one of the main ingredients of stud cattle rations. It was also handy to have a good supply of feed oats on hand for feeding to sheep in dry times. Later, when he had his merino stud set up, David proposed to show his sheep.

When Nell came out of quarantine, David took her for three months and re-educated her to his commands. These were quite different from the whistle commands she had known in Scotland, but because she was only young and not yet been completely broken in, David didn't have a great deal of trouble with her. He found her very quick to learn and it didn't take her long to work out that she had to move fast to head merino sheep. Unlike the previous border collies Angus Campbell had imported, Nell was not a natural 'clapper' and instinctively stayed on her feet rather than dropping to the ground to eye the sheep. This was one of the things about her that had appealed to David when he saw her work for the first time. He liked a smooth-working dog that stayed on its feet and was ready instantly for anything a sheep might decide to do. Clapping was all right on the slower-moving Scottish sheep, but on merino sheep, some of which broke very fast, it was a damned nuisance. Australian sheepdog breeders had largely overcome the clapping trait by introducing kelpies into their border collie strains – either openly or under the lap. The kelpie had also been responsible for reducing the amount of coat carried on the body and legs. David knew that the late Bill Marshall had twice used kelpie in his Herdsman strain of border collies and had had great success.

It was not that a handler couldn't overcome the clapping trait – there were handlers who could do it, but Angus Campbell wasn't one of them. His dogs had always been too slow to react and as he was also slow, he couldn't win good trials. Nell was the answer to his first problem but after David had her schooled to his commands, he then had to coach Angus in how to work her. This took a couple of months. He told Catriona that her father would never be a great handler but he might be able to win a trial with Nell. Nell wasn't up to Belle as a trial bitch but she was pretty good and a lovely bitch to work.

Two months later Angus won a Novice Trial with Nell. She scored the highest points Angus had ever recorded with a dog. He sent David and Catriona a case of champagne to mark the occasion. David couldn't abide champagne, but Catriona said she had no doubt it would come in handy before too long. Of more consequence to David was the fact that Angus had given him the cow he had promised him for handling Nell.

The night that Angus came to tell them he had won the Novice Trial wasn't the first surprise David received that evening. They had finished dinner and were about to do the washing up when Catriona sprang her own surprise.

'Have you ever given any thought to what you might call our first baby, darling?' she asked.

'Not really, Cat. I'll give the matter some thought when he or she is imminent,' he said.

'I thought Dougal might be nice for a boy and Moira if it's a girl,' Catriona said. 'As we're both from Scottish families, it would be nice for our children to have Scottish names.' David still hadn't caught on. 'There could never be another Andrew MacLeod so I think Dougal would be nice. And I've always liked Moira. You couldn't abbreviate it like you do mine. I mean, Mo would hardly be appropriate, darling.'

'Are you trying to tell me something, sweetheart?' David asked with some urgency, turning to her.

Catriona nodded. 'It's confirmed,' she said.

'Crikey, Cat,' he said, and engulfed her in a mighty embrace.

'That's all right for now but you will have to be a little more restrained by and by,' she said.

'Crikey,' he exclaimed for the second time, his eyes shining. 'I'm going to be a father. Does anyone else know?'

'Only the doctor,' she answered.

'Let's clear this washing up and go up and tell Mum,' he said.

'You mean right now?'

'Right now. Mum will be over the moon. She's got grandchildren on the brain.'

Catriona could never refuse David anything, so of course they had to walk up to the old homestead.

They found Anne watching television and she looked up with some concern on her face as they walked in on her. 'There's nothing wrong, is there?'

'There's nothing wrong, Mum. It's just that we've

got some news for you. The first is that Angus won a Novice Trial with Nell. He's pretty excited about it.'

'That's nice, dear,' Anne said. 'And when is the baby due?' she asked.

David's mouth fell open. 'How did you know?' he asked.

'I could see it on Catriona's face as soon as you walked in. That's wonderful news,' Anne laughed, and kissed them both. 'Now I have something really special to look forward to. And Kate will be thrilled, too. Have you told Angus and Jane?'

'Not yet. You're the first. As soon as I told David he said we had to come and tell you,' Catriona said.

Anne flashed her son a quick smile. 'That was very sweet of you, David. I'm sure Catriona would have liked to tell her own parents first. Oh, this is truly wonderful news. A grandchild on the way!'

So of course they had to stay for supper and discuss names for the baby, which David thought (privately) was a bit silly. Nothing, though, could affect his excitement because his future plans were so much built around the children he hoped to have. He would have to start looking for a pony for the youngster, because he had been on one when he was only two. Anne had to ring Kate and pass on the news and then relay her reaction back to them. It was all very exciting and he couldn't be happier, he thought, sitting there with Catriona and Anne.

Later, as they walked back arm in arm through the orchard Catriona expressed what David had been thinking. 'My goodness, Anne is sharp. Were you ever able to hide anything from her?'

'Not very often, sweetheart. She was always sharp as a tack and she's still much the same. I believe Mum was very bright at school and they say she was one of the best teachers ever to come to Merriwa. Your mother told me that. Well, we've made Mum's day so we had best get over to Inverlochy in the morning to give Angus and Jane the news.'

The following morning at Inverlochy Angus was still on a high over his trial win and confident he could go on and win his first Open Trial. David felt Angus had a long way to go before he could win an Open but didn't like to dampen his father-in-law's enthusiasm. While there, they had to inspect Nap's son bred from a bitch by the imported collie, Toss. This was the dog Angus proposed to breed to Nell. David reckoned that Angus would be better advised to mate Nell to Nap or Clancy but the thought of breeding an imported bitch to a kelpie was too revolutionary for Angus to contemplate.

With her baby on the way, Catriona began to experience the first manifestations of pregnancy. She had some morning sickness but it didn't persist for too long. It was the fact that she couldn't ride with David that affected her most. For a young woman who loved her husband to the extent Catriona did, to be deprived of his company was not a situation she liked at all. She pottered about her garden and took trips with her mother to Tamworth to buy baby clothes, but often found herself walking up the track to be with Anne. If David was going anywhere by vehicle she would accompany him, but he always had jobs to do and had to leave her. Later, as she grew bigger, David became so anxious about her that she had to tell him there was no need to worry. Given what had happened to his mother, David was concerned that nothing should go amiss that would prevent Catriona from having other children.

Catriona realised that giving David the children he had set his heart on was probably the greatest contribution she could make to his future happiness. She had no doubt that he loved her, but children would be the manifestation of their love. All David's work and planning, his dream of building a network of properties for his children, would be to no avail if she failed to produce the children he sought so dearly.

Motherhood, Catriona realised, would probably be the first great challenge of her life. She had had a confrontation with her parents about marrying David, but motherhood was something entirely different – having and rearing children would occupy most of her attention for at least a dozen or so years, at which time the first child would be off to boarding school. Catriona knew that she would have a battle ahead about the children attending boarding school because David would want them home with him. He did not put the value on a boarding-school education that she and her family did. Like Anne, he would think parting from his children was too great a sacrifice. But in Catriona's opinion there were definite advantages in a boarding-school education, and she would have to convince David to make sacrifices for the sake of his children.

Unlike a lot of modern young women, Catriona didn't warm to the idea of having her husband present at the birth. The very thought was abhorrent to her. She had always prided herself on her appearance and the thought of David seeing her giving birth was too awful to contemplate. Not that David had said he wanted to be present.

Jane Campbell was also very much opposed to husbands being present at childbirth, and expressed her forthright views to Anne over morning tea. Jane was on her way to have lunch with Catriona but usually called in to see Anne.

'It's all very fine to say men should see what their wives go through and to talk of commitment, but I for one had no desire to have Angus present at the births of our children. There are some things a woman has to put up with in this life, but having one's husband there when one presents such a diabolical picture is not one of them,' Jane said firmly. 'I mean, Anne, it's one thing to flounce about one's bedroom in fancy lingerie when one is young and has a presentable figure but it's quite another to be seen at one's worst. Childbirth is such a messy business.'

'I should think it would be up to David and Catriona,' Anne said gently, disguising her smile.

'Well, I can assure you that Catriona doesn't want David to be present and I agree with her entirely,' Jane said.

Jane had been a young, pretty blonde woman when she married Angus Campbell. She was from a notable grazier family and after her marriage to Merriwa's leading member of the 'squattocracy' Jane assumed, certainly in her own mind, the mantle of the district's leading lady. The townies thought Jane to be, when they thought about her at all, 'a snooty bitch'. She was sometimes referred to as Angus Campbell's 'silvertail missus' and, in coarser terms, as being 'too much up herself'. One old local said that if he could buy Jane Campbell for his price and sell her for hers, he would make a lot of money.

Jane had not received any tertiary education after boarding school so, unlike Anne and Catriona who both had Arts degrees, she did not have a great knowledge of any subject at all. She was an indifferent pianist and did not knit or crochet. Nor was she very proficient in the kitchen, because she had never had to be. Despite her lack of expertise and experience, Jane considered herself a competent judge of many things and because she was Angus Campbell's wife, she had the ear of a lot of people.

Her views on many things were forthright: she detested rock and pop music and musicians, and blamed rock music for many of the problems affecting modern youth; she professed utter contempt for abstract art; and she was also a vocal critic of Labor politicians and what she described as sloppy dressing. However, if anyone had ever asked her to speak in any depth about these subjects, the gaps in Jane's knowledge would have been fatally exposed. Because she was Angus Campbell's wife, nobody ever did.

Jane had liked Anne MacLeod from the time she had first come to Merriwa, but she had always adopted an air of superiority towards her. Anne, being Anne, accepted this with an amused tolerance. Kate was less benevolent towards Jane Campbell. 'For a person with no talent of any kind, Jane Campbell has the most inflated opinion of herself of anyone I have ever met,' Kate said openly on one occasion.

Kate's pronouncement wasn't precisely correct. Jane did have one characteristic that stuck out a mile; she had class, ingrained class. Jane was a perfect hostess, dressed beautifully and was a great organiser of charity functions. Class had been drummed into her from when she was a small child. Appearance mattered. There had hardly been a jarring note in Jane Campbell's whole life until her daughter became enamoured of David MacLeod. Jane had dreamed of Catriona making a brilliant marriage and yet all her daughter wanted was David. But when David MacLeod looked at her, Jane was woman enough to understand why Catriona wanted him. Jane also knew that Catriona wasn't the only girl who wanted David – Susan Cartwright also wanted him, and Jane hoped she would get him because that would solve the problem. When David didn't reciprocate Susan's feelings, Susan married Michael Hunter instead.

It had been pointless trying any longer to dissuade Catriona from marrying David. The Campbells had sent Catriona overseas and to university for three years and it hadn't made a scrap of difference to the way she felt about him. Jane's greatest fear was that Catriona would do something silly like becoming pregnant, which would make Jane and Angus the laughing stock of the district and would have a diabolical effect on her son's romance with Carol Leonard, who had all the right attributes to make her a perfect wife for Stuart.

'No, Anne, childbirth is definitely not the place for a young husband. It is an obnoxious business. All that pushing and screaming. A husband should see his wife all nicely freshened up and in a pretty nightdress.'

Anne wondered whether Andy would have wanted to be present at David's birth. She doubted it.

'It is quite different now, Jane,' Anne said. 'I understand they give you a needle and there isn't any screaming. Or very little.'

'No matter, Anne. It isn't the place for a man. Quite unnecessary.'

Catriona agreed with her mother. She need not have worried because David told her he didn't want to be in on the birth. He said it would distress him too much to see her in pain, so Catriona left it at that.

When Catriona gave birth to a nine-pound boy David was overjoyed. Here was the son who would take over what Andrew MacLeod had begun and passed down. David had haunted the hospital until the news of the birth came to him and then he phoned his mother, Angus and Jane, and Kate. Angus and Jane found him holding Catriona's hand at her bedside. She seemed very pleased with herself.

Visitors came from far and wide to the hospital and later to High Peaks where Dougal MacLeod was installed in a nursery room with a nurse. Two people who came infrequently to High Peaks because of their age were Anne's father and mother, Jack and Mavis Gilmour. Jack had sold his printing company some fifteen years earlier and the couple had retired to live at Coffs Harbour where Jack indulged his passion for fishing and watched his beloved St George rugby league team when they were featured on television. Jack still drove and appeared very sprightly for his age. The couple seemed slightly overwhelmed by the fact that they were great-grandparents. Andy and Jack had got on very well because they were both no-nonsense men not given to airs and graces. David had not seen as much of his grandparents as he would have liked to but he was obviously delighted that they had come to visit his son. Of course, they had come to see Anne and Kate and himself and Catriona but it was the baby that had brought them together, despite the long drive from Coffs Harbour. Jack's visit was in fact his last to High Peaks as he had a fatal heart attack later that year.

When Dougal was a little boy there was a birth of a different kind that brought two other visitors to High Peaks. David had bred his great race mare Ajana to a son of Star Kingdom called Star Lover. Not being thoroughbred-minded, Andy and David had previously bred Ajana to stockhorse stallions, and while the mare had produced some lovely offspring Angus had pushed them to pair her with a thoroughbred stallion. The foal – which David had promised Angus could race – was a bay filly, and David and Catriona named her Starana.

Very shortly after David had bred Ajana to Star Lover, he rang Wilf White at his north-coast home and told him what he had done. The news had a huge effect on old Wilf. When he left Poitrel to live on the coast, it was thought he would not last long. However, under the care of his sister Gertie, Wilf got his weight down and was walking each day, and, despite a couple of scares, he was still battling on. Gertie had tried to persuade him to have heart surgery but he had refused pointblank. 'No, by gum, Gertie, I won't. I've had my day and if my heart fails, it fails.'

Now, with no further urging from his sister, he asked her to arrange for him to have the operation. There had to be a reason, she thought. Gertie rang David one night and asked if he could tell her why Wilf had suddenly changed his mind.

'It could be, Gertie, that it was because I told him we had bred Ajana to a Star Kingdom horse,' he said, and laughed.

'The foxy old devil. I might have known it would be a horse,' Gertie said.

But she went ahead and organised Wilf into hospital where he had his operation and, amazingly, came through it quite well. And so it was that when Ajana's filly foal was about three months old, Wilf, driven by his sister, came back to High Peaks. It was their first visit since Andrew MacLeod's funeral.

When told of Wilf's intended visit David had had a quiet word to Julian Miller. 'If you're thinking of doing a camping trip for some sketching I'd suggest that you do it over the next two weeks, Julian. Wilf White is coming back to see us and he's sure to want to come to Poitrel, his old home. I think it might be best if you're elsewhere – Wilf wouldn't understand this partner business. He'll want to see Jean because he thinks a lot of her and Kate. You follow me?'

Julian followed, all right. Besides, nobody argued with David MacLeod. It wasn't only that David owned Poitrel but Julian realised that he and Jean were on a good wicket. It wasn't any great sacrifice to clear out for a couple of weeks – he had wanted to take a trip, anyway.

David cushioned his suggestion with a sweetener. 'How would you feel about painting my mother, Julian?'

'Well, er, I haven't done any of that sort of thing for a while, David. I've concentrated on landscapes,' Julian said.

'Can you do it or can't you?'

'I reckon I could if I set my mind to it.'

'I'll pay you to do it,' David said.

'No need for that. Letting me stay here with Jean is sufficient payment. Will you arrange it with your mother?'

'Certainly. You can begin when you come back,' David said.

He thought his mother would be pleased about the portrait. He hadn't discussed it with her but it was something that he had had in the back of his mind for some time. One day she would be gone and he wanted something that would perpetually remind him of her.

It wasn't Wilf White's old red utility that came up the track to High Peaks homestead. Nowadays it was a comfortable sedan with Gertie at the wheel. David had hung about the woolshed and yards doing odd jobs to be on hand for Wilf and Gertie when they arrived.

It was a leaner Wilf White who got out of the car as Anne came down the steps to join her son. Wilf, leaning on a stick now, was smiling broadly as he took David's hand. 'By gum, it's good to see you again, David,' the old man said.

Gertie embraced David in a huge hug and whispered in his ear. 'Thank you, David.'

'For what, Gertie?' he asked of the big woman who had once given him piggyback rides. She had been a redhead in those days but was grey now.

'For mating that bloody mare, David! That's what persuaded him to have the operation. Wilf's got a fresh lease of life because of the damned foal.'

'Well that's a by-product I didn't count on,' David said, and laughed. 'We're very pleased to see you – for whatever reason.'

'Of course we are and Kate will be over later, Wilf,' Anne added.

Wilf and Gertie were staying with Anne but first it was afternoon smoko. 'One small piece of that cream sponge will be enough for Wilf, Anne.'

'By gum, but she's tough on me, David,' Wilf said.

'I think Gertie needed to be, Wilf. I saw what you used to eat and if you had kept on like that you wouldn't be here now. I think you owe a lot to Gertie,' Anne said.

'That's right, David. All Wilf does is complain, but he would have been dead if he'd carried on like he was doing. We eat a lot of fish these days and I think it's doing us a lot of good,' Gertie said.

Although Anne pressed Wilf and Gertie to have a rest after smoko that wasn't what the old chap wanted. It was to be straight down to the mare's paddock to see Ajana's foal. David led Ajana up to the fence and Wilf stroked her neck while he inspected her foal.

'By gum, I think she's a bottler, David,' Wilf said at last. 'Too young to tell, you'd probably say, but I like the look of her. Look at the way she moves already. She'll be a sprinter, mark my words.'

'She'd have to be a sprinter the way she's bred, wouldn't she, Wilf?'

'You bet. What I'm saying is that she will be a *real* sprinter. Look at the way she floats over the ground. That's how Ajana moved at her age.'

They could see that the old chap was pretty excited by their foal. Horses had always been his weakness. Everything else could go hang, but the horses had to have the best of everything.

'You should be keeping this filly, David,' Wilf urged. 'She's too good to let go.'

'I promised Angus he could race her for three

seasons and I won't go back on my word, Wilf,' David said firmly.

'Of course you wouldn't. Andy's word was his bond, too. Maybe you could race her in partnership?' Wilf suggested.

'I'm not a thoroughbred man, Wilf. I've promised Cat Ajana's next foal and she can race her if she wants to,' David said. 'Maybe after that we'll put Ajana out to pasture. She's done a great job for us. She's earned her retirement.'

'There's others who would breed from her a lot longer than that, David.'

'Oh, well, they might too, Wilf. But money isn't everything. You gave her to me and she means a lot to me. I've got good stockhorses from her and I've sold a couple for decent money. If this filly is a good one, she'll be a prospective brood mare.'

'This filly will go places, David. Foals from her will one day be worth gold. Maybe I'll be gone by then, but you bear in mind what old Wilf tells you.'

Wilf and Gertie then went to see Catriona and the baby. Catriona held Dougal up for them to inspect.

'My God, he's Andy all over again,' Gertie exclaimed.

Anne nodded. That had been her unspoken thought for months.

'By gum, maybe you've got two champions in the making, David,' Wilf said, and chuckled. 'And this fellow has been on a decent paddock by the size of him.'

The little boy looked up at the two unfamiliar faces and then buried his face in his mother's hair.

'Is he a good child, Catriona?' Gertie asked.

'Very good, Gertie. Actually, he's a very quiet fellow. My brother's boy is just the opposite.'

The party returned to the High Peaks homestead for Wilf and Gertie to have a rest before dinner. To welcome them back to High Peaks, Anne prepared a meal that she knew Wilf, in particular, would like. She had David bring her a piece of sirloin from one of his feedlot steers and she carved it wafer-thin so that the meat melted in the mouth. It was served with roast potatoes, cauliflower, cabbage and Anne's special gravy, and was followed by trifle and cream. Gertie sanctioned the main course, but rationed dessert.

Next morning David would take Wilf and Gertie to Poitrel and then across to meet Lew Hooper. Lew had half-a-dozen mares now. Wilf had advised him to concentrate on quality rather than quantity.

The following morning Catriona told David that she would like to accompany him when he took Wilf and Gertie to Poitrel and Glen Morrison.

'We could be away all day, Cat,' David said.

'That's all right. Lottie is perfectly reliable,' she replied.

'If that's what you want, sweetheart,' he said.

'Wouldn't you like me to come with you, darling?'

'Sure, I love having you with me. I just thought you might not want to leave Dougal all day,' David said.

'It won't harm him a scrap not to have me for a day. I've left him before to go shopping,' Catriona said.

David had agreed, not without an argument, with Catriona's suggestion that she pay for a nurse–housekeeper when the baby arrived. Catriona had considerable money invested from her share of Inverlochy. That was the first victory Catriona had won, if it could be called a victory because David was fiercely independent when it came to money.

Lottie Hann had been recommended to them by a friend of Jane Campbell's. She was born of a German father and Australian mother and she had married another German who migrated to Australia. Günter Hann had been killed in a car accident and although money had come to Lottie, it was not a great amount so she had taken up looking after children. Lottie, a woman in her early forties, was quite a gifted artist and what spare time she had, she often put into sketching and painting. She had a flat at the back of the house and she looked after herself and helped Catriona in the house. A biggish, well-made woman with blonde hair and blue-grey eyes, Lottie was a perpetually cheerful person and Catriona was very pleased to have her around. She was to stay with David and Catriona for a number of years.

With Wilf beside David and Catriona beside Gertie, the group left for Poitrel. Both David and Catriona knew it would be a traumatic day for the old chap because he hadn't been back for so long, and there were still several of Wilf's old mares running on Poitrel. With David's hand under his arm Wilf negotiated the steps up to his old homestead. Kate was there to greet him and Jean was standing further back.

'Sister Kate,' the old chap said, as she took his hand.

'Not any more, Wilf. I'm a manager these days,' she said.

'What's David got you doing, Kate?' Wilf asked.

'Oh, just about everything, Wilf. For starters, I cleaned up the big shed which was in a mess. I've set up a central control system that tells us what tools, drenches, fencing material, horseshoes, wool packs and so on we have at any given time. I feed bulls and rams and I can plough a paddock. I also look after bull buyers. And I do a whole lot more than that, but that will give you some idea of my role with the High Peaks Pastoral Company,' Kate said.

'By gum, but that's wonderful,' Wilf said with admiration.

Kate chuckled. 'I don't know about it being wonderful, Wilf. Women everywhere are pulling their weight on the land. There's women who are doing far more than me. You just don't hear about them.'

'And there's Sister Jean. Don't tell me young David here has you managing a place?' Wilf asked.

'I look after Poitrel, Wilf. Well, a lot of its animals, anyway. Gertie, how nice to see you again.'

Presently, they took Wilf to see his horses. The old chap, leaning on his stick, told them the name and breeding of every old mare they showed him. It was a formidable feat of memory.

'We had to put three or four of them down, Wilf. We couldn't let them go on any longer,' David told him. 'Jean feeds them every day. We bred some nice horses from some of your mares. Catriona's black horse would be one of the best horses we bred. Cat won Champion Hack awards on him. You can see him tomorrow.'

They then took Wilf and Gertie up to the shearing shed they had erected after they bought Poitrel. These and new yards had been two of the major improvements they had made to the property.

Kate and Jean laid on a big smoko, but Gertie wouldn't allow her brother to eat too much. Wilf looked wistfully at the cream sponge as Jean cleared away the plates.

'No, Wilf. It's no good you looking like that,' Gertie told him. 'If I had allowed you to go on eating like you used to, you'd have dropped dead long ago. I have to watch him, Kate. Wilf will sneak stuff away if he can!'

'You can have a lean steak for lunch, Wilf,' David said, and laughed.

They were to lunch at Glen Morrison, with Lew Hooper. First stop was the cattle preparation shed where a grinning Shaun Covers was on hand to greet the visitors.

'G'day, Mr White. Long time since I saw you last. G'day, Mrs Blake,' he added, nodding at Gertie.

'By gum, if it isn't Shaun Covers,' Wilf declared. 'You still going to campdrafts, Shaun?'

'Not so many these days, Mr White. Young Greg is the main drafter now.'

'Shaun still wins a draft or two, Wilf,' David said. 'He's my stud manager these days. We're just about ready to start showing our cattle. The first of them are in the shed.'

Catriona took David's hand as they walked into the shed. She was very proud of what he had achieved, and especially so in the case of the Herefords. The red-and-white cattle were tethered at feed troughs and they looked a picture. Through a wall in the shed were some young heifers that were being prepared for showing.

They continued down a gravelled path to the feedlot where Hereford steers were being fed, and David explained that these were being fed so that he could ascertain the meat quality of his cattle while the pick of them would probably be shown as steers. Next they took Wilf and Gertie for a tour of the property by car. The first calves by the Sydney champion bull were on the ground and looked like red-and-white mushrooms dotted about the paddock. Further out they also inspected the draft of Aberfeldy steers being topped off for market.

'By gum, they're a different-looking beast,' Wilf observed.

'Yes, they're different, Wilf. Dad used to call them yaks. They weren't his cup of tea at all. But they're hardy and they're valuable in ticky areas. We've got to improve them a fair bit, and we will.'

It was then back to the Glen Morrison homestead, where Lew Hooper joined them. He and David cooked home-grown steaks and they sat about drinking mugs of tea and talked about life on the land, and horses.

After lunch David and Catriona took Wilf and Gertie across to Lew Hooper's block. Lew now had a shed up which served as temporary accommodation for when Lew and his wife stayed at Glen Morrison overnight. The balance of the shed was used for storing feed and property requisites. Lew also had a nice block of lucerne established.

Wilf's main interest was Lew's horses, because he had had a hand in advising Lew which mares to purchase and which to leave alone. Lew had the breeding of the six mares in a folio and the two men discussed future breeding options for the best part of an hour. There were three foals on the ground from the first three mares Lew had purchased but because Lew did not have the financial means to pay for the best sires, he had had to use lesser entires of reasonable breeding.

'If they aren't top class I should still get one or two mares good enough to breed from, Wilf,' Lew said.

David's next words took Lew aback. 'If Ajana has a colt maybe we'll keep him and Lew can use him. What do you think, Wilf?' David asked.

'By gum, you must be reading my mind, David. I was going to suggest the same thing,' Wilf agreed. 'If that filly foal you're going to call Starana is as good as I think she will be, a brother could be the very thing. And maybe worth a lot of money, too.'

They left Lew and drove back to Poitrel for afternoon smoko with Kate and Jean and listened to Wilf talk about David's father, Andrew, and Andrew's mother.

'By gum, what a great woman she was. No wonder Andy was so straight. Straight as a die, he was. And what a worker. And Mrs Mac over there is a good 'un too. She wasn't bush-reared but she's a bottler woman. There's plenty of good people about. Look at Kate and Jean here. David tells me Kate is as handy as any man.'

Wilf was clearly enjoying himself. 'Ah, by gum, I wish I were young again. Life is too bloomin' short. David is going places and Ajana's foal is going to win big races or my name's not Wilf White. I knew it was right to let you have Poitrel, David. You've looked after my horses just as Andy promised you would. And it was damned good of you to let Lew Hooper have that block, David. A big thing, David.'

'You let us have Poitrel, Wilf, and I was left a fortune with Aberfeldy. It wasn't much to let Lew have two hundred hilly acres. Besides, I wanted a good neighbour to keep an eye on Kate and Jean,' David said, and laughed.

'You can't fool old Wilf, David. Always wanted to hide your light under a bushel, as the saying goes. It was a big thing cutting that block off for Lew. A big thing, wasn't it, Gertie?'

'Yes, Wilf, a big thing,' Gertie agreed. 'Catriona, did you know that I used to give your husband piggyback rides?'

'So Anne told me, Gertie,' Catriona said as she took David's arm.

'What a boy he was. There never was such a boy for dogs and horses. Andy told me that if Anne knew what he got up to on horses, her hair would turn grey.'

'David used to think I was a little pest, Gertie,' Catriona said. 'If he knew I was coming to High Peaks he'd clear out on his pony. That's how I came to grief on Yellow Rock. I went looking for him on my new pony because I was going to show him that I wasn't just a pony club rider.'

Wilf laughed uproariously. 'By gum, so that's how it was. And the young scamp rode your pony off the mountain when everyone else wanted to put her down. That's when I knew David was something special. Took a fall and hurt your shoulder, eh, David.'

'It wasn't much, Wilf,' David said sheepishly. 'I knew Cat wouldn't want to lose her pony. It's true I thought she was a little pest but she was the pick of the little pests.'

'Thanks a lot, David,' Catriona said, and slapped his arm.

'Well he woke up, didn't he?' Wilf said, and winked at Catriona.

'Finally, and with a lot of prompting, Wilf,' Catriona answered. 'I think even Anne had given up on David ever asking me to marry him.'

'Well, by gum, I shouldn't say it because it will give David a swollen head, but you've got one of the best young men the Australian bush has ever bred and the best one I know or am ever likely to know,' Wilf said.

'You'll give him a big head, Wilf,' Catriona said, glowing with pride.

'Got to say what I think, girlie. Won't be around to

say these things too much longer . . . not even with the new pipework in me! The MacLeod family was always very good to us. Real decent bush people, Catriona. Never let you down and always ready to do you a good turn. Not enough of that in life, and the old ways are passing. People are too greedy now.'

'We had better get you back so you can have a rest, Wilf,' David said.

'I suppose so,' Wilf said, and they could tell he was reluctant to leave Poitrel.

Out at the car the old chap stood for a few moments taking in the hills beyond the homestead and then, finally, the paddock where the last of his horses grazed contentedly.

'Well, it wasn't a bad life, even if I lost my brother and I didn't breed a Melbourne Cup winner,' Wilf said. And then he got in the front of the car beside David. If he had looked sideways he would have seen that both Kate and Jean were crying. It seemed to both women that this would be the last visit Wilf White ever made to Poitrel.

'By gum, you must be proud of David, Mrs Mac,' Wilf said that night. They had had another hearty dinner and were sitting in the High Peaks lounge room where Andrew MacLeod's trophies still took pride of place.

'Oh, Wilf, I am full of admiration for what he has achieved and the way he has developed personally. He has such big plans for the future and such hopes for his children,' Anne said. 'Yet sometimes I wonder if it wouldn't have been better for him just to have had this place and Poitrel and to go to his dog trials and campdrafts. Of course, being left Aberfeldy made a huge difference financially. It also made a big difference to the Campbells,' she said, and laughed. 'David wasn't the son of a battling hill grazier and shearer any longer; he was a wealthy man.'

'By gum, you're telling me.'

'I do admire the way David has tried to get on with Angus Campbell for Catriona's sake. And to give Angus his due, he has been very helpful to David. He helped him with stud cattle and introduced him to his sheep classer. David has learnt a lot from Angus. Of course, David has helped Angus with his dog handling and breeding. Angus can still be difficult as the Campbells think themselves better than anyone else, but David won't abide that nonsense.'

'I reckon he wouldn't. Can't tell you how impressed I was by what I saw today. Everything tidy and then those lovely cattle at Glen Morrison. I said when I gave Ajana to David that he would be a legend one day. Your son is going to be a great man, Mrs Mac. Andy would be a proud man if he were here.'

'We believe Andy is never far away, Wilf. I've seen David up on the knoll looking down at Andy's grave and I know that he will never forget him. He was very depressed after Andy died, Wilf. Depressed even with his lovely new wife. But he came out of it and he has never looked back. I just hope that his children are all that he expects they will be. David doesn't need to expand his interests further but he will because he says his children will need more land with the way costs are these days. The next thing he wants is a big place further out where he can breed replacement wethers and top off more of the Aberfeldy cattle. More land and animals means more worry, Wilf.'

'Well, by gum, so it might be, I see that, but would you hold David back? Better to work for something than sit on your tail!' Wilf said.

'David is hardly sitting on his tail, Wilf. He's got four properties to keep an eye on. Then he's got his dogs and horses and now stud cattle. Stud sheep will be next. What if his children don't want to stay on the land? It's a possibility. Andy always said that he was very lucky to have a son cast very much in his own image and with the same stock skills, but David shouldn't bank on his children being the same as him. He'll be awfully disappointed if they aren't, Wilf.'

'I wouldn't worry too much, Anne. I'm sure David will have some land-minded children. He tells me he would like four or five,' Gertie said.

'Catriona doesn't want four or five, Gertie. Two would be plenty for her. She might go to three for David. Having a boy first up put David on cloud nine but I have told him that girls are not to be discounted as they're doing just about everything today. Sure, they might not want to dig post-holes but who digs post-holes any more? There's digging machines for holes now.'

'And women like your sister Kate make good role models,' added Wilf.

'Yes, Kate came to the land in her thirties and David says she's as good as any man. She can ride and draft cattle with almost anyone and she's absoluely super with keeping track of drenching programs. David says girls marry and you lose them and only sons can be relied on to keep the properties going. Well, there have been a few sons in this district that have been anything but reliable and they had decent parents. David has such dreams of a MacLeod dynasty and I don't want him to be disappointed. He's my only child and I am very proud of him – and proud too that good people like you, Wilf, and Tim Sparkes recognised what was in him and helped him. David and I talk a lot and he realises that he has been lucky and that you should use good luck to better yourself. David wants the MacLeod name to mean something substantial in grazing circles. It really is quite amazing just how much David has progressed. He leaves me quite breathless at times,' Anne said.

'By gum, I wish I had been able to have a son like him, Mrs Mac,' Wilf said. 'I've been a silly old fool for most of my life. Just wasted it messing about with horses. I went to pot when Wesley was killed in the war. Very close we were, Mrs Mac. Never bothered with people much after that. Andy was different. He shore my sheep and never worried much about money straight off. Andy handled my horses, too. He was the best man with a horse in these parts. Andy's father wasn't up to much, though I heard he did good things in the war. Andy's mother was a bottler, like I told them all today. She came to see me after Wesley was killed. Rode round the road and brought me cakes and biscuits. Damned fine woman, by gum. Taught Andy well, too. He knew right from wrong.'

'Oh well, we shall have to just wait and see, Wilf. David has his dreams just as he once dreamed of winning the National Trials for his father. He did that when we all thought it was virtually impossible and he has come on a treat since then. For a boy who hated school what my son has absorbed in the way of agricultural knowledge just floors me.'

'That Starana filly could help you a lot, Mrs Mac. By gum, I wouldn't have offered to lease her to Angus Campbell. You should be racing her yourselves. I could be mistaken but I reckon that filly could do anything,' Wilf said.

'We aren't thoroughbred people, Wilf. Angus has been at David for years to breed Ajana to a blood horse, and even offered to pay the service fee. David's going to lease the filly to him for a while as a kind of thank-you gesture for letting him have such a good lot of Hereford cows to begin his stud. David wouldn't go back on his word.'

'I never had much time for the Campbells, Mrs Mac. They never came near me when Wesley was killed. I heard that Angus called me an old fool for letting you people have Poitrel. By gum, I wasn't going to let Angus Campbell have it. It's you people who should be getting the good out of Ajana.'

'And we have, Wilf. We have some lovely horses from her. David is giving her next foal to Catriona and she can race her if she is so inclined. I believe she wants to.'

'Angus is David's father-in-law, Wilf,' Gertie said sharply. 'Catriona is a lovely person and David wouldn't want to do anything that would make her unhappy. Obviously Angus has accepted David now and David appears to be doing his best to have a good relationship with the old silvertail.'

'By gum, it goes against the grain knowing that old swank is going to profit from one of my horses,' Wilf said fiercely. 'The old bugger has been after a top racehorse all his life and unless I've lost my touch, Ajana is going to give it to him.'

'Only for a couple of years, Wilf,' Anne pointed out.

'Ah well, I can see the difficulty for David,' Wilf said more mildly. 'What else could he give him but a decent horse?'

'Well, he did handle the border-collie bitch Angus bought in Scotland and after he handed her over, Angus won a Novice Trial with her. Angus was tickled pink about that, Wilf,' Anne said with a smile.

'That filly out there will do a lot more than win a sheepdog trial,' Wilf said.

'You can't be sure of that, Wilf. You weren't always right about horses,' Gertie said.

'By gum, I was right more often than I was wrong,

Gert. I was right about Ajana and this filly moves just like her.'

'Well, what will be, will be,' Gertie said.

Wilf and Gertie stayed at High Peaks for two more days before leaving to go back to the coast.

'I must say that Wilf looks remarkably well for a man who had a bad heart when he left Poitrel. The operation has given him a new lease of life,' Anne remarked, as they watched Wilf's car disappear around the bend.

'It says something for a fish diet, Anne,' Catriona said.

'It certainly does. A fish diet and a martinet in the shape of Gertie who watches Wilf's diet like a hawk!' Anne added.

'It was great to have them here but now there's work to be done,' David said.

'What do we do first, darling?' Catriona asked.

David looked at her with a puzzled look on his face. He had thought that when Dougal arrived Catriona would spend most of her time with him. She had fed him for a while but now Lottie looked after him more than Catriona. As soon as she had weaned Dougal it was business as usual for Catriona. Whether it was a trip to look at stud cattle or sheep or a muster in the hills, Catriona was with her husband. David did not do as much hill country mustering as he used to because Greg Robertson did a lot of that kind of work now. However, there were still some excursions, such as when they were crutching. Greg had learnt to shear and crutch and David paid him the extra money to crutch. On these occasions David would be involved in the mustering and he would take sheep back to the hills. Catriona liked nothing better than to boil the billy for lunch somewhere up in the hills. She would lie with her head on David's shoulder with a dreamy, contented look on her face as she listened to him talk.

Believing that mothers transferred most of their love and affection to their children, David was puzzled when Catriona indicated her preference for being with him rather than with their son. Nor did her behaviour alter after the births of their other children. It was not that he did not like having Catriona with him – far from it. But having her was a bonus he did not expect. The fact was that while David was an extremely knowledgeable stockman and judge of animals, he did not know very much about women. Catriona loved her husband far more deeply than he ever realised, and David never fully grasped the lengths to which his wife went to keep him interested in her. Catriona was determined that no woman was ever going to lure David away from her.

Chapter Five

On the occasions when Catriona saw her husband walking up the track towards her, her heart would usually beat a mite faster and her stomach would flutter. David was a handsome man and he was her man.

While Catriona had many admirable qualities, she had her fears, faults and frailties like everyone else. One of her secret fears, which she had never expressed to anyone, was that she would lose her looks and figure and that perhaps David would look at other women. Her insecurities were totally unwarranted, but they coloured Catriona's thinking for about thirty years of her married life. Although she knew that she was expected to have children and wanted to please David, she was secretly fearful that pregnancy and nursing would ruin her figure. She had seen several women deteriorate quite remarkably after producing a family; the bigger the family, the worse it seemed to be. This was the reason Catriona didn't want the number of children David had in mind. After Dougal was born, Catriona installed an exercise bike and running machine, and exercised every day.

Catriona's fears were accentuated when she was over seven months pregnant with Dougal. Catriona and Susan Hunter, who had been Susan Cartwright, still maintained a close friendship and visited each other regularly. Catriona was staying at home a lot now, so Susan often came to High Peaks for lunch. On one particular occasion David had told Catriona he would be back for lunch and the two young women were gossiping while they prepared the meal.

'Have you thought about starting your family, Susan?' Catriona asked.

'Not much,' Susan replied with startling candour.

'Don't you want children?'

'Not for some years, Catriona. I feel like I haven't had any life yet myself,' Susan said. 'Well, I haven't, being away at school for all those years. At least you had a trip overseas.'

'What does Michael have to say about you not wanting to start a family?' Catriona asked curiously.

'Oh, he's not too concerned for the moment. You know what young men are like – give them that and they're happy,' Susan said. 'Besides, Michael and I are very much in demand on the court.' Susan couldn't resist making a reference to her tennis prowess because it was about the only area where she had superiority over Catriona.

'It seems to me that tennis is a poor substitute for

a family, Suse,' Catriona said. 'Look, Susan, we've been friends a long time and talked girl talk from way back. Is something wrong?'

'Oh, it's all right for you, Catriona. You've got a dreamy husband and you love him,' Susan said fiercely.

'Are you saying you don't love Michael, Susan?'

'Marriage isn't a bed of roses for everyone, Catriona. I married Michael when I knew I couldn't have David,' Susan stormed.

'Now, hang on, Suse. If that's the case then you've got nobody to blame but yourself,' Catriona retorted.

'Well, what else could I do? I didn't want to go to university and I certainly didn't want to do a boring secretarial course. They didn't need me at home and I'm not quite good enough to play tennis professionally. Marriage seemed the best option at the time. I don't have to work at a boring job and Michael is still doing well enough to afford good clothes and nice holidays. But as I said, it's not a bed of roses, Catriona.'

'Well, you made it so you have to lie in it, Susan,' Catriona said a mite tartly.

'Don't be like that, Catriona. So I made a mistake. I'm not the only one. If I was with the right man, I'd have a family like a shot. I know that must sound awful, but you don't know how lucky you are to have David. All the girls say so. Playing house and having a family with David must be a dream come true. I mean, he is such a hunk.'

At that moment the hunk, as Susan called him, came up the front steps. He was whistling and presented a very cheerful picture. In grey gaberdine trousers and a blue shirt he was the personification of the picture-book young grazier.

'Darling, you're right on time,' Catriona said, and kissed him.

'Susan, you're looking well,' he said. Susan kissed him with what Catriona thought was a little too much enthusiasm. Susan had sat near David at the little primary school down the road and had had tender feelings for him for years, which grew the day David came to the girls' rescue when Wade Missen and Stanley Masters had tried to attack them. Well, it had been Catriona they were after first, but Susan knew they would have got to her, too.

Catriona watched this display of affection with some trepidation. Susan always carried on like that with David. The way she had kissed him at Catriona's own wedding had been over the top, and then there was the way she had behaved the day she married Michael. Of course, Susan had let too much champagne go to her head that day, but that was really no excuse.

And it seemed to Catriona that David's compliment about the way Susan looked gave Susan reason to gloat. It was not that David had said anything wrong but he had highlighted Susan's appearance which she felt, in comparison to her own heavily pregnant form, put Susan at a distinct advantage. In crimson trousers and a red-and-white blouse, Susan looked slim, stylish and very attractive. It had always been said that next to Catriona Campbell, Susan Cartwright was the best-looking girl in the district. But Susan wasn't looking and feeling seven months pregnant – she had been playing a lot of tennis, and was trim, taut and terrific. That was what Catriona thought as she looked at her old school friend engrossed in an animated conversation with David. There would always be attractive young women like Susan ready to turn on the charm for David. Cartiona burned. She wanted to say 'Don't kiss David like that, Susan.' But she knew Susan would laugh and reply 'Like what, Catriona?' Catriona would look foolish and appear as if Susan's kisses mattered.

A glowing, energised Susan monopolised the conversation over lunch. Catriona felt that a lot of it went over David's head. At one point, he looked across the table at her and winked, and Catriona took pleasure in the secret knowledge that her husband was merely being polite to her lunch guest. While she took some comfort from that, it did not alter the fact that Susan looked great. Catriona knew that perhaps later, years later, there would be other attractive women who offered more serious competition than Susan.

David talked politely for a few moments after lunch and then announced that he would be at Glen Morrison for the afternoon. Susan got up and kissed him goodbye. She could have just *said* goodbye, Catriona thought. David bent down and kissed Catriona and told her to take a rest because she looked a little bit tired. So I don't look fresh and glowing like Susan, Catriona thought.

Susan stood at the window and watched David walk

down the front steps and then out to his utility. Yes, I would willingly start a family with David MacLeod, she thought. She had once believed she had a chance with David but it was only ever Catriona that he wanted.

Catriona's pregnancies were planned and executed with clinical perfection. Her second baby was born two years after her first – a girl, whom they named Moira. Again Catriona fed her for a short while and then turned her over to Lottie and resumed her exercise routine. Catriona was happy to have produced a son and a daughter. David loved the cute dark-haired little girl but he also wanted more sons, and made no secret of the fact. Catriona's love for her husband transcended the discomfort of pregnancy, and even overcame her fears about losing her looks.

'I'll make a deal with you, darling,' she said. 'I'll have another baby and if it's a boy, that will be it. If it's a girl, I'll try once more.'

'You're a bottler, Cat,' he said, and kissed her affectionately. He knew he would have at least three children and perhaps four.

'If they're all girls, you'll just have to make do with them,' she said.

Catriona did not show any greater interest in her daughter than she had in her son. They were never neglected in any way but Lottie was responsible for more of their early upbringing than Catriona. The truth of the matter was that Catriona's feelings were less maternal and more directed to pleasing her husband.

Two years after Moira was born, Catriona gave birth to her second son. In an act of unequalled generosity, so thought Catriona, David agreed to call the boy Angus, which delighted the Campbells. David now had his three children. More particularly, he had two sons to take over the activities of High Peaks Pastoral Company. He didn't have any expectation that his daughter would remain permanently with them.

Catriona was immensely relieved to be free of any further pregnancies. She threw herself into a strenuous program of calisthenics and aerobics and monitored her weight every day. It was wonderful to hear people tell her that she looked fantastic. She had had three children and was still a young woman. Now she could ride with David to her heart's content. She rode King only occasionally because David had presented her with a great new bay filly, Ajana's second thoroughbred foal, which David actually liked better than Starana. Catriona called her Davana, in acknowledgement of David's gift and the great mare that produced her.

David still handled a horse occasionally, but most of the breaking was done by Greg Robertson; Shaun Covers' time was mostly taken up with the stud cattle. It was Greg who had handled Starana before she was turned over to Angus Campbell's horse trainer. Originally David had told Angus that he could race her for two years, but he increased the period to three years.

Starana won her first three country races with such ease that Angus sent her to Sydney where, after being blocked badly, she ran a fast-finishing second. At her second race in Sydney, the filly won by three lengths. It was an important day for the Campbell and MacLeod families but most especially for Angus. It was one thing to win on a country track but to win at Randwick was something else again. David and Catriona had accompanied the Campbells to Randwick, in all their finery, to mark the occasion.

In her second year of racing, Starana won two country cups and then blitzed a good field of horses in her return race at Randwick. Angus was delighted – there was no telling how far Starana would go. But in her next race the golden mare broke down and was forced to return to Inverlochy for a prolonged spell. Starana had bowed a tendon, stretching it beyond the normal. She was raced again, but once again broke down. Reluctantly, Angus returned her to High Peaks – Starana would never be able to race again.

Greg handled Davana and she was raced only a couple of times the first year. She ran a second and a third, but David felt that she was a lot better than that. The filly was still growing, so they spelled her and brought her back to the track as a three-year-old. Racing in Catriona's colours, Davana won her first country race by four lengths. Her jockey told David and Catriona that she won it 'on the bit', meaning that she had a lot more in reserve. The race marked the beginning of a run of successes such as neither David nor Catriona had imagined possible.

The success of these two fillies from Ajana gave Wilf

White enormous pleasure. While Starana had broken down she had been a fine racehorse and there was no doubt in his mind that she would make a great brood mare. He knew that sometimes, just sometimes, a combination of sire and dam produced wonderful horses.

At the close of her first year of racing Davana had won Catriona a bag of money. Davana was being compared with the greatest mares in Australian racing history, so it was not surprising that great racing figures tried to buy her from the MacLeods. The money they were offering was stupendous.

'What am I to do, darling?' Catriona asked her husband.

David, like his father, wasn't a man to beat about the bush. 'If Davana were mine I'd let her go. You saw what happened to her sister. Davana could break down at her very next race or fall and break her leg. We've got Starana to breed from, so we've got the blood.'

'Darling, what's mine is yours. If you think we should sell Davana, we'll sell her. It would be nice to keep racing her and to see what she could end up achieving but we'll see that anyway. And as you say, anything can happen to a horse.'

Catriona had never had to go without money for a day of her life but she had been staggered by the amount she had been offered for Davana. Ajana's next foal was a colt named Western Star and that would be her last, too, because David felt she had done enough for any mare. People were already offering to buy the colt but Catriona doubted that David would sell him.

He could see the stud possibilities for a colt that was brother to Starana and Davana. Moreover, Western Star gave promise of being a great looking individual. Unlike his dam, the colt was a liver chestnut with a white strip on his head and two white rear stockings.

So they let Davana go. David rang Wilf White and told him of their plans to sell Davana. He did not want Wilf to learn about the sale after it was made. Wilf was disappointed that they were not going to keep Davana but recognised that there were risks and that Catriona had made a good business decision. And it was not as if they did not have the blood, because there was Starana with her breeding life ahead of her. There was also the chestnut colt which, Wilf predicted, would be one of the boom sires of the future. Releasing Davana was not done without a pang because Catriona loved horses, and Davana was a very special horse. She recognised, though, that David's advice was sound. Davana could go on winning races and amassing prize money but she could just as easily break down or be injured in a race fall. It had happened to other good horses and it would continue to happen for as long as horses were raced. But Davana did not break down. She went on her winning way and amassed much more prize money than Catriona had received for her. That was the luck of the business, and neither Catriona nor David had any regrets about selling the mare.

But Starana, the horse that held the MacLeods' strongest hopes for breeding, did not get in foal. Not the first year and not the second year. David had her inspected by a horse veterinarian and was not very thrilled by what he heard. He had never had much trouble getting their mares in foal and it looked as if they might have a lot of trouble with Starana. He was told she could be afflicted with any one of a number of problems. The first was what was referred to as 'silent' heat. The remedy involved getting a vet to examine the mare two or three times a week in the breeding months. Another possibility was that Starana could have an infection.

The more David heard from the experts, the less he liked the idea of messing about with Starana. He put her in the paddock to retire with her mother and more or less forgot about her. Well, not exactly. Both mares were exceptionally quiet and he would feed them from a bucket two or three times a week. Starana would rest her head on his shoulder while he stroked her neck.

The truth of the matter was that David had greater concerns than a thoroughbred mare that would not go in foal. He was not a thoroughbred man and although their foray into the business with Davana had turned out successfully, it had not convinced him to get stuck into breeding thoroughbreds. He was well aware that for every winning horse there were probably hundreds that never won a race. And the costs were prohibitive – the only way the average person could ever race a horse was with syndication, whereby a group of people all put up so much money to buy and race a yearling. Later, if the chestnut colt from Ajana turned out satisfactorily and won races, he might stand him at stud and Greg could look after the business. He, David, certainly did not have time to mess about seeing to the mating of mares.

It was about this time that David received a phone call from Troy Hamilton asking if he could come to see him. Troy and his son Walter owned Strath Fillan, the property that adjoined Poitrel. It was mostly wether country, though the Hamiltons also ran Hereford cattle. David knew that his father, Andrew, had shorn at Strath Fillan and had got on well with Troy and Walter. Troy had been a commando on Timor in the Second World War. They were a family that kept very much to themselves. David had heard that Walter was having health problems. There was also a daughter, but she had married and lived somewhere in Sydney.

Troy was a strong man who had once been rather good-looking. His hair was now grey, which matched his grey eyes. There were lines under his eyes and he had fallen away somewhat since David saw him last. Troy had always attended the annual show and that was where David remembered seeing him.

'G'day, David . . . Catriona,' Troy said, as he came up the steps.

'Good to see you, Troy,' David answered as he shook hands.

'I've been meaning to ring you to ask about having a dekko at your cattle down on Glen Morrison, but never got around to it. Ah well, it doesn't matter now,' Hamilton said wistfully.

'What's the problem, Troy?' David asked. He sensed there was something wrong.

'No good beating about the bush, David. I've been diagnosed with cancer. I'm going to have an operation, but they don't give me much chance. That's one of my problems. The second is that Walter has this Parkinson's thing. He's had it for a while but it's got worse. He's got a job to hold things now.'

'Crikey, that's bloody tough, Troy. How can we help you?' David asked.

'I'm wondering, only wondering, if you'd be in a position to buy Strath Fillan from us, David. I realise it's not a good time to sell properties now with wool the way it is, but I reckoned if I could sell it privately I would save on the commission. The agents have had plenty of commission from me in the past but I want as much money as I can get to give it to Walter. Well, Walter mostly. Beth has to get her share. Walter and I would like you to have Strath Fillan, David. Your father was a good man and we've seen what you've done with Poitrel and Glen Morrison. You know this country, David. You've got the dogs and the horses to work it and I reckoned Strath Fillan would fit in nicely with your other places – Poitrel, especially.'

David looked across at Catriona who had been listening to everything Troy had said. 'I'll get a cup of tea,' she said.

'What do you reckon, David?' Hamilton asked. 'Would you be interested in buying the old place?'

'To tell you the truth, you've caught me on the

hop, Troy,' David confessed. The acquisition of more land always excited him but his plans for expansion had not led him in the area of Strath Fillan. He was even now looking for a grazing property further out; a property where he could breed replacement wethers so that he didn't have to continually buy them in. Strath Fillan was principally a wether place so that meant even more wethers. And then his mind clicked into gear. Sure, it was a wether place but it was also nearly perfect for horses, hilly and well watered. It would be just the place to stand a stallion and to breed horses. And then there was Greg, who had a girl and wanted to get married. He could put Greg on Strath Fillan. The big problem was that he couldn't really afford to buy Strath Fillan as well as a property further out, and he needed the latter more than he needed Strath Fillan. It wasn't that acquiring Strath Fillan didn't excite him – putting High Peaks, Poitrel and Strath Fillan together would give him more than eleven thousand acres of hill country. Then there was Glen Morrison on top of that. Aberfeldy he regarded quite differently, even though he was topping off some of its cattle on Merriwa country.

'I'll have to think about it, Troy. I'm grateful that you've come to me and I'm really sorry to hear of your health problems – no one deserves so much bad luck, Troy,' David said. 'I've been on the lookout for a property further out where I could breed replacement wethers rather than having to continually buy them in. If I bought Strath Fillan I'd have to put off buying the breeding place for a while. That's my problem, Troy.'

'Good of you to put your cards on the table, David,' Hamilton said. 'It's what I'd expect of you. I reckoned with what you've got here and that big place in Queensland the banks would be pretty sympathetic.'

'Look, I won't make a decision now, Troy. Can you give me a few days and I'll let you know one way or the other?'

'No worries – that's fair enough. I didn't expect an answer today. Thanks, Catriona,' Hamilton said, as Catriona handed him a cup of tea and offered him a plate of biscuits. 'By the way, how is the family?'

'Very well, thank you Troy. They're out the back with Lottie right now. Three children can be a bit overpowering at times,' Catriona said.

'Tell me about it. Beth brings her three up a couple of times a year and they just go mad. Probably does 'em a heap of good out here in the bush after Sydney. The city's not my cup of tea but I've got to admit it's where the good doctors are. The best doctors, I mean. I've been healthy all my life, even survived the war, and now this. No rhyme or reason for it.'

'Jean Courteney, you know, Sister Jean down at Poitrel, says there's a theory that too much meat in the diet can cause some cancers,' Catriona said.

'Well, I've certainly eaten a lot of meat in my time, Catriona. And I knew old fellows who never ate much else but meat and bread and lived into their nineties.

I suppose these scientist fellows are finding out more things and maybe they'll find a cure for cancer, but it won't do me any good,' Hamilton said.

David was still thinking about Troy's offer. 'Troy, it's a long time since I was on Strath Fillan. Dad took me there once when I was very young. Do you mind if I poke on down and have a look at your place?' David asked.

'Any time, David. Bring Catriona with you. Louise was only saying a few days ago that she hadn't seen Catriona for ages.'

'I've been a bit busy having babies these last few years, Troy. Thank you for the invitation.'

They talked on about wool and cattle prices and then Troy said he had to go to town, and left. David saw him to his car and then came back to the lounge room.

'Well, what do you think about that?' Catriona asked, as he sat down.

'I don't know what to think, Cat. Troy's offer takes me back to the day old Wilf visited and offered us Poitrel. We only had High Peaks then and it seemed the most wonderful news we had ever received. Owning more land was what Dad dreamed about, yet it killed him in the end,' David said with emotion in his voice.

'But you can buy Strath Fillan,' Catriona said. It was a statement more than a question.

'Oh, yes, we could buy the place, but it isn't really the direction I had in mind for the business. If I buy

Strath Fillan I couldn't afford the breeding place out west. I haven't found it yet, but the place I want would cost a lot more than Strath Fillan. I couldn't afford the two. The whole idea of buying a breeding place is so we can breed replacement wethers. If we buy Strath Fillan without the breeding place then we would need to buy more wethers than we're doing now.'

'If it made good sense to buy Poitrel and then Glen Morrison because of their proximity to High Peaks then surely it also makes good sense to buy Strath Fillan, which adjoins Poitrel. It would give us three adjacent properties with Glen Morrison across the road,' Catriona said.

'I'm well aware of all that, Cat. It would give us over eleven thousand acres of hill country, plus Glen Morrison. And values are down now with the wool market the way it is, but I'm betting things won't stay that way. If I wasn't so keen to get hold of a good breeding place I'd probably say yes to Troy right now. He wants us to have the place just as Wilf wanted us to have Poitrel. Of course, Anne and Kate will have to be consulted. I know they're happy to leave these decisions to me but they're directors of High Peaks Pastoral Company so I can't ignore them,' David said.

'Of course you can't,' Catriona agreed. 'I think we should go and have a look at Strath Fillan. If you think it's a good proposition, buy it.'

'Then I'm up the creek for money to buy the other place. Sure, I could go to the bank but interest rates are too high now to make borrowing an option. There are good land people in lots of trouble over these high interest rates.'

'I don't know why you're worried, darling. You can have my money to buy your breeding place. What's mine is yours. I've told you that many times before. I wouldn't have had Davana except for you. What I got for her would buy your breeding place, wouldn't it?'

'Close enough, Cat. But I don't like using your money,' David said.

'Don't be silly, darling. I have other money invested. Take Davana's money. It's for a worthwhile purpose,' Catriona said.

David looked at his wife and broke into a grin. 'You're a bottler, Cat. And to think I once thought you were a little pest,' he said as he bent down to kiss her.

Catriona knew that David did not throw praise around in an extravagant fashion. When he called someone a bottler, which was not very often, it was just about the highest compliment he could bestow.

'But you always came to my rescue,' she reminded him with a dazzling smile. It was the kind of smile that usually stopped him in his tracks.

'So I did. Well, you were worth rescuing, Cat,' he said.

Catriona smiled broadly. The truth was that she really lived for David. He had always been the light on the hill for her. One of the things she most admired about her husband was that money hadn't changed the way he treated people. He was just as likely to take Greg or Shaun to a stud sale as her father or brother. David had been lucky, but luck and money hadn't changed him.

David sat down in his lounge chair beside the fireplace and held out his hands towards her. Catriona got up and went across to him. She hadn't sat on his lap for a while because the children were always underfoot. That was why she liked the privacy of the hills.

'There's another thing to consider,' he said, as he kissed her cheek.

'What is it, darling?' she asked.

'It's Greg. He and Liz want to get married. On top of that, I've been trying to think of a way to upgrade his job – Greg is a good colt and I don't want to lose him. I've put a lot of effort into making him a good stockman. When he came to us all he knew much about was horses and, while he's still horse-mad, he's not as one-eyed as he used to be. Liz is as horsey as he is but I think she's a great girl. If we bought Strath Fillan I could make Greg manager there and he and Liz would have a place to make their home. The cottage is all right, but it's only three rooms – not ideal for a young married woman,' David said.

'That's a marvellous idea, darling,' Catriona agreed.

'I'm pleased you think so. I've got a pretty good idea what the property is like. I've looked at it from Wallaby Rocks. Some of it is top-of-the-range stuff but it's got good valleys and a decent creek. On top of wethers and some cattle it would make a great horse place. Apart from Wilf's remaining old mares and Starana, which have to stay on Poitrel, I reckon we could shift all the other horses to Strath Fillan. We could possibly stand Western Star there and Greg could look after all the mares. It would be another source of income and probably suit Greg and Liz down to the ground.'

'You're a genius, David,' Cat said, and kissed him. 'Daddy once said that you were a genius with stock and he was right.'

David smirked. 'If Daddy said it, it must be right, eh?'

'David, don't you dare make fun of my father!' she scolded.

'Wouldn't dream of it, sweetheart. You know we get on very well these days.'

The next day David and Catriona took two horses in a float down to Strath Fillan. It was the first time Catriona had been on the property. She had met Louise a couple of times and her son, Walter, only once. He was a quiet, middle-aged man who had never married. His arm shook as he extended his hand to David.

'We brought horses and I thought you might show us around a bit,' David said, nodding at the float. 'Can you manage that, Troy? I mean, are you well enough to ride?'

'I'd sooner die on a horse than in a bed, David,' Hamilton said proudly.

Louise watched as David and Catriona mounted. She had always envied Catriona's horsemanship. She had seen Catriona win Champion Lady Rider and Champion Hack awards and no woman she had ever seen rode a horse with more skill and beauty than Catriona MacLeod. Wilf White had told them that for sheer horsemanship David took some beating but Catriona certainly rode extremely well. She always had the best of horses to show her off, and the bay horse she was riding now was a beauty.

Troy Hamilton took them through all his paddocks, though they didn't attempt to ride to the tops. There were good grassy valleys and the timber was much the same as on High Peaks . . . ironbark, kurrajong, gum, and stringybark. David thought it was a better property than Poitrel, though it didn't have the flat area that made Poitrel quite valuable. It was a fair sort of hill-country property suitable for wethers and cattle – the Hereford cattle they saw were in fine condition.

They came back to the homestead mid-morning, flushed and enlivened from the ride. Across from the main house there was a smaller dwelling which, on enquiry, Troy told them had been the overseer's cottage when the property had been much larger. It needed renovating but was structurally sound.

The main homestead at Strath Fillan was similar to their own High Peaks house, timber with an iron roof. There was a gauzed-in verandah on three sides and one portion of the verandah had been converted into a sleepout-cum-bedroom. It was a comfortable country home with sweeping views of the surrounding country, and the kitchen was fitted with an Aga stove.

The shearing shed was of three stands and again much like their own shed. It would hold several hundred sheep, probably close to two days' shearing. There were stables in good nick, a feed shed and a cluster of other buildings – one of which, David noted, was a smithy.

'Do all my own shoeing and make other things in my spare time,' Troy explained.

David nodded. He had heard that Troy Hamilton was regarded as a tough-as-teak bushman. David reckoned he would have made a good commando. It was a damned shame about the cancer. And about Walter's Parkinson's. A decent family like the Hamiltons shouldn't have to face those sorts of problems. Sometimes life seemed brutally unfair.

'How is your mother, David?' Louise asked.

'Well, thanks, Louise. The garden and grandchildren keep her busy. And of course she still does all our books,' David answered.

'I met Anne in town one day and she told me you had a landscape gardener come and set a garden up for her,' Louise said.

'And for Catriona too,' he said, and grinned, 'though Cat's garden is more easy-care than Mum's. Mum always wanted a nice garden, and now she's got it. She needed something to take her mind off things after Dad died.'

'I've only ever worried about a vegie garden here,'

Louise said. 'I wouldn't mind a more extensive garden but I don't have much time, what with the writing and the quilting.'

David and Catriona were both aware that Louise wrote children's books and produced lovely quilts in her spare time. There was always something about Louise in the local paper.

'I must come down one day and have a look at your quilts, Louise,' Catriona said, as she and David were about to leave.

'You'd better not leave it too long because Troy wants to sell up here as soon as he can, Catriona. He wants everything cleaned up so that if he goes, Walter and I are fixed up satisfactorily.'

That afternoon David and Catriona met with Anne and Kate at the High Peaks homestead. David told them that Strath Fillan was on the market and that he had been offered first crack at the property.

'Do you need more land, David?' Anne asked. 'It seems to me that you've got quite enough to look after.'

'You can never have too much land, Mum. You do the books, so you would be well aware how much costs have gone up over the last few years. I've heard that good farming properties reckon ninety per cent of their incomes are going in costs. The smaller places are going to have a real battle replacing their farm machinery.'

Anne and Kate listened intently as David continued. 'In a few years' time there will be three children to educate and two of them – the boys for sure – will want to stay here, and they will have to be paid a share of what we make,' David said.

Anne had said more than once that David shouldn't bank on his children staying on the land. They might want to be anything but landowners but she bit her tongue now.

'You only have to look at what's happened in this district,' David went on. 'A hell of a lot of young people have had to leave their places because there's not enough profit there any more. I've been lucky and have been able to acquire more land to build the business up, and now Strath Fillan has fallen into my lap. It fits in very well with what we've already got. There's also the fact that Greg and Liz want to get married. If we buy Strath Fillan, I could put Greg there as a manager, which is the upgrade I've been wanting to give him,' David said.

'That's a good point,' Kate agreed.

'I thought you wanted to buy a place further out to breed replacement wethers?' Anne asked, a little confused.

'So I do,' David said.

'I don't see how you can buy two places,' Anne said flatly.

'Catriona wants us to buy Strath Fillan and she's offered to give me the money to buy the other place. It will come from what she received for selling Davana,' he said proudly.

'*Catriona!*' Anne exclaimed.

'I've always told David that what's mine is his, Anne. David is trying to build a future for our children, so it's an investment. I wouldn't have had Davana to sell only that David gave her to me. A property for a horse seems to me to be a very good exchange.'

'Well, I must say that it was a very fortunate day for you, David, when you came to your senses and proposed to Catriona,' Anne said.

'Hear, hear,' Kate chipped in.

'That's ancient history. Well, are we in agreement that we should buy Strath Fillan?' he asked.

'It seems we should,' Anne said.

'I agree,' Kate said.

'That's the first and major item settled. What about my suggestion that we give Greg the manager's job on Strath Fillan? He's been in this little cottage a long time and I reckon he and Liz would be tickled pink to go there.'

'I think that's a splendid suggestion,' Anne said.

'Me, too,' Kate agreed. 'He's certainly earnt it.'

'My thinking is that we should move most of the horses to Strath Fillan and maybe stand Davana's brother, Western Star, there one day. Greg and Liz are both horse-mad and that sort of thing would be right up their alley,' David said.

'That seems a good idea to me,' Kate said.

'Right, I'll talk to Troy Hamilton and then to Greg. I reckon Greg and Liz will set their wedding date real quick when they hear the news,' David said, and grinned.

David and Catriona drove straight down to Strath Fillan to give the Hamiltons their decision. Relief spread across their faces. They knew that David MacLeod was the straightest man they could do business with and that they would get the fairest of fair deals. They made an appointment to meet with Hamilton's solicitor next day, and High Peaks Pastoral Company bought Strath Fillan on a walk-in-walk-out basis.

Before he and Catriona left Strath Fillan David pointed across to the old overseer's cottage. 'I'm going to renovate that cottage, Troy. When it's done, you can tell Beth that she'd be welcome to keep bringing the kids up here on their holidays. The same goes for you people if you would like to spend some time here.'

The Hamiltons looked at him in open-mouthed surprise. 'I'll fix it with the new manager,' David said.

He and Catriona got in the car and drove away. When they had driven a little way down the road Catriona asked him to stop the car.

'Why, Cat?'

'Will you just stop the car, David,' she asked again.

He braked the car to a standstill and Catriona leant across and showered him with kisses.

'What's that for?' he asked.

'What you just offered to the Hamiltons – the use of the cottage – was one of the nicest things I have ever heard. For a supposedly tough, hard man, the son of a tough, hard man, you can be very soft at times, David MacLeod.'

'Ah, well, those grandchildren of his would be very disappointed about not being able to go to Strath Fillan for their holidays. Maybe they'll accept my offer and maybe they won't. Given that Troy gave me first offer of Strath Fillan it's the least I could do,' David said. 'Can I start up now?'

'If we were out in the bush I'd –' Catriona began.

'And you the mother of three children,' he said, as he started the car.

David usually gave Greg his instructions for the following day on the previous evening. They would meet when Greg was feeding the horses, which was when David fed his dogs.

'I'd like to see you in the woolshed at nine tomorrow morning, Greg,' he said.

'Anything wrong, David?' Greg asked.

'Nothing is wrong, Greg. It happens I might have some good news for you.'

'Crikey, I like the sound of that.'

'See you at nine, Greg,' David said, as he walked away.

The two men sat on wool bales in the shearing shed. 'How long have you been with us, Greg?' David asked.

'A fair while, David. A year or so before you won the National and nine years since,' Greg answered.

'Happy here?'

'Bloody oath. Learnt a lot, too,' Greg said enthusiastically. 'Been a second home for me.'

'Okay, where do you want to go from here?'

'Well, I don't really want to leave, David. I've been offered other jobs but I don't reckon I'd be any better off. You give me extra money when I do any crutching or shearing and then there's the horses. You do want me to stay, don't you, David?'

'Of course I want you to stay, Greg. The thing is that we've just bought Strath Fillan. The sale is going through now. We've bought it on a walk-in-walk-out basis so we keep all the stock. If you're feeling up to it, I'd like you to have the job of looking after Strath Fillan, Greg. I'll make you the manager, which would mean you'll need to live there. I guess it also means that you and Liz can get married as soon as you like – seems no point to delay it any longer. And there's a pretty comfortable house on the property.'

'Crikey. I don't know what to say, David,' Greg said warmly.

David eased his back against a wool bale. 'I've a notion to send all but the working horses up to Strath Fillan and breed the foals there. I also have a notion to maybe stand Western Star, that chestnut colt from Ajana, at stud. Of course, we'd have to race him first. If he won well, we'd pull him out and stand him. With sisters like Starana and Davana, he ought to pull in a lot of mares. Think you could handle that?'

'I reckon I could. David, would it mean that Liz and I could still go campdrafting?'

'You might not be able to attend as many camp-drafts, Greg. There is always a price to responsibility.

Of course, you don't have to take this job – you could stay here at High Peaks and go on just as you're doing. I could send Kate to Strath Fillan and Shaun could take over Glen Morrison or vice versa. I'd rather he stay where he is looking after the stud cattle and I'll have stud sheep there before long. Camp-drafting is all right, Greg, but you've got to think of your future. You only get a win in your turn at that game because there are so many drafting these days. I've had to curtail my activities in that area. How many drafts have you seen me at lately? Or trials either, for that matter. The local trial is about my limit now. A fellow's family must come first, Greg,' David said.

Greg considered carefully all David was saying. 'I'd like to take you up on your offer but can I ring Liz first? If I say yes without asking her I reckon that would be a pretty bad way to start a marriage,' Greg said.

'It certainly would. Of course you can ring her. Do it now if you like. There'll be an increase in your wages too, Greg.'

They walked up the slope to the house and David waited with his mother while Greg rang Liz. His face was wreathed in a broad smile when he came out of Anne's office.

'What did Liz say, Greg?' David asked.

'First she screamed, and then she said, "Yes, yes, yes. Take it!" Then she said if she were here, she would kiss you,' Greg said, grinning.

David put out his hand. 'Well done, Greg. You've worked hard here and you've done a good job for us. You've earnt this promotion. Now it's up to you. You know me. If you let me down, I'll come down on you like a ton of bricks. But I'm sure you won't disappoint me.'

'I won't, David. This is the opportunity I've been after – it's just meant for me. Liz is really excited about it,' Greg said.

'Good. I'll take you down there next time I go. I'd say take Liz with you next weekend but I don't like intruding on Troy and his family too much. They've got big problems, Greg. Troy has cancer, and Walter has an advanced form of Parkinson's disease. Troy wanted a quick sale and preferred it was with someone he knew. That's about the size of it, Greg.'

'Gee, that's bad luck. Dad told me that Troy Hamilton was a pretty tough fellow ... a commando or something.'

'That's right, Greg. It's a bad show. Meanwhile, we've got a lot of work to do. You had better go down to Poitrel. That new lot of wethers is due to arrive after lunch. There's some crutchings you can press while you're waiting. Better take some lunch with you, just in case Jean's on duty.'

'So that's that,' Anne said, joining David as Greg went to his cottage to make up some lunch.

'That's that,' David agreed.

'Five properties. When I came here if someone had

said to Andy that one day the MacLeods would own High Peaks, Poitrel and Strath Fillan, not to mention Glen Morrison and Aberfeldy, he would not have believed it. He hoped we might acquire Poitrel but that was the limit of his thinking,' Anne said.

'Dad started it all off, Mum. It was the way Dad and his mother treated Wilf that put Poitrel in our hands and it was Dad's friendship with Tim Sparkes that put Aberfeldy in mine.'

Anne smiled at her son's wisdom – she knew he was right.

'I've got to get going, Mum,' David said, hurrying off. But a few minutes later he was back again.

'What is it, David?' Anne asked.

'It's Nap. He's dead. He was lying with his head pointed up here and I thought he was asleep,' said David, white-faced.

'Oh, David,' was all Anne could manage, but there was a wealth of meaning in her words. She knew full well what Nap meant to her son. Of all the dogs David had owned and handled, none meant more to him than Nap. Not even Clancy, who had won the National. 'He was very old, and very tired lately.'

'It doesn't make losing him any easier, Mum. I doubt I'll ever have a dog like him again. I know Clancy won the National and he's a brilliant dog, but Nap had an extra dimension to him.

'I'll ring Kate, and Bruce McClymont – asks about him every time he rings,' David said, and went out again.

Nap had been growing weaker for months and although he dragged himself after David when he took the other dogs for their runs, it was clearly an effort. Only his heart kept him going. Catriona, Anne and Kate all fed him titbits and gave him eggs but sixteen was a good age for a dog, even for a kelpie. David had been going to have him put to sleep but kept deferring it.

Belle had gone before Nap and was buried with a row of other MacLeod dogs, but David decided to bury Nap beside his kennel, and Kate made a plaque and inscribed on it the following words: *MacLeods' Nap. He was more human than dog.*

Kate rang the local paper and Bruce McClymont rang just about everywhere. The following article appeared shortly after.

Canine Hero Dies, Aged 16
Nap, one of the kelpie stars of the film The Call of the High Country, *died recently at High Peaks, Merriwa, NSW. The red-and-tan kelpie, considered by his owner, David MacLeod, to be the greatest of all the great MacLeod kelpies, made national news on two occasions. On the first Nap carried a message across miles of rough mountain country with the news that the part-owner of the property had broken a leg.*

The kelpie came to the rescue a second time when he shepherded a small mob of sheep into a cave and saved them from a bushfire. No greater loyalty to man was displayed by any other dog.

This generous tribute to a dog could probably be described as an epitaph for all of the faithful, hard-working stock dogs who did not make the national news.

David had dogs that were the sons and daughters of Nap, and Angus Campbell had Nap's blood in his border collies. But no other dog occupied Nap's kennel in David MacLeod's lifetime. The old dog had meant more to him than he could ever put into words. He could talk to Nap and know that the dog understood pretty well what he said. A lot of people wouldn't believe that about a dog, but they would be people who didn't really understand dogs. David knew that occasionally, very occasionally, a dog would come along that was super-intelligent. It was the same with dogs as with humans. There are the Michelangelos, the Galileos and the Einsteins and there are their canine equivalents. Nap had been one of those equivalents.

Nap's passing was the prelude to three other deaths. Anne's father died in April, and her mother in October. That she hadn't seen more of her parents in recent years caused Anne much guilt. They had come to High Peaks once or twice a year but her father, particularly, felt out of his element in the bush. He liked to watch league football and to fish. Anne regretted that David had not seen more of her parents but he was just as much out of his element where they lived – first in Sydney and then on the north coast of New South Wales – as Jack was in the bush.

A loss of a different kind occurred when Gertie Brooks rang Anne and told her that her brother had died that day. Wilf White held a very special place in the hearts of Anne, Kate and David, for Wilf had allowed them to purchase Poitrel on very generous terms, because of his respect for Andrew MacLeod.

David had a special reason for remembering Wilf White because, apart from selling his family Poitrel, he had given the MacLeods Ajana, a flying machine and a great brood mare. Wilf had lived on the successes of Starana and Davana, Ajana's two great fillies. Gertie told them later that Wilf considered what these horses had achieved on the racetrack justified the money he had invested in thoroughbreds. David thought of Wilf with deep affection. 'He was a great gentleman, Mum. Some people thought he was a bit funny but this family owes Wilf White a damn lot.'

It was a solemn group that drove to Coffs Harbour for Wilf White's funeral. Anne, Kate, David and Catriona sat with Gertie in the front pew of the church. David gave the eulogy and though he spoke in a church with a view of the Pacific, his memory of Wilf White was of the old chap at Poitrel, feeding his beloved horses.

Later, at the wake, David took Gertie by the arm. 'I . . . *we* will never forget Wilf, Gertie.'

She nodded, and rested her hand on his arm. 'Some will, but I believe you won't, David.'

But Wilf White's death removed another link with the past. Anne told David that death came to everyone – that was why a person should make the best of things in the time one had. Not, she assured her son, that he wasn't doing that.

David was indeed very busy. With Greg Robertson installed on Strath Fillan, David did not have him to fall back on for jobs at High Peaks. He had transferred most of the breeding horses to Strath Fillan, leaving only their own working horses and Ajana and Starana on High Peaks. While he had competent people on the other four properties, he was now back to looking after High Peaks on his own. He needed another Greg Robertson, but there was nobody like Greg to be had.

Catriona was secretly pleased with this situation because it meant that David was home more often and that she could go mustering with him. Anne was relinquishing her role as keeper of the books to Catriona, who had mastered the computer she had installed and was putting all their financial records on disc. At first sceptical, David was convinced when Catriona was able to retrieve masses of information at the touch of a key. Keeping the books for one property was one thing; keeping a record of inputs and outputs for five properties was quite another. And if David acquired his merino breeding property, this would add to the financial transactions.

'I wish the children would grow up faster, Mum,' he said to his mother. She was working in her beloved garden and David was standing beside her.

'You shouldn't,' she answered.

'Shouldn't what?' he asked.

'Shouldn't wish for that,' she said. 'Childhood is such a wonderful time. Children grow up fast enough as it is. Then the problems arrive. You should enjoy your children. I certainly enjoyed your childhood. If I hadn't had you I would have missed an awful lot. I used to worry about you when you were away on your ponies because if anything had happened to you, I knew I couldn't have another child.'

'Sorry, Mum, to put you through that grief,' he said, coyly.

'You aren't at all, David. You would do it all over again no matter how much I worried. You were very much a boy where horses were concerned. Your father aided and abetted you. I know he did. Well, he got what he wanted – though he wanted two or three Davids and a couple of daughters as well.'

'And what did you want, Mum?' David asked.

'I wanted to give Andy what he wanted, dear. I couldn't, so we had to be content with you. You have a lovely family, David. Three is nice,' Anne said.

'Catriona would have had another baby if we hadn't had Angus,' he told her. 'She made a deal with me. If she had a second son, that was it. If she had a second daughter, she would try once more for a boy.'

'I know, David. Catriona told me. Your mother was right about Catriona, wasn't she? I always knew she was the girl for you,' Anne said.

'Well, as I've said on more than one occasion, you were a pretty grouse mother. It was just that I had more things than girls on my mind in those days,' he said.

'You could have lost her, David,' Anne said.

'If she had been so easily put off, she wouldn't have been the girl for me, Mum,' he said, with the simple logic that was difficult to challenge.

'To change the subject, I'm wondering if you would be up to camping out with us next weekend. Cat and I are taking the kids up to the hills for their first night out. Lottie is having the weekend off. I want to get the kids used to the bush. We'll have a singsong. You could bring your guitar and play. Do you think you're up to sleeping in a swag?' he asked.

'I'm not exactly geriatric, David,' Anne said.

'I realise that, but I don't want you to come just to please the kids and me . . . not if it's too much for you,' he said. 'I don't expect you to go eel-bashing.'

'And I wouldn't be,' Anne said with a laugh. 'Are we riding?'

'The kids and Catriona can ride. I'll take the Fergy and the trailer with the gear. Think you could sit on the trailer?'

'Now you're putting me to the test, dear. I think I would prefer to ride than to be bounced around on the trailer. Have you thought about asking Kate? I fancy Kate might feel a wee bit left out of things, and it wouldn't hurt to ask her. Of course, you should talk it over with Catriona,' Anne said.

'I will,' David said. 'It won't be many years before Glen Morrison will be too much for Kate. That's one

141

of the reasons I need the children to grow up.'

'You will be very disappointed if the children have other ideas,' Anne said. 'I've warned you before not to expect that your children will naturally want to stay on the land.'

Anne's words would prove to be prophetic.

Chapter Six

Camping out was a new, exciting experience for the MacLeod children, and to camp out with Nanna and Auntie Kate as well as their parents was a real treat. It was an outing David had been promising them for some time. Up until now Angus had been considered too young to camp out, and he was the most excited of the three children.

David had pitched the tent and a large tarpaulin very close to the spot Andy had taken Anne for her first lunch with him all those years ago. It was adjacent to the creek where Andy, Anne and Kate had gone eel-bashing. It was a warm evening and the children, watched over by Anne, were allowed to paddle in the creek while David, Catriona and Kate set up camp and began preparing the meal.

The planning of David and Catriona's family had all been so carefully done, Anne thought, as she watched the children squiggle their toes in the mud, squealing with delight. The three children were spaced out two years apart – seven, five and three. To look at Catriona one would never know that she had produced three children, Anne thought to herself, her figure was so youthful. Of course, Anne would never have guessed the lengths that Catriona had gone to to maintain her appearance in David's absences.

With parents as handsome as David and Catriona the three children were all fine-looking, all dark-haired like their father. The two boys had grey eyes, while Moira's eyes were chestnut brown. In nature, the children were all quite different.

Dougal was a very quiet boy, and nothing like David had been at the same age. At the age of seven David had been pony-mad, and was in the hills with his father at every opportunity, while Dougal was more often found buried in a book or perhaps ensconced in Anne's poultry shed examining the newly hatched chickens. A new litter of pups was a special delight and he would spend hours watching the pups playing and sucking at their mother's teats. Anne, who was considered the oracle where children were concerned, described Dougal as 'solemn'. The eldest child certainly took everything very seriously.

Dougal established very early on that both Ajana and Starana were especially receptive to titbits of bread and sugar. The little boy would tempt the horses with a piece of sugar and then wander down to their shelter shed. There he would sit down on bales of hay and Starana, in particular, would nuzzle up to him looking for more morsels. Although Dougal had his own pony,

Starana had a special place in his heart, with her velvety soft muzzle and lovely eyes. His mother had told him that Starana won races but that she couldn't have a foal. They had kept her at High Peaks because of old Mr White. He had owned Ajana and made a gift of the mare to David, and Starana was her daughter.

David had expected that Dougal would want to ride with him but if Dougal could get out of riding into the hills he would do so, and lose himself in a book instead. Likewise, at shearing and crutching time David expected that his son would be eager to help with yarding the sheep and penning up, but Dougal showed little interest. He spent a lot of time with Nanna and seemed more interested in how she made a cake than the activities down at the shed.

It was Anne who discovered how bright Dougal was. He had asked her a question about something and she had dug out a book that contained the answer to his question. She handed him the book and after he had looked at it for a few moments he handed it back to her.

'Does that answer your question, Dougal?' Anne asked.

'Very well, Nanna,' he said. He then proceeded to detail from memory what he had just read in the book.

Anne picked up the book and studied the page in question. Dougal had read off the three or four paragraphs almost word perfect. She tested him on another subject and again he repeated what he had just read. There was no doubt about it; the boy had a photographic memory.

Unlike David, Dougal loved school, and attended the primary school in Merriwa where David and Catriona were once students. David's old principal, Mr Carruthers, had long gone but his replacement, Miss Barwick, never had to complain that Dougal did not have his heart or his mind on his school work. Academically, Dougal left all the other children of the district in his wake.

David MacLeod was perhaps less impressed with his son's achievements at school than he should have been. David himself had won a local sheepdog trial when he was only ten years of age and had run second in a junior campdraft when he was not a great deal older. Dougal had no such ability to speak of – there was no way that Dougal could bring straggler wethers down off Yellow Rock as David had done.

'What are you doing, Dougal?' Anne called to him. The boy was stretched out on a dead tree that overhung the creek.

'There's a dead eel underneath, Nanna. I wonder what happened to it,' Dougal mused. He stood up with the eel hanging by its tail from one hand. He thrust it towards his grandmother and his siblings so they could examine the creature at closer quarters.

'Poo, it smells,' Moira said with disgust.

'Poo, it mells,' Angus said, copying his sister. Angus copied her a lot because of his two older siblings, she was closer to him. Dougal was four years older and seemed to occupy a different world.

'Yes, it smells, Dougal,' Anne concurred. 'Throw it back into the creek and the yabbies will eat it.'

Dougal let the eel dangle from his hand for a few moments before reluctantly dropping it back in the creek. 'Now wash your hands, Dougal,' Anne told him.

The boy was certainly different from his father, Anne thought, as she watched him. Where David had done things instinctively, Dougal questioned everything. For example, why had Starana broken down? Why couldn't she be healed? Why couldn't she have a foal? Of course, Dougal asked about a lot of things but Starana was his main concern because, as he told his grandmother one day, 'Starana is my friend.'

'Why is she your friend, Dougal?' Anne asked him, curious.

'Because she talks to me with her eyes,' Dougal told her earnestly. 'I can talk to her and she looks at me as if she knows what I'm saying.'

Anne loved the three children but she had a big soft spot for Dougal because she felt he needed more understanding than his brother and sister. Dougal, she told Kate, was a square peg in a round hole.

Moira was like a piece of quicksilver. She had her father's dark hair, her mother's brown eyes. As a child she wasn't as pretty as her mother had been, though her features were handsome. Anne felt that she would blossom into a striking girl later, which was exactly what happened – Moira grew more beautiful with each year that passed.

From when she was only a tiny girl Moira adored her father. David would carry her in front of him on his saddle with one great arm wrapped around her and the other holding the reins. Before long Moira's little hand took the reins. David bought her a pony and led it round with Moira perched on top just as his own father had led his first pony. Moira would put on a turn if her father left without her. David had great difficulty in explaining to Moira that a day in the hills was too much for the little girl.

When Catriona finished 'baby-farming', as she called it, and began accompanying David again, Moira saw no reason why she should remain at home with Lottie. Lottie was nice, and good to her, but could never compare to her father, who did all kinds of exciting things. A trip to Glen Morrison was about the zenith of Moira's expectations at that period of her young life. Hand in hand with her father, she would walk up and down the big show shed where his red-and-white cattle were housed. Often there would be a small red-and-white calf sucking away at its very large mother. Lottie could offer nothing as wonderful as this.

Moira, Anne noted, possessed some of David's innate stockmanship. She did things instinctively. You didn't have to tell Moira not to push sheep too hard through a gate, but to let them draw through steadily – it was something she had picked up from watching her father in the yards. David used to carry her there and sit her on a big strainer post while he worked sheep through the yards. So, without really knowing why her father did things in a certain way, Moira followed suit.

At the age of ten, Moira could muster sheep down off Wallaby Rocks to the Poitrel shed. David wouldn't allow her to muster Yellow Rock without him and she would not have been able to bring stragglers down as he had done, but she was, he told his mother, 'a pretty damned good kid'. In actual fact, David was thrilled to bits about Moira. The only reservation he had about his daughter was that one day he would lose her, for that was the fate of daughters. Moira's passion for the land made up for Dougal's lack of interest, in David's eyes. And while Catriona fretted to Anne that Moira was too much of a tomboy, she reasoned that boarding school would straighten her daughter out.

Of the three children, Angus was the closest in nature to David and the most reckless of the trio. Angus could do everything his sister could do and then some. He broke his arm falling off a horse at eight and experienced concussion at ten. This frightened the life out of David and he read the riot act to Angus. There was nothing the fearless boy would not attempt and of the three children he was by far the most gifted with sheepdogs. As a teenager he could run rings around Angus Campbell, who had been working sheepdogs all his life. Angus still hadn't managed to win an Open Trial though he had come close a couple of times. 'Grandpa doesn't think fast enough,' Angus confided to his father. David recognised that this was a telling statement. He had known for years that Angus Campbell wasn't a natural stockman but it was remarkable of his young son to recognise this failing.

The youngest MacLeod was known to everyone as Young Angus. Once, Angus Campbell had been called

Young Angus and his father Old Angus, and the old man was delighted to have a grandson to carry his name. The boy was born to love the land – which he did with all his heart and soul. Horses, cattle, sheep, sheepdogs, it didn't matter: Young Angus thrived on them all.

Young Angus differed from his father in one respect – he was a very nice-looking boy and he liked girls, and girls liked him. Dougal didn't pay girls much attention and in this respect alone he was like his father had been at the same age. However, Young Angus had a steady stream of girlfriends and discarded them with the same speed with which he picked them up. It was all a great joke to Young Angus. David attempted a couple of very serious discussions with his son but they didn't do a lot of good. That was until, returning one night from a B & S ball, Angus just about wrote off a utility and put himself in hospital. Young Angus knew he had pushed his father's patience too far, and was grounded for six months. No balls, no shows, no nothing except work. 'I'll cure him or kill him,' David told Catriona. Of course, he didn't mean it literally. He had plenty of liking for his younger son but he was a mad bugger at times. David didn't want to kill his spirit but the boy had to learn some sense. He reckoned if he could get him over this wild period, Angus would be the goods. After the boy finished boarding school, with much foreboding, David sent him off to the pastoral college at Longreach. He hoped the teachers there would be able to handle him. He also hoped Angus wouldn't get into too many fights over girls.

But of course all of this was years down the track. Yet even now Anne could see vast differences in her son's three children, and it was exciting to ponder what paths they would take. She hoped she would live long enough to see it. In the meantime, she entirely approved of these 'bonding' excursions, as Catriona described them, and enjoyed herself thoroughly around the camp fire. 'Oh, Andy, I wish you were here to see the children', she sighed to herself. But perhaps he did see them from up above High Peaks.

After they had eaten, they all sang until the children fell asleep under the stars and were put into their swags. When they awoke the next morning their father had the billy boiling on the fire and they had a hot breakfast of sizzling bacon and eggs. Then they pulled camp and rode home.

The children loved these camping trips. Anne, David and Catriona all felt that there was no place like the bush to rear children. Reality would come all too soon but it was important that children had a happy upbringing and that they experienced simple pleasures before they had to tackle the harder lessons of life. So camping trips figured strongly in the childhoods of the MacLeod children.

When the children were older, they rode to Wallaby Rocks and camped in the big cave where Nap had taken the sheep to shelter during the great bushfire. There,

Catriona confided to Moira, David had at last asked her to marry him.

'In the big cave?' Moira breathed.

'Yes, it was there that he told me he had been left Aberfeldy and that we could get married and I knew that we would. I would have married David even though I knew Daddy and Mummy didn't approve,' Catriona reflected wistfully.

'But don't they think Dad is rather wonderful?' Moira asked.

'They do now, but they didn't know about Aberfeldy or Glen Morrison at that time and they had other plans of grandeur for me.'

'But how could any other man get within a bull's roar of Dad?' Moira asked.

'Moira, please. Some of your expressions are distinctly earthy. But, to answer your question, of course no other man could come close to your father. He was the only man I ever loved and wanted and as it has turned out, I was right to want him so much. I'll let you in on a little secret, Moira. I wasn't the only woman to have eyes for your father. Susan wanted him, too.'

'You mean Susan Hunter?' Moira asked, shocked.

'That's precisely who I mean. Susan was always my best friend, and she carried a torch for David for years. When she couldn't have him, she married Michael on the rebound. That's girl talk just between you and me, Moira.'

'Whew,' Moira breathed. It was quite exciting to be let in on old secrets. It made a girl feel very grown-up.

'Sometimes a girl marries a man she doesn't love because it is a way out of difficulties. She decides that although she doesn't love the man in question, she can live with him. My view is that you have to decide whether you can live without a certain man. I didn't want to live my life without David. It was as simple as that. I would have done just about anything to be with him forever,' Catriona said.

'Anything?'

'Just about anything,' Catriona reiterated.

'Holy moley,' Moira exclaimed, in a long drawn-out breath. This disclosure had elevated her mother to a higher level of esteem. Moira knew that her mother was a super horsewoman with a seat and hands second to none but to now know that she would have gone to almost any length to win her father was something else again.

'Well, of course, Dad is rather special, isn't he?' Moira said at last.

'He was always rather special, Moira. He fought for me twice and he helped to save me when I went over the ledge on Yellow Rock,' Catriona said. 'Both Wilf White and Tim Sparkes realised that your father was rather special, Moira. That's why Wilf gave him Ajana and why Tim left him Aberfeldy. And he hasn't let them down. Of course, David sets high standards for everyone, including his children, and he is disappointed when people let him down.'

'I hope I shall never let Dad down,' Moira said earnestly.

'I'm sure you never will intentionally, sweetheart. Daddy thinks you're rather special. Dougal isn't what he hoped for, though he is terribly clever. Angus is extremely talented with animals but rather wild, and Daddy is worried how he will end up. You're his surprise packet. But he is determined not to hope for too much from you.'

'Why is that, Mum?' Moira asked.

'Because one day a fine young man will sweep you off your feet and take you away from High Peaks. That's what happens to daughters. A man needs sons to run the kind of operation David has put together. If Angus had been a girl, I promised Daddy I would try for another boy. I didn't want to have another baby but when you love a man and you know he wants something, you try and give it to him. That's what women do, Moira. If you don't feel that deeply about a man, you shouldn't marry him,' Catriona said firmly.

'Gosh,' Moira said. So many confidences at one time. She really felt she was growing up. She also knew that she would never let her father down.

'You see, dear, it's fairly clear that Dougal isn't interested in being on the land and he was Daddy's big hope. He looks so like Grandfather Andrew but is nothing like him in character or disposition. You're next, and because you're a girl, you may well be gone in a few years. As for Angus, well the jury is still out on him. If he doesn't kill himself off a horse, he could be all right. Daddy needs Angus because Shaun can't go on forever. He really misses Kate but her arthritis has become so bad she can't carry on much longer. High Peaks Pastoral Company is a pretty big operation, Moira. It was built up on the expectation that one day there would be sons to carry it on. Otherwise why work so hard? Daddy could sell up everything, invest the money and not do a hand's turn of work. Of course, it's not in his nature to do that but you see what I mean, Moira?'

'But what if I don't marry, Mum? What if I stay here and help Dad run the properties?'

'There's hardly an unmarried girl in the district, Moira, and suitors will soon come calling on you. Few women who choose to live on the land remain single. And you are likely to fall in love one day – it's the nature of things. Daddy knows this is the way it will be. Of course, you will always come back to us but you will have your own family one day.'

This was all heavy stuff and left a deep impression on Moira. And if David felt any apprehension about losing his daughter he didn't exhibit it in his actions. Dougal was a dead loss as far as working on the land went, but David pitched Moira and Angus into every junior judging competition in sight – sheep and cattle. Both children were taught how to parade cattle and how to show sheep. There was a judging ring adjacent to the show shed at Glen Morrison and David, Angus Campbell and Shaun Covers drilled Moira and Angus in judging techniques. They had to explain why they put certain cattle up and certain cattle down. When they went on and won junior judging competitions, David was over the moon.

David's frustration with his elder son gradually grew to disappointment. This would have been more acute had it not been for the fact that the two younger children were so extroverted and so obviously mad on animals and the bush generally. As Dougal grew away from his father, Moira and Angus grew closer to him. Moira, in particular, idolised her father and Angus would run to do his bidding.

'They're the kind of kids Dad would have loved,' David said to his mother on one of the many occasions he called in to see her. This was virtually daily, and sometimes even twice a day.

Anne looked at her son and smiled. What a man he had turned out to be. While Andrew had set his heart on having a big family, what he got was one outstanding son of whom he had been very proud. Of course, David had his faults; chiefly, that he expected his children to be cast in his own and Andy's mould.

'You are too hard and unreasonable where Dougal is concerned, David,' she said. 'It comes from having preconceived ideas and expectations about your children. All children are different. They're individuals, so you can't treat them all the same and you can't expect the same of them. You should understand this from all the dogs and horses you've trained. Have there ever been two the same? Dougal has qualities and talents Moira and Angus don't have and they have leanings and qualities Dougal doesn't possess. I suspect that one day Dougal will do something quite remarkable and you will be very proud of him. If you keep criticising him, he will grow further away from you.'

'A lot of my hopes were based on Dougal, Mum. I say *were* because it is becoming increasingly more obvious that he isn't interested in stock work. Do you know that he boxed two lots of sheep because he was watching some new bird that appeared out of nowhere? His mind just wasn't on the job,' David said with feeling.

'Poor Dougal. And of course you would never have boxed two lots of sheep?'

'You're damned right I wouldn't have! Dad would have given me a thick ear quick smart if I had done that,' David said indignantly.

'Have you seen any of Dougal's schoolwork, David?' Anne asked.

'Can't say I have, Mum. Been too busy lately. Cat tells me it's pretty good.'

'Not just good, David. It's just about perfect. I saw Jill Barwick at the school fete a few weeks ago and she told me that Dougal is the cleverest child she has ever taught. I should think that ought to make up for some boxed sheep,' Anne said with a wry smile.

'What is Dougal's cleverness going to do for us here at High Peaks, Mum?' David asked, exasperated. 'We've got five properties to look after and there are more things I want to do. You need sons on the land today. I've got the places and the money to give them a good honest living. There are plenty of challenges for a young fellow. It's no good pinning my hopes on Moira because she's such a pretty girl that some fellow is likely to snap her up and before I know it she'll be gone. That leaves Angus. While he's terrific with dogs and horses he's a bit mad-headed. I wanted more children but Cat said three was enough to look after. She would have had another for me if Angus had been a girl. But one son to look after all I've got is a big ask,' David said.

'Andy wanted more children, too, but when I couldn't have any more after you were born he never once complained because there was only you. Andy was simply grateful you were the kind of boy you were,' Anne chided.

'Dad didn't have five properties to look after. At that stage he only had High Peaks and when we bought Poitrel and he went away, Kate and I did the work,' David reminded her.

'I doubt he would have complained, anyway. It seems to me that you should be grateful for what you've got and make the best of it. You've got three wonderful children and a lovely wife plus the five properties, and that's a lot more than most people have,' Anne said.

David paused to consider all his mother was saying. 'You, as usual, are right,' he admitted with a rueful smile. 'It's just that I expected so much from my elder boy. To look at him, Dougal is Dad all over again and yet he's really nothing like him. He might as well be away at school because his heart isn't in the bush.'

This wasn't the most accurate summation David ever made because although Dougal wasn't bush-mad he was intensely interested in animals – not so much in training them but in what made them work. He would willingly worm the dogs and feed the pups and he had reared a couple of orphan calves. The first really severe confrontation Dougal had with his father was over Starana. This occurred just before Dougal went away to school.

The only issue that divided David and Catriona was the schooling of their children. Catriona had registered the children into Sydney boarding schools virtually as soon as they were born. She was determined that they would have the same kind of education and opportunities as she had received. It would stand them in good stead for the remainder of their lives, and was one thing her father and mother were adamant about.

David acquiesced when it was time for Dougal to go to boarding school but he hit the roof about the very notion of Moira leaving the property. For Moira was his trusty shadow, and now Cat was proposing that she leave them for five long years.

'You're only thinking of yourself, David,' Catriona told him. 'If you had Moira's best interests at heart, you would recognise that she should go away to school. She needs a boarding-school education in order to become a polished young woman. It will help her make a good marriage.'

'What absolute bunkum,' David roared. 'I didn't go to boarding school and you married me. You've still got some of those same snobby values as Angus and Jane or else you wouldn't sacrifice the most interesting years of a child's life.'

'That's not fair, David. A child simply doesn't receive the same kind of education at a government school. It's a well-known fact that a child educated at a boarding school is thought of much more favourably when it comes to going for a position. I simply want what is best for our children,' Catriona said.

'I don't believe that one iota! I read the *Sydney Morning Herald* and I'm struck by the number of men and women in top positions in this country who went to government schools – even High Court judges,' David said with considerable heat.

'Brilliant people will always come to the top no matter where they were educated but by and large children educated at boarding school are usually favoured by employers over those from the public school system – certainly by many employers. Furthermore, boarding school is a wonderful life experience. It's selfish to want to keep Moira here rather than allow her to develop to the best possible advantage,' Catriona said.

'I love her, and if I'm being selfish wanting her to stay here, well, that is too bad. My people didn't want me to leave them because they loved me and wanted me with them. It didn't do me any harm not going to boarding school,' David said angrily.

'Your people couldn't have afforded to send you away even if they had wanted to, and they only had you. I can understand why they didn't want to let you go,' Catriona replied.

'My mother knew that I would be totally out of place at boarding school. She was right, too – I would have hated it! I don't understand how any mother would want to give up their children during the most rewarding years of their development. Damn it, Cat, I don't.'

'So, I'm a bad mother now, am I? Nothing like as good as Anne? Well, I don't agree, David. Children are sent away for their own good. And it isn't as if they are away for a year at a time. They have long holidays. You don't have to pay for it. I've had money put by for years to educate them properly,' Catriona said. She was close to tears but was determined to make her point.

'It's got nothing to do with money, Cat. I just don't want to send Moira away. Dougal was another matter because his heart wasn't in the land. He can do whatever he wants to do, but Moira and Angus are different propositions. We rear them up and just as they become really interesting, we send them away. My mother said it was barbaric to send some children away and I agree with her,' David said. He was still fuming at the thought of losing his daughter.

'That's silly, David. Try to be open-minded – boarding school isn't barbaric at all. Was it barbaric to send me away? Boarding school did me a lot of good and it will do Moira a lot of good, too. She will certainly progress far more than if she stays here and follows you around like a shadow,' Catriona said.

'Following me around hasn't done Moira any harm so far. Everyone says she's a bottler. When I'm finished teaching her she'll be ready to judge any sheep and cattle show in Australia, Royals included. The papers will be writing heaps about her. She'll have so many marriage proposals it will be a circus,' David said, and laughed.

'This is the first time I have ever asked anything of you, David, the very first time. I wanted only two children and I had Angus just for you. I would have had another if he hadn't been a boy. I think it is mean and selfish of you not to agree with me over boarding school. We have never argued over anything and I hate arguing with you now but I feel strongly about this matter. I thought you were bigger than putting your own interests over those of your daughter,' Catriona said, as the tears started to stream down her face.

'That is a miserable thing to say of me, Cat. All my efforts have been directed towards building up properties so that our children will have a decent future. You don't see me running off to dog trials and campdrafts and, God knows, I love the damned things. I think you're worried that Moira is going to intrude too much into your territory. You couldn't push the children off onto Lottie fast enough so you could be with me. Well let me tell you, Cat, this isn't a competition for my affections between you and Moira. The fact that I love my daughter doesn't mean that I love you any the less. It does mean that you have to share me with Moira to some extent and it seems to me that you have a problem coming to terms with that,' David said evenly. He was cooler now and thinking more. 'With Moira away at school you have me to yourself,' he added.

Now there was more than a ring of truth in what

David said. Catriona had watched her daughter twine herself around her husband's heart. Her long-held fear that some other woman would take David from her was never far from Catriona's mind and, as Moira grew up, Catriona sensed that she would become more and more a part of her husband's life. The simple truth was that Moira adored her father. Catriona knew that with Moira away at boarding school, she would have David to herself. This wasn't the sole reason, or even the major reason, for wanting her daughter to go to boarding school but it was a factor, and unwittingly David had hit on it.

'That is absurd. It's a rotten thing to say, David. How could there be any competition between Moira and myself?'

'That's the way it looks to me, Cat.' And with that he turned and stormed out of the house. Catriona saw him walking up towards High Peaks and a few mintues later he rode past and headed for the hills. She watched him with a pang in her heart until he was lost to sight. He hadn't taken any lunch or even stopped to unclip a dog.

Behind her the phone rang and she answered it automatically. It was Anne. 'Catriona, is something wrong? David didn't come in this morning.'

'Oh, Anne, we've just had a big row – our first ever. It was about me wanting Moira to go to boarding school,' she sobbed.

'Oh, dear. I think I had better come and see you,' Anne said.

Catriona was on the verge of telling her mother-in-law not to come, that it was a matter between David and herself, when she recalled just how many times Anne had given her wonderful advice. Unlike her own mother, Anne always had the gift of seeing both sides of an argument. As far as the issue of schooling was concerned, Jane believed that boarding school was the natural progression from the local primary school – it wasn't a matter for argument at all.

Anne noted Catriona's red eyes and ascertained that her argument with David had been no small thing. To the best of her knowledge David and Catriona had never fought before. This was remarkable because as much as she had loved Andy, and he her, there had been arguments. They had mostly involved David, who was so precious to her.

Over a steaming cup of tea and some of Anne's home-baked biscuits, Catriona poured out her heart. 'I can't make David see that boarding school is by far the best education for a boy or girl. He told me that I still had the same snobby values as Daddy and Mummy. That isn't true, Anne. I'm not a snob. I simply want what's best for my children.

'David didn't mind in Dougal's case because his heart wasn't in the land, but Moira is a different matter. She adores her father and there's no doubt they are very close. Dougal was a big disappointment because David had such hopes for him taking over here. David argues that not going to boarding school didn't hold him back but he was a special case, wasn't he, Anne?'

'That he was, Catriona. Even if we had been able to afford to send David away, there was no way either Andy or I could have parted with him. I have a lot of sympathy for David's views on this matter, and I can understand why he wants his children to stay here. I can also understand why you would prefer them to go to boarding school. You were brought up to believe that boarding school is an indispensable part of one's education. Your people also had the money to make this possible. Like all things in life, you get what you pay for. Originally, part of the reason why Angus and Jane vetoed David was because he hadn't been to a GPS school. That, and the fact that his father was a battler and a shearer. They wanted what was best for you. You were bigger than that and I've always given you credit for standing up to your parents. You know that I always wanted you for David. I have never regretted it either,' Anne said warmly.

'But what am I to do, Anne? I so much want the children to go to boarding school and yet I don't want to fight with David. He has been my life from way back. We can't both win on this matter. I can't make him see that it is important for children to have the best possible education because he believes that what he can offer them here is more worthwhile than that. He is determined to make Moira a female version of himself. He already predicts she will judge at Royal Shows. Moira needs the experience of boarding school to widen her horizon and give her some balance, Anne.'

'You may very well be right, Catriona. It is possible

that too much David would not be to her advantage. It could be that Moira needs to see how the other half lives so that she can make up her mind what she wants to do,' Anne said thoughtfully.

Catriona was relieved to hear her mother-in-law's good sense. 'Oh, that is what I like so much about you, Anne. You are always so very fair. Mummy only ever looks at one side of an argument – her own. It would be useless me going to her about this row,' Catriona said.

'We haven't resolved it, Catriona. Either you or David will have to give way. If it is David it won't be because he believes he is in the wrong but because of his love for you. If it comes to the test, as it will, he will put you before Moira. I would bet my life on it. He might be as sore as blazes that you want Moira sent away but he will agree because he loves you,' Anne said.

'Oh, do you really think so?' Catriona asked anxiously.

'I really think so, Catriona,' Anne said and patted her daughter-in-law's arm. 'I know my David.'

Up on Wallaby Rocks David sat on his horse and let his eyes wander across the great expanse of hill country all around him. For as far as he could see to the left and in front of him, the country all belonged to him. Once there had been only High Peaks. And then there was Aberfeldy in Queensland, which made more money than any of the other properties.

It was not properties that concerned him now but

the situation at home. For the first time since their marriage, he and Cat had quarrelled. They had a conflict of views that was not to his liking, not something he had ever envisaged. He thought of all that Cat had given him, of how she had offered to have another child for him if Angus had been a girl. She was right – this was the first time she had asked anything of him. And it was more than the pure snobbery of Angus and Jane: Cat genuinely believed it was advantageous for children to be educated at a boarding school.

Well, maybe it was. It hadn't mattered in his case because he was left what amounted to a fortune.

After an hour of cogitation, David knew that he would have to let Cat have her way. It wasn't what he wanted and maybe it wasn't what Moira wanted, but he didn't want to be at war with his wife, the woman he loved more than anyone. Cat had stood up to Angus and Jane for him and would have married him even if he hadn't been left Aberfeldy. He was going to miss Moira a hell of a lot but, as Cat had said, there were long holidays and he would have to make the best of them.

Presently, he turned his horse and rode down off Wallaby Rocks to the boundary gate between Poitrel and High Peaks. It was mid-afternoon when he arrived back at his homestead.

'Have you had lunch, David?' Catriona asked as he walked in. She had resolved to try and stay calm and to act as if the morning's incident had not come between them.

'No, I've been up on Wallaby Rocks. Look Cat, I've been thinking, if sending Moira to boarding school means so much to you, she can go. It's not what I want but as you pointed out, it's the first favour you've ever asked of me. I'll be back later.'

David turned on his heel and walked out.

When Moira and Angus got off the school bus later that afternoon, their father was waiting for them. 'Angus, you run on home to your mother. Moira, I want to talk to you,' he said.

The children thought their father looked very stern, which suggested that something had happened. 'What is it, Dad?' Moira asked.

'We'll go down to the shed, Moira,' he said. 'I won't keep you long because I know you're always hungry when you get home from school.'

They sat on wool bales and David let his daughter have it straight from the shoulder. The children never had any difficulty understanding their father. When he had something to say, he said it clearly and forcibly.

'Moira, your mother and I had our first row today – the first argument we have had in our marriage. It was about you. Cat wants you to go to boarding school next year and I don't. I thought about it all day and I've told your mother that if it means so much to her, you can go.

'What I want to tell you is that it isn't my wish that you leave here but I don't want to be at war with Cat over this matter. Mum thinks it's an advantage for you to go to boarding school and she may well be right.

I happen to think that it's not essential that you go, but I'm giving way to your mother for the sake of peace. I'll miss you a lot but, as Cat tells me, there are nice long holidays and we'll have to make the most of them. What do you say?'

He looked at his pretty almost-twelve-year-old daughter, on the face of it still only a child, but close to womanly happenings.

'Poor Dad, you couldn't win, could you?' Moira said with infinite wisdom for a girl of her age.

'That's what happens when a fellow has more than one female in the house,' he said. 'And sometimes you don't even need two.'

'Oh, well, if I have to go, I have to go. It could be fun for a while. And in a few years I shall be home for good,' Moira said determinedly.

'No, you won't, Moira. Some young fellow will take you away to another life and you'll break my heart all over again. I'm going to miss you an awful lot,' David said.

'You'll have Angus for a couple of years, Dad,' Moira said with simple logic.

'If he doesn't break his neck in the meantime. Well, you'd better run home and have some smoko. I'll see you later, sweetheart.'

She put her arms around his neck and kissed him. 'You're a lovely Dad,' she said.

There was a certain coolness between David and Catriona for some little time following the argument. Catriona felt this more than David. David had always made love tenderly and enthusiastically, but now it seemed he could not bear to touch her. This was not something Catriona found easy to cope with; nor could she talk about such a delicate matter with anyone else. It was a matter only she and David could resolve.

As things turned out, it was another family's tragedy that brought David and Catriona together again.

Chapter Seven

The defining moment in Dougal MacLeod's life occurred on one of his early holidays. He had gone away to boarding school where he breezed through his lessons with astonishing ease. Or so it seemed. In actual fact Dougal worked very hard behind the scenes to build on his natural intelligence. At that stage he wasn't sure what career he wanted to follow after he left school. But he was soon to find out.

In the days when Catriona was competing in riding events and winning Champion Girl Rider all over northern New South Wales, there was a young woman by the name of Emily Holland who held the title for the leading Lady Rider. For years Emily Holland was Catriona's idol, until the day came when, after graduating from the junior ranks, Catriona defeated the older woman for the title of Champion Lady Rider.

At about this time Emily Holland was wooed by an older wealthy man, Rod Matheson, who had interests in breeding and racing thoroughbreds. When Rod proposed to Emily and was accepted, he bought her as a wedding present a property on the Merriwa–Scone road known as Glengarry. This was a mix of hills and valleys, and the ideal location for a small thoroughbred stud. Fortunately, in the light of what happened later, the property was indeed in her name. It was a small but useful property and Emily ran a herd of Herefords while she and Rod built up their thoroughbred stud. Rod had an office in Sydney and drove up to the property almost every weekend.

With time, Rod and Emily had two daughters, Dianne and Sarah. Everything seemed to be going well for the family. They had plenty of money and the girls were booked into a Sydney boarding school from a young age, where they were when David and Catriona had their row about the schooling of their own children.

Catriona and Emily had maintained a friendly relationship from their triumphant days in the show ring. Emily had bought a couple of bulls from David. She had many times looked wistfully at Ajana and Starana because, despite her exceptional knowledge of equine matters, Emily was not having much success in the thoroughbred business. This did not matter greatly while Rod's business was thriving. The cattle more or less paid for the property's expenses and the thoroughbreds were a hobby she loved.

Then things started to go wrong for the Mathesons. First of all a snake killed Emily's prized stallion and shortly afterwards she lost two good mares. But the worst was yet to come. Unbeknown to Emily, Rod had lost a great deal of money – more money, in fact, than he possessed. Rod Matheson had been an inveterate gambler for most of his life, but up until now he had always been lucky. He had managed to hide this fact from Emily though he had had to prevaricate when she suggested they buy a stallion to replace the horse they had lost. 'We'll have a good look around, darling,' he said.

When the police came and told Emily that her husband had been found dead in his car, Emily could not believe it. She very soon had to because, apart from the property, still in her name, a few of her own mares and a small truck, she lost everything they owned together. Emily had very little money of her own and so the two girls had to be taken out of boarding school, the fees now being out of the question. Dianne and Sarah were instead enrolled in the local high school in Scone.

Catriona had heard all of this from Emily herself, and had invited the older woman to come and visit her. Thus it was that a day or two after 'the row', Emily phoned and said she and the girls would like to come to High Peaks.

David was genuinely sorry to hear of Emily's misfortune because he liked her as a person, and respected her as a horsewoman. David had a lot of time for the people he described as 'professionals' in their fields and he considered Emily to be a real professional. And Emily just loved horses.

By the time Emily came to High Peaks she had put her grief behind her and had accepted what had happened. She knew she had to make the best of things. The two little girls, one blonde and one brunette, were pretty young misses but still a little bewildered by what had happened to their father and their life. One moment they had been at boarding school and the next they were hauled out and brought back home. Of greater magnitude was the fact that they had lost their father. It was not easy to come to terms with a shock of that dimension.

Catriona was especially concerned by what had happened to Emily and her girls because of her own belief in the superiority of a boarding-school education. To lose such an education half-way through would have to be traumatic in the extreme. The scenario the Mathesons faced assumed even greater intensity for Catriona because of the current difference of opinion on this very matter between herself and David.

Catriona had asked David if there was any way they could help Emily and her two girls. 'I don't know, Cat. I'm thinking about it,' he said, lost in thought.

David and Catriona had travelled to Sydney for Rod Matheson's funeral and Catriona had visited Emily and talked to her on the phone, but this was the family's first visit to High Peaks since Rod's suicide. When the Mathesons arrived at High Peaks Catriona and Emily embraced, and Catriona hugged Dianne and Sarah in turn. David received a kiss from all three. Emily Matheson admired and respected David MacLeod – in fact there was no man Emily respected more than David. The two girls were a little in awe of him because he was so big and because they had heard he owned so many places. By comparison their own property seemed minuscule. Of course, when they had had money, the size of the property hadn't mattered because Daddy had a successful business in Sydney. Mummy could breed her horses and cattle and it didn't matter whether they made money or not because Daddy had an endless supply of money. Not that they discussed money with their mother; having money was simply an accepted part of their life.

Over afternoon tea Catriona and Emily discussed several topics while David talked to Dianne and Sarah. He could see that they were still in shock and it was difficult to know how to handle them.

After they had eaten a little he took them outside and down to where he kept his working horses. Ajana and her daughter, Starana, were in an adjoining paddock and he called them up and gave them oats from a bucket, so the girls could pat the majestic mares.

Presently, Catriona and Emily joined them. Emily looked wistfully at the two mares. 'I could do with an Ajana or Starana right now,' she said. 'It would make all the difference in the world. If I could produce one big winner that could be all I need.'

'Well now, Ajana's days are nearly over and Starana won't breed, Emily. I've had several tests done and short of spending a small fortune for perhaps no result, there wasn't much more I could do. I wasn't interested in thoroughbreds at that stage but we're going to stand Starana's brother, Western Star, up on Strath Fillan and maybe try and breed a few thoroughbreds. After what Starana and her sister did Catriona is all fired up,' David said.

'If you're not doing anything with Starana would you sell her to me, David?' Emily asked.

'What on earth for, Emily? The mare isn't a breeder,' David exclaimed.

'Maybe something could be done, and right now I need a miracle, David.'

David looked at Emily, then at her two little girls and finally at Catriona. 'I won't sell her to you, Emily. You can take the mare but when she is old I want you to bring her back here because I want to bury her alongside her mother,' David said gruffly.

'Oh, David, that is sweet of you. I can assure you that Starana will be very well looked after, won't she, girls?'

The girls hardly knew how to answer. It seemed that David had just given their mother a mare that had won races. They knew that because their mother talked racehorses all the time. Daddy had been mad on racehorses and had talked about breeding top horses to win the Golden Slipper and even the Melbourne Cup. But so far their horses had only won country races.

'You can put her in one of our floats and take her away with you, Emily. Someone can go over and pick up the float,' David said. 'I'll leave you with Catriona as I have to scoot over to Glen Morrison.'

Catriona watched her husband walk away from them. She was very touched by what he had just done. But, she reflected, David was always likely to come up with something unexpected.

'That was a very sweet thing you did for Emily,' Catriona said, when he came into the house that evening.

'Was it? The mare won't breed so Emily won't do any good with her,' he said.

'That's not the point, David, and I think you know it. Emily and the girls are down on their luck right now and they need a helping hand or two. Horses are Emily's life. They always have been. She'll devote all her energies into trying to get Starana in foal and that will take her mind off what has happened,' Catriona said.

'I reckoned on that,' David said.

David's benevolence towards Emily provoked a far different reaction from Dougal. He had always had a soft spot for Starana and asked his father several times to give him the horse, but each time David had refused. The last time he had been fairly short with his son.

'Why can't you give her to me for my own horse?' Dougal asked.

'What for? To look at? She's not a good-footed mare in the hills and there are horses here that would leave her for dead,' David said, frustrated with his eldest child.

'She won races, Dad. Grandpa Angus said her sire is by an old Star Kingdom horse,' Dougal persisted.

'I know all about that, Dougal. I spent money on her and we could spend a heap more and not get her in foal. It's not as if we don't have Ajana mares. We do.'

'But not by a thoroughbred sire,' Dougal said.

'You can have a bigger horse any old time and one that won't let you down in the hills but not Starana,' David said flatly.

When Dougal saw Starana being loaded onto the single horse float, he could not believe his eyes. As Emily's utility and the float disappeared down the road he ran to his mother. 'Where are they taking Starana?' he asked anxiously.

'Your father has given her to Mrs Matheson, Dougal. The Mathesons are very down right now after the tragedy of Rod Matheson's death. It was a very sweet thing to do. They needed a lift,' Catriona said.

'Dad *gave* them Starana? How could he? He wouldn't let me have her and now he's given her to a stranger! The only thing I've asked of him and he wouldn't let me have her. He knew how much she meant to me – Starana was my friend,' Dougal said, his eyes filling with tears.

'The Mathesons are hardly strangers, Dougal. Emily is one of my oldest friends. Starana won't go in foal. You have to be careful of shy breeders,' Catriona said, trying to calm Dougal down.

'We don't know that she's a shy breeder, Mum. Dad could have spent more money on her. He could afford it. Starana was the only horse I really liked. Dad could have let me have her.'

'Starana is going to a very good home, Dougal. She'll be rugged and fed. I know how well Emily looks after her horses. I used to ride against her. And the two girls are horse-mad too. Emily had to bring them home from boarding school because she can no longer afford to keep them there. You'll be away at school and Dianne and Sarah will be home,' Catriona tried to reason with him.

But Dougal was inconsolable. The loss of Starana was a defining moment in the boy's life because from that day he knew what he was going to be: a vet. He was going to be a top vet, so good that people would come from all over the country to ask him about horse problems. Moreover, he was going to be a vet because that would mean he could do exactly as he liked and not have to do what his father wanted. When he was a top vet he would be able to solve horse problems such as Starana's inability to have a foal.

Dougal thought about this new-found resolution as he lay in bed, devastated and angry. He was to go back to school the next day and he resolved that he would do everything possible to get himself to vet school. There was another boy at school who had told him that he wanted to be a vet and Dougal decided he would talk more to this boy. He would show his father that he didn't need him or his land to make a living – he would do it by his own efforts, and be the maker of his own success.

Meanwhile, Catriona was still ill at ease because David was, for the very first time in their married life, noticeably cool towards her. She couldn't say that he was sulking – David never sulked – because of her insistence that all three children attend boarding school. She had heard via Kate that David was at a loss to understand how a mother could put children's attendance at boarding school over the desirability of having them remain at home. Because he was now a wealthy man, David considered that his children didn't need the benefit of a boarding-school education and whatever advantages that did or didn't bring. He simply wanted his children to stay at home. David thought that Catriona's point of view was based on latent snobby values continually reinforced by her parents. Angus and Jane considered it unthinkable that the children not attend boarding school; it was a *fait accompli* and therefore not a matter for discussion. Catriona knew that it was up to her to break the ice. She had to do something to bring David back to her. David was her life.

Once a week Catriona went over to Inverlochy to have lunch with her parents and to visit Stuart and Carol. She usually went on her own because David was always too busy for long lunches. He would go for dinner, but daylight hours were too valuable.

Jane Campbell was now reading more books than had been her practice in the past. The smart young married set could all talk about art and books and Jane had been feeling a bit peeved because she couldn't contribute. Even her knowledge of art was only elementary, and the young women who had been to university knew far more than she did. So Jane now had a very presentable library of both fiction and non-fiction, and now and then Catriona would borrow a book or two. On this occasion she went to her mother's shelves and began looking idly at the titles on the spines. One title caught her eye, and she drew it from the shelf. It was a book devoted to love and marriage, by an author called Stopes, and the inscription inside told her that it had been a present to her mother from her grandmother. There were a few words scribbled above Grandmother Ellen's name: *I hope this helps, Jane.* Catriona put the book between two others and slipped them into her bag. It was probably too old-fashioned for today's climate, but might make interesting reading.

Catriona read the book through without David's knowledge. He was still remarkably cool towards her – civil, but cool. There was still no lovemaking. David would collapse into bed and fall asleep almost immediately. Of course, he rose at dawn and never stopped, and he was an older man these days, but that had not stopped him from being a loving man before their argument.

A couple of days later when David announced he would be in for lunch and to make a phonecall to Victoria, Catriona knew what she had to do. Before she put on the lunch she spent longer than usual freshening up. She put on a pretty checked shirt and oyster-grey denim jeans she knew David particularly liked and set about preparing lunch.

David enjoyed steak and salad when he had lunch at home so she gave him the best piece of meat she could find and cooked it the way he liked it, just a wee bit rare. It was obvious to her that he enjoyed it. He made his phonecall straight after the meal, so Catriona knew she had to act quickly before he left. It was time to tell if what she had read in her mother's book actually worked.

When David gulped down the last of his tea he took his cup and plate to the sink and then turned to leave. Catriona was standing in the doorway, unbuttoning her shirt. She dropped the shirt at her feet, unhooked her bra, and tossed it to the floor. Her sandals were kicked to one side and the jeans came down leaving Catriona attired in only her knickers. She slipped out of her knickers and stood facing her husband with nothing on at all. Even in her middle age, Catriona had an inviting figure preserved by exercise and a lifetime of being outdoors.

'Cat, what do you think you're doing? Mum or Kate could walk in any moment – you know what they're like' David said, flustered.

Catriona didn't answer but simply held out her hand. David had been looking for a way to end the rift between them and now she had shown him. To refuse her now would drive them further apart. And it was very difficult for a man to refuse his wife when she took her clothes off in the middle of the day.

He walked towards her and bent to pick up her clothes. If his mother or Kate walked in, what would they think?

'Leave them, David,' Catriona said, beckoning him with her eyes as she took his hand. 'I need you.'

There, she had said it. She needed him.

David looked at her and smiled. It was the first time he had smiled at her for days.

She led him into their bedroom and began unbuttoning his shirt. Any coolness David felt towards her melted away – for good.

When Catriona took the books back to Inverlochy Jane asked her if she had enjoyed them. 'Oh, very much so, Mother. Very interesting.'

Stopes might be considered very old hat but she had solved Catriona's problem. The solution had been so very simple but the execution of her advice had to be done right. Catriona felt she had done it exactly right.

Chapter Eight

Emily Matheson was in unfamiliar territory. Never before had she had to worry about money because her father and then her husband had ladled it out with sufficient generosity to provide Emily with a very comfortable lifestyle. Financial security had been one of the major factors in Emily's decision to marry Rod Matheson in the first place. Rod had money, and his ambitions included breeding a Melbourne Cup winner.

Emily's family, who had been on the land for generations, had been far from happy about their daughter's proposal to marry the Sydney money man. Rod Matheson was more than twenty years her senior to begin with, and Emily could have married any one of several younger men from good grazier families. But not one of those younger men had Rod Matheson's money, nor his ambition to build a great thoroughbred stud that would produce classic winners, all of which was most appealing to Emily. What Rod Matheson got in Emily was a good-looking younger woman who was a very good horsewoman and able to look after Rod's horses while he took care of his business interests in Sydney. Their union was an arrangement that suited them both for an array of reasons.

What Emily didn't know about her husband was that he was an inveterate gambler. Rod Matheson gambled on shares and property and also, of course, on the horses. He was a big-time punter and he could afford to be when everything was going his way. But when things started to go wrong, Rod's judgement also went awry. One of his last desperate acts was to take money from a joint account he had set up for Emily and himself and bet the lot on a horse he had been told was a sure thing. When this 'sure thing' was beaten into fourth place, Rod Matheson knew that he was finished.

When Emily assessed her available funds she discovered that the joint account she shared with her husband held only $500. Over $50 000 had been withdrawn just prior to Rod's suicide. This was a huge blow because apart from this money there was only a little over $6000 in the main account used to pay bills relating to the property. The funeral expenses still had to be paid, there was an account owing to the vet and the shire rates were due. Apart from these funds there was $5000 in each of the girls' accounts. Rod had set up these accounts after a big win on the track. The only other money Emily could lay her hands on was about $1000 in cash, which Rod had posted to her the week he died. A brief note that accompanied the money stated that the cash might come in handy. There was no other explanation for its delivery.

Apart from the property, which was hers and could not be touched, the only real cash-generating assets was the herd of Hereford cows, of which there were about seventy, and the thoroughbred yearlings. But the receiver soon discovered that most of these yearlings were in joint names, as were their dams, so a large portion of the proceeds after sale went the way of the rest of Rod Matheson's property. The receiver couldn't touch Starana because David MacLeod transferred her to Emily.

The cattle produced about $18 000 a year, out of which the family's living expenses, shire rates, property and vehicle maintenance, and schooling were to be paid. Emily was aghast when she sat down and worked out what she actually owned and what money she had to live on. She herself had no skills that would enable her to obtain a worthwhile job because she had never had to work. True, she had helped on the family property when she wasn't riding horses in the show ring but that experience didn't count for much in the eyes of potential employers.

She had tried to explain the family's changed circumstances to her daughters; that because their father had lost a lot of money she had had to withdraw them both from boarding school, and they would have to attend the high school in Scone from now on. This was a big enough shock, but to see the horses they had loved taken away shattered both girls. It was a situation so new and unexpected that for a time Dianne and Sarah had trouble coming to grips with it.

It was against the background of her reduced circumstances that Emily accepted David's gift of Starana with heartfelt relief. She had no real belief that she could succeed in getting Starana in foal because if it had been possible, David MacLeod would have done it. What Emily needed was a morale booster for her girls and a horse they could focus their attention on after being told they would lose their own thoroughbreds. Starana, her famous sister Davana and the great mare that produced them were household names in the district. Starana's grandsire, Star Kingdom, was known throughout the country.

Emily wasn't destitute. She owned a 700-acre property that was free from debt, but it was not capable of giving Emily the lifestyle to which she was accustomed. It would take very careful stewardship to carry on. The alternative was to sell the property, which would allow Emily to buy a house in town and invest the remainder. When she proposed this to Dianne and Sarah they would not hear of their mother selling up.

'You mustn't, Mummy,' Dianne pleaded. Dianne was fourteen-and-a-half and Sarah was just thirteen. 'I can leave school at fifteen and get a job,' she said. 'I can do a secretarial course. Sarah is much smarter than me and she can stay at school to finish her leaving certificate,' Dianne said magnanimously.

'That's very sweet of you, Dianne. Well, we shall see. I must say I don't want to leave here and go to town,' Emily said.

'Oh, no, Mummy, we don't want to leave here,' Sarah chipped in.

'Then we'll just have to make the best of what we have,' Emily said with a forced smile. 'Losing the horses is a real blow. We are almost back to scratch.'

This was true, because the only horses they would be left with were those that Emily could prove actually belonged to her. There were a couple of her old show horses and three other mares she had acquired from her own resources.

'But now we have Starana,' Dianne said.

'We mustn't build our hopes up too much on Starana, sweetheart,' Emily said as she hugged her. 'If the MacLeods couldn't get her to go in foal, you may depend it probably isn't possible. David MacLeod is the best horse and dog man in these parts.'

'He's gorgeous, isn't he, Mummy?' Dianne said and giggled.

'He is rather, isn't he?' Emily agreed, smiling to herself.

'I should like to marry a man just like David Mac-Leod,' Dianne said.

'That's a very worthy ambition, darling,' Emily said, and laughed. She hadn't felt like laughing these past few months. 'I'm afraid the David MacLeods of this world don't grow on trees and there are always girls like Catriona who win their hearts. Not, I must say, that you won't be very pretty, Dianne. I am very proud of my two girls. I shall always be grateful to your father for giving me two such sweet girls. And you must remember your father for the way he loved you both.'

It was a tough transition for mother and daughters, but somehow they managed to make ends meet. Emily could have gone to her family for help but in the light of their opposition to her marriage to Rod, she was too proud to do that. Instead she skimped and saved where she could. She had plenty of clothes and made do with what she had so she could give Dianne and Sarah new clothes.

Dianne left school at fifteen and completed her secretarial course. She was a blonde, pretty girl, though not as classically good-looking as her sister. Her enthusiasm and her attitude landed her a job with a stock and station agent and it was not long before several young graziers took to calling in regularly on some pretext or other.

It was during the first couple of years following her husband's suicide, when things were toughest, that Emily and her daughters had most reason to be grateful to David MacLeod. Like his father before him, David would help anyone he thought worthy of a hand up. Emily and Catriona had become very close friends and visited each other fairly regularly. Catriona was disturbed when she heard how little Emily had to live on and that she was going to lose her horses. She went back to David and told him what she had learnt.

'Is there anything we can do, darling?' she asked.

David looked away into the distance for a while before answering. 'I suppose we could buy back some of Emily's mares. The receiver will put them up for sale. They probably won't make a lot of money. It's a forced sale so might not attract much interest. If we can get some of the mares back – the best ones anyway – I'll let her have free services to two or three of them when we pull Western Star out of racing.'

'What a splendid idea, darling. Let me buy the mares back as my contribution,' Catriona said.

'If that's what you want, Cat. I'll get Lew Hooper to look into it and go and bid for them. He's got plenty of time on his hands now he's retired. The sort of job Lew would like no end,' David said.

Catriona was in awe of her husband's capacity to organise things in difficult situations. He had had this gift from boyhood. It had come to the fore when she went over the ledge on Yellow Rock and again when Kate broke her leg on Wallaby Rocks. It was David's organisational skills that allowed him to handle five properties just as easily, or so it seemed to Catriona, as some people managed one. Given that David controlled stud cattle, sheep, horses and dogs, it was little short of amazing that he was able to keep so much in his head.

David went to see Lew Hooper who, since his retirement from the police force, had done several jobs for him. Hooper was a tough man who didn't respect many people but he respected David MacLeod and would have done almost anything for him. He now had a very nice cottage on his 200 acres and a dozen good mares to keep him occupied.

'I've got another job for you, Lew,' David said. 'It's right up your alley.'

'Sounds interesting. What is it, David?' Hooper asked, curious.

David outlined the circumstances relating to Rod and Emily Matheson and added that the mares had been jointly owned and taken over by the receiver. 'We want to buy back the best half-dozen for Emily. There might be one or two that would suit you, too. I want you to have a look at the list and when the sale comes up, buy them for us to give back to Emily. Cat will go with you to pay for them. You can pick up our truck at High Peaks and when the sale is over deliver the mares to Emily, if you wouldn't mind. Can you do that for me, Lew?'

'On my head, David, no worries at all. Will Mrs Matheson be at the sale?'

'No, she told me she couldn't bear to see the mares sold. There's some good stuff in those horses, Lew. When Rod had money they didn't stint on what they spent. They should have bred more than they did – maybe they used the wrong sires. Can you afford a couple more mares?'

Some people would have been offended by this question but Lew Hooper knew that David MacLeod didn't beat around the bush. If he told him that he couldn't afford the mares, David would offer to pay for the mares until Lew sold a horse or two and had the money to spare.

'I got a big super, David. I can afford a couple more mares,' Hooper said and grinned.

David nodded. 'Just thought I'd check. Pity to see

good mares go elsewhere. Let me know what I owe you.'

'You'll owe me precisely nothing for this job, David. I'll be glad to do it for Emily. If I buy any of her mares, I'd like to use your truck to bring them back here – that's all I ask,' Hooper said.

'Of course, by all means. If you've got any time on your hands, I'll have a couple more jobs for you, Lew,' David told him.

'Not like this one, I'll be bound,' Hooper said with a grin.

'No, a lot different, Lew. I want you to set up computer programs for us to keep record of the livestock side of things. Advise on what system to buy and all that sort of thing. Cat has taken over the bookwork from Mum and has mastered the financial aspect of the business electronically, but I think we can take it further. I want to put all the stud stock on computer discs because with the cattle, especially, there's weight-gain figures and the like that need recording and accessing easily.'

David knew that Hooper was something of a computer expert and that he had set up a system for himself that gave him instant access to thoroughbred pedigrees from around the world.

'Sounds interesting. I wonder what Andy would have thought of that!' Hooper said. It was his summation of how far David had come in a relatively short space of years.

'An interesting observation, Lew,' David said, and grinned. 'Dad took Aberfeldy in his stride so I reckon he'd see the value of computers. Nobody could be bushier or more stock-minded than me and I can see how they will help us – so long as I don't have to work the mongrels! Sitting down in front of a screen isn't my go. Once we're on top of the computer business I'll see about getting someone else in to handle it a couple of days a week. I want Cat to learn the software so that someone in the family is computer-literate rather than an ignoramus like me!' David said. What he didn't tell Hooper was that he already had someone in mind for this particular part-time job.

Hooper laughed. David MacLeod might be an ignoramus where computers were concerned but he was the smartest man with livestock that he knew. It seemed to Lew that David knew things instinctively while other people tried all their lives to amass the same degree of knowledge.

So it transpired that with Catriona sitting beside him Lew Hooper acquired what he considered to be the best six mares in the receiver's catalogue of Matheson horses. He bought a couple of mares for himself, as well, but not until he had purchased the best six horses for Emily. As David had predicted, there weren't a lot of people present at the sale but there were a couple of 'sharpies' who knew the value of some of the horses. Fortunately people like the Inghams and their ilk were not represented. Even so, Catriona outlayed a tidy sum for the mares.

When Hooper, driving the High Peaks International, drove in to Glengarry with the mares and began unloading them, Emily and the girls couldn't believe their eyes. Lew had once judged Emily in the show ring and she had met him several times since then. The last occasion was when David and Catriona had taken her over to Glen Morrison to see the shedded cattle and they had visited Lew.

'What is this, Lew?' Emily asked, astonished. 'These are our mares?'

'David and Catriona bought them back from the receiver. I bought a couple, too,' Hooper said, a little gruffly – he wasn't a man to show emotion but it was hard not to looking at Emily and her girls.

'They bought them back? For me? Oh, how could they? Did they make much, Lew?'

'Some did and some didn't,' Hooper said.

'This is unbelievable. How shall I ever thank the MacLeods for their generosity?' The girls couldn't believe that the mares were back because they had believed them lost. It seemed awful that people could take horses from you but that was what had happened. Now, six of them were back.

'And I see you bought Cindy and Lady – that's what we called them, Lew,' Emily said, 'I'm so pleased to see them go to such a good home,' as she peered in through the stock crate.

'I bought for you what I thought were the pick of the bunch, Emily. That's what David asked me to do. When I had done that, I bought these two. I'll look after them and you can come and have a look at them and their foals any time you like,' Hooper said.

'Thank you, Lew. Oh, I must phone and thank David and Catriona,' Emily said brightly, overwhelmed by the goodwill of her friends.

'I think Catriona actually bought them, Emily. I reckon David has something else up his sleeve,' Hooper said, as he got in the cabin of the International.

Emily stood with her daughters and watched the red truck as it went down her road. 'Well, it looks as if we are back in the thoroughbred business, girls. How we are ever going to repay David and Catriona I have absolutely no idea. Let's get the mares back in their old paddock and then I must phone Catriona.'

'You go and phone, Mummy. Sarah and I will take the mares down,' Dianne said.

'Very well, Dianne. I really do want to ring Catriona straight away.' Emily walked back to the house with a renewed spring to her step.

Catriona gave her husband the credit for the purchase of the mares but admitted that she had paid for them. 'It was David's idea, Emily. I offered to pay for them. David will talk to you about the mares.'

'How on earth can I ever repay you?' Emily asked.

'We aren't worried about that, Em,' Catriona said.

'Bless you, Catriona. And do thank David. I'll give him a hug when I see him,' Emily said brightly. 'I'll think of some way to repay you both.'

'You'll breed a top yearling one day or race a horse that wins a heap, Em. You can pay us back then,' Catriona said and laughed.

'That could be a long way off, I'm afraid,' Emily said.

'Don't worry about it, Em. We certainly aren't. You're a good friend, and we're pleased to be able to help you.'

Back at High Peaks Lew Hooper set up a computer system that provided David and Catriona with details of pedigrees and all the figures relating to the stud sheep and cattle. It didn't take long for Catriona to master the system. As David had said, she preferred to be away with him but she realised he depended on her to handle this side of the business. Anne had looked after the books almost from the day she had come to High Peaks as a new bride and it was now Catriona's turn.

But the following year David pulled another rabbit out of his hat, which more or less relieved her of the bookkeeping chore. It came about when David and Catriona went across to Glengarry to have lunch with Emily and her girls.

'I hear you're doing well at the agency, Dianne,' David said over lunch.

'I think I am, Mr MacLeod,' Dianne said.

'Know your way about a computer too, I'm told,' he said.

'You get a good grounding on computers at school these days, Mr MacLeod. They're not hard once you know the basics,' Dianne said.

'They didn't have them at school in my day. What do you do at weekends?'

'Oh, this and that. Help Mum. Do my washing and

ironing so that I'm set for the week,' Dianne said with a smile.

'What about all the fellows who, so I'm told, find the agency a very interesting place to visit?' David asked.

Dianne blushed. 'I'm too young to worry about boys, Mr MacLeod.'

'The boys don't seem to think so. If you're not too busy at weekends how would you like to come and work for Cat and me? How would each Saturday appeal to you?'

Dianne looked from David to her mother. 'What would you want me to do at High Peaks?'

'Take over our bookkeeping. We've got everything on computer now, stud figures and all. Cat's been doing it but her heart's not in it. She'd sooner be with me and I don't want her doing something she doesn't like. It's quite a big job with five properties to account for. I thought you might like to earn a few extra dollars,' he said.

'It sounds wonderful,' Dianne said.

'Personally I wouldn't call sitting in front of a small screen all day "wonderful", but I appreciate the technical significance and I shall use it to our advantage,' David said. 'You would be doing us a favour if you could spare the time,' he added.

Emily guessed that Catriona could have managed the computer very well and probably would have carried on. This was another initiative to help her and the girls, and it had David's imprint all over it. But if Dianne wanted to do it, Emily certainly wouldn't stand in her way.

Dianne was now making an important contribution to her family's support. She was very unselfish with her wages so any extra money would come in handy. So virtually every Saturday Dianne drove the Mathesons' utility over to High Peaks for her day's work and each week David filled the vehicle with petrol on top of what he paid her.

It didn't take Dianne long to realise that the High Peaks Pastoral Company was a significant operation. There were over 3000 head of cattle on Aberfeldy, about 300 commercial breeding cows on the three hill-country properties and a hundred stud Hereford cows. Then there were the sheep, about 12 000 all told. And as a minor consideration there were about thirty stock-horse mares plus the working horses.

Of course, the expenses, which included wages, shearing costs, fuel, stockfeed and a host of other expenses, were considerable. There was also tax, including provisional tax, which David complained was very unfair. It all amounted to a considerable operation and Dianne could understand why David needed a better system of control.

'I don't know what my father would have thought of computers, Dianne, but the fact is that it's getting very difficult to keep up with everything now. I was born a hill-country boy but I'm not wedded to the old ways. You need to be abreast of the changes. In the old days a lot of graziers recorded their stock information in a little red Cooper's notebook. These days there's a lot more to running a successful grazing operation. You

198

need to be able to call up details of your stud sheep and cattle enterprises. I could see that computers could make me a better operator.'

After a few weeks Dianne felt that she had become part of the High Peaks operation because she often had to ask David to explain some aspect of management. Recording the bull figures was difficult at first. However, after a while she absorbed what was being done and became so proficient that she had no difficulty understanding the jargon tossed around by cattlemen in the agency office – quite an achievement for a girl of her age.

What made Dianne's visits to High Peaks so enjoyable was that both David and Catriona were unfailingly kind to her. They would often send her home with a piece of beef or a side of lamb from Catriona's coolroom. Emily would phone and thank them and tell David or Catriona that they didn't have to send anything as they were managing quite well but it made no difference. Emily wanted to do something to repay their kindnesses but as much as she racked her brains, she couldn't find a way to do it.

The three MacLeod children all expressed some interest in David's computer program. They had all been introduced to computers at school and knew their way around them, as the saying goes. The degree of interest varied from child to child. Moira, in her quicksilver way, was very quick at picking up anything, and if her father was expounding some point to Dianne she would sit and listen with interest. However, as soon as

David left the scene Moira would follow. Angus took a perfunctory interest but horses and dogs had greater appeal so he would never hang about for long. As he grew into his teens Angus was more interested in Dianne than the computer but she was several years older than him and her put-downs finally quenched his interest.

Of the three children Dougal was by far the most computer-literate, and Dianne found him an interesting boy and enjoyed his company. Dougal had absorbed the technical aspects of bull recording, and having all the bull records accessible via the computer was something that appealed to his intelligence. He was also very courteous, and would ask Dianne if she minded him sitting alongside her while she worked. This early experience of livestock recording was to stand him in good stead in later years.

When the children returned to boarding school Saturdays were much quieter. David and Catriona often went away for the day after giving Dianne the accounts and whatever else they wanted put on record.

Dianne's visits to High Peaks continued for some years, until Moira finished boarding school and took over the computer. By this time Dianne had a very nice boyfriend and was quite happy to relinquish her Saturday excursions to High Peaks. The money she had earnt had been a big help to herself and her mother and she was very grateful to David and Catriona for their help. What Dianne managed to save went towards sending Sarah to Longreach Pastoral College.

David and Catriona marvelled at Dianne's selfless-
ness, but also wondered how Sarah would cope at
Longreach with its preponderance of male students.
Sarah was a striking girl and sure to attract a lot of
attention. She had come to David for advice about
her schooling, and told him that she wanted to work
with sheep, cattle and horses rather than farming. David
suggested Longreach because it was more pastorally
orientated than some of the other colleges. Longreach
was where he intended to send Angus when he finished
at boarding school – David reckoned that would round
him off nicely and perhaps settle him down, too.

Although David was unhappy about Dougal's decision
not to return to High Peaks after finishing school, he
was not altogether unhappy about the boy wanting to
be a vet. If he had to do anything besides working on
the land, being a vet was the best option by far. There
would be certain advantages in having a son who was
a vet. David had plans to utilise artificial insemination
for his sheep and to create an elite Hereford herd using
embryo transplantation. Dougal could specialise in
these areas and become an integral part of the overall
High Peaks operation as David had always hoped he
would be. But Dougal had other ideas.

Moira came to David midway through her final year
at boarding school. 'Well, Dad, not long to go now.
What do you want me to do when I finish school?'

David looked at his daughter in some amazement.
It was hard to believe that she and Dougal were

brother and sister. Dougal wasn't at all interested in what his father wanted whereas Moira was just the opposite. He wondered how the blazes he would be able to keep Moira with him because except for the dark hair she was Catriona all over again – in short, a knockout – and David feared a young man before long would sweep her away from High Peaks. David had pushed her and Angus into every judging competition in sight in their holidays and they had loved it. The boys had loved Moira, too, but she had kept them all at arm's length.

David decided to take an entirely different tack with Moira. Rather than try to steer her his way he would allow her free rein.

'Well, now, sweetheart, you must do whatever you wish, just as Dougal is doing.' This comment was a bit below the belt because Moira knew how disappointed her father was over Dougal's 'defection', having set up a mini-empire of properties with the expectation that Dougal would be on hand to help him run them and eventually take over.

'The thing is that I don't really want to go to uni or away to college like Sarah Matheson. What I'd really like to do is come home and help you run the show. Maybe take over the showing of the cattle and sheep.'

David beamed. 'Nothing I'd like more, Moira. But what say you do one of these external courses? Dianne was telling me that you can do them from home by correspondence and only have to go away for short periods. Anyway, have a think about it,' he said.

'I'd like to take over the recording from Dianne. I know you and Mum gave her the job to help the Mathesons but the thing is that Dianne has a boyfriend and I think she'd be happy for me to take over,' Moira said.

This was even better, David thought. 'What about some riding?' he suggested.

Moira wrinkled her nose. 'I don't think so, Daddy. I shall never be in Mum's class and getting togged up in a fancy outfit isn't my go. I'd prefer to help you with the stock. Shaun can stay at home and we can show away.'

Moira's words were music to David's ears. There was nothing he wanted more than to have Moira with him. Of the three children Moira looked the pick. Dougal was too academically inclined and his heart wasn't in the place and Angus had a lot of growing up to do before he could take over. The big drawback with Moira was that she was a girl. If he grew to rely on her too much, he would be awfully disappointed when she left. He couldn't see how she wouldn't be whisked away by a handsome beau because she was too spirited and damn good-looking for fellows to ignore. He secretly thought that a fourth child would come in handy now. But there was no fourth child and he had to be content with what he had. Maybe he would have Moira for a few years, by which time Angus would be ready to take her place.

Having established that he would have his daughter with him for some time, at least, David knew it was time to take the next step – perhaps the final step – towards making the High Peaks Pastoral Company a really worthwhile operation. Most people would have thought it was that already but David still had visions of building on what his father had started so long ago. For a long time he had wanted to purchase a merino breeding property so that he could source his replacement wethers, as he was buying wethers in virtually every year. Most of these wethers came from the larger merino properties in north-western or western New South Wales or even from the Riverina. Because they were nearly all Peppin strain sheep, some of them were too strong in the wool for David's liking. A lot of the Peppin sheep carried too much colour and in a wet year, the flies gave them curry. You could jet and minimise the problem to some extent, but David was committed to using fewer chemicals wherever possible.

His chief objective was to use the rams he was breeding on Glen Morrison in a commercial ewe flock and to bring the annual wether drop back to his three hill-country properties. If he could do this he would get more of the kind of wool he was seeking and he could market the wool from the three places under the same brand, which would be a great advantage. As it was, the three clips were now branded under the various property names.

David reckoned that with wool down in price, the time was ripe to hunt out a decent-sized merino breeding place before the cotton boys grabbed the best of them. Some of the best places in recent years had already been utilised for cotton production because cotton gave such good returns, so David was aware that competition for good land was fiercer than ever.

He put his idea forth to the other directors, Anne and Kate. Anne thought David had quite enough on his plate without an additional property, but Kate supported him. She saw the merit of what David was trying to achieve and that a merino breeding property would complement the existing operation. Finding the right place was something else again.

Angus, meanwhile, suffered a little by being the youngest of David and Catriona's three children. A free spirit by nature, Angus often went to extraordinary lengths to get himself noticed. He broke an arm in a fall from a horse and he would ride up to the peak of Yellow Rock just as his father had done. He was a good handler of sheepdogs, and his ponies could do all the tricks David had taught to his own ponies. Like his father, he had no trouble guiding straggler wethers down off Yellow Rock. In short, on the score of natural ability, Angus was just about all that David had hoped for in a son. Except for one thing – responsibility. There were times when Angus didn't care whether the cow calved or busted, to use an earthy bush saying, so long as he was enjoying himself. David had given him a few wallopings and he hoped that the boy would change as he grew older.

Falling off a horse was one thing but playing the devil in a motor car was quite another. Angus, like his father, and like most bush children, could drive a tractor, truck or car long before he reached the legal age to acquire a vehicle licence – the problem was, Angus was far less skilled behind the wheel than he thought. It was Lew Hooper who wised David up to his son's shenanigans.

'You should have a word in your young fellow's ear, David. He'll kill himself in that old utility. I know a lot of young people in the bush can drive long before they're old enough to get a licence and the police don't worry much while they stay off public roads, but young Angus has been driving on a public road and he's been skylarking,' the former police officer said.

'What's he been up to, Lew?' David asked.

'For a start, he's been driving too fast. But he's also broadsiding the vehicle as he comes to the Poitrel and Glen Morrison entrances. Puts it in a big skid to turn the damned thing.'

'Is that so? I'll have a word to him, Lew. And thanks for the tip-off.'

Hooper nodded. 'He's a hell of a good kid with dogs and horses but a bit wild, David.'

David had more than a few words with his younger son. He tore strips off him, and threatened him with a hiding if he heard another adverse report about his driving. But when Angus ran David's near-new utility off the road, David was ropeable.

'Damned young idiot. That's it. He can stick to horses until he learns some sense.'

Angus wasn't allowed to touch a vehicle until he gained his licence.

'It's your own fault, Angus,' Moira told him.

'That's all right for you to say, Moira. You're Dad's pet.'

'That's not true. I just don't go around smashing up expensive motor vehicles, that's all. Dad is expecting a lot from you and you keep letting him down. I shouldn't have to carry all the weight for my two brothers,' Moira said.

'I don't expect you to carry me, sis. I'll do my share when I finish at school,' Angus said.

'I should hope you would,' Moira said. 'I should remind you that Dad was doing a man's job looking after High Peaks and Poitrel when he was your age. And he was part of the reason we own Poitrel today, let alone Aberfeldy.'

'Oh, yes, he was a bloody marvel. You're a bloody marvel too, Moira. You get a boyfriend Dad doesn't like and you'll see his true colours,' Angus said sulkily.

'Don't be so childish, Angus. You're far better with dogs and horses than I am – and you're smarter, too. You simply need to grow up a bit. And I don't envisage going out with a man Dad doesn't like,' Moira added.

When Angus finished at boarding school and acquired his driver's licence – as well as a taste for beer – matters got worse. Catriona was worried every time Angus drove off – all over the country – to a dance. She found it difficult to sleep until she knew he was home safely. She always left the outside light and the verandah lights on so that Angus could find his way in. On one particular occasion Angus had gone to a dance in Merriwa and he told his parents that he should be home by one a.m. The grader had been along earlier in the week and gravel was banked up along the edges of the road from near Inverlochy to the low level crossing below High Peaks, which gave Catriona further reason for concern. She had found it quite skiddy if you took the road too fast, especially the one big bend half-way between the two properties.

This particular night the girl Angus had set his heart on conquering had told him that she had heard too much about him to be seen dead with him – the first time he had been turned down flat. When he left the dance, girl-less, to drive home, he was cursing the injustice of the situation. As he turned the bend towards High Peaks, driving too fast as usual, two roos jumped from the side of the road not far in front of him. Two roos could make a mess of a vehicle as Angus well knew, and he slammed on the brakes. The utility skidded on the fresh gravel, left the road, hit a rock and then slammed up against a tree. Angus heard the windscreen splinter before he blacked out.

David awoke from a deep sleep to find Catriona shaking him. 'What is it, Cat?' he asked sleepily.

'Angus isn't home, darling,' she said.

'What time is it?' he asked.

'It's after three,' she said.

'The young devil said he'd definitely be home by one,' David said.

'Something tells me that he's had an accident, David. It really does,' Catriona said. 'I want you to go and look for him.'

'Will I ever be free of worry where Angus is concerned?' he grumbled as he got out of bed.

'Would you like me to come with you?'

'No, Cat. I'll handle this one,' he replied.

It took David only three or four minutes to reach the utility. David left his car lights on and walked across to the smashed utility. His son was unconscious inside. Unconscious, or dead. A brief examination suggested he was still alive. David swore softly and then walked back to the car to dial the ambulance and Catriona. Moira drove her mother down to the site and the trio waited anxiously for the ambulance to arrive.

'Well, he's got bad concussion, at least,' Eric Wood said. Eric had been one of the ambulance officers who had ridden up to Wallaby Rocks to treat Kate when she broke her leg. Eric was growing old in the ambulance service. 'If he doesn't come out of it, they'll probably send him down to Newcastle, David.'

Catriona travelled with Angus in the ambulance, while David and Moira watched its lights disappear around the bend. It was very quiet. Moira took her father's hand and squeezed it.

'I'm sure Angus will be all right, Dad. Footballers get concussion and they don't take long to get over it.'

'Any hit on the head is serious, Moy. It could be concussion and it could be a coma. The young idiot was probably driving too fast. Lordy, I hope he's going to be all right. There's a lot of good in him if only he wasn't so mad-headed at times. He seems to be intent on trying to kill himself. He's got a big job ahead of him to run all our properties one day. I didn't acquire them just for Cat and me,' David said.

'You've got me, Dad,' Moira said.

'Thank goodness for that, Moy.'

The following morning Moira watched her father leave the homestead and walk up the stone path that led to the consecrated knoll where his father was buried, presumably to tell him about what had happened. She knew that if they lost Angus, or if he never came out of a coma, which amounted to the same thing, she would be the only one left to carry on her father's work. It was a sobering thought. Damn you, Angus, she thought. Why did you have to do this to him?

Later, at the hospital, they waited for news of Angus's condition.

'How do I get him to change, Moy?'

'If he meets the right girl, he might change, Dad,' Moira suggested.

'That's a profound suggestion, Moy,' he said.

'You aren't being condescending, are you, Dad?' she asked.

'Not a bit, sweetheart. I was thinking how much more mature you are than your brother. If only . . .'

'I wasn't a girl?' she suggested.

'Cut that out, Moy,' he said sharply. 'I've never regretted the fact that you're a girl. You're as good as any boy and more conscientious than most, and I would have missed an awful lot not having a daughter. It's just that I thought I'd get at least one son who was a bottler fellow just like you're a bottler girl.'

Moira put her arms round his neck and kissed him. 'Angus is almost a bottler, Dad. He's better than me with dogs and horses and he's smarter than me. Because he's the youngest, he's probably been noticed the least. Mum and I both think that he does mad things to be noticed. When he comes out of this, you should make him more of a mate, Dad.'

David looked at his daughter in astonishment. Moira had grown up very fast. Once again her insight had left him flabbergasted.

Angus was unconscious for three days. It seemed like an age to the other MacLeods, but eventually he came to and smiled weakly at his mother. 'It was two roos, Mum. I swerved to miss them because I reckoned Dad would go crook if they damaged his ute. The ute skidded on the new gravel.'

Catriona rang home to tell David and Moira that Angus was conscious and that he had swerved to avoid hitting two roos. David and Moira immediately left for Newcastle to see him.

'I'm sorry about the ute, Dad. I tried to miss the roos and it skidded.'

'Vehicles can be repaired or changed, Angus. That's why we have insurance policies. Don't worry about the ute. How are you feeling?'

'Not as good as I could be,' he said and grinned.

'You'll be as good as gold before long. Maybe I'll

order you a tank and you can drive that,' David suggested.

'Don't make me laugh, Dad. It hurts too much,' Angus said.

This accident kept Angus reasonably quiet for a couple of months, after which David sent him to Yeppoon for a holiday, and then arranged for him to spend some time with Don Morgan at Aberfeldy. But a week after Angus arrived at Aberfeldy David had a phone call from Don Morgan to tell him that Angus had a broken arm.

'How in blazes did he manage that, Don?' David asked.

'Well, he, er, had a go at riding a buckjumper at the local rodeo. It threw him against the iron gate. I'm sorry, David. I know you said to watch him but I couldn't watch him all the time. I didn't know he was going to have a lash at the buckjumping until after it was over,' Morgan said.

'It's all right, Don. I'd better come up and get him and bring someone to drive the utility home. I presume his arm is in a sling.'

'It is, David.'

David put the phone down and looked into Cat's anxious eyes. 'It's Angus?'

'He's got a broken arm, Cat. Tried to ride a buckjumper and it threw him against the iron gate. I suppose it could have been worse. We'll have to go up and get him. You can drive the car and I'll drive the utility home.'

He had been thinking he might keep Angus home for another year but this didn't seem the right way to go in the light of recent events. The mad bugger would probably be better off being busy at college. It wouldn't stop him getting into scrapes, but Longreach would keep him fairly well occupied. And there was always the chance that he might meet a really decent girl who might motivate him to behave himself. If Angus didn't toe the line at Longreach, David would bring him home. So off to Longreach Angus went.

Chapter Nine

David MacLeod was a sheepman by breeding and inclination, while his father, Andrew, had been a sheepman first and foremost. Many people swore at sheep, but Andrew MacLeod swore *by* them. He had shorn at some of the top merino properties in the land, and knew how good merino wool could be. But he also recognised that it wasn't wise to put all your eggs in one basket. He ran beef cattle as a sideline and would have increased his cattle holding, but High Peaks wasn't suitable to finishing off any more cattle than could be run on the more congenial country surrounding the homestead.

David followed his father's example. He graded up the beef herd on Poitrel and then, after he had established the Hereford stud, he used his own good bulls to upgrade all of his cattle. This was one reason for establishing the Hereford stud in the first place. Another reason was that he wanted to be able to sell stud and herd bulls to provide additional income. But the third reason for setting up the cattle stud was less obvious – David wanted it as a vehicle for promoting his children. Stud cattle breeding had more glamour to it than most rural enterprises, ranking second only to the breeding of thoroughbreds in prestige. However, David knew you could easily spend a million dollars on setting up a cattle stud and still not produce a Royal winner.

David was fiercely determined to stamp the MacLeod name on the Australian pastoral scene. The best way to do this was by having his children exhibit high-class sheep and cattle. They would then be asked to judge, and David wanted to see them judge at Royal and State sheep shows. He reckoned that he would be invited to judge and planned to take along Moira and Angus as associate judges to give them experience and put them in the limelight. And that was more or less how it happened. When Moira accompanied David, ageing stud masters sighed and wished they were young again.

Moira was philosophical about her effect on men. 'I know when I'm judging sheep they're more interested in checking me out than in my judging ability. It's hardly fair though, is it? For a man, it's how he judges and the decisions he makes that are important; it's just not the same for a woman,' Moira said.

'The most important thing is that you are being asked to judge at shows, sweetheart,' David answered. 'And you are very attractive,' he added. 'I used to gaze at your mother quite a lot in the days when she thought I wasn't interested in her.'

Moira slapped his hand playfully. 'Now the secrets are coming out, Dad. From what I've gleaned from Mum, she was very concerned that you weren't looking at her at all! Anyway, if they want to look at me, let them.'

'That's the stuff, sweetheart. Think positively. If you were three axe handles across the beam nobody would want to look twice,' he said, and grinned.

'You are a devil at times, Dad,' Moira said, and hugged him.

Catriona viewed Moira's closeness to David with deepening concern. Ordinary affection was one thing, but to be David's shadow was quite another. If she and David went somewhere Moira nearly always wanted to join them. Catriona knew that Moira had always idolised her father and until some young man came along and claimed her daughter's heart, he was the biggest thing in Moira's life.

All three MacLeod children had a great eye for livestock. Even though Dougal seemed to lack real interest in High Peaks' activities, he had little trouble selecting the pick of a herd of animals. Moira and Angus also demonstrated a flair in this area from an early age. Their father talked livestock continually and they would have had to have a few screws loose not to pick up a lot of what he said.

David's huge advantage over most other people was his instinctive grasp of all things related to animals. He had transferred his exceptional ability with dogs and horses to his breeding of sheep and cattle. What he drilled into his children was the importance of having a mental picture of what a top animal should look like. Some people couldn't do this, and these people never made top breeders.

There were some fundamental tenets that applied to the breeding of merino sheep that provided the foundation for all subsequent knowledge. David had learnt these fundamentals in the first instance from Hugh Pfeffer, Angus Campbell's sheep classer, and later from other sheep classers and studmasters. The first consideration was structure, which included the feet and legs. A sheep had to be built correctly to carry a heavy fleece of wool. When merino sheep carried only three or four pounds of wool, structure had not mattered so much, but now that rams were carrying thirty pounds of wool and some ewes in excess of sixteen pounds, structure was very important. The second consideration was size – put simply, big sheep produce more wool than small sheep because the larger the area of skin, the more wool-producing follicles. Because wool production was determined not only by an animal's genetic makeup but also by what went down its throat, diet was the third consideration. When he started to feed sheep in the shed David learnt that sheep needed a ration of about 12 per cent protein to fully capitalise on their genetic potential. Under paddock conditions sheep seldom had access to pastures providing this level of protein, so it was important to supplement the diet.

'One of the big secrets to the merino business is finding out which strain of sheep suits your area or even your individual property,' Hugh Pfeffer had advised David. 'Some strains suit certain areas very well. For example, by and large Haddon Rig blood sheep do extra well in the Walgett district but might not do as well in other places. South Australian strains are big sheep but you need the nutrition to maintain a big sheep and to allow it to produce to its potential. It's hard to be dogmatic, David. Some strains of sheep do no good at all in hill country and some thrive in it. What it comes down to is that a sheep needs to be able to thrive on what you give it, and some strains do better than others in certain areas. Follow me?'

'I understand,' David replied.

'It's hard to produce sheep that will suit every condition. If you're going to breed stud sheep, first get the structure right. Then try and pack on that structure as much wool of the type you want as you can get a sheep to efficiently carry. Bear in mind that different people have different ideas about sheep. Some people are looking for what are called "easy-care" sheep. These have little or no wool about the head. If one person is looking after 10 000 sheep, which is the go on some places, easy-care sheep appeal to them. If you're on a smaller place you might be looking for a sheep with a lot more wool about the head and legs. On clean country you can run sheep with wool to the toes whereas in the bigger country this leg wool gets stripped off by burrs and bushes,' the old classer advised.

David looked about a lot and studied old books and photographs before embarking on his big merino project. It seemed that having families of sheep was important because some strains, even within the same stud, exhibited superior quality for certain factors. It might be length of wool, crimping or softness. What David knew was that you could not select for a single characteristic because if you did, other important features suffered. Two factors which were receiving a lot of attention were crimp and softness. Crimp is the natural wave formation that exists to a greater or lesser extent in the wool of most breeds of sheep. Generally speaking, the closer these waves are, the finer the wool. Crimp is a factor in wool's elasticity. The value of softness, although stated as a plus factor for wool, was receiving more attention than in the past because wool's 'prickle' factor had long been a negative selling point for the fibre. Stud breeders were actively breeding for soft wool and virtually all fleece tests now gave details of the prickle factor. Because of the many traits necessary to make up a top sheep, it was very difficult to purchase sheep that had every desirable quality. When one such animal was offered at auction, it invariably made a big price.

With Catriona by his side, David made trips to virtually all the main sheep-breeding areas of eastern Australia. He concentrated his efforts on the studs producing the finer-woolled merinos. He bought enough ewes to register a stud and then added to this original fifty as he came across ewes he liked. He was taken aback to discover that some fine-wool breeders wouldn't offer old fine-wool ewes on the open market but consigned them straight to abattoirs so that other studs couldn't acquire their bloodlines. This wasn't a universal practice but it did happen.

David used Glen Morrison as his sheep base. He built an annexe on the existing woolshed and started feeding the pick of his young crop of lambs. This was very much a learning experience, and David learnt an astonishing amount. Some rams looked good but didn't sire well; other rams bred better progeny than themselves.

What David also learnt was that in chasing high-quality or elite wool, some stud breeders were allowing the structure of their sheep to fall away. This was evidenced in bad legs, goose rumps and shallow ribbing. With his usual foresight David sensed that if breeders kept chasing superior wools at the expense of structure it wouldn't be long before there would be some very funny-looking sheep on properties. He also sensed that if he concentrated on big-girthed sheep, the kind of sheep that were in evidence at Sydney sheep shows after World War II, he would have a very valuable sheep to promote.

It was several years before David made his entry into show circles. His first show was at Merriwa, where he and his father had won so often with kelpies. There wasn't a lot of competition except from one stud with a big name, that conducted an annual on-property sale. David won every major award on offer – a stunning entry into the stud merino business that resulted in a flood of enquiries for rams. He followed up this initial success by winning six successive Grand Champion Ram awards. The beautiful, richly crimped white wool attracted a lot of attention but to David's surprise, not a single person had commented on the depth of his sheep. It seemed that the quality of the wool had blinded them to what he regarded as his major achievement, which was the improvement in girth.

Later, after they took the show team back to Glen Morrison and the sheep were in their pens feeding, David's excitement over his success at the show boiled over and he turned to Catriona and took her in his arms. 'Wow, we did it, Cat. Grand champion ram and grand champion ewe. It's what we've been working for and now we've done it.'

'You've done it, David,' Catriona said. 'I didn't contribute anything to the sheep side of things. I know a little bit about Hereford cattle but not much about the finer points of merinos.'

'Cat, you've helped in more ways than you can imagine. This isn't just my operation, it's ours. We've always worked as a team. You're entitled to any success we achieve,' David said.

'It's sweet of you to say so but you've done the work with the sheep. Now all the work and the money you've expended is starting to show results. Congratulations, darling.'

Once the merino stud had been established on Glen Morrison, David and Catriona began their search for a merino-breeding property.

'What are you actually looking for in this merino

property, darling?' Catriona asked. She, Moira and David were sitting on the front verandah having afternoon tea. David had been commenting on various properties advertised in *The Land* newspaper.

David put down the newspaper and looked up at the ceiling while he collected his thoughts. He knew precisely what he wanted in a property but how to get this across to his wife and daughter without appearing long-winded and patronising concerned him quite a bit.

'The thing is that there are certain districts that are recognised as being better sheep-growing areas than others. There's the Macquarie country, the Riverina and north-western New South Wales, and they produce good-sized sheep though they're mostly of the earlier-maturing Peppin strain. There are other places that also produce good sheep because they have reasonably assured rainfall and can grow improved pastures. The problem is that this inside country is pretty damned expensive. A lot of the bigger inside places that have been sold have been subdivided into smaller areas to attract city people to purchase properties, and these smaller areas attract more money than the land would if sold in a complete parcel. Any property with water rights is dearer again and a big whack of the best flatter country is being put under cotton – or is already growing the stuff,' David said.

'But there must be some suitable places left?' Moira said.

'Sure there are, Moy. Sometimes one will come on to the market out of the blue – like when the owners decide to retire. But if you can grow cotton on it, it puts the place out of our league, cotton giving such big returns.'

David wasn't overly concerned as he reckoned he would find what he wanted sooner or later. One of the earliest pieces of information on land that had come his way was that the ideal property had a mix of red and black soils. Red country needed less rain than black to bring feed away but folded quicker. Black country needed more rain but held better. An old grazier and kelpie man from western New South Wales had vouchsafed this information to David's father. The same man had said that the ideal country for breeding and finishing cattle should have long creek frontages and plenty of shade trees. These 'gems' from past days stuck in David's head. Some were useful and some were not.

Catriona enjoyed the process of hunting out the right property. She and David looked at a lot of places together and met some fine people. In some cases properties were being sold because of an owner's age or because the owner felt there was no future in the land. Inability to finance bank loans was another reason. Poor seasons were sometimes also a contributing factor in an owner's decision to sell.

One of the reasons Catriona liked these visits was because she had David to herself – unless Moira had prevailed upon her father to allow her to accompany them. Moira was passionately interested in David's objectives because he had made her part of his plans since she was a child. To now be a party to her parents' conversations as they discussed properties they had inspected removed the last traces of pure girlhood that had remained when she left boarding school. Moira was now in every sense an adult.

So the three of them, and sometimes just David and Moira, ranged far and wide looking at sheep properties. They went out as far as Nyngan and along the Lachlan country below Forbes. Some places they inspected were in flood country – lovely grazing country in dry weather because of countless inundations, but a different story when the river flooded.

All three were amazed just how much the country-side varied, not only from district to district but even within the same area. The old experienced landowners would speak of 'soft' and 'hard' country and of how sheep and cattle would do so much better on the former. One old flat-country grazier told David that when he saw hills, he saw sour country. It was generally felt that no hill country could approach the Macquarie and Riverina areas in sweetness and productivity.

Both David and Catriona felt privileged to meet and talk with graziers who had spent a lifetime breeding top-quality sheep and were only retiring, very reluctantly, because of advancing age. They shared their knowledge and love of the land. David was impressed by relatively poor country transformed and made more productive by the introduction of saltbush or lucerne. But what really astonished him was that people were running stock, both sheep and cattle, on widely different country. Some of it was heavily timbered and some of it hardly grew a tree at all.

Elders and other agents were continually phoning David with news of new properties being placed on the market. Cattle prices were down and high interest rates were creating big problems for farmers who had opted for the 'get bigger or get out' advice they had swallowed from rural consultants. Some interest rates were as high as 24 per cent, which was financial suicide with low commodity prices. Elders property rep Joe Morton had taken David and Catriona to several properties, but none he had seen appealed to David. It was Joe who rang and told David about Molonga, a property that was coming on the market. It hadn't been advertised but Elders had the place to offer.

'The fellow's been there all his life, David. Old age and the tough times have caught up with him. It's not as big as you're looking for but it's a really nice place and Len Murray has bred good sheep there,' Joe told him.

David listened patiently. He had heard variations of this spiel probably thirty times. 'How big is it, Joe?'

'About three and half thousand acres, David.'

'Not big enough, Joe,' David answered quickly.

'I realise it's not as big as you're after but it's a really good place, David. Got a long creek frontage and some great farming land, too. Len is keen for a quick sale. You'd like the place. We've sold his sheep for years and they've got a great name. Trust me, David. You should have a look at this place,' Joe said with some urgency.

'Oh, I don't know, Joe. I want a place to run five thousand ewes. You know that. I haven't got time to look at unsuitable places,' David said firmly.

'You shouldn't miss this place, David. I kid you not,' Joe said.

'Okay, Joe, I'll go and have a look at it. You set it up and come back to me with the details.'

'Great stuff, David. You won't be sorry,' Joe said with a chuckle.

'Hmmm. We'll see about that. Where is it, Joe?' he asked.

'It's at the foothills of the Nandewar Range – sort of between Narrabri and Barraba.'

'Well, we haven't looked there before,' David said.

'I'll be talking to you, David,' Joe said.

David put the phone down and looked at Catriona.

'Joe has another place for us to look at, Cat. Reckons it's the bee's knees. Well, it's not big enough to begin with so why the blazes I should go and look at it I don't know. Only thing in its favour is that it's been owned by the same people for a long time. They probably wouldn't have stayed there if it hadn't given them a living. Oh well, I said I'd look at it.'

When Joe came back and told David he had arranged an inspection for the following Saturday, Catriona told him that she and her mother were going to Sydney for a few days. 'You know that Mum's heart has been causing her some concern, darling. She's been putting off tests she must undergo in Sydney, and they can't wait any longer. I'm her only daughter and it's my place to go.'

'Of course, Cat. Has Jane got worse?' David asked.

'She hasn't got better, darling. I'm sure that Moira will jump at the chance to go with you' Catriona said with a wry smile.

And, of course, Moira did. To go away with her father was Moira's present conception of heaven. People everywhere looked up to her father and to be introduced as his daughter really meant something. And it would mean that he would discuss with her what he would have discussed with her mother.

Molonga was everything Joe Morton had said it was. The property was at the foothills of the Nandewar Range and spread out into gently undulating-to-flat country traversed by a creek. The timber was predominantly box and ironbark, with some pines and a few old majestic red gums along the creek. The homestead sat in a kind of horseshoe between hills. It wasn't grand, but a very comfortable big house, and there were solid improvements all around it, such as a decent three-stand shearing shed and a row of grain silos.

Len Murray reminded David in some indefinable way of his own father. It began with the strong handshake. Then there was Len's slow, deliberate way of talking.

'I put some woolly ewes in the yards for you to look at, David. I thought you'd like to see what we've been running here,' Murray said.

'I appreciate that, Len,' David said.

Murray was a tall, spare man with hair in the transition between grey and white. He had clear blue eyes framed by a web of tiny wrinkles.

Joe Morton had told Len a great deal about David MacLeod. He knew that David was a big-shot grazier with multiple properties and would probably want to be called Mister. But David soon shattered that notion, and it wasn't long before both men and Moira were sitting on the fence rails yarning about sheep. David had complimented the older man on the quality of the sheep and their wool.

'They're largely Egalabra blood, David. Egalabra and Rossmore, actually. Been on the mix for years. Seems to suit this country,' Len said.

Presently, Len took David and Moira for a drive around the property. Joe said he'd go and have a yarn to 'the missus'. Everything David saw was in first-class condition. The cattle were a mix of Angus and Herefords and looked to be doing very well. They were strung out along the creek and there wasn't a poor animal in sight. It was a great place, David reflected, but it wasn't quite big enough. He needed a bigger property to be able to keep replacing his wether flocks.

Moira whispered in his ear, 'I like this place, Daddy. It's beautiful, and it's produced fine stock.'

David asked Len to stop the utility one paddock out from the homestead and he got out and leant on the gate. About a mile across to his left was another homestead, red-roofed and with a thin plume of smoke spiralling skywards from a chimney.

'It's a damned nice property, Len. Everything is in great order and there's nothing here that needs attention. The problem is that it's not big enough. I'm looking for a place that can run five thousand ewes. I want to breed replacement wethers and maybe some of my stud ewes and rams. I'd take it if it could handle that number of ewes,' David told him.

'I appreciate your honesty, David. Let me make a suggestion and don't repeat it in front of Joe Morton. You see that homestead?' Murray pointed to the red-roofed house away to the left, as a flock of cockatoos flew overhead.

David nodded, and Len continued in a lowered voice, despite their isolation in the middle of the paddock. 'The fellow who owned that was killed a year or so ago. Got on the spree and turned his car over. He was a mad bugger at times. You ever hear of Jack Barden?'

'Jack Barden? Now let me think. Wasn't there a Jack Barden who was a rodeo champion and campdrafter?'

'That's the fellow. Horse-mad. You've got to be a bit mad to want to ride bulls and buckjumpers. When he inherited the place from his father, Jack turfed out all the sheep and replaced them with cattle. He used to spend hours working his horses on cattle. Good style of a fellow when he wasn't on the grog.

'To cut a long story short Jack married a bonzer girl. Linda was a sister at the hospital. There's five kids aged from fifteen to four. Jack bought an extra bit of country and then interest rates went up to blazes and cattle prices went the other way.'

'It's bloody criminal, Len,' David sympathised.

'The bank is pushing Linda pretty hard. She's back doing night duty at weekends when Kitty, that's the oldest girl, can look after the others. I've helped Linda a bit but she tells me she'll have to sell. What I suggest is that you go and see her and maybe make an offer. You could do it privately and that way she wouldn't have to pay commission on the sale,' Len said earnestly.

'You think she wants to sell?' David asked.

'I doubt there's any alternative. She can't keep up the repayments on their loan. A damned shame, really – they're a great lot of kids. The oldest boy is a real goer. What I suggest is that while you're here, you talk to Linda. If you could buy her place and this one you would have any amount of country to breed your ewes. And there hasn't been a sheep on the place for twenty years or more.'

'How big is it?' David asked.

'I reckon with the Meredith block there'd be about four and a half thousand acres,' Murray said.

'What's the country like?'

'Every bit as good as ours. They're running about four hundred breeding cows and growing some wheat. Jack put on a share farmer to grow the wheat as he hated engines. You wouldn't get Jack to touch a combine or a harvester.'

David walked up and down while he thought about

the situation. The two places combined amounted to around eight thousand acres, which was about what he had in mind. It was actually more than he had in mind, but that didn't matter.

'Len, I'm in a bind because Joe brought us out here. I can't get loose of him decently as we don't have our own vehicle. You talk to your neighbour and I'll phone you tonight. If she's interested in selling, Moira and I will come back tomorrow morning. We'll leave early and be here about ten. If you give me the offer of your place until tomorrow night, I'll finalise the deal one way or another. Is that okay with you?'

'You've got my hand on it,' Murray said.

'Right, now we can head back for home,' David said.

'You'll have time for some lunch, won't you?' Murray asked.

'I don't want to give your wife extra work,' David said with a smile.

'It isn't every day we have a bush legend here,' Murray said with a grin. It was his first grin of the morning.

'A bush legend, eh? I thought a fellow had to be dead before he was described as a legend,' David said.

'You're a legend in your lifetime, David. There's hardly a sheepman anywhere who wouldn't have heard of your kelpies. That's for a start. Then there's what you've done with horses and cattle and now stud sheep. Yeah, I reckon you're a legend right enough. I'd like to say that if anyone is to buy this place, I'd prefer it was you.'

'Thanks, Len. Well, we'll see what eventuates.'

Elizabeth Murray, who asked to be called Beth, because that was what everyone called her, was in David's view the quintessential country woman. She was at the front door to greet them and insisted that it was no trouble at all to have them stay for lunch.

'I suppose you've been feeding Joe scones or pikelets while we've been out looking at the place?' David said.

'Well, now that you mention it, Joe did show a liking for my scones,' Beth replied with a laugh.

'A fellow never knows when he'll get his next feed in this game,' Joe defended himself.

'In this case it will be in about ten minutes,' Beth said.

Lunch consisted of roast lamb, crispy baked potatoes and beans followed by home-baked apple pie and cream. 'That should do us until dinner tonight. A great meal, Beth,' David said.

'Yes, thank you Beth – a lovely meal,' Moira seconded. 'Dad is a great one for baked dinners. Mum complains he's boring to cook for as he doesn't like pasta and rice and, oh, lots of things.'

'That stuff wasn't around when I was a boy. Or if it was, I didn't see it. I got plenty of baked dinners and –'

'Heaps of chocolate cake and cream sponges!' Moira added.

Sitting around the table yarning about sheep, wool, cattle prices and shows was all very pleasant until Joe announced they had better be going, as he had phone-calls to make that evening.

'Great pair, aren't they?' the Elders man said, as the trio drove away from Molonga.

'It must be a wrench to leave the property after all the years they've been there,' David said.

'There comes a time and all that,' Joe said. 'Len doesn't want Beth to have the worry of selling the place should he die first.'

That night David rang Len Murray, who told him that Linda Barden was agreeable to him coming out again the next day. She had confirmed to Murray that she intended to sell the property.

'You want to come out with me again tomorrow, Moira?' David asked when he put the phone down.

'Try and stop me, Dad,' she said quickly.

'Then you had better duck off to bed. I want to leave by five. Think you can be ready then?'

'Of course. I presume you want something to eat before we leave?'

'You know me,' he said, and smiled across at her.

'That means getting up before four. Do you think you'll buy Molonga, Dad?'

'I'm certainly thinking about it, sweetheart. It isn't big enough on its own but the two places together would be beaut. Maybe just what I want. Len Murray's sheep certainly looked pretty good,' he said.

'Eight thousand acres means a lot of money, doesn't it?' Moira asked.

'It does, sweetheart. It would mean a lot more if cattle prices were better and wool not in the doldrums.

It's the dead right time to buy a place, Moy,' he said.

Moira loved it when he called her Moy. She went across to his big chair and bent over and kissed him. 'Goodnight, Dad. I'll be ready in the morning.'

'You'd better be, or I'll leave you behind,' he teased.

It wasn't much after five when they left High Peaks. Moira looked her usual immaculate self in white mole-skin trousers, cream blouse and white Akubra. She had thrown a tweedy coat over the blouse as the morning was cool.

An hour or so along the road, David stopped the car and asked Moira to drive. 'You'd better get used to driving longer distances, Moy,' he said.

Moira drove for a couple of hours before David took over again. 'I must say, a cup of tea and a few pikelets wouldn't go astray,' he said, as he took the wheel. 'Being on the road makes a fellow hungry.'

'Nanna says you're always hungry, whether you're on the road or not,' Moira said.

'We might stop in Barraba and get a cuppa and a toasted sandwich,' David suggested.

They did stop in the small town of Barraba before driving on again for the Barden property. It was reached by the same road as Molonga and in fact adjoined it for nearly three miles. The name on the gate was 'Wirrewarra'.

'There was a terrible massacre of Aborigines not all that far from here. A place called Myall Creek,' David said.

They drove on to Wirrewarra in silence, both deep

in thought. Eventually, the homestead came into sight.

'Oh, look there's the house. And there's a boy with the gate open for us,' Moira said.

The boy closed the gate behind them and then ran after the car as it cruised towards the big homestead. Children and dogs in about equal numbers seemed to appear from nowhere.

'Careful, Daddy. There are dogs running towards us,' Moira warned.

'I can see them, Moy. This place could do with a traffic cop,' he said.

'Oh, look at the ponies,' she said, and pointed to a paddock not far from the homestead. A small black Shetland pony and two larger ponies, one bay and one brown, were tethered to the back fence.

'I like the look and feel of this place, Moy,' David said. 'It's obviously a family place.' They pulled up beside the back entrance to the house. There was a tall fence surrounding the back lawn, which was strewn with various toys.

As David opened the door of the car a little tan-and-white terrier thrust itself into the vehicle. A small tow-headed boy grabbed the terrier by its wildly wagging tail and extracted it from the car. 'His name's Rowdy – he's very friendly,' the boy said.

'I can see that,' David said with a smile. 'And what's your name, young fellow?'

'I'm Bob,' he said.

'Come away from there, Bob,' a feminine voice called from inside the yard.

Moira joined her father and they pushed open the gate to meet Linda Barden. She was a slim, blonde woman who was still very pretty although she would have been quite a beauty in her youth. Her figure belied the five children she had produced, and only the lines on her face testified to the years and maybe the stresses Linda Barden had endured. Her yellow dress displayed evidence of flour, which the apron she had obviously taken off in a hurry, and was still holding, had failed to catch.

'Mr MacLeod, I'm Linda Barden,' the blonde woman greeted them.

'This is my daughter, Moira, Mrs Barden,' David said, as he took his daughter's arm.

'And I can see you're very proud of her,' Linda said, and laughed. 'I would be too.'

This congenial greeting set the tone for their visit.

'This is Kitty, Mr MacLeod. Kitty is my eldest daughter. Bob you've met. Fiona has the jam on her face and the little fellow is Jack, like his father. The boy who opened the gate for you is Tim. He's fifteen.'

'Did you say Tim?' David asked.

'Yes, Tim,' Linda said. 'You must be hungry after leaving so early.'

David looked over at the boy she had said was Tim. It took him back over the years to his old friend Tim Sparkes who had taught David how to defend himself and then had left him his property. Tim Sparkes had made David a wealthy man.

'We had a cuppa and some toasted sandwiches in Barraba but I wouldn't say no to another cuppa,' David said.

'Dad is ready to drink tea and eat any old time,' Moira said.

'Well, he's a big man so he probably takes some filling,' Linda observed.

'You're a woman to be treasured, Mrs Barden,' David said.

'Come along then. You children play outside while we're talking.'

It was a big, comfortable house and remarkably tidy considering the five children and the litter that adorned the back lawn. Two sections were connected by a covered walkway, and a long gauzed verandah stretched along one side. But the most notable feature was the huge kitchen, which opened onto the verandah and suggested many meals were shared there.

Linda Barden's scones were first-class and David murmured his appreciation. After some comments on the weather and the season he brought the conversation around to the reason for their visit.

'I don't really want to sell the property but I have to. It's beyond me. Len Murray probably told you that Jack borrowed a fair bit of money to buy an adjoining block. The interest is killing me. Cattle aren't much good right now and I can't keep up the payments. I hate the idea of selling because the children love it here, especially Tim. But I'm going to make sure that Tim has a profession or trade anyway so that he can make his living at something apart from the land. Maybe when the children are older I could buy a place for them, but with these interest payments and five children to educate I can't keep this place. I really can't. I'm back doing night duty at weekends when Kitty can mind the children, and it's a help but not nearly enough. If I sell this place I'll be able to invest money and that will help us to live,' Linda explained.

David nodded his understanding. 'Could Tim show us around the place?' he asked.

'Of course he could. Would you like to go now?'

'Yes, I want to be back home tonight. My wife is away in Sydney with her mother, and so there are chores waiting for me back there.'

Tim proved to be a very capable and informative guide. He was a mine of information about the various paddocks and the cattle in them. When they stopped at a gate Tim was out of the car like a shot and had the gate opened in the winking of an eye. Of course, he was fifteen and full of energy, as Moira reminded her father later.

There was not a fault with the property or the cattle, either. They were in just as good condition as Len Murray's cattle next door. A lot of the cows were lying up and down the creek.

When they arrived back at the homestead Linda took them into the office. There, David saw with interest old ribbons behind glass that revealed that a Barden had once exhibited championship fleeces off the property.

'That was Jack's grandfather. He was a great sheep-man by all accounts. Jack's father had sheep too,' Linda said.

'The property must be capable of producing good wool. The sheep Len showed me had good wool and there's hardly any difference in the country,' David said.

'A lot of our neighbours had sheep and some still do but many went in for cropping when these districts started to grow wheat in the fifties,' Linda explained.

'Would you mind calling Len for me? I'd like to speak to him about coming over here if that's all right with you, Mrs Barden,' David said.

'Of course it is. Len and Beth are dear friends as well as being wonderful neighbours,' she said.

She dialled the number and then handed the receiver to him. 'It's all yours, Mr MacLeod.'

'Thank you,' he said, and took the phone from her. 'Len, David MacLeod here. Could you and Beth possibly come over here fairly soon? I'd like to talk to you and Mrs Barden together. You can? Thank you – I do appreciate this!'

David turned to Linda. 'Maybe Tim could show me around the sheds while we're waiting for Len and Beth?'

'He'd like that. I'll call him for you,' Linda replied.

The tall, fair-haired boy listened to what his mother said and nodded.

'I'd like to have a look at the old shearing shed first,' David told him.

'It hasn't been used for shearing for ages,' the boy warned.

239

'I realise that, but I'd like to have a look at it anyway,' David said.

'Dad used it to store a lot of things, so it's in a bit of a mess,' Tim said as they walked down the track. He was conscious of Moira beside him but all his interest was focused on the shearing shed.

The sheep yards surrounding the woolshed had seen better days but the shed itself was substantially sound. It had originally been a six-stand shed, which suggested that at one time the property had been much larger than it was now. Some of the internal pens were in disrepair but wouldn't take much renovating. The wool room was full of items of station use, from fencing to drench. The wool press was an old Koertz, its red paint very faded. There was even an old wool book beneath a stack of weights.

David and Moira, trailed by Tim, walked outside where David had a longer look at the sheep yards. They weren't worth repairing, as much of the timber in them was old and rotten. Some of the big posts were still solid, but really the whole lot needed pulling down to make way for a new set of yards. Conversely, the adjacent cattle yards were in A-one condition with a modern crush and even a set of scales, making it apparent where the late Jack Barden's real interest lay.

'That's interesting,' David said, and pointed towards the scales. 'Did your father weigh his cattle before selling them?'

The boy nodded. 'Dad sold some of his cattle off the place. He used the scales to weigh them and also for the steers he showed. We won a lot of steer awards.'

'Did you now? Are you a cattleman like your father, Tim?'

'I don't mind sheep. I go over and help Mr Murray sometimes. It's just that we haven't had sheep here while I've been alive. Dad got rid of them all when he took over the place,' Tim said.

'What's that shed there?' David asked, and pointed off to their right.

'It's a hay shed. Dad used to buy hay when it was cheap. It's about half-full right now.'

'I see. What do you think about your mother selling the place, Tim?'

'I don't want to see it sold but we owe a fair bit of money and cattle aren't much chop right now. It's too much worry for Mum, and she's working too hard. There's five of us to rear, and Mum's had to go back nursing at weekends,' Tim said.

'I can see you lot have had it tough,' David said sympathetically.

'We've had a bit of bad luck all right, but that'll change, Mr MacLeod. I sure will be sad to leave this place, but one day I'll buy another place of my own,' Tim added.

Tim Barden impressed David considerably. He was a very level-headed boy who seemed to have genuine concern for his mother. Boys like Tim Barden didn't grow on trees. A glimmer of an idea began to form in David's brain.

'Ah well, this looks like Len and Beth,' David said,

and pointed to where a green car had just rounded the hill in front of the house.

'Yes, that's their car – a green Holden,' Tim confirmed.

They met up again in the big lounge room where the children were hustled outside in Kitty's care, the door shut behind them.

'Thanks for coming at such short notice, Len and Beth,' David began. 'I wanted to talk to you in company with Mrs Barden because the business in hand involves the three of you.

'First things first,' David said, and smiled. 'I'm prepared to purchase both properties but the purchase is contingent on me getting both of them. If for some reason one party pulls out, the sale is off. The Molonga sale has to be through Elders but as you, Mrs Barden, hadn't put Wirrewarra on the market, it can be a private sale and there won't be any commission. I'll pay the same price per acre for Wirrewarra as for Molonga.

David could have negotiated a lower price for Wirrewarra by arguing that he'd have to put in a new set of sheep yards, but he wasn't the kind of man to take advantage of a widow with five children.

'Len, I'd like to purchase all your ewes. I don't have many commercial ewes and if I don't buy them from you, I'll have to buy them elsewhere. There won't be enough to stock both places but they'll be a good start. There's a lot of years of breeding behind them and I'd be foolish to let them go,' David said.

'Well, I reckon we can come to the party on the sheep,' Len said.

David nodded. 'Great stuff. Now as regards your cattle, Mrs Barden, I'm not sure which is the best avenue for their disposal. The way cattle prices are right now you won't get top value for them. Maybe Len here could advise you how best to sell them. Don't try and sell them until we finalise the purchase of the properties. We'll get the bank out of your hair and then worry about selling your cattle.'

David paused for a moment and looked at the boy sitting next to his mother. 'I'd like to put a proposition to you, Mrs Barden. It seems to me that Tim here and his brothers and sisters ought to be out in the bush. They like ponies and I reckon Tim is a really handy fellow on the place. I'm prepared to let you stay here free of rent. I won't need this house as I'll have the Molonga homestead. I'm also prepared to pay Tim something to keep an eye on things for the time being. I don't know who will be coming to Molonga but even with a full-time manager there'll be times when he'll need a hand.'

Linda Barden was speechless, so David continued. 'Tim, you're a fine boy with your head screwed on tightly, and you know a lot about the land. Your mother says she wants you to do a course in something. You do that and when you're through, if you still want to stay on the land, I'll give you a job. Maybe one day you could be back here managing both places. How does that appeal to you?'

By the time David had finished talking, Linda Barden's eyes had filled with tears. Moira, sitting beside her father, felt a flush of love and pride for him.

'The bottom line is that you won't have to worry about getting out of here if you don't want to, and we will try to get you the best possible price for your cattle. If you invest your money wisely, you should have enough to live quite comfortably,' David said.

'I don't know what to say,' Linda Barden began. 'I never expected anything like this.'

'You could put the kettle on and we'll have a cup o' tea,' Len Murray suggested.

'Len,' Beth scolded. 'It's lunchtime.'

'Oh dear, so it is. I was going to put on a nice lunch. Would cold meat and salad be all right, Mr MacLeod?' Linda asked.

'Anything would be all right, Mrs Barden,' David said with a smile.

'I'll give you a hand, Linda,' Beth suggested.

Linda was still overwhelmed. 'Len, I think I should be passing out drinks all round but it seems too early for that. My mind is in a whirl. I had resigned myself to leaving here and the children wanted to keep their ponies. Tim, it looks as if your future is assured one way or the other. Oh, I don't know what to say.'

She went out dabbing at her eyes and Tim followed her.

'That's a very generous offer, David,' Len Murray said. 'And here's my hand on the deal.'

'Maybe you could look after things this end. There'll

be no hurry for you to get out even after the sale goes through. Take all the time you need. It sometimes takes a while to find what you want. I'll talk to you more about the sheep a bit later down the track,' David said.

Murray nodded. 'I'll look after the sheep until you're ready to take over. No problem there.'

After lunch David and Len walked up the road to have a look at the boundary fence between the two properties. 'As the crow flies the two houses are not much more than a mile apart, but it's about five miles around by road,' Murray explained.

'What I'm thinking is that I'll put in three or four grids and gates so I can move stock easily through both places. I'll get a quote on gravelling a track direct from here to your house. It might come in handy,' David said.

'That's a good idea if it doesn't cost too much,' Murray agreed.

'It would save a bit of time, especially at shearing and crutching. I'll have to put in a new set of yards to use the shed here. It might be easier to put all the sheep through Molonga shed . . . for the time being, anyway. It wouldn't be much longer to take them there. Plenty of time for that later. I won't have sheep here for a while.'

After Len and Beth left, Linda and Moira were together in the kitchen. Linda turned to Moira and smiled. 'Your father is really something. If I were your mother I'd keep every female well away from him or never let him out of my sight.'

'I doubt Dad has ever looked at another woman, Linda. Mum said she couldn't get him to look at her for a long while – although I think he looked all right, but had other things on his mind. Dad is a wonderful man but he can be tough as iron when he has to be,' Moira said.

'I sensed that about him,' Linda agreed. 'Your mother is very fortunate to have him for a husband.'

'I think I'm very fortunate to have him for my father,' Moira said, and laughed. 'We're good mates as well as being father and daughter. My oldest brother is away at university studying vet science and there's some doubt about whether or not he'll return to the property, so I'm more or less taking his place. I have a younger brother too, but he's still at school. Dad wanted plenty of sons because he reckoned daughters would marry and leave him.'

'Which they do . . . mostly,' Linda said, and laughed. 'When Jack was killed I didn't think I'd ever be able to look at another man. Not that he was a perfect husband or lover. Jack had a lot of faults, and you wonder whether it's worth what you go through. Then I see someone like your father and I know if I could find someone like him I'd probably try again. But I doubt there are many men like your father. He's handsome, certainly, but he's a good, decent man, as well.'

Moira had never considered her father from the point of view of his attractiveness to women. The hair at his temples was becoming flecked with silver, but her father was still a great-looking man – a big man in good shape, with not an ounce of fat on him. But a man of his age being attractive to women, that was a new thought. He was not yet fifty and didn't look his age.

Linda Barden kissed David goodbye and thanked him for his extraordinary generosity. 'You've made Tim so happy,' she said. 'He's a very good boy. He has been a great help to me since Jack was killed. It will mean the world to him not to have to leave Wirrewarra, and to know that he will always have a place on the land after his studies.'

'Tim is the kind of boy the land needs, Mrs Barden,' David said.

'I wish you would call me Linda,' she said.

'If the sale goes through it's a deal,' he said.

Then he and Moira left Wirrewarra and headed back home. Len Murray was to ring Elders and tell Joe Morton that the sale had been made and that David would ring him that night.

'I think you made a hit back there, Dad,' Moira observed after they had been driving for perhaps half an hour.

'If I did it was unintentional,' David said.

'I know that, Dad.'

'The thing is, sweetheart, that Linda Barden is like most women in that she needs some affection. She's battling along there with five children and no man to lean on. It must get her down at times. So I come along and make her a decent offer and she thinks I'm a great fellow. But she should sleep all right tonight because she knows things are going to pan out okay. I don't

247

need the house and it will be better to have that family in it than to leave it empty. And I reckon that Tim will make a decent man if he's given the opportunity. He's got the makings of a really good man.'

When she returned from Sydney Catriona wanted to know all about the purchase of the two properties. David sketched out the bare facts, so Catriona went to her daughter for more details. She listened attentively as Moira gave her impressions of both properties and the people who owned them.

'Linda Barden must have been very nice-looking, Mum. She still has fine features but she's a bit careworn. There's five Barden children aged from four to fifteen and she's had the worry of the bank pushing her. Dad came along like a white knight. She was so relieved she kissed him goodbye,' Moira said ingenuously.

'She kissed David goodbye?'

'Mmm. Linda thinks Dad is fantastic. Of course, he is, isn't he? When he told Linda that she and the children could stay there free of rent, she couldn't believe her ears, and her eyes filled with tears. It must have been such a relief to have all her worries swept away.'

Catriona's long-held fear that another woman would win David from her surfaced again. This grateful and evidently good-looking woman was going to be where David would be from time to time. The prospect didn't please her at all. Yet she could not be unimpressed by what David had done.

'You were very sweet to make that offer to Mrs Barden,' she said later. 'What's she like?' Catriona added tentatively.

'She seemed a nice person,' he said. 'She's got a nice lot of children. The eldest boy might be a ripper. A woman left widowed with five children needs some help.'

So she had produced five children. That would appeal to David, who had always wanted a large family.

'You'll meet her next time we go out there,' David said.

Catriona wondered whether seeing Linda Barden in the flesh would ease or aggravate her concerns. She was determined that if she could not be with her husband when he went off to his new properties, Moira would accompany him.

But the challenge for David's affections, when it came, was not from Linda Barden. It came from an entirely different direction.

Chapter Ten

The sale of Molonga and Wirrewarra went through smoothly and both properties were now owned by the High Peaks Pastoral Company. David purchased the Molonga ewes and the first cattle had been sold for Linda Barden. Len and Beth Murray were still in residence at Molonga and undecided whether to stay in the country or opt for the coast.

David had had to borrow money to buy the two properties and although property values were down, so were wool and cattle prices. The other properties he owned were paid for so he had a lot of equity, but the wool market was a worry. The reserve price had encouraged a lot of woolgrowers to produce more wool but it had also sheltered a lot of inefficient and indifferent producers. For as long as the government sustained the reserve price with taxpayers' money, many woolgrowers were sitting pretty. Only the percipient foresaw that an unsold stockpile of millions of bales of wool hanging like a sword of Damocles above the marketplace would act as a depressant on prices.

David wasn't 'political' in any sense because he believed a fellow's first duty was to provide a decent living for his family. It was all right for the Angus Campbells of the world to belong to farm organisations and the like because he had been handed a property that was debt-free and in great order. David could have become involved at this stage of his life but he was still building up his property interests and argued he hadn't the time for anything else. What he was convinced of was that the wool industry had been well and truly set off the rails. Huge amounts of money had been poured into research on wool yet it commanded less than 4 per cent of the total world fabric market. Likewise, too much promotion had been directed towards the high-fashion market, whereas everyday woollen articles of good quality were increasingly difficult to come by. Some school pullovers he had seen were so rough and prickly that schoolchildren were likely to retain a poor opinion of wool forever.

Yet despite the present atmosphere of doom and gloom David believed that the wool market would come good; otherwise, he would never have borrowed money to buy Molonga and Wirrewarra. The best-quality wool was still making fair money, but the problem was that costs were so high that it was considered 600 cents per kilogram at least was needed to cover costs. Traditional woolgrowers were turning away from wool or using some of their ewes to produce prime lambs. It was a depressing scene, yet David was determined to resist becoming depressed.

David and Catriona were enjoying morning smoko and a chat on their front verandah. They had made several additions to the house since they moved into it after their honeymoon twenty-odd years earlier. Part of the front verandah had been closed in to provide a sleepout and the remainder of the verandah had been gauzed. There were steps from the verandah to a paved front area with low shrubs that didn't spoil the view across the creek and up to Yellow Rock. Catriona's garden had flourished, and all around the house there was an explosion of mostly Australian natives, and particularly hakeas and grevilleas, filling the garden with blossoms and native birds.

In the paddock below the house that skirted the creek there were a few mares and some Hereford cows. It was a tranquil scene and David and Catriona never tired of gazing out at it when they had a quiet moment together. On this day they were alone because Moira had taken the day off to visit an old school friend. This was a rare event because to some extent Moira had taken over from Catriona as David's companion. Catriona's time was increasing spent with her mother, who stubbornly resisted having bypass surgery.

Catriona had made a point of accompanying David and Moira when Molonga and Wirrewarra were officially sold to become part of the High Peaks Pastoral Company. She studied Linda Barden very closely, and found her much as Moira had described her – a woman in her late thirties who had once been very attractive and who still cared about her appearance. It wasn't that Linda had acted in a way that was threatening to Catriona, but she did want David to notice her, to admire her and to like her. It was there in the way she dressed and put on fresh makeup when they went back to Wirrewarra for meals or smokos. Linda had discovered that David liked Anzac biscuits, and she made sure her biscuit tin was always full.

Catriona imagined that if she were not on the scene Linda would make a more direct move to win David's affections. But of course Catriona was pie-eyed when it involved her husband. Now her mother was making such demands on her that she could not go with David to Wirrewarra. For the first time she had to be thankful that Moira would be with him.

As they sat on the verandah looking out across High Peaks they discussed the issue of securing a manager for Molonga and Wirrewarra. They would need someone to live at Molonga when Len and Beth Murray moved out, and before long there would be several thousand ewes on the two places. Angus was at Longreach Pastoral College, Shaun Covers looked after Glen Morrison and Greg Robertson was tied up at Strath Fillan and helping at High Peaks and Poitrel. The absence of Dougal was now making itself felt, as David had foreseen. It seemed there was no alternative but to employ an outsider, something David had never wanted to do. He regretted that young Tim Barden wasn't a few years older.

It was while David and Catriona were discussing what to do when the Murrays left Molonga that they saw a white utility come across the grid into their house paddock. It wasn't a vehicle that David recognised and he stood up to obtain a better view of the driver. It wouldn't be a rep, because they all drove late-model vehicles. It was more likely to be a dog or horse crank because such people dropped in on a regular basis.

'It's a woman, a young woman,' he said, as he watched the driver of the utility get out of the vehicle. 'What do you know, it's Sarah Matheson, Cat.'

Catriona got up and stood beside him. 'So it is. Sarah was due home a week or so ago. She's just finished at Longreach, and apparently she's done very well.'

As Sarah Matheson came up to the front steps, David held the screen door open for her. He scrutinised her as she walked through.

'Hello, Sarah, this is a pleasant surprise,' Catriona greeted her. 'Nothing wrong at home?'

'Nothing that money wouldn't fix, Mrs MacLeod. How are you, Mr MacLeod?' Sarah asked.

'I'm fine, Sarah. Finished at Longreach?' he asked.

'Yes, finished. Look, you must think I've got a frightful hide coming here unannounced, but Mum said she was sure you wouldn't mind.'

'Mum's right. Try some of Cat's orange cake, Sarah. It's very good,' David said pulling out a chair for her and passing her the plate.

It was obvious that Sarah had gone to some trouble

with her appearance. Her white moleskins were spotless and her blouse was nicely ironed. Even her brown elastic-side boots were bright with polish. But the young woman herself would have stood out in just about any kind of clothes. Both Dianne, a blonde, and Sarah, brunette, had been nice-looking girls in their early teens, but Sarah had truly blossomed with age. She was wearing just a hint of makeup and her dark, wavy hair was thick and shiny, tied low at the nape of her neck. Her figure was just as good as Moira's, which was saying something, and by David's calculation she would be almost twenty-one.

Emily had told David and Catriona that Sarah had been the most affected by her father's suicide and the subsequent removal of herself and Dianne from boarding school, together with their vastly reduced financial circumstances.

'How was Longreach, Sarah?' Catriona asked.

'It was all right, Mrs MacLeod. Like Mr Mac said I think it was the right place to go, with its focus on livestock. And the horses were a bonus. The boys were a bit of a problem – if you know what I mean,' Sarah said, and looked meaningfully at Catriona.

Catriona laughed. 'Don't you like boys, Sarah?' she asked.

'Not particularly – especially when you find out what they're really after. They all drink too much. I prefer horses. Oh, I know there are some decent men – like you, Mr Mac, and like your father must have been. I'm aware of how much you've helped Mum and

Dianne. That's why I've come here today. I'm wondering if you can give me a job. Mum said you've bought another couple of properties and I know Angus is at Longreach and Dougal is at university. I'd really like to work for you, Mr Mac. I can do anything a man can do, from shoeing horses to inseminating them. And sheep, too,' she said.

David and Catriona exchanged glances.

'I'm not a vet but I can do a lot of things a vet can do,' Sarah implored, keen to impress them.

'Why did you come here specifically, Sarah?' David asked.

'For several reasons, Mr MacLeod. Nobody else in this district has the name you have. You're doing big things with sheep and cattle. Furthermore, Mum says that she'd trust you where she wouldn't trust a lot of men,' Sarah said.

'It's a comfort to know that I'm regarded in the wider community as morally reliable, Sarah,' David said, and smiled at her. Today's young women were very upfront and candid in their views, and yet he instinctively liked Sarah Matheson. She appeared to be an innately honest young woman. In fact, he hadn't met another young woman exactly like her.

'Are there any openings for me at High Peaks Pastoral Company?' she asked in her direct way.

'I'm not going to give you an answer right now, Sarah, but I will think about it. No doubt you've had a solid grounding and I'm sure you'd be very reliable but I have to be honest with you and say I have some doubts about employing a woman. I doubt I could employ you where I could employ a man, in terms of looking after an isolated property. It wouldn't be right. Do you appreciate what I'm saying?' he asked.

'I don't agree with you Mr MacLeod, but I know where you're coming from,' Sarah sighed. 'It always gets back to the same thing: a woman is disadvantaged because she is a woman. Well, I'm sorry if I've wasted your time. Mum said to come here first.' She knew she could have raised the legalities of sexual discrimination, but thought better of it in the light of all David MacLeod had done for her family.

'Don't get on your high horse, young lady. I haven't said I won't give you a job – I said I would think about it. How are you off for money?'

'I put all I had from Dad into that secondhand utility so I could get around. I can't ask Mum for anything. Di works but she'll be getting married in the near future so there'll only be Mum and me. I want to do things with the horses – breed some winners. You can't do that without money,' she said.

David and Catriona listened carefully to all Sarah was saying.

'We can't afford to send mares away to good sires because we don't have the money. There are some good old mares going to waste – not to mention Starana, who probably has some kind of internal problem that a good vet could fix. I could cry when I look at her and the other old mares.'

This *cri de coeur* touched a chord in David's heart.

257

He and his father had never tried to get into thoroughbreds for the very reason Sarah had just revealed – a
lack of money. They had been lucky with Ajana and
Davana. David knew that. Wilf White had done the
work and they had benefited. David knew, as his father
had known before him, that you could spend a lot of
money on thoroughbreds for very little – if any –
return. The only way most people could indulge their
dreams about owning racehorses was by syndication.

'Have you thought of putting together a syndicate
to purchase services?' he asked.

'It's a lot harder to do that than to form syndicates
for yearlings on the ground, Mr MacLeod. With a yearling there's something to see, something to offer people.
I'll give you that syndication is a great way for people
to get involved in racing horses because the costs are
too much for the average person, but a service is another
matter. Without money you can't use the sires that
produce a lot of winners,' Sarah said.

'I realise all that, Sarah. But I wouldn't turn away
from trying to form a syndicate for the purchase of a
service. I remember that one of the mares Lew Hooper
picked out to buy back was a cracking mare on breeding. She ought to produce something good to the right
sire. The challenge is to produce a great horse without
it costing a mint. There are any amount of instances of
top horses being bred from inexpensive stock. If I
remember right Flight didn't cost much and Bernbor-
ough was another. The way they're reared is a big factor.
Then there's the ability to pick a good horse. You

should go and talk to Lew Hooper. Lew picked up a lot from Wilf White, who knew thoroughbreds and their pedigrees better than anyone around here,' David said.

'Mum told me about Wilf White and Ajana. We thought we might have been lucky enough to get her daughter in foal but we never have. It might have made all the difference. I think Mum would have mortgaged the place if Starana had been a breeder. We'd have bred her to a top horse,' Sarah said. She stood up and looked at the view through the fly mesh that enclosed the front verandah. 'It's a lovely view. That's Yellow Rock, isn't it?'

David nodded.

'It must be something to ride over that country. No wonder you've got such good-footed horses. Everyone talks about your stock horses,' Sarah said.

'That was one of the reasons we let your mother have Starana, Sarah. She was a bit clumsy in the hills. So was her mother. Of course, it was a different thing on the racetrack. Horses for courses, Sarah,' he said, and smiled.

'Well, thanks for your time, Mr MacLeod. It's nice to see you both again. Mum is always talking about you. She said that even if you wouldn't give me a job, you wouldn't throw me out on my ear.'

'Never that, Sarah. I admire what you're trying to do. I'll have a think about where we're going and whether I could find a position for you. I'll be in touch,' David said.

Catriona stood with him and together they watched Sarah as she walked down the path to her utility.

'You like her, don't you, David?' Catriona asked.

'Yes, I like her, Cat. There is a lot to like about her. Sarah is the kind of girl the bush needs. Imagine what kind of wife she would make for the right man – supposing one man could win her. She seems to have a set against men right now,' he said.

'Wow, Sarah must have impressed you. You couldn't employ her, though, could you,' Catriona said – and it was more of a statement than a question.

'Is that what you think, Cat?' he asked.

'It wouldn't look right, darling. Sarah would be working with you and people would talk. You know what they're like. You may be a bush icon but you're a man, and still a very presentable one at that. Imagine what people would say if they saw you and Sarah working together on a fairly constant basis. Sarah is a very tasty morsel. Tasty enough to fuel a lot of gossip,' Catriona said decidedly.

'So you wouldn't trust me with her – is that it? You think I'm at that funny age when I might need a bit of variety, that you're not enough for me?' he said, and raised his eyebrows.

'It's not a matter of trust, darling, it's a matter of appearance. You could behave impeccably and people would still talk. It's the nature of people – especially those who live in small country towns. They're good people, but they love to gossip.'

'Mmm,' he said.

'And aren't I enough for you, darling?' she asked.

He took her in his arms and kissed her along her

neck. 'You've always been enough for me, Cat. You should know that. I hear what you're saying, and you're right: people would talk. However, having given this some more thought, I think it's a damned shame if I can't employ a person with Sarah's credentials simply because she happens to be a female. There's also the fact that we have two sons and –'

'You cunning fox. I didn't think you had it in you, David MacLeod. You want to employ her, don't you? You really do want Sarah?'

'I'll think some more about it, Cat. Sarah could be the answer to what we need but I admit the gossip could be stupendous. It seems so unfair that a girl who's done a pastoral course should be discriminated against because of her sex. Besides, technically speaking, you can't do that, Cat. You can't advertise for a male manager of a property – not these days. Of course, you don't have to give the job to a woman because you can always say that the man had the best credentials. In Sarah's case it could be that she's a damned sight better proposition than most fellows. She'd probably be more conscientious. I like the fact that she wants to do something with their horses. And I'll bet she hasn't smashed up a vehicle like our youngest offspring.' This incident still rankled, as Catriona well knew.

'I could send her out to Molonga,' David went on. 'That would get her away from a lot of the gossip.'

'Send a girl her age out to manage those two places? That's a big ask, David. Quite apart from the work, would it be fair to expect a young woman to live on her own so far from home?' Catriona asked.

'I'm going to put in a gravel road between Molonga and Wirrewarra. It's only about a mile as the crow flies. I dare say Sarah and Linda would get on very well.'

'You don't know that, darling. I think you're tough expecting a girl of her age to manage two places. There'll be crutching and shearing and lamb marking; teams of men and she on her own.'

'She won't be on her own. I'll be out there for those occasions,' David told her.

'The country isn't like it was, David. Women have been taken off places before now. If it's known that Sarah is there on her own, she could be at risk. Anyway, I think you should talk to Anne and Kate before you make up your mind about Sarah,' Catriona said.

Catriona had a lot of reservations about the wisdom of employing Sarah Matheson. Her husband might never have looked at another woman, but he had never before worked alongside the likes of Sarah. Right now David was only concerned with Sarah's competence and with the fact that she had the right grounding to suit his future plans for more and better wool production. But what about when they were inseminating sheep and sharing meals together? Linda Barden was one thing, but Sarah Matheson was quite another. All of Catriona's old fears resurfaced at the thought of this young woman working with her husband. David was still a strapping man and he was a bush legend. He had been the biggest thing in her life and still was. The children were lovely

262

in their own way but they had their own lives to live –
David was a constant and she couldn't envisage her life
without him.

Later that afternoon Catriona communicated her
reservations to Anne and Kate. She didn't put into
words that she saw Sarah as a danger to her happily
married life but concentrated instead on what she
regarded as her unsuitability for the job David had in
mind. Anne, still acute despite her age, could see both
sides of the picture and, in fact, saw more than Catriona
had intended to give away. Anne had always wanted
Catriona for her son and the couple had been very
happy. They didn't need a hiccup at this stage of their
lives. So she was well aware of the situation when David
came to talk to her and Kate just before dinner.

'I think it's very unfair if I can't employ Sarah
Matheson because of the possible gossip it would
create,' David said. 'That's allowing other people to
influence your decision, something I have always
resisted. Under these new laws you can't refuse employment on the basis of a person's sex. If Sarah is the best
person for the job, she should get it,' David said
forcefully.

'There are no other applicants, David. It's not as if
there were a dozen and she was the best. There would
certainly be gossip and there are people who would like
to pull you down. It's the tall poppy syndrome that
permeates Australian society. If you were seen simply
helping Sarah over a fence that would be magnified in
the telling. I've lived in this area for over fifty years and

263

there are some great people here, but there are many who love to gossip.

'Also, you have to consider Catriona's feelings,' Anne went on. 'A lot of the gossip would come back to her, and how do you think she would feel? I realise you think it's unfair, but why create a potential problem? There must be young men who are just as qualified and competent as Sarah.'

'That isn't the point, Mum. If everyone took that view no girl would ever be employed. I think Sarah has a lot in her. She says she isn't interested in men and wants to help her mother breed top thoroughbreds. They've had a tough time since Rod's death. You know I helped them by employing Dianne to do our books. What's so different with Sarah?'

Anne looked at Kate and smiled. 'First, as for Sarah not being interested in men, there is hardly a woman in the world who isn't interested in men – or a man, anyway. Once the right man comes along, Sarah will react in the same way as any other young woman. David, it's your mother talking to you. I have to say this: what Catriona is concerned about is that Sarah might become too interested in you. Young women fall for older men and you're still a very presentable and impressive fellow.'

David shook his head. 'I've only ever been interested in one woman and I've got her. Kate, what do you think?' he asked.

Kate, thus appealed to, responded in her usual forthright manner.

'I agree with you, David, that it seems a great shame you can't employ Sarah because she is female. It certainly isn't fair, or logical for that matter, that Sarah should be denied employment because of possible gossip. Yes, I can understand Catriona being apprehensive about the situation. It's only natural that a happily married woman would feel that way about her husband working with a young, attractive woman. You would have to consider Catriona's feelings, David. It isn't inappropriate for Sarah to be employed here. Young women work in all kinds of situations today. They're in all the armed services and although it must be very awkward for them at times, they have the right to be there.

'You're right about not being able to refuse a woman a job on the basis of sex, David. You can opt to employ a man if you feel he is the best candidate for the job but what you can't do is refuse a job to a woman simply because she is a woman. A woman can have you on toast for doing that. What you have to decide is whether there is a position here that Sarah could fill. You need a manager for Molonga and Wirrewarra but you could hardly send Sarah out there.'

Although he had spoken to Catriona about possibly sending Sarah to the new properties, he had never really been serious about it.

'I appreciate all that, Kate. I could use Sarah, no doubt about that. To employ her I'd have to shift Greg out to the new places and he may not choose to go. So, until I speak to Greg I can't say that I'd have a job for Sarah.

'What I'm looking for, what we've always looked for, are reliable, capable people for the job at hand. We gave Don Morgan a go at Aberfeldy following Tim Sparkes's death and he's been terrific. Likewise, Greg Robertson and Shaun Covers. And, not to put too fine a point on it, you, Kate, as well. You've come up trumps, Kate. Now I've got new plans and I see Sarah Matheson fitting into them very well, but I'm told I can't use her because she's a woman. Did you ever experience any problems with men while you worked here and at Glen Morrison, Kate?' David asked.

'Not here, David. But I wasn't married, and you are. Personally, I think it's between you and Catriona. As much as you might like to employ Sarah, if it is going to affect your relationship with Catriona, you might have to give it a miss,' Kate said. 'If you can work that out satisfactorily then I'd say go ahead and employ her.'

'I suppose if Sarah had a face like a horse and was three axe handles across her backside, nobody would object to me employing her,' David said vehemently. 'Sarah is being penalised because she's attractive. What's in her head doesn't matter.'

'It's not Kate and I that you have to convince, David,' Anne said. 'I'm all for women being given every opportunity to advance. But human nature being what it is, people will talk. They don't need an excuse to gossip, but if you give them one they will gossip even more. You might be able to ignore the gossip – and men seem to acquire an added lustre if thought to be randy – but it could be very hurtful to Catriona.

Besides, no woman likes to think of her husband being with another woman. So, as much as we've moved on a very great deal in so many ways, the fact is that men and women still get up to hanky-panky and always will.'

David shook his head. 'I'm perfectly happy with Catriona. The fact is, as I said to Cat, I reckon Sarah would make a great mate for one of the boys. She's a bit older than Angus but younger than Dougal.'

'You can't make plans for other people, David,' Anne said, and touched his arm affectionately. 'Not with the best will in the world.'

'Perhaps not, but if you put two people together there ought to be some chance they will hit it off,' David said, grinning.

'You are a real schemer, David,' Kate said.

'I want this place and the other properties to be in good hands after I'm finished here. A decent wife is worth more than winning several lotteries. A man needs the right wife to make a proper go of things. Dad knew what he was about when he picked you, Mum.'

'And didn't I worry until I knew he did want me,' Anne, said, and laughed. 'Your father didn't try to kiss me until the day he asked me to marry him up on Yellow Rock! Mind you, when he did kiss me I thought all my birthdays had come at once,' Anne said, and winked at her sister.

'Now the secrets are coming out, Kate,' David said, and grinned. 'Well, I reckon I picked a pretty decent wife myself. And if picking the right women is a trait that we MacLeod men excel at, you will understand why I think Sarah Matheson is too good a prospect to let slip through our hands,' he said.

'You'll have to sort that out with Catriona. She's the one who will be most affected if you choose to employ Sarah, both personally and by the inevitable gossip. However, for what it's worth, I applaud your motives,' Anne said.

David got up from the table and bent and kissed his mother and then his aunt. 'I couldn't have had a better mother or a better aunt,' he said. The two women both felt there was a catch in his voice as he spoke. Together, they watched his tall figure walk through the orchard to the dog yard.

Anne sighed. 'What a boy he was, and what a man he has become. Andy would be so proud of him.'

'Andy was proud of him from the day he was born, Anne. He couldn't have been any prouder of David than he was after he won the National,' Kate said. 'Oh, dear, growing old is such a nuisance. I would so much like to go on for a long time yet. I hate the thought of leaving all this behind. Do you understand what I mean, Anne?'

'Of course I understand. I think about it every day. Do you think I want to leave this place that has meant so much to me for so long, the people I love? If I could be sure I was going to be with Andy again I could face the future with greater fortitude, but I can't be sure of that, Kate. Through all the years since Andy left here I've felt that he was very close to me. I can still picture him as he was when I first came here. The first time I saw him at that dance something inside me turned over and I said to myself "There's the man I want". I think Andy must have felt the same way. What a man he was, Kate.'

'He sure was, Anne. If you had turned him down, I would have snapped him up quick sticks,' Kate laughed, with a twinkle in her eye.

'I knew that, Kate. But I've got to say that as good a man as Andy was, David has surpassed him. Andy battled to pay off High Peaks and then Poitrel, and now we've got six properties.'

'David has great vision, Anne. For a person who didn't go to college or university, David is quite remarkable.'

'Yes, of course you're right,' Anne mused. 'Will the boys be as successful? Angus is very gifted with animals, but a bit wild. He needs a strong woman to take him in hand. Dougal is very clever and will no doubt become an excellent vet. His future is assured. As for Moira, who can say? She adores her father and has a lot of his gifts.'

'Of the three children she is perhaps the pick,' Kate added, 'though one shouldn't say so. Strong, spirited women are certainly a force in this family.'

Anne sighed, and smiled. 'Certainly, but I have a lot of time for Dougal because he was strong enough to stand up to David over his choice of career. Ah, Kate, it's all so very satisfying. When I came to Merriwa to teach I never envisaged my life would proceed as it has done. Well, I must say it has all been rather wonderful.

Losing Andy was a great blow, but I couldn't show what I really felt because I knew what David was going through. He missed his father terribly and it would have been worse for him if he hadn't had Catriona.'

'Yes, what a wife she has been for David. I knew you always wanted her for David but I admit that at first I had my doubts about the wisdom of that, the Campbells being so uppity. I would have given anything to be a fly on the wall the day David dressed old Angus down, telling him he was a damned snob, and worse. Well, I must say Angus and Jane turned out better than I imagined. Of course, David is a more important bush figure than Angus now,' Kate said.

'Yes, and didn't Andy think it was great when David told him what he had done. I must say I wouldn't have blamed Catriona if she had told David to get lost, he took so long to ask her to marry him. Having Aberfeldy and all that money certainly made a difference where Angus was concerned,' Anne said.

'The damned old snob,' Kate said, and laughed.

'Yes, the damned old snob,' Anne agreed. 'Well, Angus and David became very pally and if Angus finally wins at his last trial he will owe most of it to David. He has put in a lot of time with Angus. And with Stuart, too. Angus has been trying to win the Open all his life. And for an old silvertail I have to say Angus has been a very good neighbour. He and his father before him. It's time that Angus retired, though. Time to feed the chooks and gather the eggs, Kate. That's about what I'm reduced to now.'

'At least you don't have arthritis, Anne,' Kate said.

'No, thankfully – just old age and a fraction of the energy I used to have. Life is so very short, Kate. It disturbs me no end to see so many young people wasting their most precious years in idleness – or worse.'

That evening after dinner, with Moira away with an old school friend, Catriona asked David what Anne and Kate had said about employing Sarah Matheson.

David had been waiting for the question. 'They said that by and large they agreed that a woman shouldn't be discriminated against because she was a woman. But,' and here he paused and looked intently at Catriona, 'they were firm that it was really a matter for you and me to decide. I must say that they were very fair about it. They both said they foresaw there would be gossip if we employed Sarah, and they also said they understood why you would be concerned.'

'So where does that leave you, David?' Catriona asked.

'I wouldn't do anything to cause you concern, Cat. You seem to have the idea that I could be attracted to Sarah. I don't know why you should because there were girls eyeing me off when I was young and randier than I am now and I never touched one of them. Susan was coming on pretty hot and strong for one. You were the only girl I ever wanted and, if you remember, even when you volunteered to get pregnant so we could marry, I didn't take you up on it. I have a lot of difficulty trying to understand why you think I should be tempted now.'

David's words beat like hammer blows against her heart. Everything he said was true. David was so much bigger in every way than her that he made her feel suddenly small and petty. How could she answer him without disclosing her lifelong fears about losing him? She knew that many men cheated on their wives and that some wives cheated on their husbands. It happened in Merriwa just as it did everywhere else. David had inferred she didn't trust him not to cheat on her. He hadn't said as much but what else could he imagine? After all these years and all their closeness, she didn't trust him.

'David, I . . .' she began weakly, before her voice trailed off. She wanted to say that she loved him too much to risk losing him to a younger woman, but that again would mean that she didn't trust him.

'We'll let the matter rest for a while, Cat,' he said and picked up a newspaper and began reading it.

Next morning, David announced that he and Moira were going to Glen Morrison to meet a ram buyer, and asked Catriona if she would like to accompany them.

'I might take Danny for a ride, David,' Catriona answered. Danny was a bay gelding Greg had broken in for her. 'It's a lovely day and he could do with the work.'

David nodded. 'We should be home for lunch at one.'

'If I'm not here can you get yourselves some lunch, darling?'

'I'm sure that between us Moira and I can manage some lunch,' he replied. 'After lunch I'm going over to see Angus.'

Catriona waited until David and Moira had left before going to the stables to saddle the beautiful bay gelding, Danny. He wasn't up to King, but he was a nice horse Catriona knew would come better with education. He was from the first crop of horses bred at Strath Fillan and, according to Greg Robertson, probably the horse most likely to suit Catriona.

Catriona rode down to the creek, crossed it, and then headed up the paddock towards Yellow Rock. It was all uphill and fairly tough going for a horse. When she got to where the track cut across the face of Yellow Rock, Catriona dismounted and hitched Danny to the branch of a kurrajong. It was at this very spot that she had paused all those years ago to ponder whether to take her grey pony across the mountain, or simply wait for David to join her. Now she set out on foot to walk the track she had ridden Princess on before they both fell over the ledge.

It was David who had come to her rescue back then. He had sent a dog down the ledge to stay with her and had then ridden for home to get help. Later, before anyone could get to her, he had come down off the ledge by rope to be with her. Later still, when everyone else wanted to destroy her pony, David had ridden Princess off the ledge and brought her back to High Peaks. Just a little boy and he had behaved like a man. It was from that time that she knew in a girl–woman way that she wanted him to be her boy.

Catriona's thoughts then turned to the night the two Missens and their odious mate, Stanley Masters, had tried to rape her. It had happened the night of the Debutantes' Ball and Roger Cartwright had been her escort. The trio had forced their car off the road and they had hit a post. Roger had concussion, and was no help. The young men had dragged Catriona from the vehicle and stripped off her lovely white gown. That was as far as they got because David arrived on the scene and took on the three men. One of them had hit him over the eye with a branch and opened up a big gash that bled profusely but he had beaten the three of them and locked them in their vehicle until her father and Stuart and the police arrived. If David had not intervened her life would have been very different.

Catriona looked up at the vast expanse of blue sky and sighed. This matter of Sarah Matheson was, she recognised, a defining moment in her married life. She had already hurt David by intimating that she didn't trust him with a younger woman. He had never given her the slightest cause to doubt his love for her, yet she had hurt him. She knew that by his silence.

As Catriona stood there on the face of Yellow Rock, she realised that if she was to regain her husband's respect, she would have to take the lead in the matter of Sarah just as she had done when she and

David had their first big row over the children attending boarding school. This time it could not be solved by daytime lovemaking and telling David that she needed him. She would have to overcome her long-held fears about losing David by agreeing to employ Sarah Matheson. This decision would be the real test of her married life. It would prove whether their love meant anything. It would also prove whether David was as fallible as other men when a younger woman appeared on the scene.

For one last time Catriona looked at the mound of rubble below her. She owed David more than she could ever repay, and the thought that she might lose him to Sarah was like a knife thrust through her heart. Life without David would hardly be life at all. Her marriage had to survive this new challenge.

Catriona retraced her steps down the track. Danny was standing patiently where she had tethered him and she gathered the reins and vaulted into the saddle. The downhill trip was easy after the uphill slog. Catriona's mind was also easier now. She had come to a decision and she would make it known to David.

Back at the homestead, David and Moira had had lunch and cleaned up. David had left a note telling her that her mother had been asking for her. It was signed *Love, David*. Catriona studied the note. It was just a simple message, yet the last two words seemed especially significant today. David had left notes before but not for some time. Was he trying to tell her something?

Moira was with them for dinner that night. Moira was experimenting with new recipes and was anxious to try them out on her parents. Catriona had told her several times that David didn't like fancy Asian and Italian dishes but Moira kept stretching his taste by trying new cuisines.

'Darling, I've been thinking about Sarah Matheson a lot today,' Catriona began. 'I agree it would be unwise to miss out on employing her – she would be very handy with all this new work you're doing with sheep. I've got reservations about sending her out to Molonga, but perhaps that is a matter for Sarah to decide. I realise you need a manager out there but I wouldn't feel comfortable sending any single woman to such a place,' Catriona said.

David looked at her intently before he answered. 'I wouldn't put her on without your complete agreement,' he said.

'Then you have it,' she said quickly. 'I realise women should be given every opportunity to get on. And besides, who knows? Angus may fall for her,' she added, with a wicked smile.

'Thank you, Cat,' he said. 'I'll talk to Greg tomorrow. Then I'll talk to Sarah.'

'Greg?' Catriona said, and raised her eyebrows.

'About going out to Molonga. I'll have to offer it to Greg before anyone else. It will mean a rise in salary. Shaun is too tied up with the studs and too valuable, besides being a bit on the elderly side for out there. If Greg doesn't want the position, I'll have to bring someone in,' David said.

'So you wouldn't be sending Sarah out there?'

'Not on your life. I only said that to get a bite out of people,' David said, and grinned.

'Grr,' Catriona growled. It broke the ice to a large extent, and brought Moira into the conversation.

'Don't you feel you could hit him, Mum?' Moira said.

'Occasionally, dear,' Catriona said.

'I think I'll like working with Sarah,' Moira said.

'She isn't here yet,' David reminded her. 'She might have thought better of the idea. Might already have a job, for all we know.'

'Ha, I'll bet she's haunting the house waiting for you to ring her, Dad. Of course, she doesn't know what a slave driver you are,' Moira said, and gave her father a flashing smile.

'That's why people stay with me so long,' he said.

Greg Robertson was a mite worried. Nearly all the farmers he knew were complaining about how crook things were on the land these days. Cattle were down, wool was down, wheat cost too much to grow and the politicians kept introducing more and more ridiculous regulations. The last time Greg had been talking to David he had told him that all their returns were down and that the wool industry had been well and truly shot to pieces. Properties that had employed two and three people were now being run by husband and wife and, in many cases, either husband or wife was working at a job off the property.

'I sure hope it isn't going to affect us, Liz,' Greg said to his wife.

'Surely not, Greg. David has just bought two more properties. Why would he do that if things weren't going well?' Liz asked.

'People are doing away with full-time employees and using casual labour, Liz,' Greg told her.

When Greg received a phonecall from David telling him he and Catriona were coming down to see him the following day, Greg grew even more despondent. He had worked for David MacLeod virtually from the time he left school, and he didn't fancy working for any other man.

Liz was more worried about getting the house cleaned up in time because although David didn't worry if it was a bit untidy, it was a different matter entertaining Catriona. Although Catriona was always very nice, the fact remained that she was once a Campbell.

The three Robertson children were about the wildest kids in the district. They had been reared on Strath Fillan, which was a pretty damned good place for them to run wild. The two boys had both broken arms and collarbones coming off ponies, and their sister was the biggest tomboy for miles. Greg had walloped all three so many times he lost count, but they took wallopings in their stride. Before David and Catriona were due to arrive, Greg told his terrible trio that if they put one foot out of place he would use the stockwhip on them, take their ponies from them and lock them up for two days. He had found that locking them up for a day worked better than a walloping. The children were so high-spirited that being confined to their rooms was the most awful punishment they could endure.

Faced with this threat and conscious of the fact that their father was unusually grim-faced, the children contented themselves with riding flat out alongside David's vehicle as it came through the gate into Strath Fillan. Then they took off into the hills, as Greg had told them to do.

Liz noted that Moira had accompanied her parents, so there would be two women to inspect the interior of the house. It was fortunate the kids had left some of the fruitcake to go with the scones she had just made. Liz knew she wasn't a good housekeeper. She spent most of her time outside with Greg as he worked with the horses. Liz wasn't a show rider like Catriona had been but she could sit just about any horse or bull in the country.

It wasn't that Catriona and Moira were ever hoity-toity with her, but they were always dressed beautifully, even when in working clothes, while she never was. Liz got on very well with Anne and Kate but was somewhat in awe of Catriona and, to a slightly lesser extent, Moira. David was a different matter. He was a millionaire a few times over with what he owned, but it hadn't changed him one little bit. He would sit in the kitchen and drink tea and eat scones with Greg and her just the same as anyone else. She knew that he could be tough and that nobody argued with him. But if you did the right thing by David, he left you alone. He told you what he wanted and he expected you to do it.

Liz was attractive in a less polished kind of way but she had never placed much importance on the way she looked; nor did she have the sense of style that set Catriona and Moira apart. She had never made her debut, nor ever wanted to, because she wasn't that kind of girl. She had a heart of gold and was in every sense the perfect mate for Greg. It was only when faced with people she acknowledged to be superior to her that Liz felt inadequate.

Catriona always sought to be especially friendly because she realised that Liz felt awkward entertaining her. She usually took biscuits or a cake and sometimes special treats for the children.

'There's an apple charlotte, Liz. It's probably not very good as it's the first time I've made one. There's a chocolate cake, too. It's Anne's recipe so I can vouch for it,' Catriona said.

'Thanks, Mrs MacLeod, that's real good of you,' Liz said. She felt a little relieved that Catriona couldn't do everything perfectly. 'They look delicious, and the kids will love them.'

She noted that although the two women weren't dressed up and were in fact for them in what passed for working clothes, they both looked fantastic. Catriona was in dove-grey slacks with a blue top and Moira was in white moleskins and cream blouse. They made her blue jeans and grey shirt look distinctly second-rate.

David, as usual, took command of the situation by handing over a pack of a dozen bottles of beer. 'There's a little bonus for the job you did on that last filly, Greg,' he said. And in the next breath, 'You're looking well, Liz.'

Oh, she could have kissed him. Liz reckoned that David was the most wonderful man she had ever known. There wasn't a man anywhere that came near him. He and his mother were just lovely people. They had helped Greg and her so often she had lost count. On one occasion she had been so overcome by one of David's kindnesses that she had actually kissed him, and he hadn't minded in the least. Next to horses, she and Greg talked about the MacLeods more than anything else.

'I hope you haven't gone to any trouble, Liz,' Catriona said. She noted the set table in the lounge room, which had a vase of native flowers as its centrepiece.

'Oh no, it's no trouble at all,' Liz said, as casually as she could muster.

Greg felt a little easier. This didn't seem to be the forerunner to the sack. Catriona and Moira would hardly come to hear David tell him that he was finished.

David sat down in one of the big lounge chairs that

Greg and Liz had just finished paying off. Presently Liz was at his elbow with a steaming cup of strong tea, just as she knew he liked it, and a plate of hot date scones lashed with butter. He nodded his thanks and took a scone.

After some desultory conversation David switched to the real reason for their visit. 'Still like it here, Greg?'

'It's been great, David. Good place for the horses – and for the kids, too,' he said, and laughed.

'What about you, Liz?' David asked.

'It's a real nice place, Mr MacLeod. The house is very comfortable and the property is beautiful. Horses do well here. As well as the sheep,' she said.

'You know that I've bought two properties the other side of Barraba. I bought them principally to breed replacement wethers for these three places so I don't have to continually buy them in. There are good homesteads on both properties and I'm allowing the former owner of one of the places, Wirrewarra, to stay there. She's a widow with five children. Her eldest boy is a good colt and could have a future with me later. The thing is that I need a manager for both places. The manager would live at Molonga, which has a very nice old homestead.'

Greg wondered what David was getting at.

'I'm offering you the job, Greg. It's a much bigger position than what you're doing here so there would be an increase in salary, but we'll talk about those details if you want the job. If you don't want the job, I'll have to bring someone in from outside. You don't have to accept it, and before you make up your mind I'll take you and Liz out there so you can see what it would be like. How does that sound to you?'

Greg was temporarily lost for words. This wasn't the sack, but a promotion.

'It sounds great, David. But what about the horse side of things? You want to keep Western Star here, don't you?' Greg asked.

'Yes, of course. You can have a few horses out there to keep your hand in but Strath Fillan will remain the main horse place. I've bought those two places to try and breed top merino sheep, Greg. Maybe run a few cattle, but sheep will be the priority. As I said, there are five children next door. It's only a mile or so from one homestead to the other. I've put in a gravel road to link the two.

'The thing is that I've got a young person in mind who could come here but hasn't the experience to go out there. You'd think me lousy if, after all the years you've been with me, I didn't offer the job to you and brought an outsider in. However, it's up to you and Liz. If you're interested, we'll go out there in the next day or so. If the job doesn't appeal to you, say so and you can stay put here.'

Greg looked at Liz, whose eyes were shining. 'I reckon we should go out and have a look,' he said.

David nodded. 'I thought you'd say that. We'll go the day after tomorrow. Have you got anyone who can look after the children?'

'I'll ask my sister to come out for the day,' Liz said quickly.

'Right, that's that.'

So it was that David and Catriona took Greg and Liz out to see Molonga and Wirrewarra. The Murrays had left and Molonga homestead was bare. David had rung Linda Barden and told them what he was doing and she had insisted they all come for lunch.

'If Greg and Liz are going to be our next-door neighbours, I'd like to meet them and make them welcome,' Linda said.

And see David again, Catriona thought as she listened to her husband talking on the phone.

It was a four a.m. start. Moira said she would stay back at High Peaks so there would be someone to feed the horses and dogs that evening. They drove straight to Molonga and inspected that property before driving on the new gravel road to Wirrewarra.

David shared his plans with Greg and Liz. 'There's two shearing sheds but I reckon it would make good sense to put all the sheep through the Molonga shed. It will be one big clip and there shouldn't be much variation, if any, in the wool once we get Wirrewarra stocked. One bonus is that after twenty-odd years running cattle, there shouldn't be any sheep worms to worry about on Wirrewarra.'

Liz, although not an inside person, liked the big Molonga homestead. She also liked Linda Barden and the five Barden children, who would be good mates for her trio. The country was different. There were

284

hills behind the homesteads but most of the country was undulating to flat. David said it was much better country than at Strath Fillan. Not so good for horses, but much sweeter country for breeding sheep and cattle.

Linda Barden thought that having three children next door would be a great asset. That three children could be wilder than her own didn't come into her head; they would simply be good company for her brood. She had no doubts at all about Greg Robertson. David had told her that Greg had been with him almost since leaving school and was totally reliable. Liz could do anything a man could do and sit just about any horse in the country, and Linda knew she would enjoy the company of the younger woman.

Greg reckoned he had to take the job. As David had said, it was a lot bigger job than managing Strath Fillan. Ewes were more trouble than wethers. There was mulesing and lamb-marking, too. David said he would look at the economics of bringing in a team to assist with these operations. There would also be some artificial insemination, because David intended using his top rams to upgrade both the Molonga ewes and those he bought to help stock Wirrewarra.

After lunch David and Greg walked down to look at the Wirrewarra woolshed. From there they drove around the property to give Greg an idea of the country it covered.

'I'll take the job, David,' Greg said as they were driving back to the homestead.

David nodded. 'I reckoned you would, Greg. It's a more important job than the one you've been doing. I know how you feel about horses and you can have some out here but they'll be only a hobby here, Greg. I've got big plans for these two places. Maybe breed some of the rams here and finish them off at Glen Morrison.'

Despite the way Linda Barden looked at her husband, Catriona could not help liking the blonde woman. She was so very friendly and hospitable that it would have been churlish of her to be standoffish. Besides, Linda was hardly the first woman to look at her husband in a hungry kind of way. She supposed it was something to have a husband other women wanted but she would have preferred it not to happen. Anyway, it wasn't Linda Barden she was worried about, but the looming opposition at home. Catriona had come out in favour of employing Sarah Matheson because she felt she had to, but she wasn't looking forward to her working for them.

The following day David rang Sarah Matheson and asked her to come to see him. She came that afternoon, and David met her on the front verandah. They sat down and David told her that he could employ her under certain conditions.

'First, I'm shifting Greg out to manage the two new places the other side of Barraba. That leaves a vacancy at Strath Fillan. It's mainly wethers with some cattle but we've put most of our horses there, and Western Star is at stud there, of course.'

Sarah's eyes were bright with interest.

'You'd be managing Strath Fillan and living there. I'll take you down and show you the place and you can decide if it will suit you. It's amongst the hills and may be a bit lonely for a young woman. If that doesn't worry you, it's quite a picturesque place. Moira has said that she would go and stay with you for the first week or so if you would prefer that.'

'It sounds perfect, Mr MacLeod,' Sarah said.

'Later, I'll have the homestead painted and renovated a bit. As it is, I'd need you to move in as soon as Greg and Liz move out because of the horses. As well as looking after Strath Fillan, you'll be involved in the stud work at Glen Morrison. I'm particularly keen to use your expertise in inseminating stock. How does that affect you?' he asked.

'I'm overwhelmed,' she said. 'I was sure you had decided against employing me, let alone giving me a manager's job.'

'It isn't much of a manager's job, more a glorified overseer's position, but it could lead to bigger things later on. And you will be doing much more than looking after Strath Fillan. You could be showing sheep and cattle some of the time, though Moira is doing most of that these days. And you'd be looking after the mares that come to Western Star. Think you can handle it?' David asked.

'I'll do my best,' Sarah said.

'That's all anyone can do, Sarah. The thing is that

if you want to be treated the same as a man, you'll have to perform the same as a man. Well, almost. I wouldn't expect you to dig post-holes all day,' he said and smiled. 'Still want the job?'

'You bet, Mr MacLeod,' she said.

'Right. Come back here in the morning and I'll take you down to Strath Fillan. When can you start?'

'When do you want me to start?' she asked.

'Soon as you're ready to come. You can stay at the cottage near Mum's until Greg moves out. You'll need to tucker yourself, although I'll keep you in meat. There's a coldroom beside the cottage. Oh, and you'll need bedclothes. On your way out stop at the petrol tank and fill your utility,' he told her.

'Thank you, and thank you for the job,' she said.

'It might not suit you, Sarah,' he warned.

But her reply was earnest and eager. 'I'm sure it will, Mr MacLeod.'

'How are you off for money?' he asked.

'I don't have much, I'm afraid,' she said.

'Well you need a vehicle. I'll give you a cheque now so you can buy tucker and whatever else you need. We'll take some out of your wages each week to pay it off,' David said.

'That is very generous of you, Mr Mac. You don't mind me calling you Mr Mac, do you?'

'I reckon I could live with that. Go to town tomorrow and get what you want. The day after will do to start. That all right?'

'Suits me,' she said.

'Right. Be here at eight and I'll take you down to Strath Fillan.'

When he handed her a cheque for $500 she looked at him blankly. 'This is far too much for food.'

'It will tide you over for a while,' he said, and turned away before she could say thank you. It was the first of many kindnesses she was to receive from him.

Two days later Sarah was at High Peaks shortly after seven and she made several trips carrying in food, clothes and sheets and blankets before David appeared.

'Got everything stowed away?' he asked, as he looked about the cottage.

'For now, Mr Mac.'

'Righto, as you're here we might as well get going. You won't need anything as I'm just going to show you where you'll be if you take the job. You can still pull out if you don't like the place,' he said, and smiled.

'I'm on the payroll now, so I can't pull out,' she said.

'Pile in the Toyota and we'll hit the track,' he said.

On the drive down to Strath Fillan David used the time to show her the various boundaries that divided the four properties. 'We'll call in at Poitrel and Glen Morrison on the way back, Sarah.'

At Strath Fillan they found Greg and Liz in the throes of packing. There were boxes, tied and untied, in the middle of the lounge room.

'Sarah, this is Greg and Liz Robertson. There are three small Robertsons but I presume they're at school.'

'Thank goodness,' Liz said. 'They keep pulling things out of boxes after I've packed them. Nice to meet you, Sarah.'

David had told Greg that Sarah would be coming here. After getting over his initial surprise that Sarah was to succeed him, and after he had listened while his boss detailed the girl's credentials, he conceded that she might be okay.

'Welcome to Strath Fillan, Sarah. We know you're going to love living here – we've certainly had some great years at this place,' Greg said warmly.

'Thank you, Greg – I've got a good feeling about it already.'

After they had looked through the big homestead David took her over to the stables where they saddled two horses for a quick ride up the valley. Greg had no reason to doubt his boss's judgement when he saw Sarah in the saddle. She and Dianne had been riding horses since they could walk and she had learnt a lot more about handling horses while at Longreach. After riding around the various paddocks they rode back to the yards and unsaddled the horses. 'Shall I feed them, Mr Mac?' Sarah asked.

'No, Greg and Liz will do that later. What do you think? Still want the job?'

'Of course,' she said. 'This place is perfect.'

'There's some outside work I want to do before

any renovations to the house. Buying those two places has left me a bit short of money and what I've got has to be spent on a priority basis.'

This was the first of many confidences David shared with Sarah and she appreciated him being honest with her.

'Right, we'll poke up and have morning smoko with Jean and Julian at Poitrel. Julian is a bit offbeat, but he's quite a nice fellow and Jean herself is a darling, as Mum puts it,' he said.

'Is Jean the same age as Kate?'

'A wee bit younger, but not much. Jean is an elderly lady now but doesn't look her age.'

Jean, warned by Anne that David would be bringing his new employee for morning smoko, had buttered teacake ready. Julian had discreetly disappeared, as was his habit when he knew beforehand that someone was coming to see Jean.

'This is Sarah, Jean. She could be coming here quite a lot in future. Not for you to look after, I hasten to add, but for mustering and drenching. Sarah is taking over at Strath Fillan so she'll be your neighbour. If something goes wrong and you can't get hold of me, you should phone Sarah.'

'I hope you'll be very happy working for David, Sarah,' Jean said.

'I'm sure I shall. Oh, what do I call you?'

'You must call me Jean as everyone else does. Dear Mr White always called me Sister Jean but I am not a Sister now. Just Jean, dear.'

Later, after a tour of the stables and an inspection of the old mares and poultry they left for Glen Morrison.

'Jean seems a very nice person, Mr Mac,' Sarah said.

'Indeed she is, Sarah. She has looked after Poitrel very well for a long time. I told her she could stay for as long as she wants to. I fancy she's been happier at Poitrel than anywhere else. Beats me why any man would want to hit a woman like that,' he said.

'Is that what happened?'

'I believe so. Her husband used to get on the booze and become violent. Jean eventually left him, but never remarried or had children. She told Mum she wanted to have children,' David said.

Glen Morrison was surely the jewel in the MacLeod 'empire'. It was David's stud property and the most highly improved, and he was very proud of it.

'This is Sarah Matheson, Shaun. Sarah – Shaun Covers.'

'Pleased to meet you, Sarah,' Shaun offered, tipping his hat.

'And you,' she replied.

'Sarah started with me today. She's been at Longreach Pastoral College. You've met her mother and sister. As I told you, Sarah is taking over from Greg and she'll be coming here quite a lot. I want her to get to know the stud business.'

Sarah was entranced with the quality of the sheep

and cattle in their preparation sheds and with the steers in feed. David then drove her around the property and showed her what he had been doing to improve the quality of pastures. There were small mobs of ewes in some of these paddocks and she thought they looked wonderful.

After an hour or more wandering through the paddocks they went back to the homestead where Shaun told them if they waited a few minutes he would 'burn some meat'. Sarah, who didn't usually eat a big midday meal, ravished her steak and said it was delicious.

'So it should be, seeing what it came from,' Shaun grinned.

After lunch David took her back to the ram shed where he spent two hours with her while she gave her opinion on the various sheep he held for her to inspect. He was agreeably surprised with the extent of her knowledge. It was much better than he had expected.

From Glen Morrison it was back to High Peaks to meet with Anne and Kate and then down to have afternoon smoko with Catriona and Moira. 'I've been eating all day, Mr Mac,' Sarah protested when told where they were going.

'You don't have to eat anything. I simply want you to meet with Cat and Moira so you get to know them better.'

Catriona felt a pang of apprehension as David walked in with Sarah. She had wanted to be with

David as he took Sarah about but realised that it wasn't appropriate.

'What have you seen so far, Sarah?' Moira asked.

Her question saved Catriona from temporary confusion. Sarah was simply too young and too attractive for Catriona not to worry about her being with David. But if Catriona was concerned she didn't show it to Sarah. Her outwardly friendly greeting shielded her apprehension. She knew that there would be times when David and Sarah were alone, but she resolved to make these as few as possible.

Conversely, Moira welcomed Sarah with an open heart. It was going to be decidedly more interesting working with a female near her own age, and she immediately offered to stay with Sarah for her first week at Strath Fillan. She had discussed this suggestion with her father who had agreed wholeheartedly.

Quite apart from her own feelings regarding her husband and Sarah being together, Catriona still had reservations about a young woman being on her own in what she regarded as a fairly lonely location. Certainly, it was not all that far from Poitrel and Glen Morrison but it was at the end of the road and enclosed by the peaks of the range.

'Can you handle firearms, Sarah?' David asked.

'I don't like firearms, Mr Mac,' Sarah said.

'Maybe you don't, but I'm going to insist that you keep a shotgun in the house and another in the utility. Moira can show you how to use a shotgun. You may never need to use it, for snakes or anything else, but not to put too fine a point on it, there are some real mongrels about now and, like it or not, women are vulnerable. If somebody threatens you, a shotgun is the most potent deterrent you can have. If there's a real threat, shoot the mongrel in the legs,' David said firmly.

'I don't think I could,' Sarah said, and frowned.

'Then think about what happened to some of the girls taken by creeps. If it's your life at risk, you have every right to defend yourself. That's what I've told Moira and Cat. It's better to have a gun and not need it than not have a gun when you are in trouble,' David insisted.

'I suppose so, but I really don't like guns,' Sarah said.

'They're very necessary items in the bush. I suggest you do as I say or we'll have our first disagreement,' David told her.

'Yes, Mr Mac,' Sarah said meekly. She appreciated that her new boss was concerned for her welfare, which did touch her.

'I've told David that I think he's being very tough expecting you to live at Strath Fillan on your own,' Catriona said. 'Daytime isn't so bad, but I would be frightened there at night.'

'We'll put a big chain and padlock on the front gate and Sarah can keep a key,' David suggested.

'There's no need for that, Mr Mac. I'm not at all frightened of staying on my own. If a woman wants to be treated the same as a man, she has to behave the same as a man. I don't want any favours,' Sarah said.

'Well, I'll let you have a dog, which you'll need for mustering, anyway. I've got a nice young dog going fairly well,' David told her.

'What Sarah needs down there is a cattle dog,' Catriona suggested. 'Not for working but for a watchdog.'

'She can have a cattle dog if she wants one,' David agreed.

'I'm sure I'll be all right,' Sarah tried to assure them.

'Well, I'm going to stay with you for the first week,' Moira said. 'We'll have lots to talk about and we can try some new recipes. Dad is an old stick-in-the-mud when it comes to new recipes.'

And that was Sarah Matheson's first day at High Peaks.

Chapter Eleven

The morning the Robertson clan left Strath Fillan was brilliantly clear and crisp. This was Greg's favourite time of the day. Their furniture truck was ahead of them and Greg was pulling a double horse float to transport the last of his horses. He had taken the children's ponies in the High Peaks truck a few days earlier.

An hour or so later David drove in to Strath Fillan with Moira and Sarah. Sarah's possessions were in the back of the utility together with a bed, refrigerator and small wardrobe. David, with the two young women as eager helpers, manhandled the fridge and wardrobe into the house and then left the girls alone. He returned later with Catriona and a table and chairs. He noted with satisfaction that everything from the first load was already nicely in position and that Sarah and Moira seemed to be getting on very well.

What he found later was that Sarah didn't know much about mustering in hill country, but she was a quick learner. When he showed her how to do something, she never forgot it. She would drench sheep all day without complaint and then get on a horse and take them back to their paddock. No day was too long for her. But where Sarah really shone was in actually looking after animals. She would sit up all night with a mare due to foal and she was as good as any vet when it came to difficult births.

Not long after Sarah came to Strath Fillan she went up to Glen Morrison to help Shaun with an old stud Hereford cow that was in trouble. David had retained the cow well past the age at which the cows were usually culled because she had bred exceptionally well and he wanted to try and get one last calf from her. Shaun rang and told him the cow was going to have trouble calving, and David called Sarah and asked her to go to Glen Morrison to lend a hand. It was after dark when he arrived and he found Sarah and Shaun hard at work on the cow. The poor old cow couldn't deliver the big heifer calf and they were using tackle to pull it out. Sarah was covered in blood and Vaseline but there was a gleam in her eye as the calf was pulled clear. She pulled it around to the cow's head and presently the exhausted cow began to lick her newborn.

Sarah looked up at David from where she was squatting beside the cow.

'You've got your calf, Mr Mac, but this will be the last from this old girl,' she said. She got up slowly, but her legs gave way and she fell against David. He held her and then picked her up and walked her across to a bale of straw and sat her down on it. 'Stay there, Sarah,' he ordered her.

'You be right now, Shaun?' he asked.

'Yeah, I'll be right. I'll stay here with them for a while and then leave the light on all night. Sarah's all in, David. She's a blooming marvel at this game,' Shaun said, clearly impressed.

David looked across to where Sarah sat looking at the cow and calf. 'I reckon she is, Shaun.'

He walked back to where the girl sat wearily on the bale of straw. It was the first time he had seen her exhibit any trace of tiredness. He put out his hand and pulled her to her feet. 'Go and wash your face and hands, Sarah. I'll take you up to Cat and Moira and you can stay there tonight.'

'I couldn't, Mr Mac. I haven't fed Charlie or Tex,' Sarah said hurriedly. Charlie was the kelpie David had given her to work, and Tex was the horse she used.

'They won't starve until morning, Sarah. I'll go down early and see to them myself. Go and have a wash.'

There was a small partitioned-off room at one end of the cattle shed that enclosed a toilet and hand basin. David had installed it for the convenience of ram and bull clients who travelled long distances to inspect and/ or buy his stock. Sarah walked slowly across to it. When she reappeared the only blood on her was on her clothes.

'Mrs Mac will have a fit if I walk in looking like this,' she said.

'Hop in my ute, Sarah,' David said.

She had found that there were times when you could put your point of view to David and he would listen very attentively. There were other times when it didn't pay to argue with him. This was one of those times.

Catriona and Moira knew that David had gone down to Glen Morrison to help with a difficult calving, so when he walked in with a blood-spattered Sarah they didn't turn a hair.

'Sarah needs a bath and a drink and then something to eat. I want her to stay here tonight. Moira, can you find her some pyjamas and a dressing gown – and she'll need some duds in the morning.'

'Will an omelette be all right for you, darling?' Catriona asked.

'That will be fine, Cat,' he said, as he watched his daughter shepherd Sarah out of the room. 'That girl is all in. First time I've seen her knocked up. It was a damned difficult job with that old cow. She was up the night before with a mare.'

About half an hour later a much brighter-looking Sarah appeared wearing pink pyjamas and slippers and a crimson dressing gown. David handed her a brandy and soda and watched her drink it slowly. 'Feel better?' he asked.

'Much better, thank you,' she replied.

'Good. You'll feel better still after one of Cat's famous omelettes.'

When Sarah had eaten and had warmed up by the fire the colour had come back into her face. 'I want you to have a lie-in tomorrow, Sarah. Then I want you to go home and spend a day with your mother. You can come back to Strath Fillan the following morning.'

'I'm perfectly all right, Mr Mac. I got a bit tired because I was up with Gretel the night before,' Sarah protested.

David sighed and looked at his wife and daughter. 'You will damned well do as you're told, Sarah. You've hardly had a day off since you came here. Go and spend some time with your mother.'

'Yes, Mr Mac,' she said meekly. Tough hard men didn't argue with David MacLeod, she thought to herself, so what chance had she to change his mind?

'That's the shot. Take my utility, as yours is still down at Glen Morrison. I'll bring it back here for you to pick up on your way back through in a couple of days, and you can leave mine here.'

'There's meat in the fridge for Charlie, Mr Mac,' Sarah said.

'Go to bed, Sarah.'

David was gone when Sarah woke next morning. It was after eight and she felt much refreshed. There were jeans and a blouse and jumper on the chair beside her bed. She was about to get up when Moira appeared in the doorway. 'Hi, feeling better?'

'I'm feeling great. I was just about to get up. Thanks for the clothes. I'll bring them back tomorrow.'

'No hurry. What about a shower and then some breakfast? We're having it in the kitchen.'

'That sounds wonderful, Moira.'

'Just come out when you're ready, Sarah.'

'I suppose Mr Mac has gone?' Sarah asked.

'He left at six this morning, Sarah. Dad has a big day. He and I are going away for a few days to look for some ewes to stock Wirrewarra. Mum doesn't want to leave Grandma for that length of time.'

With her health increasingly on the decline, Jane Campbell had become very capricious and demanding of late. No amount of persuasion could convince her to have the heart operation and she was convinced that if she didn't overdo things she would be perfectly all right. Although Jane got on very well with her daughter-in-law it was Catriona she wanted to see every day. So to go away for several days was out of the question. Catriona was disappointed because she loved trips away with David. She had no doubt that Moira was delighted to be going in her place.

Although Catriona was still apprehensive about Sarah working for them, so far nothing had happened to give her any real cause for concern. She wasn't even anxious about David bringing Sarah to the house because the poor girl was exhausted, and to send her back to Strath Fillan would have been a bit tough. She was compensated to some extent for her fears by the fact that she and Moira had reached a new plane of understanding.

Quite by accident, Moira had discovered Catriona's secret. She, like many other people, marvelled at the way her mother held her figure. She had seen her in a swimsuit when they were on holidays at Yeppoon and her figure was fantastic for a woman of her age. Catriona could almost wear Moira's clothes. Moira knew that her mother watched her diet very carefully and she worked out on the exercise bike every day but those things alone didn't seem enough to be responsible for her sculpted form. In actual fact Catriona was working out very strenuously almost every day with her aerobics regime. It was always done when David and the children were absent.

Moira had left to go to Muswellbrook on a shopping excursion and to have lunch with an old school friend from the area. She was almost at Inverlochy when she realised she had left her wallet behind. It was the first time she had ever done this and she was frustrated with herself. She turned the car around and headed back and the sound of Catriona's taped music masked the car's approach.

Moira heard the music as she got out of the car. It was not the kind of music she associated with her mother. She walked up the side path and entered the house by the back door. The music was louder now. It was coming from what she had known as their rumpus room. Her mother's back was to her so she did not see Moira, who looked on in amazement as her mother, gyrated to the beat of the music, in skimpy shorts and bra top, perspiration dripping down her arms and legs.

Stunned, Moira watched her mother for a few moments before switching off the tape recorder. The music stopped abruptly and so did her mother's movements. Catriona turned quickly and Moira felt she saw relief on her mother's face, which was streaming with sweat, running in rivulets down her neck.

'How long has this been going on?' Moira asked.

'Since I weaned Dougal,' Catriona said.

'You're kidding.'

'I'm not, Moira.'

'Does Dad know?'

Catriona shook her head as she picked up a big towel and began wiping the sweat from her face.

'Why?' Moira asked. She could now understand how her mother had kept her figure for so long.

'I couldn't risk losing him,' Catriona said.

'You love Dad that much?'

'David is my life, Moira. He's been my life since I was a little girl.'

'But Dad wouldn't leave you if you put on a bit of weight – he loves you. You're the only woman he ever wanted. I doubt he's ever looked at another woman. Dad is a decent man,' Moira said indignantly.

'I've seen the way women look at him, Moira. And a young woman can be hard to resist,' Catriona replied.

And then the penny dropped because Moira remembered her mother's initial opposition to her father employing Sarah Matheson.

'You don't think that Dad and Sarah would . . .?' The thought was so awful she couldn't finish the sentence.

'I sincerely hope not, Moira. It would kill me if that happened. I once went through a very difficult time when I knew Susan was chasing David. Men are men, sweetheart. I've tried to stay fit and young in body so I'll be attractive as long as possible.'

'Dad wouldn't touch Sarah. I'd bet my life on it. Are you sure all this strenuous exercise is healthy?' Moira asked, concerned.

'I have regular full check-ups and I'm in perfect condition,' Catriona assured her.

'And you've been doing this for twenty-odd years?'

'As I told you – from when I weaned Dougal. I couldn't do it when I was pregnant with you and Angus but I did it in between and as soon as I could,' Catriona said.

'Wow,' Moira said, as she temporarily forgot her tongue and her boarding-school training. 'Have you finished?'

'I'm only about half-way through,' Catriona said as she put down the towel.

'Has no one else ever caught you at this?' Moira asked.

'Lottie knew about it. She used to take you children for walks so I could work out.'

'Good heavens. How blind I've been not to wake up before now. I should have known you couldn't keep your figure on dieting and a little bit of bike work. Not *your* figure, Mum.'

'Thank you. Maybe one day you'll love someone enough to make this kind of effort. It *is* an effort, Moira.'

'I can see that,' Moira agreed, as she eyed her mother's sweat-soaked towel. A lot of things made sense now. Like the clothes her mother wore, chosen to show off her trim, taut condition.

'Do you think it's worth it?' Moira asked.

'It's worth it when David tells me I look fantastic, and when I catch him watching me and know he still thinks I'm desirable,' Catriona said, and smiled.

'Wow,' Moira said for the second time. She could see she had a lot to learn about the love game. 'I guess if I had a husband like Dad I might go to similar efforts to keep him.'

'You might and you might not, sweetheart. The important thing is never to take your man for granted. Weren't you going to Muswellbrook?'

'I can take a hint,' Moira said, and smiled. 'You want to get rid of me.'

'No, I don't want to get rid of you; I simply want to finish my routine, have a shower and then go to visit Mother,' Catriona said, and patted her daughter's arm.

'You're amazing, Mum,' Moira said, and picked up her wallet and set out again.

Moira thought about her mother most of the way to Muswellbrook. This was a surprising change because most of the time she thought about her father. She realised that people in love often made sacrifices but she had never thought her mother was in that category. Nanna Anne was supposed to have been very much in love with Grandfather Andrew but she couldn't imagine her doing aerobics to maintain his interest in her. She would bet any money that her father would never touch Sarah – or any other woman for that matter.

Catriona finished her routine and after a shower she drove across to Inverlochy. She often had lunch with her parents. They still had a housekeeper, so Jane didn't have to prepare any meals. Angus didn't do any work now. Stuart really ran Inverlochy. Angus worked his dogs and still went to occasional meetings but he was as good as retired. The big question was whether he and Jane should retire to Port Macquarie or stay put. There were points for and against both options. Jane didn't fancy being too far from her family – particularly Catriona, upon whom she leant fairly heavily. Angus didn't like the idea of leaving his dogs at Inverlochy or not being able to look at his bulls when he wanted to. He certainly didn't like the idea of not being able to talk to Stuart and David on a regular basis. He reckoned they had probably left it a bit late to retire to Port Macquarie. Angus had lived all his life at Inverlochy and it was going to be a wrench to leave the property, if that's what they ended up doing.

Jane had never achieved anything particularly remarkable in her life but she still considered her-self the district's Queen Bee, even though she had resigned from all her committees. Most of her old friends were elsewhere – some in Sydney and others on the coast; others had passed on. Jane felt the loss of her old friends and thought life would be even lonelier on the coast. There would be no Catriona to come and see her regularly. Stuart and Carol might get over to the coast a couple of times a year but with all of David's interests Catriona would be lucky to make it once a year. Jane was no fool where her daughter was concerned. She was well aware that David was the biggest thing in Catriona's life. She had once been prepared to defy her parents to marry David MacLeod and it was clear that she was still in love with her husband.

On this particular day Jane was in a pensive mood. After lunch, when Angus went to have a rest before working a dog, Jane and Catriona went into the lounge where a cheery fire was crackling away in the big fireplace.

'I want you to know that I think you were right about David, and Angus and I were wrong all those years ago,' Jane began. 'Our concern for you clouded our judgement quite badly. David is an exceptional man and you were wise to see it,' Jane said to her daughter.

'Is this your absolution, Mother?' she asked with a smile.

'Don't you dare mock me, Catriona. I was wrong about David and I want to tell him so while I can. I realise I may not be living a lot longer and I will feel better for getting that off my chest. You have the best husband a woman could wish for; a man to be proud of, as Angus says.'

'I was proud of him from the age of ten, Mother,' Catriona said firmly.

'It seems to me that Moira takes after David very

much, Catriona. That is, as much as a girl can take after a man.'

'Moira is potent competition for me, Mother. She thinks she owns her father. Moira is always very willing to take my place.'

'But that's a daughter–father thing, dear. When Moira meets a nice young man, she'll transfer her affections to him and you'll have David to yourself again,' Jane said.

Catriona rolled her eyes to the ceiling. '*When* is the operative word, Mother. Moira sees herself as the real heir to High Peaks. David told Kate that he regards Moira as "the pick of the bunch" which, considering how much he wanted sons, was – is – a very considerable compliment. David has built Moira into his life with her judging achievements and all the rest of it. It isn't going to be easy for a nice young man to take her away from High Peaks. There aren't many David MacLeods in the country and only that kind of man will appeal to Moira,' Catriona said.

'Oh dear, life is so complicated,' Jane said with a sigh. 'I have seen so many changes in my life. Once upon a time it seemed so much easier.'

'It was only easier because girls were expected to make a good marriage. They didn't have the options they do today, Mother. I'm not going to worry if Moira doesn't want to get married early. A lot of women are in their mid-thirties before they marry and have children. Even if they marry earlier than that, a

lot don't have their children until even the late thirties. Many women want careers before they have
children. Moira has plenty of time.'

'It's all so different now. I don't know what my
mother would think if she were here to see it,' Jane
said.

'I'll probably make the same comment when I'm
your age, Mother. Now, have you had any more
thoughts about the operation?'

'I'll consider it, dear. Angus says that the next
show will be his last with dogs. He would so very
much like to win that big trophy he gave to remember
Andrew. I won't do anything before the show. As it
seems to mean so much to everyone, I shall probably
have the operation after the show,' Jane said.

'Thank goodness for that. If you get that over and
done with you can decide then whether you're going
to stay here or live at Port Macquarie. I wouldn't
worry about it until you get well over the operation,'
Catriona said earnestly.

'That's good advice, dear. Now you go back to
your lovely man and I shall have a little sleep,' Jane
said, and smiled. 'Anne and Kate are coming to see
me tomorrow.'

Catriona smiled to herself. Her mother couldn't
stop herself from making this last remark. All her
married life she had sought to make herself the centre
of attention by having people come to her. First there
had been the tennis parties and, later, the garden
parties and the art discussion group. In later years still

it had been a literary group that met at Inverlochy. Now this notion that people still wanted to come and see her.

'That will be nice for you, Mother. Anne was always my ally and is a very special person, and Kate is part of what makes High Peaks such a wonderful place. Kate is up there very close to Anne in David's scheme of things. I'll try and see you tomorrow, Mother,' Catriona said.

That night as Catriona and David lay in bed David folded her into his arms and told her how much he would miss her while he and Moira were away looking at ewes. Catriona turned to face him.

'Would you do me a big favour, darling?' Catriona said.

'What is it, Cat?'

'Could you manage to be somewhere else for this year's Merriwa sheepdog trials?' she asked. Catriona was aware that David never missed these trials. He had won Angus Campbell's trophy awarded in his father's memory several times and when he didn't win it he was always asked to present it to the winner.

'Why, Cat?'

'This is going to be Daddy's last year. He has so much wanted to win the Open and never has. He believes he can never win it while you compete. It would make me so happy if you could find a legitimate reason not to be there,' Catriona said.

David chuckled at the request.

'I'm not the force I was, Cat. I don't have the same time to train dogs that I used to. And even if I don't show there are plenty of really good handlers these days. Trialling is a big sport now.'

'I understand all that, darling. It's you that Daddy finds most intimidating. He thinks Rob Roy and Jamie are the two best dogs he has ever had and he would like to go out with the Merriwa Open under his belt. It's been such a sore point that he could never win it,' she said.

'I suppose I could invent a sudden reason to be at Aberfeldy. I've been promising to take Moira up there.'

David's suggestion was bittersweet – Catriona loved to accompany David to Aberfeldy because they usually spent a couple of days at the Yeppoon house. She had David to herself there and it was always like a mini-honeymoon, and it gave her the excuse to wear a swimsuit and show off her figure. Moira would be in seventh heaven to go in her place. But if that was what it took to keep David out of the trials so be it.

'Elders want to talk to me about sending some of the cattle overseas via Karumba,' David said.

'That should do it,' Catriona agreed.

'I could say I was also looking at a property in New England except that we can't afford another place,' David said. He had a dream that some day he would buy a property in New England so he could send his finest-woolled sheep there to try and attain top wool prices. He could use these prices as promotion for his stud rams.

Catriona lowered her face and kissed him. Aberfeldy will be fine,' she said.

'It will have to look like a last-minute decision, Cat. I'll enter dogs and scratch them the day before. How's that?'

'Brilliant idea, darling. I'll make it up to you,' she promised.

'You do every day. I don't need to be there. You can present the big trophy in my place. I'll suggest it to Bob Howe, the chief steward of the sheepdog trials.'

'You're a genius, darling.'

'I also have to get away early in the morning,' he said.

'You will remember me to Bruce, won't you?' she asked.

He and Moira were taking in the Riverina and making a long-delayed visit to Bruce McClymont who had leased his great dog Nap for three years. Bruce was an old man now but still breeding kelpies as enthusiastically as ever.

'Of course, sweetheart.'

'Do you remember how Bruce and Daddy argued over who was going to shout dinner that night after you won the National and we held hands under the table in the caravan?' Catriona asked.

'And rubbed legs too, as I recall. It was especially thrilling after all the excitement of the afternoon.'

Catriona sighed and rested her head on his shoulder. 'I will miss you, darling. Don't be too many days away.'

'I'll be as quick as I can, Cat. I have to stock Wirrewarra to help pay off the loan. Right now nothing is much good but it's the right time to buy sheep. Wool will come good again and then we'll be sitting pretty. I can't have Wirrewarra not pulling its weight.'

'I understand, darling.'

They fell into a deep slumber in each other's arms.

Chapter Twelve

Merriwa show time had finally arrived and sheepdog enthusiasts from near and far had come to work their dogs. Although not considered a top trial, it was still very popular – there was almost no trial that failed to attract some of the leading handlers. Sheepdog trialling had become a very popular sport in recent decades.

Back some distance from the oval there were dozens of triallers' 'camps'. Some competitors had their own caravans and some had campervans. Tied up around these camps were sheepdogs of countless hues and types – border collies with prick ears like kelpies and an odd one with a white head and wall eye. The kelpies, though not as numerous as the border collies, were of different colours and types and there were the occasional kelpies with a lop ear, which would have disqualified them in the show ring. However, every dog on show could work sheep and some could do it exceedingly well.

Angus Campbell had his two dogs, Rob Roy and

Jamie, in a crate in the back of his utility. They were tall black-and-white dogs which conformed to what had become known as the Australian border collie type. Both dogs differed markedly from the dogs Angus had imported from Scotland after he took over from his father, Old Angus, at Inverlochy. Those dogs were much heavier in coat and some of them clapped (lay flat) a lot. Angus got walloped every time he worked those dogs at Merriwa. He could never get within a bull's roar of beating Andrew or David MacLeod, which was a significant prick to his ego.

Luck had changed for Angus when he reluctantly accepted David's advice and infused kelpie into his border collies. David allowed him to use his great dog Nap and later, Clancy, the dog with which David had won the National. The two crosses of kelpie made a startling difference – they lightened up the coat and produced dogs that worked on their feet, while retaining the collie's calmness and biddability. And instead of breaking wide they had more hold and drive, which was a big plus when holding sheep at the obstacles.

David had spent countless hours coaching both Angus and Stuart in how to train and trial dogs. Neither man had innate ability or natural stockmanship. David knew that if he owned either Rob Roy or Jamie he could win trials with them but it was Angus who wanted to win with them. The Merriwa Open Trial was the last prize Angus sought to win before he retired. Both dogs were capable of winning it if they got fair sheep and if Angus didn't make mistakes. David had gone over with him any number of eventualities, but nobody could anticipate every move sheep might make. What he had stressed to Angus in preparation for the show was the importance of a dog getting sheep on side from first contact so that the dog completed its cast and finished behind the sheep. Ideally, a dog shouldn't cast too close, but rather stop and then make a cautious 'lift' so that the sheep turn away rather than bolt. Sheep were supposed to be driven in a relatively straight line to the handler at the far end of the ground. If a dog allowed sheep to wander too far from a narrow pathway, points were deducted for being 'off course'.

A sheepdog trial is one of the truly 'bush' events run at an agricultural show. Merriwa had once been a great sheep district and sheep still featured very strongly in the area. Most people who worked sheep had owned sheepdogs and these people took a perennial interest in sheepdogs. There was a fair crowd around the ring before Angus went out to work his dog. Most onlookers were locals or from nearby districts, but there were also some fellow competitors sprinkled among the crowd. Not every show conducted sheepdog trials so it was a matter of prestige to conduct a trial. Moreover, even before Andy and David MacLeod came to the fore with kelpies, there had been some notable sheepdog handlers in the district, including Tom Bower and Paddy Cronin. Angus Campbell had always tried to maintain the trials and to encourage young handlers to compete. He was desperately keen to add his name to the list of people who had won the Merriwa Open Trial.

Both Jamie and Rob Roy had won small Maiden trials but it was a big step up to Open-class company. Angus did fairly well with Jamie until they got to the pen, when Jamie moved quickly, startling the sheep, and one sheep ran out. The ninety points he scored was one of the best rounds Angus had ever completed but it wouldn't be good enough to get him into the final. Six dogs ran ninety-one and a real class dog ran a ninety-three, which put the pressure right on Angus and Rob Roy. Catriona, who was with her father for most of the trials, could see that he was very uptight.

'Just relax, Daddy. Remember what David told you – a dog can detect if you're nervous. Have a small whisky before you go out.'

Angus had a drop more than a small whisky to calm his nerves, and suddenly he felt that he was going to do all right.

In the next round everything fell Angus's way, and Rob Roy performed to perfection. He ran a ninety-three to be equal top dog, and Angus realised he had a chance of winning the Open. He had done everything David had drummed into him and it had all worked. Catriona kissed him and told him he had done very well. Stuart, who had run second in the Improver Trial, nodded his agreement.

As he walked Rob Roy back to his utility, fellow workers were calling to him 'Good round, Angus'. For the first time Angus felt one of them. He realised he had always been regarded as an easybeat because he had never done well in the trial ring. People had used the blood of the dogs he had imported and had reasonable success, but he never had. With a ninety and a ninety-three on the scoreboard, Angus suddenly had confidence he had never had before. He also had confidence in his dog, which he recognised was streets above anything he had ever owned before. He remembered working Toss for Andrew MacLeod and how diplomatically Andrew had told him that the dog didn't have it for Australian conditions. He owed both Jamie and Rob Roy to David's expertise and his kelpies. He had been too biased and ignorant to use kelpie in his borders until David blasted him and called him pig-headed, which no other man had been game to do. It was a shame Jane wasn't here to see him work his dogs, the show being too strenuous for her. He was pleased she was going to have the operation. He reckoned that he had a few years left in him to enjoy his retirement and so should Jane.

That night David rang from Queensland and Catriona told him that her father was on equal top score with ninety-three and had run a ninety with Jamie.

'Give Angus a big well done from me, Cat. Tell him not to forget to talk softly and encouragingly to Rob. He'll know what I mean,' David said.

David had taken Rob Roy and handled him for Angus. The dog had a lot of ability but lacked confidence. By urging, encouraging and praising him with lots of 'good dog, Rob', David had got him responding very well. Rob would cast half a mile and he had great distance off his sheep. He had the knack of adjusting his distance to the pace of the sheep he worked – a valuable attribute in a trial dog, especially in the face of touchy sheep.

It was touchy sheep that put paid to most of the dogs in the Open final. The dogs worked too close, frightening the sheep, and the sheep ran all over the ground. Catriona sat with her brother and father and watched as the three first finalist dogs foundered. Catriona had picked up a lot about sheepdogs from David. He had taught her how to work a dog and she had watched him at work with Rob Roy.

'You'll have to keep him right off, Daddy. These sheep are very touchy. As soon as a dog gets close to them they run.'

Angus nodded. He knew what he had to do but anything could happen on the trial ground.

Catriona watched anxiously as her father walked through the gate onto the oval. Angus was in his eighties and white-haired and this was the last time he would ever walk onto this oval. Ever since he took over Inverlochy from his father, Old Angus, her father had been the leading man of the district, but he had never won an Open sheepdog trial. David had to convince him that it wasn't the size of the property or the number of sheep that mattered but the keenness and expertise of the handler. You didn't need a lot of sheep and tons of work if you had the right strains of border collies. Kelpies needed more work and it was harder to get trial dogs from them unless you had certain key traits in your dogs. What David had done was blend the best traits of both breeds. And while a lot of Australian border collies had kelpie in them, not many people had kelpies like Nap and Clancy. That was what Rob Roy had going for him today. He had the blood of two great kelpies mixed with some of the best available border collie strains.

As Angus Campbell walked out to the peg it was David MacLeod's injunctions that were uppermost in his mind. 'If you're faced with touchy sheep keep your dog well out and well off them. If he casts narrow, he'll spook them straight off.' It had been David's insistence on keeping Rob Roy until he was satisfied he would 'run the fence' that would help to make the difference now. Everyone else had failed to score above eighty-two in the final simply because they couldn't handle the jumpy sheep.

Angus sat Rob Roy well behind him and waited until the bell rang. He had noted that the wethers came out with their heads in the air and were certain to be lively. He let them wait and settle a little before casting Rob Roy to the right. True to his training, Rob ran the fence and finished a good twenty-five metres behind the three wethers. They had seen him but he was too far clear to give them any immediate cause for concern. When Rob stopped, they turned and looked at him. The next time they looked he was a few metres closer. They edged away and stopped and Rob crept cautiously towards them. The lead wether ran a few steps but as the dog hadn't come on, he stopped again. This procedure went on all the way down the ground. Here the sheep had to be taken around a peg and they came fairly close to where the handler stood. Another of David's injunctions popped into Angus's consciousness: 'On touchy sheep or near sheep of any description, don't make any sudden movements. Don't wave your hand quickly or speak loudly.' So here he commanded Rob to back off as the wethers wheeled at a run to clear the peg.

That was the first tricky peg negotiated. It was now on to the race that would be a real test because if you tried to put too much pressure on touchy sheep they were likely to break up and run down either side of the race. Every time sheep left the mouth of the race the dog lost points. Rob lost a couple straight off because the lead wether broke, and although Rob stopped him before he had run right round, it was still points lost, maybe two, possible three. It was up to the judge.

It took some time to get the three wethers through the race and then it was on to the bridge. Again the lead wether broke and again Rob turned him back. The three sheep had their rear ends to the bridge and Angus shifted Rob to try and get the lead wether to turn away so that he didn't have to bring his dog in. The trio of wethers found the bridge more inviting than the black-and-white horror facing them. The lead wether with the odd-sized horns ran up the ramp and then across it and his mates followed him.

The final test was the pen. The wethers ran past the pen before Angus could get into his circle. Rob gathered them and placed them a few metres out from the pen and then began his hold-and-drive routine. He would move a little to one side and then as the sheep moved, he would come back to his original position. It was Clancy all over again, bamboozling the sheep with his footwork. They didn't know which way to run because every time they moved, the dog was there. So slowly, ever so slowly, Rob moved them into the pen. Angus left his circle and shut the gate. He stopped his watch and saw that he had only just made it, with only a bare ten seconds left. He had put in a lot of time on the lift and pull – bringing the sheep down the ground to the handler – but it had made all the difference.

'Good boy, good dog,' Angus said softly, as he patted Rob Roy's head before letting the wethers out of the pen.

It was only at that moment that he became conscious of the sound of clapping and from out of the crowd he heard someone call 'Good on yer, Angus'. He had no idea who had called but the words warmed his heart. Nothing he had ever achieved with his cattle came near to how he felt at that moment.

When he had put the sheep away he walked slowly around the oval to where he had left Catriona and Stuart. They were walking briskly towards him and as he got closer he saw that Catriona was crying. She was crying because she had just heard that he had won the Open Trial. Rob Roy had won it by seven points. Beyond his children he saw his daughter-in-law, Carol, who looked as if she was close to crying too.

'Oh, Daddy,' Catriona sobbed as she hugged him, 'you were absolutely brilliant out there!'

'Did I win it?' Angus asked unbelievingly.

'You won it, Dad, you've won. Well done!' Stuart assured him.

Angus had won the Open at last. He had won it because he had taken David MacLeod's advice, and because David had done the spadework on his dog.

'Did you see Rob at the pen? Just like Clancy, wasn't he?'

Catriona nodded. Nobody who had seen Clancy score the 100 points at the National would ever forget him.

'David would have been very proud of you, Daddy,' Catriona said through her tears.

'I wish he had been here to see it. I couldn't have done it without David's help,' Angus said.

'What matters is that you've done it.'

'By God, I have. Jane will get one hell of a surprise when I walk in and tell her,' Angus said.

'She certainly will,' Catriona laughed.

Later, at the presentation of trophies, Catriona felt tears well up again as she stepped forward to present the Andrew MacLeod Memorial Trophy to her father.

'It gives me enormous pleasure and pride to not only be asked to represent the MacLeod family but to present the Andrew MacLeod Memorial Trophy to my father, Angus Campbell. This trophy was inaugurated by him to honour the memory of Andrew MacLeod, whose dogs won so many trials on this ground.

'This is one of the few trophies that have eluded my father since he began exhibiting animals in his own right fifty-odd years ago. My father has always loved sheepdogs and imported border collies from Scotland and some of you here today probably have the blood of those dogs in your own dogs. This is my father's last trial, as he is retiring. To win it caps a lifetime of breeding high-class animals. I know there is nothing that could give him greater pleasure than to take home this award,' Catriona said.

Angus was clearly affected by his daughter's words and it took him a few moments to compose himself and respond. Finally he mustered a weak smile as he stepped forward to accept the trophy.

'Catriona has stolen my thunder because she has said what was in my heart and mind to say. There is nothing that could give me greater pleasure than to be able to say I won the Andrew MacLeod Memorial Trophy because I donated it to honour the memory of the first man who showed me how to work a sheepdog. If I had not been so pig-headed, maybe I would have won the Open here many years ago. I stuck out for pure borders until my son-in-law, David MacLeod, took me to task and persuaded me to use his two great kelpies Nap and Clancy with my borders.

'This is my last trial, but it's a fairytale ending. And it isn't the last you'll see of the Campbells because my son Stuart will carry on with the dogs and there is a grandson, Angus MacLeod, who can work a dog a long way better than I can. So, to use the words of the old

Campbell march, *Baile Ionaraora* ("The Campbells are coming") ... *Cruachan!* (the war cry of Clan Campbell).'

Angus shouted drinks for the triallers and then in a high state of euphoria, compounded by four stiff whiskies, set off for Inverlochy. He was followed, for safety's sake, by Stuart and Carol, who had seen him imbibe the whiskies.

At the Inverlochy homestead Stuart and Carol left Angus to break the news of the Open win to Jane. Angus let out his dogs and after tying them up he picked up the big trophy and sash and walked a little unsteadily up the back steps. The house was still and quiet. It was the housekeeper's day off, and there was no sign of Jane.

'Jane,' Angus called, 'Jane, I'm home. Jane, you'll never guess what happened.'

But there was no answer from Jane.

Angus walked from the kitchen to the lounge room, to find Jane lying on the big sofa with an arm trailing on the floor. It almost held the book she had been reading. Angus stiffened and put down the trophy on the table. His first thought was that his wife had fallen asleep and he shook her slightly to check if he was right. When she didn't respond, he sat down on the floor beside the sofa and began to stroke her hair. Presently, he got up and went into the bedroom for a covering. He came back with a blanket of the Campbell tartan that he had bought on his last trip to Scotland, and placed it over his wife's body.

He then went to the phone and rang Stuart. He told him that his mother had passed away, and asked him and Carol to come to the homestead. Catriona was evidently feeding the dogs and he had to wait to give her the news.

Catriona got through to David at Aberfeldy. He listened gravely as his wife gave him the news of Jane's death.

'What is it, Dad?' Moira asked. She sensed it was bad news.

'Jane died this afternoon, Moy. Angus found her on the sofa when he arrived back from the trial,' he said.

'Oh no, that's terrible. Poor Grandma. And she had finally decided to have the operation,' Moira said gravely, taking a seat as she absorbed the shock of the news.

'I'm afraid she left it too long, Moy.'

'We'll have to go back in the morning, Don,' David said later to his manager. We'll get up early and hit the track. Cat must be feeling very down – Jane had leant on her so heavily of late. Not to mention poor Angus. It must have shattered him to find her like that. He won the Open with Rob Roy and had the big trophy in his hands to show Jane when he found her,' David said.

'Oh, Dad. How awful. Poor Grandpa. What will he do without Grandma?'

'Goodness knows, Moy. I'm trying to think how old I was when I first met Jane Campbell. I used to think she was very stuck-up even though she once put on a party for me, after I rescued Cat from the likes of Stanley Masters and Wade Missen. Jane put on a heap of tucker – chocolate cake, and all that sort of stuff. Then she sent what we didn't eat home in a big box.'

'Was that after they gave you the saddle?' Moira asked.

'Oh, yes. Jane thought they were better than us but she came good at the end. She asked me to go and see her because she had something she wanted to tell me,' David said.

'Which was?' Moira urged.

'It was a private conversation, Moy. I think your grandmother knew her days were numbered. All I will say is that it took a lot of guts on her part. I reckon Jane had more to her than what showed under that society veneer.'

So they returned to High Peaks after detouring first at Inverlochy to see Angus and Stuart. Catriona was with her father and helping him to make arrangements for the funeral.

Anne was much saddened by Jane's death because, as David had told Moira, her first outings in the Merriwa district were tennis parties at Inverlochy. She and Jane had been friends ever since those days and although there had been some acrimony because of the Campbells' objections to Catriona marrying

David, Anne had weathered that and had seen her son accepted well and truly by the Campbells. True, Jane had often come across as superior and patronising, but at heart she and Angus were good people. It had been Angus who had looked after Anne after her fall just before David was born while Andrew had been away at the Forbes sheepdog trial.

Dougal and young Angus came home for the funeral, as did Stuart and Carol's children, so all the younger generation were in the church for the service. Some very complimentary things were said about their grandmother. There was reference to her standing in the district and her interest in art and charity work. It was a very big funeral and some Campbell relations had come all the way from Scotland to attend it. David met many of Jane's relatives for the first time. Some were very posh indeed. After the funeral there was a great gathering of friends and relatives at Inverlochy. It was as if Jane had brought them to her for one last occasion. Angus felt that Jane would have approved as she always liked to have people around her.

Those closest to Angus were most concerned about what he would do now. He immediately rejected the idea of going to Port Macquarie to live on his own. He wanted to stay close to his kin. He had a housekeeper and he said that if he got too useless to look after himself, he would employ a nurse. Catriona was much relieved by this edict. Her father was within reach at Inverlochy and she could keep an eye on him there a great deal easier than if he were on the coast.

Jane's death ushered in one of the most depressing years David had experienced. This was an admission of a nature not usually associated with David because he was regarded as one of the most positive people anyone could meet. Cattle prices remained low, wool was 'on the nose' and at the end of the year he had an almighty row with Dougal.

David was not against Dougal being a vet. If he had to be anything, a vet was the best choice, for Dougal could become involved in David's artificial insemination program for his sheep flocks, and advise on lifting the standard of his Herefords even higher through embryo transplantation. Sarah Matheson had intervened to help with the AI program but embryo transplantation was another matter.

But Dougal had ambitions which were beyond the scope of David's plans for him. He finished vet school equal first and immediately left for South Australia to do a course in embryo transplantation, though not because of anything David wanted. He then spent six months with a large horse practice and announced that he was going to the United States to do a special course in equine reproduction. David hit the roof and there was a blazing row.

'Bloody ungrateful, I call it. You've been looked after and had everything paid for you so you could become a vet and now you want to leave and do another course. When is it going to end? Well, things are tough right now and I'm not going to give you another cent,' David said heatedly.

'That's a very short-sighted attitude. I'll come back from America with more qualifications. What's wrong with that?'

'How many damned qualifications do you need to practice veterinary science? Is it your aim to have more degrees than any other vet in the country? Topping the course would be enough for most people,' David said.

'You're just crooked because I'm not here helping you run your little stock empire. That's your real problem, Dad. You wanted your children to be just like you and because I don't fit into your calculations, you won't forgive me. There'd be any amount of fathers very proud of what I've done but you never gave me any encouragement to do what I wanted to do.'

'What absolute bloody nonsense,' David said angrily. 'Who paid for you to do all you've done? I could see that you weren't cut out to be a stockman and I never stinted on anything to get you through. Sure, I was disappointed you weren't going to be here but we've got by without you and we'll continue to get by without you.'

'I never had any encouragement to be a stockman. You sent away Starana when I asked you to keep her,' Dougal said. He couldn't help referring to this long-felt grievance.

'You don't mean to tell me that if I had kept Starana here, you would have suddenly become committed to staying with us? I won't wear that.

'You disappoint me, Dougal. I don't want to lay it on about the money but you've had the best education any young man could have and you don't seem particularly grateful. You should take a leaf out of your sister's book. Moira has done more than I could expect a daughter to do and she's been pleased to do it.'

'It's me you're crooked on. It's because I'm the eldest son and you thought I would be just like you and grandpa. It shot all your plans down in flames. Well, I'm an individual and that's all I wanted you to recognise,' Dougal said, his voice rising.

When Dougal told Catriona what he wanted to do and why he had to go to the US, she gave him the money he needed. It was the first time she had ever gone behind her husband's back to do anything, but Dougal was her son and she realised he was far too clever to hold back. Furthermore, High Peaks was a more peaceful place when Dougal and his father were separated by distance.

Before Dougal left for the US David had calmed down sufficiently to ask him why he needed another degree or diploma or whatever it was he was after, when he had an honours degree already.

'There are areas I need to specialise in and the US is the place to go. Money is no object to thoroughbred breeders over there. It will give me greater clout when I come back here and start my own practice,' Dougal answered.

'So you won't be coming back to be part of this operation?' David asked.

'Afraid not, Dad. Of course, I'd be happy to help where I could if you haven't begun your embryo program,' Dougal said.

'Very generous of you,' David said gruffly. However, as much as he was disappointed that his elder son would not be around to take over the properties he had worked so hard for, David was secretly rather proud of the fact that he had a son with an honours degree in vet science who would one day, undoubtedly, be one of the best horse vets in the country. He wondered what his father would think of that achievement. Maybe, like everyone else in the family, Andrew MacLeod would think it was pretty damned good. But he would have given Dougal a lot of strappings on the way and told him to keep his mind on the job in hand. Dougal would be damned handy right now but they would survive without him.

Catriona was enormously proud of Dougal and his achievements, while Anne said that Dougal reminded her of Andy more and more each year. Although Catriona liked to have Dougal at home she was happier when he left because there was always some degree of tension between him and David. Dougal realised that Moira was doing what his father had expected him to do, which was help run their properties. When he was home he heard his father give instructions to Moira and pointedly leave him out of everything. Catriona's first interest was David's welfare and giving Dougal the money to study in the US was a small price to pay for that.

Dougal's first meeting with Sarah Matheson in her employment at High Peaks was not propitious. He learnt that she had done the first artificial inseminations of his father's stud ewes and he asked her what lambing percentage had been achieved. When Sarah told him that it had been seventy per cent he said that it should have been higher than that and that she couldn't be doing it right. This got right up Sarah's nose because David was standing beside her at the time.

'It was our first try at the business, Dougal. We used a back-up ram anyway so all told we had ninety-eight per cent,' David said.

Sarah could have kissed him, but David hadn't finished. 'We didn't have the benefit of your expertise, Dougal, and I think Sarah did a damned good job under the circumstances.'

It was the best put-down Sarah had heard for ages and it completely silenced Dougal. Sarah thought he had a very superior attitude towards everyone, which was surprising considering it was David who had paid for him to be a vet. Little by little, everything David MacLeod did took on special proportions in Sarah's world.

Jane's death was a forceful reminder to David that both his mother and Kate were over eighty. God, he would miss them when they went. Kate had become almost as close to him as his mother – she was a real true-blue woman. Her transition from being a theatre sister in a city hospital to property manager had been a remarkable achievement, and illustrated to David that a person could do anything with sufficient determination. A young Kate Gilmour would be very handy.

Chapter Thirteen

The days Sarah Matheson worked for the MacLeods were among the happiest of her life. It was only after she left David MacLeod's employ and looked back on her time with him that she fully realised how carefully and skilfully he had mentored her to become an exceptionally knowledgeable manager and stock judge.

When David was happy that Sarah had mastered one aspect of her work, he presented her with another challenge. Sometimes she worked in tandem with Moira; for example, she and Moira practised truck driving together and gained their licences on the same day. David had said that it was no use depending on him or Shaun to always be on hand to drive the truck – he needed to be able to send either one of them away with stock.

In the second year of her employment David got both Moira and Sarah together and told them what shows he intended to exhibit at for the year.

'Do you think if I send you both away together it would be too much for the young men at the show?' he asked with a smile.

'I'm not interested in men, Mr Mac,' Sarah replied quickly.

'One of you can drive the truck with the cattle and the other can take a few sheep in one of the utilities,' David suggested.

'What about Strath Fillan?' Sarah asked.

'I'll worry about Strath Fillan, Sarah. I want you to learn how to exhibit sheep and cattle. There are bigger things ahead.' David was punting that the wool market would improve and that he could show sheep and cattle interstate.

Sarah had never shown an interest in boys. The memory of her father's suicide was forever with her. Her father had left her mother in the lurch – it was as simple as that. Some people disagreed. Rod Matheson had left his wife with a property fully paid for, which she could have sold. Emily was certainly better off than some other women had been. She hadn't been left with a big debt and although she lost some of her mares, Catriona had bought half-a-dozen of these back for her.

All that Sarah had heard about men suggested that they were hardly worth the bother. They drank too much, and even married men chased other women. Many boys had shown an interest in Sarah at high school and at Longreach, but she wouldn't spit on them. Sarah was well aware of the extent that David had helped her family by employing Dianne to do his bookwork, and her mother's high opinion of both David and Catriona had influenced her to ask for a job on High Peaks. It wasn't until Sarah came to work for David MacLeod that she was exposed to a man of determination and principles. For a time she was even apprehensive about David but although they were often alone together, he never behaved inappropriately. He occasionally spoke sharply to her when she disappointed him, but he also made sure he gave praise where praise was due.

What David especially liked about Sarah was her willingness to tackle any kind of job. Time, also, wasn't an issue for her – she would begin earlier and finish later than conventional working hours if something needed to be done. On occasions David had to order her home. If she had been one of his sons, he could not have expected more from her.

It wasn't until her second year with David that Sarah realised she was falling in love with him – despite the fact that he was married and more than twice her age. She had never felt anything like it and it wasn't something she had expected, or even wanted. It had happened, and she was both happy and miserable. When she was with David it was as if nothing else mattered, and when she was on her own her life seemed empty, devoid of meaning.

The hopelessness of her situation compounded her misery. David was so obviously happy with Catriona that there was no hope for her. Moreover, after all David and Catriona had done for her family it would be unthinkable that she should do anything that could threaten or destroy their relationship.

As Sarah's feelings for David grew they became increasingly difficult to hide. When she saw David get out of his vehicle and walk towards her she wanted to run to him and throw her arms around him. While Catriona had been preoccupied with her mother, Sarah had had David to herself occasionally, when Moira wasn't with him. However, since Jane Campbell's death Catriona was by her husband's side much more and Sarah knew she had to be especially careful not to give her secret away.

If David had hoped that Sarah would be attracted to either Dougal or Angus she soon diminished that hope. She found Dougal rather dour and arrogant while Angus, who was younger than her, lacked depth and maturity. David had told her that Angus was smart and gifted with animals but a bit wild and woolly at the edges. He confided that he was hoping that Angus would grow up as he had a big job ahead of him if he was to eventually take over the family business. David was hoping Longreach would sort him out. Sarah had met other boys like Angus while at Longreach and some of them had even propositioned her. She had no doubt that some girls would fall for Angus easily because although not as big as David, he was very like him in looks, and had an easy, confident charm. But neither Dougal nor Angus in Sarah's opinion was good enough to stand in David's shadow.

Moira was a different matter. In Sarah's opinion,

Moira was the real jewel among David's children – she wasn't the smartest of the three, but she was the nicest. And it didn't take Sarah long to appreciate that Moira rated very highly with David. In later conversations with her mother, who spoke regularly with Catriona, Sarah learnt that one of David's biggest regrets was that Moira was a girl, because sooner or later he knew he would lose her. Catriona had confided to her mother that David was disappointed in the two boys, albeit having some pride in their respective talents, but was delighted with Moira. Sarah also learnt that David had wanted a bigger family, especially boys, but that Catriona stopped after three children. Sarah pondered this a lot. Having children was not something she had ever thought about very much but having David's children was another matter – if he wanted four or five she would have them. Sarah fantasised about David as she lay in bed at night. He had had smokos and an occasional lunch with her at Strath Fillan and it had been heaven to look after him. If David had been a different kind of man he would perhaps have tried something on with her, but that never happened.

To Moira, Sarah was much more than an employee. The two young women exchanged confidences, and their friendship grew closer the longer Sarah stayed at Strath Fillan. David gave them plenty of opportunities to cement their friendship because they often had to work together. A couple of times he sent them both out to Molonga to help Greg Robertson with mustering for shearing and crutching.

It was inevitable that the subject of romance would come up sooner or later in their conversations. Sarah began probing in a tentative kind of way. Had Moira had a boyfriend? No. Did she want to have a boyfriend? Not particularly – not for some time, anyway. Why? Sarah asked.

'Dad expects too much from me to let him down now,' Moira said. 'He's upset about Dougal leaving and not sure how Angus is going to end up. But what man could ever measure up to Dad?'

'But don't you want your own family, Moira?' Sarah asked.

'If I met the right man that would be nice. Later on I'd like to have a couple of children. Of course, you don't need a husband to have a child these days. I could afford to rear children without a man,' Moira said forthrightly.

'Moira, I'm shocked. What would your parents think?'

'I'm sure Dad would prefer to have me here with two children than lose me. The boys might not appreciate what he has done to put together all these properties but I certainly do, and I won't leave him in the lurch. And you can see how much he depends on me,' Moira said.

'But you must have men chasing you, Moira, from all over these parts – and well beyond! You're so attractive, and you have so much behind you – High Peaks Pastoral Company, I mean.'

'Well you didn't miss out in the looks department,

either. I could ask you the same question,' Moira teased.

'Boys just don't interest me, Moy.' This was true – it was a man who had her heart. 'I want to help Mum breed some big winners on the racetrack. That's what I'm working for, and boys would only get in my way. If you want something, really want something, you have to go all out to get it. Good men, from what I can figure out, are few and far between. In my experience, once you become friendly with a boy he wants to sleep with you. Boys seem to think you should naturally want to do that. Not for me, thank you,' Sarah said firmly.

'I know what you mean and as I told Dad, I know that when I'm judging sheep men are looking at me more closely than at my judging technique. I say, let them. It's the nature of the beast, Sarah. All I know is that I would never marry a man unless I was over-poweringly in love with him just as Mum was with Dad. Mum would have defied her parents to marry him. She didn't have to do that, but she would have. Lordy, what Mum has done to keep Dad interested in her. You just wouldn't believe the sacrifices she's made,' Moira said.

Sarah couldn't imagine it being any sacrifice to do anything for David. She had always imagined that David and Catriona had an almost perfect marriage. Her mother had said as much to her.

'Ha, ha. Do you think Mum looks good for her age?' Moira asked.

'I think she looks wonderful either on a horse or off

it. I'd love to be able to wear clothes like her. I mean her figure is something else,' Sarah said.

'If you promise not to breathe a word of what I tell you, then I'll let you in on a secret. Will you promise?' Moira asked.

'I promise,' Sarah answered earnestly.

So Moira told her about her mother's secret aerobics, the exercise bike and the dieting.

'Your mother has been doing this for twenty-odd years? To keep your father interested in her?' Sarah asked incredulously.

'That's right. That's how much Mum loves him. She has the idea that if she doesn't look attractive he will look elsewhere. Which is a ridiculous notion. He's never been interested in any other woman and I'm sure he never would be. It's all in Mum's head. I know she thinks more of Dad than she does of us. Oh, she loves us but Dad has always been the big thing in her life. Mum gets her kicks out of Dad still thinking she looks sexy and terrific. She told me so. That's real love, Sarah.'

'Moira, that's almost unbelievable,' Sarah breathed.

'I'd have said so if I hadn't seen it with my own eyes and heard it from Mum's lips. It's the biggest secret Mum has ever shared with me. Well, I think it is. It kind of made us closer, Sarah. There's not many men who could generate that kind of love. I wouldn't want anything less than that. If I don't feel for a man like Mum felt for Dad then I'll just stay here helping him run this show. It's a good life and there are plenty of rewards. The papers are writing about us and about me personally. I'm being asked to judge all over and one day maybe I'll be asked to judge at Royal shows. That's been one of Dad's aims for myself and Angus. I don't feel the need for a man, Sarah. I don't mind being admired but I don't want to become a man's possession or accessory. I'm my own person and I have Dad to thank for that.'

Moira's words beat like hammer blows on Sarah's heart. It was apparent that Catriona still loved her husband excessively, for what woman would put herself through so much unless she did. It was also apparent that David wasn't a womaniser because he had never tried to touch her. And yet, at times Sarah had caught his eyes fixed on her and there seemed to be more in his scrutiny than an employer's preoccupation with his employee's devotion to the job. Inexperienced with men as she was, Sarah didn't know what to do next. She had no idea how she would respond if the unthinkable happened and David touched her. What she did know was that if anything happened, it would mean disaster. It would be disaster for Catriona, for herself, and for David and all he had put together for his family. And Moira would probably hate her forever.

Oh, God, it was an awful situation. Sarah knew that the longing she felt could only be assuaged in one way. To feel that way about a man and to have to walk away from it involved the biggest sacrifice she would ever have to make. Probably never again in her life would she feel the same way about a man. Perhaps never again would she ride the hills with a man and experience the bliss of his company.

One such experience kept recurring in her mind. She and David were mustering on Wallaby Rocks; it was the highest point on Poitrel and just above the big cave where David and his dogs had gained sanctuary when the fire swept over the ridge. It was also not far from where Kate had come off her horse and broken her leg. David pointed out these landmarks to her and then dismounted and began sniffing the breeze that blew gently across the tops.

'Crikey, I love the bush, Sarah,' he said. 'And I love this country best of all. It's not a patch on Molonga and Wirrewarra but I love it. I love the sweep of it and I love the eagles that fly above. An eagle once took one of my best pups, but an eagle has to live too, Sarah.

'Dad loved this country because it's sheep country, pure and simple, and Dad liked sheep. He reckoned sheep were great and that a fellow couldn't do anything much better than run sheep because it was an honest, straightforward thing to do. Dad would be mightily impressed with what we're doing with sheep now, Sarah. The wool we're producing these days is so much better than the wool off the wethers Dad used to run.

'I used to look at our country through the windows of the school and wish the time away so I could be back in the hills. There's nothing better in life than to be on a good, sure-footed horse with a good dog running behind and to be off for a muster in the tops.'

Sarah had seen then images of the boy David who had so impressed everyone who knew him. She had leafed through the pages of Anne's scrapbook with its stories and pictures detailing his father's successes with dogs and horses and then, David's achievements – he had been front-page news several times. Even now, a millionaire grazier and bush icon, David was still very much a boy at heart. He struck a chord in her heart because she felt similarly about horses. But where David valued horses for their usefulness, she loved them for their fleetness.

What David had revealed was that he was far more than the strong, pragmatic, determined man everybody perceived him to be. Of course, he was all of those things but at heart he was simply a bush boy who had grown up. David had been given what amounted to a fortune and he had turned it to good account. He had also been given talents and commonsense. And two great parents.

'I want to show you something, Sarah,' he beckoned. He led her down off the ridge and along a faint track to the big cave. He took her horse's reins and tied them to a sapling. 'Have a look in there, Sarah,' he said.

She stepped inside the opening and found herself in what amounted to a kind of anteroom to a much bigger cave that was accessible by an opening several feet across. Muted light partly illuminated both caves. Sarah felt hot and cold all at once. If anything was going to happen, it would happen here.

'This is where I sheltered from the fire. Nap brought a small lot of sheep here and we had them in the front cave. Clancy burnt his feet when he came looking for me. This is where Dad and Cat found me.

'And this,' he said, 'is where Cat and I became

engaged. I was able to tell her we could be married because Tim Sparkes left me what amounted to a fortune. A storm was raging outside that day and we just made it to the cave. We had lunch and I boiled the billy. And then we rode home through the glistening hills, everything clean and bright after the storm. Cat's eyes were shining because she had waited for me for quite some time while I kept her at arm's length. I told her that if she looked like that Mum would know something had happened. Mum's always been sharp, Sarah.'

Sarah knew at that moment that David would never reach out to her for anything more. Whatever he felt for her, it wasn't enough to replace what he felt for Catriona. She knew now that he had brought her to the cave to tell her in his own kind of way that he was spoken for. He may have sensed what she felt for him and used the cave and what it meant to him to illustrate that there could never be anything between them. She knew that David liked her and it was she who had fantasised there might be something more than that.

That night as she lay restless in bed, Sarah thought back over the day she had spent with David and knew that she would experience few more precious moments than had occurred that day. David had opened his heart to her and she had seen a David that few people had ever seen. She knew that men found great difficulty in opening their hearts. It wasn't the Aussie thing to be seen as soft or sentimental, and possibly only Catriona had seen this side of David. Sarah came to the realisation that she had little choice but to leave

Strath Fillan. Leaving was going to be difficult, but telling David that she was leaving would be even worse. She had asked him for a job and he had given her a job. She loved everything about her work, but she couldn't stay. Her mind and body were in torment and she couldn't endure it any longer. What on earth would she tell him?

It was while Sarah was contemplating how she could find the strength to leave, knowing she did not have the strength to stay, that Angus Campbell came to see David and Catriona one Sunday with some news. Angus came to High Peaks almost every week now and Catriona called to see him regularly. Stuart and Carol had recently taken him up to David and Catriona's house at Yeppoon and Angus was looking better now. Losing Jane had been an enormous blow and Angus had become very haggard. He was now coming to terms with his wife's death, and reconciled to being on his own. His interest in events around him was gradually resurfacing.

'Roy Missen is selling out,' Angus said.

David looked across at Catriona, who shivered. David's eyes had become ice and his expression was steely – she hadn't seen that look for a long time. David looked that way whenever anything relating to the Missen family was raised.

Angus, not as sensitive to David's facial expressions as his daughter, ploughed on. 'The Elders wool rep told me, and he got it from Roy himself. Roy is giving up and going into a nursing home. He's got something amiss internally,' Angus said.

'Poor Roy,' Catriona murmured.

Roy Missen had owned a substantial property adjoining Inverlochy on one boundary. He had mortgaged the property to secure funds for his sons' legal expenses after they and a mate, Stanley Masters, had tried to rape Catriona the night of her debut. After some years in prison Bill and Wade had started a fire on Poitrel. While running from a police car they had wrapped their utility around a tree on the Bunnan Road and both boys had been killed. Subsequently, Stanley Masters was knifed and killed in prison.

Roy and Bessie never recovered from the loss of their sons. Bessie went to pieces and became a mite peculiar. She died in her seventies and Roy lived on the old property alone. He sold part of the property to pay off the bank and bred good prime lambs and cattle. Locals thought he would sell and get out but the property was where he and Bessie had been happiest. He couldn't work out where he had gone wrong with the boys other than to have been too soft with them. Bessie had always thought so much of Bill and Wade that he hadn't liked to chastise them. If Bill and Wade had had a father like Andy MacLeod maybe things would have been different. Andy would have straightened them out.

'Are you interested, David?' Angus asked.

'Not in the slightest, Angus. I wouldn't touch the Missen place if its tracks were paved with gold,' David said vehemently. 'After what Bill and Wade tried to do to Catriona and what they did to us here, I'm surprised you'd even ask.'

'Land is land, David. You can never have too much land. Stuart has three children and two, at least, want to stay on the land. It's not every day you get the chance to buy an adjoining block. Besides, Roy is a decent old chap. He's never done anything to me. The poor chap has had a tough time of it with those boys and Bessie,' Angus said.

'Then buy it, Angus. Even if it wasn't Roy who owned it, I wouldn't be interested. If I get another place it will be in New England,' David said.

'Why would you want a place up there, David? The country isn't a patch on what we've got here. You live with a drench gun in your hand up there,' Angus said.

'I need a place to grow real top fine wool, Angus. I want to be able to send the pick of my fine-wool sheep up there. There are only a few places you can grow top spinner's wool and New England is one of them. I don't need a big property,' David said.

'I just wanted to find out if you were interested in the Missen place, David. Now I know you're not, I can go ahead,' Angus said.

'Would Roy have any objection to selling his place to you?' David asked.

'I don't see why he would. There's not a lot of demand for properties right now the way things are. Roy's not well and he needs to sell up,' Angus said.

David shrugged. 'It's your business, Angus. If you're going to buy, now is the time to do it. Wool and beef prices couldn't be much lower.'

After Angus had left Catriona took her husband's arm. 'You'll never forgive them, will you, darling?'

'Not as long as I live, Cat. Roy and Bessie were too soft on them but Bill and Wade were no damned good. They were no damned good as boys and they were no damned good as men. They came close to destroying you the night they attacked you and Roger. If I hadn't followed them, who knows what would have happened? They never showed any remorse, either. Not then and not later, when they set Poitrel ablaze. Roy was all right and he was man enough to come and apologise for his boys and offer to pay for my doctor's expenses, but I wouldn't want to own the place that had birthed the Missen boys. Not on your life, Cat.'

She laid her head against his face and he stroked her hair. There was no need for further words.

While Sarah Matheson had been working for him, David had gradually improved the horse facilities on Strath Fillan. There were new yards and last of all, a foaling shed with fluorescent lighting. The old stables had been renovated and the whole complex was now very workable. Having completed all that David now proposed to paint and renovate the Strath Fillan homestead. He shifted Sarah up to the cottage alongside his mother and employed a local painter to give the big homestead a long-overdue rejuvenation. He had some other ideas for the house he wanted to implement before Sarah moved back into it.

Kate had moved into the old High Peaks homestead with Anne when Glen Morrision became too much for her. Anne enjoyed her company, but also welcomed Sarah back to the cottage because, as she said, 'It does us old fogies a lot of good to have a young person in the house.' At the end of the day Sarah would have a sherry with Anne and Kate and then join them for dinner. She would help with the washing up and stay to talk for perhaps an hour before retiring to bed ready for her early start at Strath Fillan the following morning.

Because Sarah had always come into the homestead from her cottage by six-thirty and this particular night she didn't, Anne wondered if perhaps she wasn't well. She had heard Sarah's vehicle arrive about half an hour earlier so she knew she was home. Sarah always showered and changed and she never kept them waiting for dinner. When Sarah still hadn't appeared a quarter of an hour later Kate suggested to her sister that she go and check on the girl.

Anne walked across to the cottage where she found the front door wide open. She paused there because she heard heavy sobbing coming from the bedroom. Anne walked to the bedroom door and looked into the room. Sarah, still in her working clothes, was lying face down on the bed with her face pressed into her pillow. Great sobs were racking her body and she was unaware of Anne standing in the doorway. Anne crossed to the bed and laid a hand on the girl's back. 'What is it, Sarah?

Is David too hard on you?' This question was met with a shake of the head and more sobs. Anne now grew alarmed. Surely the unthinkable hadn't happened and the girl was in trouble?

'Are you in trouble?' Sarah shook her head even more vigorously. 'Thank God,' Anne breathed. She got up from the bed and went to the bathroom for a face washer. Back in the bedroom she sat at Sarah's bedside and stroked her hair. 'It can't be that terrible, Sarah. Here, wash your face and tell me what's troubling you.'

Eventually Anne managed to get Sarah to turn over and sit up while she massaged her face with the washer. The girl's eyes were swollen red from her crying and she was obviously distraught.

'I have to leave High Peaks,' Sarah said at last through her tears.

'You have to leave? Why do you have to leave, Sarah?' Anne asked gently.

'I just have to, Mrs Mac,' Sarah got out with some difficulty through her sobs.

'I'll ask you again, Sarah, are you in trouble?'

Sarah shook her head vigorously, 'No, of course not.'

Anne sighed. 'If you aren't in trouble, why do you need to leave us? Are you unhappy here?' This question brought on another bout of sobbing. 'How can I help you if you won't tell me what's troubling you,' Anne reasoned.

'I'm in love with David,' Sarah sobbed.

'You're in love with David. Does he know?' Anne asked.

'I don't know. Perhaps. He did something that suggested he might know but I couldn't be sure,' Sarah said in the longest coherent sentence she had uttered for a while.

'David is more than twice your age and he is very happily married, Sarah,' Anne said.

'I know, I know,' Sarah said passionately. 'You think I don't know that? It's killing me.'

'What makes you think you love him, Sarah?'

'He's in my every waking thought – I can't seem to focus on anything else. David is so much above every other man I have ever known, Mrs Mac. I don't think of him as older than me.'

'And loving him as you say you do, you can't stay here?'

'How can I?' Sarah asked through a sob.

'How long have you felt this way about David?' Anne asked.

'Some months. I've fought against it but it's no use. I love him, and that's all there is to it. I'm so miserable. David and Catriona have been so good to us for so many years now. If I did anything to spoil what they have going for them, I would never forgive myself. Yet when I see David walking towards me I want to run to him and throw my arms around him, and—'

'Oh, dear,' Anne murmured, 'we have got trouble, haven't we.'

'What am I going to say to David? What excuse can I give him for leaving? He's doing up the house for me and he's done so much to help me. I know he's depending on me to manage Strath Fillan and the stud. If I let him down how could he ever employ another woman?'

This brought on another burst of weeping, and Anne had a belated view of what she might have faced had she produced daughters.

'Ssh. You've done enough crying for now, Sarah,' Anne said. 'Wash your face and let's have some dinner. Kate will be over to check on us if we don't put in an appearance. You aren't the first woman to love an older, married man, and you certainly won't be the last. We'll have a good think about the best way to handle the situation.'

'You must see that I can't possibly stay?' Sarah said.

'No, you can't, I agree. We'll miss you, Sarah. You've become very close to us. I know that David is very pleased with you. He told me that you were as good as any man and more conscientious than he would have imagined possible. You could have had a home here for as long as you wanted it, Sarah,' Anne said.

'That's what makes me feel so wretched, Mrs Mac. Up until now I've never had any time for boys, and I have to fall in love with a married man! It's so unfair. I'll never find a place I love as much as I love Strath Fillan, or a boss like David.'

Later, after Sarah had settled her stomach with a little dinner on top of a small brandy, Anne briefed Kate on the dilemma facing Sarah. Between them, as Sarah listened, the two sisters calmly discussed her predicament. Kate agreed, regretfully, that Sarah couldn't stay, but finding an excuse for her to leave wasn't easy, and there was the matter of finding someone reliable to replace her. David could look after Strath Fillan in the short term and he and Moira and Catriona could do the mustering for crutching and shearing, but they would need a full-time person on hand to manage the stud side of things.

After a couple of hours neither Anne nor Kate could come up with a decent reason Sarah could use for leaving. What irritated Anne was that any reason Sarah could give would be a lie. A lie, if eventually unearthed by David, wouldn't sit well with him.

'The more I think about it, the more I'm convinced you should tell David the truth, Sarah,' Anne said at last. 'I really do. David is a very straight-from-the-shoulder man, just as his father was. It might be difficult for you to do that but it would be better than being dishonest. It's the most legitimate reason for leaving that you could have.'

'I think Anne's right, Sarah,' Kate agreed. 'You want to leave with respect, and being truthful is the only way to do it.'

'I don't think I could ever face David and tell him how I feel,' Sarah said.

'He won't eat you, Sarah. He would probably be flattered that a nice young girl like you should feel that way about him. My guess is that he would give you top marks for telling him the truth,' Kate said with a smile.

'I'll have to think about it,' Sarah said.

'Does your mother know how you feel about David?' Anne asked.

'No, I've managed to hide that from her. Mum and Catriona are very good friends so Mum will understand why I have to leave. She'll get a shock, but she will understand,' Sarah said.

Sarah went off to work next morning feeling more and more convinced that Anne was right. She wanted to leave with David's respect, and he wouldn't respect her if he discovered that she had lied to him. It took her a week to find the strength to eventually break the news to him. David had come down to Strath Fillan to deliver wool packs to the woolshed and to check on a couple of other matters. Sarah met him at the woolshed.

'Have you got a minute, Mr Mac? I need to talk to you,' she said.

'Has that ever been a problem, Sarah? Are you feeling okay? You look a bit peaky. When we get shearing out of the way, I want you to take a spell. You and Moira can shoot up to Yeppoon and have a couple of weeks there.'

As much as Sarah had steeled herself for this encounter, tears trickled down her cheeks. 'I can't, Mr Mac,' she sobbed.

'You can if I say so, Sarah,' he said firmly. 'What is it? Is there something I should know about?'

'I'm going to have to leave, Mr Mac,' Sarah choked out through her tears.

'Leave? Why do you want to leave? Aren't you happy here?' he asked.

'The happiest I could possibly be,' Sarah answered. 'I have to leave because I've fallen in love with you, Mr Mac. I'm in love with you and it's torturing me,' Sarah said.

This wasn't something David had expected. 'I see,' he said, deep in thought, 'but let's not do anything too hasty. You're almost one of the family.'

'I know, I know. Your mother said the same thing. But she agreed that I must leave.'

'You've discussed this with my mother?' he asked, and raised his eyebrows.

Sarah nodded, wiping the tears from her cheeks. 'She found me lying on my bed crying and she got it out of me,' Sarah said.

'Funny. Mum didn't say anything to me.'

'We agreed that the only thing I could do was tell you the truth. I didn't want to lie to you,' she said.

He looked at her and shook his head. 'Why me, Sarah? You're a young, very attractive girl with your whole life ahead of you. I'm middle-aged and I'm married. You could take your pick of a host of younger admirers.'

'The age is nothing. It's the fact that you're married that is the real barrier. That, plus the fact that you and your wife have been so good to Mum, Dianne and me. I could tell from that first day that Catriona had reservations about me working for you. What wife wants her husband running around with a young woman? If anything happened, it would destroy all that you've built up together over the years,' Sarah said.

'Nothing is going to happen. I've never put a hand on you, have I?' he asked.

'Don't you understand? If I stayed here, I would want something to happen,' Sarah almost shouted.

'Oh, Sarah, must it come to this? Quite apart from the fact that I like you a lot, I've built you into my plans for the future. I couldn't replace you.'

'You'll have to, Mr Mac,' she said quietly.

He held out his arms and she fell into them and cried against his shoulder. He bent and kissed her lustrous dark hair. 'You must understand that Cat is very dear to me. Cat has been the love of my life – I would never do anything to cause her distress. You must try to forget me, Sarah,' David said.

'I'll never forget you, Mr Mac,' she said.

'Nor I, you. When do you want to leave?' he asked as he stepped away from her.

'I don't *want* to leave – I *have* to leave,' she said. 'I need to go soon, but I don't want to leave you in the lurch,' she said.

'Now or in a month, what difference will it make? I can't replace you, Sarah – not a person with your skills and your attitude,' David said.

'I know I'm letting you down but please understand that I can't stay,' she said.

'I've accepted that. Go back to the cottage and pack your things. I'll send your money over with Cat. Do you want to keep Charlie?'

'Oh, I couldn't, Mr Mac. I don't know what I'll do next. Thanks awfully, but I think Charlie would be happier with you. He'll have sheep to work and he loves that,' Sarah said.

David watched the girl get into her utility and then drive away. He knew he was going to miss her.

When he went back to Catriona for lunch she saw that he was looking rather grim. 'Something up, darling?' After nearly thirty years she still called him darling.

'Are you doing anything this afternoon?' he asked, without answering her question.

'Not especially. Want me to go to town?'

'No, I want you to take a cheque over to Emily's. It's for Sarah. She resigned from High Peaks Pastoral Company this morning,' he said.

'She *what?*'

'She left this morning,' he repeated.

'Why, for goodness' sake. Did you have a row with her?'

'You couldn't have a row with Sarah, Cat. The girl told me she was in love with me and couldn't stay. Evidently Mum found her crying her eyes out in her room one night about a week ago. Sarah was in despair not only about that but about what excuse she could use to tell me she had to leave,' he said.

'Good heavens. This is something out of the blue,' Catriona said.

'Not exactly. Apparently Sarah has felt that way for some time. She said she had to go because she felt she had let us all down. I called in on Mum and told her that Sarah had gone. She told me that Sarah was distraught when she found her that night.'

'Funny. I sensed from the first day when Sarah came here and asked for the job that something like this might happen,' Catriona said.

'Ha. You probably thought I'd make a play for her, Sarah being young and rather good-looking.'

'David, how could you think such a thing?' Catriona asked sharply. 'If you must know I was worried Sarah would find you attractive.'

'I'm middle-aged and I'm happily married. Why would a young girl want me?' he asked.

'You're still a gorgeous, wonderful man in my eyes, and Susan says so too. I've watched the way Sarah looked at you. I'd say she's never met anyone like you. But Sarah's resignation will leave a big gap in the day-to-day running of things. Do you think we'll be able to manage?'

'I dare say we can. You and I and Moira can do the mustering. You and Moy can take sheep away while I look after things around the shed. We'll manage.'

After lunch Catriona drove over to Glengarry to deliver Sarah's cheque. Emily Matheson walked out to the gate to greet her and the two women embraced.

'Emily,' Catriona said.

'Catriona, I'm so sorry,' Emily apologised.

'Don't be, Em. These things happen. Girls will be girls. Sarah wouldn't be the only girl who's fancied David,' Catriona said.

'Sarah swears nothing happened between her and David,' Emily said, as they walked down the path.

'I know it didn't, Em. David would never cheat on me. I do know that he liked Sarah a great deal, both as a person and as an employee. We are all going to miss Sarah an awful lot. Is she here?'

'Yes, she is, Cariona. And very upset,' Emily said.

'I'd like to talk to her,' Catriona said.

Emily looked doubtful. 'Sarah may be too ashamed to face you, Catriona.'

'We've been friends, Emily. I don't want her avoiding me because of this business. I can understand her not coming to see me when she left and I want to tell Sarah that I bear no hard feelings towards her or anything like that,' Catriona said.

'That is very sweet of you, Catriona. I'm sure other women placed in your situation might not be so benevolent,' Emily said.

'Come now, Em. A young girl with no previous romantic interests has daily contact for two years with a lovely man like David. It was on the cards, Em. I give Sarah a lot of credit for leaving. Some girls would have stayed and—'

'I understand, Catriona. The pity of it is that Sarah loved being at High Peaks and she so much enjoyed looking after the stud business. Sarah loves thoroughbreds. It's a family failing,' Emily said with a brief smile.

'Hardly a failing, Emily. I have her cheque. Will you get her? Don't tell her it's me.'

When Sarah saw Catriona she stopped abruptly in

her tracks. Her eyes were puffy and red from crying, and wide with shock.

'Sarah,' Catriona said gently.

'Mrs Mac,' Sarah whispered.

'Come here, love,' Catriona said.

Sarah walked closer and Catriona put her arms around the girl's shoulders. Watching closely, Emily Matheson had never been prouder of Catriona than at this moment for had Catriona flown off the handle at her daughter, Emily would have understood and forgiven her.

'Oh, Mrs Mac, I'm so sorry,' Sarah sobbed. 'I was too ashamed to come and say goodbye.'

'Sssh, Sarah. I don't blame you for falling in love with David. I fell in love with him a long time ago and I was frustrated because I thought he didn't love me. We can't help our feelings. You did the right thing in leaving. Some girls would have stayed and made things worse. I foresaw something like this might happen when you came to us and asked for a job,' Catriona said.

'That's what makes me feel so awful,' Sarah said. 'You were all so good to me and made me feel at home and . . . well, *wanted*. I didn't want this to happen but it has. David is so much above every other man I ever met. His age didn't seem to make any difference to the way I felt. I'd live for him arriving at Strath Fillan . . .'

'Been there and done that, Sarah,' Catriona said. 'And I still feel the same way about the fellow. David is still the biggest thing in my life. I think, I hope, he feels the same way about me. Now, I've brought your cheque, Sarah. It's probably a little bit larger than you expected.'

Sarah looked at the cheque and her eyes widened. 'It's a lot larger than I expected,' she said.

'David said he added some for the holiday he told you to have before you told him you had to leave us,' Catriona said with a smile.

Sarah looked from the cheque to Catriona and then to her mother and her face crumpled. 'You see what he's like,' she said and turned and ran from the room.

Emily went to follow her and stopped. 'I'm afraid she does love him, Catriona. And rather a lot.'

Catriona nodded. 'Our hearts have a lot to answer for, Emily. Sarah needs to be kept busy in a change of scene. She's only young and she'll get over this. A nice young man would help but not just yet.'

'Can you manage without her? I mean, who will look after Strath Fillan? And haven't you a shearing coming up?'

'Moira and I will help David. We can do the mustering and transporting shorn sheep. David and the two of us can do a lot of the mustering at weekends. That's from the roughest places. Dooley Jacobs and his team go home every night. His wife looks after the lunches and smokos.'

'Will you need to put on someone to replace Sarah?' Emily asked.

'Now that, Emily dear, is the sixty-four-million-dollar question. It all depends on what our younger son decides to do with his life. We anticipate that

Angus will come back to High Peaks after he finishes at Longreach at the end of the year. David will be extremely disappointed if he doesn't. He had such hopes for Dougal and Angus. Moira is a wonderful help and makes up for the lack of interest her brothers have shown, but we know we can't count on her being there forever.'

'I suppose only time will tell, Catriona,' Emily responded sympathetically.

'If Angus comes home then we will manage. He is very good with horses and dogs. And while he's been known to be a bit wild and irresponsible, maybe he's got over that by now. Sarah really showed Angus up – she was always so conscientious and dependable – it upset David enormously that an outsider should be so much more reliable than his own flesh and blood.'

'And what about Dougal, Catriona? Has the tension eased between David and Dougal?' Emily asked.

'Even though he doesn't admit it, David is very proud of Dougal. He'd prefer to have him with us, but having a son a vet is the next best thing. And an honours vet into the bargain. He says that his father would have liked that,' Catriona said, and smiled. 'Look, I must be going, Em. Come and see us when you can. And do keep me in touch with how Sarah is coping. Say goodbye to her for me.'

Later, as he came in to shower before dinner, David wrapped his arms around his wife and looked at her. 'How did it go?' he asked.

'I talked to Sarah,' Catriona said.

'And?'

'I told her that I didn't blame her for falling in love with you,' she said.

'I doubted she'd talk to you,' he said.

'She didn't know I was there until she came into the room. Sarah is in quite a state over you, David.'

'Hmmm. That's why I suggested she leave. Better a clean break for a quick heal. I want you to know that I did absolutely nothing to encourage her, Cat.'

'Only by being you, David,' she said, and kissed him. 'Oh, and she was rather overwhelmed by the extra money.'

'She earnt it,' he said.

That brought to a conclusion Sarah Matheson's employment by the High Peaks Pastoral Company. But it wasn't the last they heard of Sarah.

The next two months were so busy that David and Catriona had very little time to think of anything but work. Eleven thousand sheep were shorn from Strath Fillan, Poitrel and High Peaks. While they were in the yards all sheep were drenched and, after shearing, treated for lice. They were now using a backliner spray to treat lice rather than the old plunge dips, which made the process much easier.

During shearing the manager of the company that handled most of the High Peaks Pastoral Company wool, Graham Bradley, called to see David. He stayed at High Peaks for one night and brought with him some interesting information. Graham was one of the most respected men in the Australian wool trade and David always listened very carefully to what he had to say.

'I've got a great mate who is the top buyer for one of the big buying firms, David. We went to school together. He tells me, very confidentially, that they're certain fine wool is going to jump pretty soon. My advice, for what it's worth, is that if you're still keen to buy a place in New England, you hop to it before fine wool goes up. If that happens, property prices there will jump too.'

David had confided to Graham that he had a notion to purchase a place that would produce super-fine wool that he could use as a promotion for his sheep stud.

'That's interesting,' David said. 'Have you got any idea when this lift in prices is likely to happen?'

'Probably from January on, when the good clips come onto the market,' Graham Bradley said. 'Of course, we've heard these rumours before and nothing has come of them but my mate seems fairly certain, and says they've got the orders now and price doesn't matter.'

David felt a stirring inside him. This was what he had always hoped for – what he had planned for. He reckoned that fine wool was the way to go and it looked as if he had been right.

'Three months,' he said, ticking off the time on his fingers. 'Not long, but maybe long enough.'

The following morning he rang Elders' property

manager, Joe Morton, and told him what he wanted. He told Joe that he had a week to find him a New England property and if he couldn't find one in that time, he would seek advice elsewhere. Joe was to fax him details of properties as soon as these became available. The first details came in the following afternoon. Joe knew David's mettle. He understood very clearly that he had a week to find a property to be assured of MacLeod business.

The decision to purchase a New England property was a bold decision but David had done his sums. Western Star's first foals had begun racing, and several had been extremely successful. One even looked like being a serious Melbourne Cup contender next year. David was going to be able to increase Western Star's stud fee considerably. Already there were many more enquiries from mares' owners than Western Star could possibly service. Over the next fifteen years David calculated that Western Star could earn at least four million dollars in stud fees. What the horse could earn per annum would pay off the New England property. And that was not taking into account the extra revenue they would have if wool prices lifted. On top of the eleven thousand sheep they were running on the three hill-country properties, there were another eight thousand or so sheep at Molonga and Wirrewarra. A year of good wool prices and he would have the latter properties paid off. This calculation didn't take into account any increase in cattle prices, which were still on the nose. As it happened, cattle prices increased greatly at about the same time as wool prices lifted.

This was the state of play as the year drew to a close. It had been a relatively tough time yet, thanks to careful management and the contributions of Davana and Western Star, David and Catriona had increased their property interests substantially. They were now poised to take advantage of the anticipated lift in wool prices.

Chapter Fourteen

The idea of acquiring a New England property consumed David. Wisely, Joe Morton was quick to act. After hanging up the phone in the office David burst into the kitchen where Catriona and Moira were washing up. 'We have to be at Tamworth at seven-thirty. Joe will pick us up at the Elders office. That all right?' he asked.

Moira did a quick calculation. 'We'd have to leave before four in the morning,' she said.

'That's right,' David agreed. 'We'll have a cuppa and a bit of toast before we leave. Maybe you could make up a thermos or two and something to eat and we'll stop just outside Tamworth.'

David didn't ask if they wanted to go; he naturally assumed they would want to, which pleased Moira, particularly, very much. The extent to which she had fitted into her father's plans sometimes amazed her and this had helped to cushion his disappointment at losing Sarah Matheson.

'Joe has two places for us to look at tomorrow. One I have got the details of and don't fancy much. The other place only came on the market yesterday and they don't have any printed material for it. It's owned by a woman whose husband died of cancer. Her two daughters have married and their husbands have good jobs in Sydney. The girls want her down there near them, so she's letting the family property go. It sounds like it could be promising.'

Anne thought David had taken leave of his senses to want to purchase yet another property. What he had put together was so remarkable that she could hardly believe it was her boy David who had done it. The boy who had worried the life out of her with the way he rode his ponies was now a millionaire, and still expanding. When would he be satisfied? Anne wondered if her son was taking on too much to handle. If Dougal hadn't left High Peaks it might be a different matter. As for Angus – well, nobody knew what he would do.

Kate understood perfectly why David wanted the New England property, just as she had understood why he had wanted Molonga and Wirrewarra, but Kate had worked very closely with David for years and thought differently to Anne. Although now frail, frailer than Anne who was older than her, Kate's brain was still working well. Everything David did had a certain logic. One operation dovetailed into another and the New England concept was no different.

David's prognosis of the two properties they were to inspect turned out to be correct. The first property they looked at was what David called a 'big, rough place'. It had a lot of acres, about half of which were fairly unproductive. The second place, known as Glenview, was at Walcha, and although it didn't match the acreage of the first place, virtually every part of the land was good grazing land. Most of the property had been supered in the past although, since her husband's death and lower wool prices, Mrs Baldwin had let a lot of the supering slip. The stock looked to be in fine condition and the improvements were in good order. The property was set in a pretty valley with a creek and there were some paddocks that had grown crop. The old homestead was solid and comfortable and there was a picturesque rose garden down one side.

'What a lovely place,' Moira said, casting her eyes over the country before her.

'It would be mighty cold in winter,' David said. 'You have to understand this country, Moy. It snows here at times. You can get caught with shorn sheep and lose them.'

From what David could see of the property, the land was a mix of basalt and granite. Granite grew wool with a fine tip, but basalt was more productive country. The sheep seemed to be in good condition – the wool was bright and fine and, according to Mrs Baldwin, it usually sold well. She told them of some of the prices they had received when her husband was alive. Obviously the property was capable of producing high-quality wool.

David sat on the fence of the sheep yards and looked

up and down the valley, and to where the hills met the sky. He reckoned that if he bought this property it would be the last one for him. He owned much more than he had ever dreamed of owning, and this place would clinch it. But was it the right place? David understood that you had to look after stock a lot more carefully in this country than in other places. Sheep worms had become resistant to some of the commonly used drenches and barber's pole worm was a real problem. However, there were new drenches and new strategies that were making a real difference to sheep production. He thought that if he bought the property he would like to give it a good spell. Super it all and give it a spell.

'You seen enough, David?' Joe Morton asked at his side.

'I've seen enough,' David answered.

'What do you reckon?'

'I'll take it,' David said.

Joe nodded. 'I reckon it's a good buy, David. If wool prices come good, this will be a cheap place. Well, if you've made up your mind, we'll go and tell Mrs Baldwin. She doesn't want to sell, but relying on other people to run the place isn't much chop.'

'Push it through, Joe. I mean that. I want delivery as soon as possible. Cut it back as much as you can.'

'I'll see what I can do, David. Do you know something I don't know?' Joe asked.

'Only a feeling, Joe,' David answered cautiously. 'I don't want this sale to fall through.' He hadn't quibbled at the price which, as Joe said, was very reasonable for the quality of the property. Quibbling would hold up the sale and he wanted the sale through before wool prices lifted.

David hadn't asked Catriona and Moira what they thought of the property, nor had they expected him to. They had absolute faith in his judgement. If David had not liked the place he would have rejected it just as quickly as he had made up his mind to purchase it. They realised he would have weighed up all the pros and cons before coming to a decision.

'Glenview would be a very nice property for a young married couple to begin on,' Moira said, when they were back in the car and on their way to Tamworth.

'Wouldn't it?' Catriona agreed.

'Yes, they could spend a lot of time keeping warm in bed over the winter,' David said.

'Dad!!!' Moira scolded.

Joe laughed. 'It's a mite cool up here in winter, no doubt about that,' he agreed.

So David acquired his New England property. He purchased it for a significantly lower price than it would have made twelve months down the track. He made what locals described as a radical decision when he de-stocked the property. Well, he didn't actually have to de-stock it – Mrs Baldwin sold all her stock and David didn't replace them with his own for some months.

It was a fairly satisfied David MacLeod who sat with his wife and daughter on their front verandah at High

Peaks on a Sunday afternoon in early December. And it was from here that he saw a white utility cross the ramp and approach the house. His first thought was that it was Sarah Matheson back to see them. It looked like her utility, but it was a dark-haired young man who got out first and went to the other side of the vehicle.

'It's Angus, our Angus!' David announced. 'And there's someone with him.'

Catriona and Moira both got up quickly and joined him. 'It's a girl,' Moira said.

'So it is,' Catriona added as she looked across at the couple with interest.

They opened the screen door and went down the steps to meet the newcomers. David stood back and let his wife and daughter go ahead.

'Mum,' Angus said, and hugged her. And then 'Moy,' and another hug.

'Angus, what a lovely surprise,' Catriona exclaimed.

David walked down to the utility to join them.

'Dad,' he said and they shook hands.

'Dad, this is Sue-Ellen. We want to get married.'

David surveyed the tall, striking, dark-haired girl at his side. 'Do you now? Is there a reason for this apparent rush to the altar?' David asked probingly.

Sue-Ellen had been told a lot about David and Catriona. She knew that David was a bush legend and millionaire and Catriona had been an outstanding equestrienne and beauty. As she looked at David, she saw a still handsome dark-haired man who was three or four inches taller than his son; a man with a commanding presence and the physique of a champion swimmer. Catriona had obviously been a beauty and was still very attractive with a terrific figure for her age. If she married Angus, as she had told him she would, these would be the two people who would most affect her future life. Angus had told her that his father could not be fooled by sweet talk and was a straight-from-the-shoulder man who respected honesty.

'In fact, until quite recently I wasn't sure that I wanted him – but once I'm persuaded there's no looking back, and we're desperate to start our life together.'

David laughed out loud. 'Good for you, Sue-Ellen. There were times when I wasn't sure that I wanted him. Come in and we'll all sit down and have a yak about everything. I suppose Angus did mention that he had a sister?'

'Many times. I believe you've been holding the fort here, Moira,' Sue-Ellen said with a smile.

'Trying to,' Moira laughed. 'The trouble is that Dad keeps buying properties and there's no one left here to run them!'

'Well, I'm home now so that should ease things a bit,' Angus announced, looking very happy with himself.

'Angus is a surprise packet, Sue-Ellen. He didn't tell us that he had someone special in his life – and you must certainly be a special girl!' Catriona said.

'I think he wanted to surprise you,' Sue-Ellen said.

'Well, he's achieved that,' Catriona agreed. 'I'll get

some smoko. I know how Angus can eat. He's like his father in that regard.'

'So you want to get married? When?' David asked, when they were sitting round the table together on the verandah drinking their tea.

Angus glanced at Sue-Ellen before answering. 'Well, er . . . that depends a bit on you, Dad.'

'On me? What's it got to do with me?' David asked.

'Because it depends on whether you want me here with you,' Angus replied.

David frowned. 'Why wouldn't I want you here, Angus? I thought the purpose of you going to Longreach was so you would be better equipped for the job here.'

'What Angus means is that he realises he behaved like a goat in the past and he has been wondering if you would hold that against him,' Sue-Ellen said. David looked at her and smiled. He liked this girl more and more. Sue-Ellen wasn't blinded by his son's looks and had her head well screwed on. He reckoned she could be the making of Angus.

'I won't dispute that Angus behaved like a goat, Sue-Ellen. I'd put it in stronger terms than that. If he's ready to settle down, I've got more than enough work for him to handle,' David said.

'Do you have somewhere we could live?' Sue-Ellen asked.

So practical, David thought. 'Do you like horses, Sue-Ellen?'

'Yes, I like horses, Mr MacLeod. I wouldn't say I could ride them as well as you people, but I can handle a horse well enough to get by.'

'She's modest as well as good-looking,' Angus joked.

David smiled, and continued. 'I can offer you the choice of two places, Sue-Ellen. I've had the homestead at Strath Fillan painted and renovated. I've also added extra horse yards and buildings. I'm standing a horse called Western Star at Strath Fillan. He won a lot of money for us when he was racing, and now his foals are turning out great. So there's a lot of demand for him as a sire and I've got a full book of mares for him. You and Angus can have the job of looking after Strath Fillan, which means that from time to time you'd be helping us here and at Poitrel. This probably doesn't make much sense to you, Sue-Ellen, but Angus can explain it to you. That's the first option.'

Sue-Ellen could not believe her ears. The choice of two properties to call home.

'The second option is Glenview, the place I've just purchased at Walcha. It's a nice little property but the winters are cold. I bought the place with the intention of growing some real super wool. It will be de-stocked for a few months. Angus hasn't seen it, but if it interests you we'll take a run up so you can give it the once-over,' David said.

He hadn't mentioned Glen Morrison because when Shaun Covers retired he wanted it for Moira, should she never marry. He hoped Angus would opt for Strath Fillan because he would be able to keep a close eye on him there. The boy was good with horses and should be able to do the job on his head.

'We can take a run down to Strath Fillan so you can see what you think of it, Sue-Ellen,' David said.

'It seems that if there is a house, we needn't delay getting married too long,' Sue-Ellen said.

'If there hadn't been a house we would have built you one, Sue-Ellen. The house part of it need never have concerned you. Is this what you want? I mean, do you want to live on the land?' David asked.

'Of course. That's why I went to Longreach. I also want to get involved in issues that affect women in the bush. I'm not a fire-breathing feminist but there are issues that I feel strongly about,' Sue-Ellen said.

'Sue-Ellen is a very good debater, Dad. She's very smart,' Angus said with obvious pride.

'Sssh, Angus. I'm not as smart as Angus, Mr MacLeod. He beat me in every subject. Mind you, he was a bit irresponsible when I first met him and I told him he'd have to shape up or forget me. I'm saying what I think because I don't want you to get the idea that I'm unaware of what an idiot Angus used to be. If he hadn't shaped up, I wouldn't be here. I'm aware that you have a lot of property and if I had wanted to trap Angus into marriage I could have done it a long time ago,' Sue-Ellen said.

'It seems to me that you might be the best thing

that's happened to Angus, Sue-Ellen. And I think you and I will get on just fine,' David said.

'Can Sue-Ellen stay here tonight?' Angus asked.

'She can stay as long as she wants to, Angus. Cat will look after that part of the business. Let's all pile in the car and we'll let you see Strath Fillan,' David said.

David was immensely relieved. It seemed to him that Angus had unconsciously chosen just the right kind of young woman to straighten him out. If Sue-Ellen couldn't do the job, nobody could. Angus might be smarter than Sue-Ellen, as the girl had said, but he reckoned she had a mile more commonsense.

When they arrived at Strath Fillan Sue-Ellen made straight for the stallion paddock where Western Star wheeled and plunged in equine splendour.

'God, what a beautiful horse,' she said with excitement. 'Is that Western Star?'

'That's him,' David said, with obvious pride.

'Angus has told me all about his mother and his sisters. Oh, and about the old man who gave you his mother. The mother of this fellow must have been a great mare,' Sue-Ellen said.

'She was, Sue-Ellen. We buried her at Poitrel, where she was foaled. I reckon old Wilf would have liked that. This fellow was her last foal, and she was very old when she had him.'

Strath Fillan looked very smart in its new paint. David had installed a new gas stove to augment the combustion stove and there was a new washing machine and refrigerator. Sue-Ellen went from room to room and then walked down the back steps and looked up at the tops.

'It is a very picturesque property,' she said.

'Is the house satisfactory? I mean, would you be happy to live here?' David asked.

'It will do very nicely,' Sue-Ellen answered.

'You should suspend judgement until you see Glenview, Sue-Ellen. It's a nice little place and Angus might feel happier there. He wouldn't have his father to contend with so often. However, it's up to you two. If you've seen enough we'll call in at Glen Morrison. Poitrel can wait for another day as I like to give Jean some notice before I take people there. Jean is nearly as old as Mum and I don't like to fuss – she always wants to put on a big feed and I don't want her to worry about that sort of thing any more,' David said.

'I know about Jean and her artist friend,' Sue-Ellen said.

David nodded. 'It seems you're fairly well acquainted with the situation here.'

'I asked a lot of questions,' she replied.

'I'm sure you did,' David said.

'I wasn't being nosey, Mr MacLeod. I wanted to find out a bit more about your family. This was after I agreed to marry Angus. I didn't want to seem an ignoramus when I came here. So he told me about your dogs and your horses and the sheep and the cattle. And he talked a lot about Moira and about

Dougal. I'm looking forward very much to seeing Glen Morrison.'

Sue-Ellen was very very impressed with Glen Morrison. She walked up and down the row of tethered cattle escorted by Shaun Covers, who positively glowed when Sue-Ellen praised them. She had been told that Shaun, who was only a few years younger than David's mother, had been with the MacLeods for many years. He had made noises several times about retiring but when David asked him if he wanted to leave, he always refused. 'Aw, I reckon I'll hang on a bit longer till you see how young Angus turns out,' he said.

Shaun was a lean old chap who cared for the MacLeod rams and bulls as if they were his own. As Moira was to tell her, 'Shaun looks after the sheep and cattle like a clucky hen looks after her chickens.'

From the bull shed they moved to the steer pens where several animals were being prepared for major shows. 'David keeps a check on the meat side of things,' Shaun explained. From this pen they walked across to the ram shed, where Sue-Ellen stood transfixed as she took in the quality of the sheep. After she had inspected the wool on several of the rams she told David they were the deepest rams she had ever seen. David was very impressed because this was one of the characteristics he had been striving to implant in his sheep.

'My Dad would love to see these rams,' she said. 'They are the best lot of rams I've ever seen. I've seen the odd top sheep but not in the number you've got here. Of course, I'm not a real expert like you, Mr MacLeod, or like Moira and Angus, but I won a couple of Junior Judging competitions before I went to Longreach. I know a good sheep when I see one. These are finer than our sheep.'

'I think fine is the way to go, Sue-Ellen,' David said.

As the day was drawing in he told her that they'd have a look at the rest of Glen Morrison next day.

Sue-Ellen agreed Glenview was a nice little property but apart from the challenge of producing some top-priced wool, to live there would be a bland existence. The real action centred about Strath Fillan and Glen Morrison, where there would always be a constant stream of visitors. This represented the hub of the whole MacLeod 'empire'. Sue-Ellen began to feel excited about becoming part of it because she would be involved in the AI sheep program.

Just outside Armidale the mobile phone pealed sharply. David had found this new technology very helpful. It enabled him to keep in touch with not only members of his family but also Shaun and Greg. Catriona took the call as David was driving. She listened intently before putting the phone down.

'It was Moira, darling. Kate has had a bad turn. Anne is with her at the hospital. They took her in by ambulance.'

Catriona watched her husband's face tighten. Kate was very special to David. She had come to

High Peaks at a very important time. They had needed help, financially and physically, and Kate had become a director and remained so ever since. She had been a second mother to David, and his trusty offsider, as well as a top stockperson and as good a campdrafter as most men involved in competitions. Over the years Kate had provided David with the encouragement and support he needed to expand the High Peaks Pastoral Company. It was arthritis that had forced her to give up managing Glen Morrison though she had battled on bravely. Younger than her sister by a couple of years, Kate had aged more in recent times.

Catriona had once been intimidated by Kate. She had been a sister at the Merriwa Hospital for some time while living at Poitrel and she had always seemed so ruthlessly efficient it was frightening. She ran Glen Morrison just as effortlessly, and instituted a store-room in which every item was classified and easily found. It was the talk of the district and many local landowners found an excuse to inspect Kate's handiwork.

Even in the narrow hospital bed Kate seemed very small and frail. Anne got up as David and Catriona came into the room. Angus and Sue-Ellen were in the small waiting room. David carried a second chair to Kate's bedside and took her small, fine-boned hand in his great paw. Kate's eyes flickered open and she gave him a weak smile.

'It looks like the last muster, Davie boy.'

'Don't talk like that, Kate. You can beat this little attack,' he said huskily.

'This isn't just a broken leg on Wallaby Rocks, David. The old bod has packed it in.' Her voice was weak and Catriona had to strain to hear Kate's words.

'You remember the day Wilf White came and told Andy and Anne he wanted you to have Poitrel?' Kate asked.

'Like it was yesterday, Kate.'

'I never did have to wallop you, David,' she said. He remembered that when Kate had become a director of the High Peaks Pastoral Company prior to his father leaving to shear in Queensland, Andrew had told him that his aunt could wallop him if he misbehaved.

'I'll bet you felt like it a few times,' he said.

'Never once, David. If I had had a son I would have wanted him to be just like you.'

David's eyes burned, as he fought back his tears.

'Thank you for making me your offsider. You made me very happy, and I feel very fulfilled. And thank you for the way you looked after me on Wallaby Rocks all those years go. I couldn't have wished for a better companion.'

She lapsed into silence for a few minutes and David and Catriona watched her anxiously. Eventually she spoke again, this time to Catriona.

'I wasn't so terrible, was I Catriona?'

'Only until I knew you better, Kate. You will always be special to me as well as to David and the children,' Catriona said.

'That is so comforting. Family is so important to me. Andy wanted a big family, and he finally got one. I loved Andy, Catriona. I would have had him like a shot had Anne passed him up. He and David . . . the best men I've ever known. You were right to wait for David, Catriona. Oh, David, I'm so tired.'

'Kate, don't talk. Angus wants to come in and see you. Will you see him?'

'Of course, Davie. Angus and his girl. Do you like her, Davie?'

'I think she will be just great for Angus, Kate.'

'Someone to take my place, Davie.'

'Nobody will ever take your place, Kate. Nobody, you hear?'

'I want you to put me up there on the knoll next to Andy, David. Me on one side and Anne on the other. Will you do that for me?'

'Whatever you want, Kate.'

'Thank you, Davie. Will you get Moira, and then Angus?' she said weakly.

When Kate next opened her eyes Moira was bent over her and tears were gliding down her cheeks.

'Don't cry, sweetheart. We all have to go sometime, and I've had a full, rewarding life. I want you to know I am so happy you've been such a wonderful daughter for Davie. He and I are so very proud of you,' Kate said, squeezing Moira's hand.

'Oh Kate, you've been such an inspiration to me for all of my life. Thank you for all you've done, all you've given, and all you've passed on to me. I can't bear to imagine the place without you,' Moira stammered.

'Hush, now, love. The land needs you, Moira. One day you'll be manager of Glen Morrison. I know you will. I'm so very tired, Moira. Can you get Angus for me?'

Angus sat with one hand clasped in his great-aunt's bony fingers and his other hand held tightly by his fiancée. 'Listen to me, Angus.'

'I'm listening, Aunt,' Angus said, tears welling in his eyes. He had grown up with this woman attending his cuts and sprains and she was something else. 'He's depending on you, Angus. Davie is depending on you, just as Andy is, from above. He's built up a great business for you. If you let him down, I'll come back and haunt you, Angus.'

'You would too, Aunt. I won't let Dad down. I know I've been an idiot at times but I'm over all that. I've got Sue-Ellen now.'

'So you have. Watch your Dad when Anne goes, Angus. He hit the depths of depression when we lost Andy. Only time Davie was ever depressed. Goodbye, Angus and Sue-Ellen. Much happiness with my family. Get them, please, Angus.'

Angus bent and kissed his great-aunt and then hurried from the room. The talking had tired her, and she looked much older when the others came back to stand beside her. When she opened her eyes she looked at David and gave what passed for a smile.

'You'll need another director for High Peaks, Davie.'

These were the last words Kate spoke. She died later surrounded by the love of her family. Once only she opened her eyes and looked at them and gave a tiny nod. David said later that it was a nod of approval.

Kate's passing was especially traumatic for Anne and David because she was so much part of High Peaks. Kate's never-failing good humour had helped to sustain them through tough times. There was no job she wouldn't tackle with a laugh. Sue-Ellen noted how much Kate's death had affected the family. She knew then if she had not known before that this was the kind of family she wanted to be part of, to belong to.

People came from near and far to farewell Kate Gilmour. One man who travelled a long way was Bruce McClymont, himself now old but still breeding the occasional litter of kelpies. Bruce had known Kate when she was at her irrepressible best and he never tired of talking about her rescue off Wallaby Rocks. So Bruce came to mourn with the people he loved and respected most in the whole country. Bruce reckoned that when it was his turn to leave the world of men and dogs, the MacLeods would come to see him off.

As is the strange way life works out, Sue-Ellen's coming was marked by Kate Gilmour's passing. Anne was now left alone in the big homestead. She resolutely refused to leave and told David she was quite capable of looking after herself. David insisted on employing a local woman to come one day a week to do the washing and general housework, and when Anne objected he said it was either that or she was to move in with himself, Catriona and Moira.

'You're very bossy to your old mother, David,' Anne objected.

'I want you here as long as possible, Mum. You're very special to me. There comes a time, Mum, and that time's now. It's outside help or you move in with us. That's unless you want to move into a nursing home,' he said.

'Perish the thought. All right, I'll have someone one day a week, and thank you,' Anne said.

David knew she would stay in the old homestead until the very end. His mother would never go into a nursing home. She would miss too much the visitors who called in to see her every day – if it wasn't one of her own family it would be a neighbour, or one of the Campbell clan.

Anne was always pleased to see Angus Campbell. Angus was a year or so older than Anne and he still had his driver's licence. Sometimes Angus would drive over on his own and other times he would come with Stuart or Carol. Angus came principally to see Catriona and to talk to David, who he now regarded as a great man.

Angus Campbell was failing in body but he was still alert mentally. Like a lot of old people he loved to reminisce. Despite the many improvements that had taken place in so many spheres, Angus still considered that the old days were hard to beat. Anne understood from conversations with Andrew that this was because just about everyone kowtowed to the big graziers. They had enormous pull with the old Country Party (now the National Party) and several pieces of legislation had been enacted to protect the interests of graziers and farmers. There was a difference between the two. The favourite reading matter for many graziers was the now defunct *Pastoral Review*. Angus had hundreds of copies of this magazine and regularly combed through them to refresh his memory about some fact or other. He knew that the old socio-economic lifestyle created by the nation's dependence on primary industry – principally wool – was fading fast. In many areas cotton had replaced merinos and a great variety of new crops had been introduced in the search for greater profitability; in effect, to stay on the land.

Angus reckoned he had seen the best of the old days. The fifties had been great because the Korean War precipitated a great increase in the price for merino wool and generated such prosperity that Australia had perhaps the highest living standards in the entire world. From that point on it had been all downhill with a huge increase in costs and many bad decisions made by incompetent politicians.

Against this backdrop, Angus viewed David Mac-Leod as really belonging to the old school because he had tried to do what many of the really successful graziers of the past had done. Certainly he had not been backward in using new technology but in his outlook he was an old-style grazier. David had a passion for top-quality stock and for a chain of properties that made up an integrated operation. By comparison his own son, Stuart, was a stick-in-the-mud. Stuart had been content to carry on with Inverlochy, which was big enough to generate a respectable living. He would not have worried about purchasing the Missen property only that Angus had pushed him into it. Angus reckoned that a fellow could never own too much land.

Although Angus had always had an inflated opinion of his own importance because of his breeding and the land that he owned, he had also come to recognise that Anne MacLeod held a position in the hearts and minds of the district's inhabitants that was far more intense than what was felt for him and for his late wife. There was nobody who would say a bad word about Anne. Anne was the mother of the district's greatest achiever, which was something, but it was what Anne had contributed in so many ways over her lifetime that was remembered by all and sundry. For Angus, seeking to remember the past, Anne was the last real link with so much that was splendid and unforgettable. She was, he now knew, the most worthwhile woman he had ever known.

Chapter Fifteen

Angus Campbell had made many attempts, all un-availing, to persuade David MacLeod to become involved in both local government and the United Farmers organisation. Stuart had replaced Angus in some positions, but David resolutely refused to become involved.

'Sorry, Angus, but no go. My first responsibility is to my family. I don't have time to devote to meetings. If I start doing that, the properties will suffer. I know someone has to do it but let it be those who are so inclined. Some people like that sort of thing, but I don't,' David told him.

Angus had a similar response when he tried to enrol David as a member of the National Party.'I don't have any time for politics and, for that matter, for politicians. If you look at New South Wales today, most of its problems – and our problems – stem from government decisions. If we had had the same rules and regulations that apply today back when the country was begun, how many would have bothered trying to set up properties? We made a country with hope, Angus, but governments are taking that away. I wouldn't waste my time getting involved in that scene. It would be like bashing my head against a brick wall,' David said adamantly.

Angus took his concerns to Anne who, he hoped, might be able to change her son's mind. He was greeted with resistance there because Anne supported David's point of view.

'David isn't that kind of person, Angus. He doesn't like working with committees. He makes all the decisions based on what he thinks is the right way to proceed. He may not be as overtly public-spirited as you have been, but David is actually supporting a lot of people. There's employees, mechanics, machinery dealers, shearers, shed hands, wool classers, accountants, transport companies, stock firms, bank employees, agricultural and veterinary companies, vets and all the local retailers plus, of course, insurance companies and local government bodies. There's probably more if one thinks about it.

'If the land is unviable, it affects all of those people and businesses. That's what politicians seem to forget. They're so busy squeezing more money from businesses they forget that if businesses and properties aren't profitable, they can't employ people. No wonder there are so many unemployed and no wonder companies are sourcing labour overseas. It's very sad, Angus,' Anne said.

Angus had to admit that what Anne said was true. He blamed the unions for a lot of what had happened but he knew deep down that governments were heavily at fault. There was very little vision today.

'Ah, Anne, life is so short. It doesn't seem any time since I came with Father to recover the body of David's grandfather from Yellow Rock. Andrew should have outlived me because he was a great cut of a man yet he killed himself with work. He should be here to see what David has done with his life,' Angus said remorsefully.

'Sometimes I think I would be just as pleased if we simply owned this place and Poitrel, Angus. I'd be happy to see David going to sheepdog trials and an occasional campdraft. It's all for his family, you know. David has the same thing in his head that Andy had. It's all about owning land. For what, Angus? Dougal has gone and will have his profession. He's lost to us. Moira is a great girl but if she marries she will probably go elsewhere. That leaves Angus. One boy. You can't tell me you need eight properties to keep one boy and his family. And will young Angus be able to manage them? Will he want to?'

Angus pondered over all Anne said but was quick to disagree. 'You can never have too much land. It isn't a matter of greed or snobbery or anything like that. In Australia you need a lot of land. The seasons are erratic and even in a good season you're never far from a bad one. We saw what happened when the blocks they gave to returned servicemen were too small. It's like what's happened with poultry and pigs. Years ago you could make a living with a thousand layers; you could do the same with fifty sows. It's a different story today. Costs are beating us, Anne. It's getting so that the smaller grain farmers can't afford to replace their machinery.'

'Yes Angus, so I understand,' Anne sympathised.

'I've talked to a lot of growers and the story is the same everywhere. There's places that used to support ten men, and the owner and his wife are running them alone now. No wonder the smaller towns are dying. We're producing the best wool and the best wheat in the whole damned world and the people who do it can't make a decent living,' Angus said, and shook his head.

Anne gave him a cup of tea and a plate of cake, which Angus took abstractedly.

'It's a damned poor outlook for young people, Anne. Those who get a taste of the big money in the cities won't ever come back to the land. Then there's this drug business, and there's no answer in drugs. Young people need to be kept occupied, Anne. Too much time on their hands and they get into trouble. No doubt about it. No drugs when we were young, Anne. How can you develop a country when they're on the dole and taking drugs?' Angus went on, sending himself into a spiral of depression.

Anne knew that what Angus said was right but he was talking from the perspective of a man who had been born with the proverbial silver spoon in his mouth. Campbell forebears had been landowners for centuries in Scotland, and had been wealthy enough to finance a younger son onto land in Australia. A canny breed, they had never looked back. Children born of broken marriages and children abused by step-parents were not so fortunate.

'Things have changed a lot, Anne,' Angus said between mouthfuls of cake. 'Do you know that at a meeting I was at, a fellow called me a dinosaur. The damned cheek of him. The chairman pulled him into gear – and so he should have. The fellow reckoned I was living in the past. Well, a lot of things were better in the past, a whole lot better. A man's word meant something then. You'd never get Andy to go back on his word,' Angus said.

'I feel much the same way about today's spelling,' Anne said with a smile. 'However, today's children have skills the children of our generation didn't have, Angus. Education standards have to reflect what the community as a whole needs to progress. Moira and Sarah Matheson came from school well able to handle computers and to set up computer programs. To me a computer is simply a glorified typewriter, except that I know it is much more than that. Change is inevitable and it is usually traumatic, Angus. My grandson and your namesake said to me one day that "you have to go with the flow". A silly statement perhaps, but probably very close to what I'm saying. We can't live in the past, Angus. Nobody can. We have moved from crystal sets to computers in my lifetime and yours. Who would wish to go back to crystal sets? I know you pine for the days of your youth because you're an autocratic old devil just like Old Angus was before you. People don't kowtow to you the way they used to and you don't like it,' Anne said. She could say things to Angus that other people wouldn't be game to.

Angus gave her a weak smile. 'No wonder David is like he is. With you for his mother and Andy for his father, he had to be something worthwhile. You've got a damned sharp brain, Anne. I suppose I was autocratic. It was the way I was brought up. Nobody argued with my father.'

There was a moment of silence before Angus spoke again. 'What's happening with Glenview? It looks as if young Angus will live at Strath Fillan so he won't be going there,' Angus said.

'It's been de-stocked and will be supered before David sends stock there. I understand that he intends going through all his sheep and sending the finest up there. As to who is going to look at it, I don't know. David is running out of managers. Shaun is overdue to retire but has been waiting to see how Angus shaped up. Dougal leaving was a big loss. Angus is very gifted with stock like his father and grandfather, and Sue-Ellen will be the making of him. Angus could solve some of David's problems. Moira is a darling and adores her father. She has restored David's faith in children, but he can't count on her staying with him,' Anne mused.

'Oh well, time will tell, Anne. I have to say that I'm full of admiration for what David has achieved. Winning the National Trial was one thing but what he's done since then has surpassed anything we could have imagined. I mean that sincerely. Andy would be very proud of him. I know that, Anne,' Angus said.

'Andy was always proud of David, Angus. David risked losing Catriona to win that trial for Andy. If Catriona had been a different kind of girl she would have told David to get lost. I must say I was very pleased that she didn't, because I wanted her for David from when she was just a small girl. Something told me that she was the girl for him. Andy told me I was silly, but I was right,' Anne said.

'I have to admit that you were, Anne. And didn't David give me the rounds of the kitchen when he came to me to get our approval to marry Catriona! Called me a damned snob when I wouldn't agree. Never had anyone talk to me like he did. Not before or since. Not much I could do about it, either. I was right to want the best for my daughter but wrong in my judgement of David. Told him so, too. We get on very well, Anne.'

'So David has told me. It takes a big man to admit that he was wrong, Angus. And you were wrong about David. He was absolutely the right man for Catriona. She knew he was and you didn't because you were looking at other values.'

'Granted. But Jane and I wanted the best for Catriona and her children. At that stage there were young men who could have given her a lot more than David had to offer. You can't blame us for wanting the best for her, Anne,' Angus said.

'I suppose not – but it's all water under the bridge now, Angus. Material benefits matter a lot to some people but I think love is important. The first time I saw Andy I knew he was the man for me. I knew it in my heart, Angus. It didn't matter that he wasn't A-one socially. Catriona felt the same way about David. I never once regretted marrying Andy or coming to High Peaks, and I still miss him after all these years,' Anne said with a sigh.

'I know how you feel – or I think I do. It's damned lonely without Jane, and you lost Kate as well as Andy. Nothing is the same when you're on your own. I've thought I might make a last trip to Scotland but without Jane it just wouldn't be the same. Old age is the very devil, Anne.'

Anne chuckled. 'It comes to all of us, Angus, and some don't get to live as long as we have. I'm thankful for every day I have because before too long I shall be gone. While one keeps reasonable health old age isn't so terrible. David and Catriona keep me well informed about what's going on and Moira calls almost every day. Now Angus is home, he comes too. I get taken to town and to the other properties so I'm not neglected. Then there are books and now and again, some good programs on television. I have some wonderful memories, Angus. Except for losing Andy so prematurely, it has been a good life. David has been a great joy for me. Yes, I would have liked more children, but that was not to be, and it was no good feeling down in the dumps about it. Other women have had worse misfortunes,' she said.

After Angus had left High Peaks he thought about what Anne had said. There was no woman he had ever met who he liked or respected more than Anne

MacLeod. There was no artifice or pretentiousness about Anne. She was essentially the same woman she had been when she first came to live at High Peaks – a woman of good sense, integrity and compassion. Her son was now one of the wealthiest and most respected graziers and stud breeders in Australia, and he could afford to put his mother into a seaside unit or whatever she desired, for that matter, yet she continued to live on in the old homestead that meant so much to her.

The next day Angus rang the travel agent he and Jane had used on their last trip overseas. He booked himself on a trip to London for the following month and then made several changes to his will.

Catriona was furious when her father told her that he was going overseas.

'It's insane,' she said forcefully. 'You aren't in any condition to travel, and certainly not on your own.'

'Nonsense. They look after you very well on the planes. I'll stay a night or two in London and then head up to Scotland. I want to see the relations for the last time and take in a dog trial or two. I'm rusting away here and Stuart is quite capable of managing everything.'

'It's madness, Dad,' Catriona pleaded. 'Can't you wait and take one of the family with you?'

'I don't want one of the young people with me,' Angus replied, indignant. 'They wouldn't be interested in where I'm going and what I want to see. I might find a good young border collie to bring back for Stuart. Be the last one, Catriona.'

Catriona sighed. Her father had always done his own thing and had never been answerable to anyone. Her mother had occasionally exerted a moderating influence but essentially her father was his own man, and would be until the day he died.

Catriona asked David to intercede with her father on her behalf but David shook his head. 'I'm sorry, Cat. I'd do anything for you, as you well know, but this is something I won't do. If Angus wants to go to Scotland, I say let him go – if it kills him, so be it. Your father has sentimental ties to his relations and to Scotland, and I can well understand why he would want to make this last trip.'

'You're no help to me, David,' Catriona said. 'I thought you would support me.'

'There's an old saying that a man has to do what a man has to do, Cat. Angus has had a good long life and maybe this is his final fling. I agree it would be good if someone was going with him but he's made it clear he doesn't want company. I say leave him be, sweetheart.'

David wondered whether his mother had had something to do with Angus's decision to make the trip. She had told him that Angus had spent a morning with her and that they had talked about a lot of things. He called in and gave her the news and asked whether Angus had given any intimation that he might go overseas.

'Angus told me that he would like to go,' Anne answered.

'I wondered if perhaps you might have said something to influence his decision to go,' David said.

Anne looked at him thoughtfully, while trying to resurrect the conversation she'd had with Angus. There was nothing she could recall that would have influenced Angus to go. Unless . . .

'Not specifically, David. I did say that I was thankful for each day that I lived because before long I would be gone from this house and this place. Or words to that effect,' Anne said.

'Ah,' he said.

'Why *ah*?' she asked.

'I think you may have unintentionally spurred Angus to action, maybe to shortcircuit him feeling sorry for being old and useless. Catriona is upset about Angus going and asked me to talk to him. I refused because if that's what Angus wants to do, let him do it. He wants to see his relations for one last time and maybe he'll buy a dog. He knows a lot more about sheepdogs than he used to. At the very least he'll feel he's doing something, which is more than he's doing over at Inverlochy.'

'You may be right, David. I certainly didn't tell him to make the trip but having made up his mind, Angus will take some dissuading,' Anne said with a smile.

Catriona tried to get Stuart on side but Stuart had talked with David and he agreed that if his father wanted to go, he should go. He was like a lost sheep without Jane, and too old to do any actual work.

So Stuart and Catriona took their father down to Sydney and saw him on the plane. David had intended to go but an urgent call from Greg Robertson sent him to Molonga instead. Jamie, the middle Robertson child, had come off a horse and had been badly knocked about. He'd been taken to Newcastle Hospital and Liz had gone with him. Greg was waiting to go to them as soon as David could get out there. Linda Barden was looking after the other two children. The devil of it was that Molonga was in the middle of crutching. So there was no hope of David going to Sydney to farewell Angus.

David called at Inverlochy on his way to Molonga. He explained why he couldn't accompany Catriona to Sydney. Angus understood David's predicament.

'Don't concern your head about it, David,' Angus said. 'These things happen. Stuart and Catriona will see me off. I suppose Catriona has told you that she's very unhappy about me going, and on my own.'

'She has, Angus. Cat tried to get me to persuade you not to go. I wouldn't be in that. If it should happen that it's too much for you and you cash in your chips, too bad. You could do that in bed here, which was how Dad died. I reckon that if you feel you want to go, you should go. I told Cat that if Angus Campbell didn't know what he was about, who did?' David said with a smile.

'That's the kind of thing I would expect from you, David. As it happens there are a couple of things I want to do before I die. I hope I get time to do them. That's besides finding another dog,' Angus said.

'You won't get another strong-eyed clapper, will you, Angus?'

'No, I won't, David. I'll be looking for something that works on its feet and covers well,' Angus said with a frosty smile.

'Good show, Angus. I'll look forward to seeing him,' David said.

'It could be a bitch this time. I've a notion to get a good bitch to put with Rob Roy,' Angus said.

'Dog or bitch, it wouldn't matter as long as the work and the nature is right. I hope you find what you want.'

'The Americans seem to be buying up a lot of the good borders now. Money is no object. I wouldn't mind seeing what the Yanks are doing with them. I believe the trial scene in the US is expanding rapidly. But maybe that's a bit optimistic on my part. I doubt I could cope with America now,' Angus said.

'I think you're better off tackling one continent at a time,' David agreed. 'You do what you want to do in Scotland and then come back to us.'

Angus nodded. 'If anything should happen to me, you'll keep an eye on the family, won't you? Stuart thinks a lot of you, David. He'd listen to you before anyone.'

'Of course, Angus, you have my word. And many thanks for your help over the years. Those Herefords you let me have made a big difference,' David said.

'You were a grand boy and you're an even grander man, David. I was a fool not to see it when you asked for Catriona. But we've been over that ground before. I'm full of admiration for what you've achieved and for the way you've lived your life. Catriona couldn't have a better man or husband by her side,' Angus said with some fanfare.

'Thank you. Coming from you that is something I won't forget in a hurry, Angus. Good trip – I hope you find what you're looking for,' David said, and shook hands with his father-in-law. Then he turned and walked away. Angus watched David's car until it was out of sight and then went back into his homestead.

The fact was that Angus had not been entirely open with David – or with anyone else for that matter – about his reasons for making this last trip to Scotland. It was true that he wanted to say goodbye to his relations and it was also true that he wanted to find a good border collie for Stuart. In so far as the dog part of his trip was concerned, what he really wanted was to try and find a good Rutherford-strain collie – he had read the history of the kelpie and it seemed that it was largely founded on Rutherford-strain collies from Sutherland. He had no idea whether the family remained to this day or if there were any Rutherford-strain dogs still being bred. Yet it would be a great coup if he could locate a dog of this family and send it back to Australia. Even David would probably acknowledge that this was an extraordinary feat.

But above and beyond these reasons for going was one that transcended all others. Angus was aware of a growing sense of his mortality. All his life he had been a great supporter of the church, like Old Angus before him – family, church and public duty weighed heavily with Angus Campbell. Although a Christian by belief, he held doubts about a life after death. He didn't see how eternal life could be possible, yet it was the major plank of the Christian faith. What Angus now sought was something that could convince him that eternal life existed.

Once, years earlier, he had been very moved when he visited the ruins of Glastonbury. Here, he felt, was a truly holy place. There was one other place he very much wanted to visit before he died. This was the island of Iona, the holy island near the island of Mull in the Inner Hebrides. On the trip he and Jane made with David and Catriona they had got as close to Iona as Oban. At the time the wind was blowing half a gale, forcing them to turn back and he had never made it to the legendary Iona.

A few days before Angus left the high country his parish minister came to see him. The Reverend James Currie had come to Australia from Scotland as a small boy. He had lost all but the occasional word of the Scottish vernacular. The Reverend Currie had a lot of time for Angus Campbell. He was not only a great benefactor of the church but a good man.

After they had been talking for a little while Angus asked him the question that had been uppermost in his mind since the minister arrived.

'Did you ever get to Iona, James?'

'No, Angus, I never did. Why?'

'I thought you might have gone there. I had it in

my head that Iona would be the place to visit for a man of the cloth,' Angus said.

The Reverend Currie looked at Angus and pondered a while before he spoke. 'Is something troubling you, Angus?' he asked shrewdly.

'As you've asked the question, the answer is yes. I'm concerned whether there is anything beyond all this,' and Angus waved one arm about to encompass the homestead and his lands.

'And you hope to find the answer on Iona? The scriptures aren't enough to convince you?' the minister asked.

'Maybe I'm looking to find something that will add to what the scriptures tell me,' Angus said. 'I felt something when I visited Glastonbury. I couldn't put a finger on it, yet it was there.'

'You have lived a good life, and you've been a good husband and father. On top of that you've been a pillar of the church and probably the most public-spirited citizen of the district. If there were more people like you upon whom I could depend, I would be a happy man. If I need help I go to you or David MacLeod and I have never been refused,' the minister said.

'Did you say David MacLeod?' Angus asked.

'I did.'

'I wasn't aware that David attended church,' Angus said, astonished. 'The only times I've ever seen him in a church have been at weddings and funerals.'

'True. David doesn't attend church, but he supports it. And very generously, Angus.'

'Well, I'll be damned,' Angus said, shaking his head.

'I doubt that you will be,' the Reverend Currie said.

'Sorry, James. It's just that so often you think you know someone and you find that you don't.'

'I would say that David MacLeod is one of the most Christian people I've known. As to this business of Iona I would say that if you believe you will find your answer there, you should certainly go.'

'I will do my best,' James. 'God willing, I shall get there,' Angus said.

'For my part I shall be interested to hear what you find on Iona. It would be trite to say to you that the Lord works in mysterious ways, but in my experience it is nevertheless true.'

'Perhaps you have put your finger on the heart of the matter,' Angus said. 'Perhaps the Lord is guiding me to Iona and perhaps He will reveal what it is I'm seeking. Anyway, that is where I am headed, James.'

Catriona had given Angus a handsome leather-covered diary, which she had asked him to use for his trip. While away at boarding school her father used to write to her two or three times a term. They were usually quite formal letters with unemotional accounts of successes gained by the Inverlochy cattle or a win by a Campbell horse at a picnic race meeting. Conversely, her mother's letters were quite bright and filled with news of her activities. So Catriona wasn't hopeful that her father would pen anything greatly interesting.

'Please write something in the diary every day, Daddy. Promise me you will,' she said.

'I'll try, Catriona,' he said.

Now he was about to leave them. He gripped Stuart's hand, and wished him a heartfelt farewell, and then turned towards Catriona. 'You've been a lovely daughter, Catriona. You've also been a lovely wife and mother. You've got the best man and husband a woman could have. I was wrong not to see that long ago. I'm very proud of you, Catriona.'

He held her close for a while and then turned and walked from the lounge. Catriona watched him with tears falling down her cheeks. She had a premonition she would never see her father again. He turned and waved and she tried to memorise how he looked that last time. There was the thick white hair above the slightly beaked nose and bushy eyebrows. Even now, stooped by age, there was the same eagle look that made her father stand out in any company. And then he was gone.

Reluctantly, Catriona turned and followed her brother from the lounge and the terminal. It was as if another page in her book of life had been turned. She had done her best to persuade her father not to go, and yet he hadn't heeded her. But Catriona then didn't know about Iona.

Chapter Sixteen

Back at High Peaks and Inverlochy, Angus's path was followed via his postcards and a few hastily written letters. Later, Catriona was to compile a fuller account of her father's pilgrimage to the land of his fathers.

Upon arrival in England, Angus stayed a couple of days in London before flying to Edinburgh. There he hired a campervan and stocked it with food before leaving for the west country. He travelled to Inveraray via Sterling and then by Aberfeldy and Kenmore along the north side of Loch Tay. He motored from there to the Breadalbane country where he stayed a night with a cousin. From here he travelled to Dalmally and thence on to Inveraray by the magnificent Loch Fyne. This was the shire of Argyll, hereditary home of the Campbells of Argyll. According to a postcard, Angus stayed two nights with his relations in Argyll, during which time he visited the old family burial ground at Kilmun.

Angus retraced his route and travelled back to

Dalmally and then by way of Taynuilt and Connel he came to the picturesque town of Oban. From Oban he crossed to the island of Mull and traversed it to reach Fionphort, at its western tip. Just across the Sound was Iona, the tiny island Angus reached by boat. What Catriona read of her father's stay on Iona was taken from the diary she had given him. Nothing he had ever written approached in any way what he wrote on this small island.

What was it about the island of Iona, only three-and-a-half miles long and one-and-a-half miles wide, that exerted an almost mystical influence on so phlegmatic a man as Angus Campbell? Certainly he was, and always had been, a regular churchgoer and a pillar of his church. He didn't go about promoting himself as a Christian, but he was a better Christian than most people. Something had happened to deepen his conviction when he visited Glastonbury, and Angus now sought reassurance that this really meant something. Other than visiting the Holy places in Israel, where better to find reassurance than Iona. For a Scot, Iona was the holiest place in the country, and a place of pilgrimage for hundreds of years. That it was in his own county, Argyllshire, added to the island's significance.

Iona, in the Inner Hebrides, was chosen by St Columba as the site of his first monastery. St Columba and some of his followers came to Iona from Ireland in AD 563. Iona became the early centre of Celtic Christianity – indeed, the cradle of Christianity for Scotland. The monastery St Columba founded was burned by marauding Danes in the ninth century, and a Benedictine monastery was established in 1203. The cathedral of St Mary, erected on the site of St Columba's first monastery, dates from about this period. The reverence held for this holy island is reflected in the fact that the cemetery of St Oran's Chapel, the island's most ancient building, contains the graves of something like fifty Scottish kings, including Duncan and Macbeth, and is also the burial site of kings of Ireland, France and Norway. The crosses and other remains bear witness to what was built here and its antiquity.

Angus's diary recorded that it was to the Cathedral Church that he went first. He seemed to have been befriended by a local fisherman or farmer, lived frugally on bread, fish and cheese, and sat for many hours in solitude at the holy places. It was all so unlike the Angus Campbell Catriona and David knew as to be almost unbelievable.

I am sitting beside a shell-strewn beach on the western side of Iona. A fresh breeze is blowing from the west, from the vast Atlantic Ocean above Ireland. Above me the gulls are wheeling and screaming and some are skimming the water for tiny fish.

As I sit here I ask myself why did St Columba come here? Why did he choose this small, poor island of all the islands he could have chosen? He would have come past Islay and Colonsay, and to the north of Iona there is Tiree and Coll and Eigg and Rum, not to mention Skye, Lewis and Harris. Was this the only island available to St Columba and his followers? Why not Mull, which lies across the Sound? Did the McLeans deny the Irish entry to Mull? Were the McLeans here at that time?

This must have been a very different coast when St Columba came to Iona. Intrepid Irish settlers had moved into Scotland, some through what is now Argyllshire and, perhaps, because of the respect held for monks in Ireland, where a burgeoning monastic system developed in the sixth century. This Irish monasticism led to missionaries going forth to Scotland, the north of England and central Europe. (You can see, Catriona, that I studied this matter before I left Inverlochy.) In those early years the Scottish kingdom was known as Dalriada. Some centuries later the Norsemen raided this coast. They were pagans, and had no respect for symbols of the Christian faith. They burned St Columba's monastery to the ground in the ninth century.

Although St Columba came to Iona following an internecine ecclesiastical dispute, I wondered whether he came here by chance or by some Divine guidance. I confess that it is the possibility of the latter that has drawn me to this holy place. As my days draw in, I feel the need to 'believe' in a stronger, fuller way.

A long time ago, nearly 2000 years ago, something extraordinary happened that caused men and women throughout the ages to pass on the message of Christianity. Many died for their belief, but there were always more to follow them and to take Christ's message throughout the world. Iona is special to me, Catriona, *because this is where Christianity began in Scotland; in my own shire of Argyll, which was Dalriada.*

Perhaps you will say that I am an old man in my dotage but this pilgrimage is important to me. I have the strange feeling that I was meant to come here. It isn't something I can put a finger on, but it is there. If it is only imagination and I find nothing, this trip shall not have been wasted because I feel very much at peace in this place. It is as if something or someone I cannot see is close to me.

As Catriona read through these evocative and personal passages she understood why her father had such a strong desire to travel to Iona.

There was a fine sea mist early and then it cleared and the sun shone between the clouds. I went to the old cemetery at St Oran's and walked from grave to grave. This was the burial place of kings, Catriona; a great many kings. They must have considered it a very special place to want to be buried here.

I walked further and came to an old cross, one of several left from the very early days. Then I walked up a slight rise and sat down. The sun had been obscured by a cloud and then the cloud passed and it shone again. There was a strange light in the sky. It was as if a golden ladder had reached down to the sea off Iona. Then there was a great rushing sound something similar to our willy-willies. When it passed there was absolute silence. Absolute. I got to my feet and looked about because I feared some sort of wind storm. But there was nothing like that. Then the golden ladder of light began to dissipate. When it had disappeared, and only then, I heard the gulls screaming and everything was as it had been. I felt curiously light and free of the tiredness that plagued me. I knew then that I had been right to come to this holy place.

I am leaving Iona now and I shall not see it again. There is something wonderful here and I urge you and David to visit Iona and to stand where I now stand, on the rise above the old cross, and find it for yourselves.

What Angus didn't write in the diary was that the pains in his chest were worrying him considerably. On the way to Iona he had called on a distant medico cousin who was also a Campbell. Ian Campbell had frowned when he tested his heart. 'It's not pills you'll be wanting but an operation, Angus.'

'Just give me something to stop the pains, Ian. I've another call I must make before I can think of an operation,' Angus said. Duncan, a cousin from Inveraray, had told Angus about a good young handler by Loch Etive, and Angus intended to pay him a visit on his return from Iona.

Ian Campbell shook his head. 'You should be going straight into hospital, I can't think what your family was about letting you come all this way in your condition.'

'They didn't know, Ian,' the old man confessed.

So Angus was now on his way to see Willie Cameron, who owned a small farm and was a rising sheepdog handler. A couple of centuries ago the Camerons and the Campbells had been bitter enemies, but all that was long ago.

It took Angus a little while to find Willie Cameron. He asked first at Inveresragen and was directed to the south side of the loch. He drove up a secondary road and found Willie close by the sleepy village of Glennoe. The north-west Highlands rose behind Willie's property, with Beinn Eunaich at the head of Glen Liver and Glen Noe.

Willie was a tall, lean man in his mid-thirties. He had inherited his farm and had been to an agricultural college before he took it over. His wife Jean was dark-haired like Willie, a buxom young woman with flashing brown eyes who seemed not at all overcome to be entertaining a landed gentleman from Australia. They talked beside a warm, crackling fire, the conversation mostly about dogs. Willie had seen several of the dogs purchased by Americans but he didn't yet have the reputation to attract international buyers. He didn't keep a big lot of sheep because he ran cattle, too.

By and by Angus and Willie left the comfort of the house and walked down to the barn where Willie kept his dogs. They were tied out on sunny days and kept inside in bad weather and at night. There was an old bitch, a retired male, a younger male and a leggy young bitch. Willie had won a trial or two with the younger male and obviously had a great regard for him. Glen was a fairly conventional type of border collie, black and white with medium coat and semi-erect ears. Willie

416

cast him around half-a-dozen black-faced ewes across the burn and brought them up by the house. Willie demonstrated his flank commands, which Glen executed perfectly. He was a clapper, going down naturally while he held his sheep. When Willie called him in, Glen showed solid force and moved the ewes to a gate. The dog did everything Willie asked of him but he did it in a mechanical kind of way.

'You've got nice handle on him, Willie,' Angus admired.

'Aye, he's not too bad.'

'The leggy bitch. What is she?' Angus asked.

'Ooch now, she's a bit lively yet. I've not had her at a trial, you ken,' Willie said.

They walked back to the outside of the barn where Angus had a long look at the young bitch. She was mostly black and tan with very little white about her, and not much coat either. One ear was erect, and one half so. It transpired that she was bred from Willie's old bitch Nan by a dog somewhere up by Ullapool. This was a noted dog in the area and being used because he wasn't related to Cap or any of the other J. M. Wilson dogs.

'She's hardly a typical border collie, Willie,' Angus suggested.

'The dog is the same colour, Mr Campbell.'

Angus began to get a little bit excited. Up north and almost black and tan. Could these be Rutherford-strain dogs?

'Do you know anything much about the breeding of the sire, Willie?' Angus asked.

'Only that the family has had the same dogs for a long time. They say that Ross can do anything with sheep. I saw him work and I can well believe it.'

'Will you let me see Meg work?' Angus asked.

'I've not put much command on her. I thought perhaps a litter would do her good. She's a wee bit fast and lively, as I said.'

'No matter. I'd like to see her work,' Angus said.

Willie and Angus walked down to the burn from where he cast Meg up a hill where half-a-dozen Cheviot-cross sheep were grazing. She brought them down a little fast because they were inclined to run more than the black-faced sheep Willie had used for Glen. Sheep and dog splashed across the burn and Meg covered them well. When they turned to break back she threw out nicely and blocked them. Angus felt his pulse quicken. At the gate of the yard Meg's holding ability was beautifully demonstrated. Angus thought of Clancy and his magic footwork. This bitch wasn't Clancy and might never be as good as him, but she was the most natural-moving border collie bitch he had ever seen. Her footwork was kelpie-like and, in fact, she worked more like a kelpie than a border collie.

'Can I see her pedigree, Willie?' Angus asked when Meg was tied up.

They went back to the house where Willie dug out Meg's pedigree and handed it to Angus. Many familiar names were featured on the dam's side but the dogs on the sire's line were unknown to him.

'Will you sell me the bitch, Willie?'

Willie was temporarily taken aback. He had expected Angus to ask for Glen and had been trying to come up with a price for him.

'Meg is not ready to trial. She's too lively yet,' Willie said.

'I don't want her for trial work. We've got trial dogs back home. Meg is the kind of bitch that would suit our conditions.' Angus said. The dopey sheep here didn't do the bitch justice. Angus could see what kind of bitch Meg would make in his range country. Moreover, he reckoned David would approve of this bitch.

'Well now, I would like to have her going a wee bit better but if you think she'll suit you, I'll let you have her,' Willie said.

'Put a price on her, Willie,' Angus said enthusiastically.

'She's not a finished dog, not much more than started really, so I couldn't put a big price on her,' Willie said.

'Forget price for the moment. I see you've got a vehicle. Would you be prepared to run her down to London — or at least to somewhere on the outskirts? The exporting firm I've used previously operates from there. I'll pay you well to do it.'

Willie looked at his wife who gave a slight nod. 'I could do that, Mr Campbell.'

Angus nodded. 'Thank you, I'll give you ten thousand dollars for Meg, which will include expenses. I'm not sure what the sterling conversion is but it's probably between four and five thousand pounds. Will that be satisfactory?'

Willie had been going to ask two thousand pounds for the bitch so he was rendered temporarily speechless. He had never thought to get anything like that price for a dog. He knew that Americans were paying prices of that order for class dogs but it was usually from well-established handlers.

'That would be very satisfactory, Mr Campbell.' He would have sold Glen for five thousand pounds but now he could keep Glen and have the cash into the bargain. The money for Meg would come in very handy.

Angus gave him all the details about the London exporters, drew a cheque on the Bank of Scotland and the two men shook hands on the deal. Willie assured him that Meg was fully vaccinated and he would worm her before he took her to London. They celebrated the deal with a lunch of roast mutton and potatoes, and shortly after Angus left for Loch Awe.

'Well, I never,' Willie said to Jean as they stood at the gate and watched the van drive up the road beside the burn.

'What a bonny man, Willie. An old man but a bonny old man. He sure knew what he wanted,' Jean Cameron observed.

'He certainly saw something in Meg that he liked, Jean,' Willie agreed.

Angus knew that he had paid more for Meg than she was probably worth right now. It was the most he had ever paid for a dog, but Meg would be the last and he reckoned Stuart would get a lot out of her. What did money matter now, anyway? This was a surprising admission for Angus because he had always been a canny man with a dollar. Stuart and Catriona wouldn't miss that amount of money. He would dearly like to know David's reaction when he saw Meg in action, but guessed it would be favourable.

The first pains of the day hit Angus about Loch Awe. He made a cup of tea and had a pill with it but there was a solid pain in his chest that he didn't like. He was making for the castle on Loch Fyne, and there his relations would look after him and get him into hospital for the operation. He drove on to the A819 that took him directly southwards to Inveraray. Through Inveraray Angus drove on to the A83. He was very tired. He knew that not far in to the left was Rob Roy's house, which he had never seen.

It was late in the evening when the big pain hit him. His chest felt as if it would explode. Calmly and methodically he ran the campervan off the road and with his last strength turned off the ignition and put on the brake. All around him was a white light, which illuminated the gathering darkness. Angus Hector Campbell's spirit had returned to the land of his forefathers.

It was the sharp-eyed local vet, Alisdair Grant, on an early-morning round to look at a sick cow, who spotted the figure slumped over the steering wheel. Alisdair opened the van's door and felt for a pulse. There was none. He called Inveraray police station on his mobile phone and then walked back to his car to await the law. The van and ambulance arrived inside the hour. The senior officer brought the diary across to Alisdair.

'Did you go through this?' he asked.

Alisdair shook his head. 'I touched nothing except the man's pulse. Then I called you.'

'This address in the front of the diary, it's a Mrs Catriona MacLeod, of High Peaks, Merriwa, New South Wales. There's a phone number too. Do you ken the mon?'

'No. That's an Australian address. I'd say by the van that he's an Australian tourist. An old tourist, but a tourist nevertheless,' Alisdair said.

The officer nodded. 'Very likely. But a tourist with a true Scottish name and travelling in Campbell country. A few phonecalls should sort this out. You can go to your sick cow now. We won't need you any more.'

The vet walked across to his car and then stopped and turned to look at the van. 'I think you'll find that he had a massive heart attack. I'm wondering if the mon came home to die,' he said.

The senior officer rubbed his jaw as he looked across to where the vet stood. 'A Campbell dead in Campbell country. It's a queer thing,' he agreed.

David, Catriona and Moira were having dinner back at High Peaks when the phone rang. David got up to answer it. Phonecalls during dinner were not unusual.

He received a lot of evening enquiries for rams and bulls and even now, for dogs and horses. People on the land were usually out all day and waited for the evening to make calls.

'Is that the right number for a Mrs Catriona MacLeod?' the Scottish voice enquired.

'It is. I'm her husband. Can I help you?' The sound of the Scottish accent had sent David's alarm bells ringing.

He listened carefully as the officer in Inveraray gave him the news about Angus. 'I'll tell her. Thank you. Give me your number so we can get back to you.'

He made a note of the number and then put the phone down.

'What is it, darling?' Catriona asked.

There was no easy way to break the news to Catriona gently. 'I'm sorry, Cat – it's not good news. Angus was found dead in his van just off the road beside Loch Fyne. He was on his way back to the castle. It appears that he had a heart attack.'

He went to her but she was very brave. 'I knew we would never see Daddy again.'

'Would you like me to ring Stuart?' he asked.

'It's my place to do that, darling,' she said calmly.

David and Moira stood beside her while she rang her brother and gave him the news. This was the prelude to a great deal of activity associated with bringing Angus Campbell home. While it would not have been inappropriate to bury Angus in Scotland, his will gave instructions that if he should die overseas, he was to be brought back and buried beside Jane. This was one of the changes to his will that Angus had made before he left Australia.

So the body of Angus Campbell was brought home and people came from near and far for his funeral. Some of the great men of the land helped to swell the church to overflowing. The Reverend James Currie conducted a polished and inspiring service. He told the mourners that Angus Campbell was a 'fine, Christian gentleman' and that he had made a pilgrimage to the holiest place in Scotland to reinforce his belief in God. This was the first time the family was made aware of why Angus had travelled to Iona, for at that stage they hadn't read his diary. When the diary finally arrived Catriona read it first before handing it to David. She took it across to Stuart who, like his sister and David, was very much surprised by the nature of its contents. Angus driving about in a van was surprising enough because he had usually stayed at good hotels or quality inns, but his pilgrimage to Iona and the way he had written about it left them baffled.

What they also discovered from his last diary entries was that Angus had bought a border collie bitch for Inverlochy and he thought she would surprise them. Subsequently the London exporters contacted Stuart to tell him that Meg was on the way to Australia and would be in quarantine for three months. There was no mention anywhere of what Angus had paid for the dog.

Catriona re-read the diary when it came back to her from Stuart, and this time she wept. She had thought she knew her father well, but he had surprised her so much at the end that she realised there was far more to him than she ever knew about.

Stuart went to Sydney to examine Meg in quarantine. Like his father, he was surprised by her appearance. She resembled a cross-kelpie more than a border collie. Stuart was even more surprised when he saw Meg work. He had asked David to come across for the occasion because David had been named a director of Inverlochy in the new will Angus had had drawn up just before he left Australia. Despite his personal liking for his brother-in-law, Stuart was a bit peeved that his father had seen fit to superimpose David onto the Inverlochy situation. Of course, Angus was a canny man and he had simply acted true to form. He knew that David was an exceptional manager and livestock judge and he had wanted him on hand as a kind of insurance.

Stuart had come on a lot as a sheepdog handler. Meg surprised him because she wasn't at all 'sticky' in eye and had a ton of go in her. In his father's diary Angus had explained that the bitch was only well started and would need more training, but he thought she was a 'natural'. He was sure David would agree.

Stuart worked Meg for David. He was conscious of the vast gulf in handling ability between himself and David and this had once worried him. It didn't so much now. There was nobody in the area who came up to David MacLeod as a handler. Stuart knew that he had improved a lot and that it had been David who was responsible for this improvement. He didn't know the commands for Meg anyway, and she had to do the job herself for the time being.

David was smiling broadly when Stuart walked off with Meg. 'You look pleased about something, David,' he said.

'The old chap got it right at the finish, Stuart. That bitch is a ripper. The best border collie bitch I've seen for a long time. I reckon that in two years I could give the National a big shake with her,' David said.

'Why don't you take her, David. I think Meg has too much dog in her for me,' Stuart offered.

'Rubbish. Work her down, Stuart. Work her down on flock work. Don't try and screw this bitch down with commands. That's the way a lot of good keen young kelpies have been ruined. I reckon maybe that's why the Scot let her go. Meg probably had too much go in her for those dopey sheep over there. I'll bet when Angus saw her he knew what I'd say about her. Meg will breed you a great line of dogs, Stuart. Never let her leave your hands,' David said.

David's ringing endorsement of Meg meant a lot to Stuart. Meg was his father's last present to him and that, too, was not something to be taken lightly.

'I'd like to know what Angus paid for this bitch,' David said. 'If you find out, would you let me know?'

'Well, in the Bank of Scotland statement there was a sum of £4000 made out in favour of a Willy Cameron, and it was Willy Cameron whose name is on the export papers. I couldn't believe Dad would give that much for a bitch that wasn't fully trained. It would be a fair price for a trained dog,' Stuart said.

'Angus knew what he was about, Stuart. I told him before he left not on any account to buy another strong-eyed clapper. Angus admired Clancy's work a lot and if you watch this bitch closely you'll see that she has some of his movements. Well, she's certainly not a typical border collie but she's a good bitch. Meg is something to remember Angus by, Stuart.'

David's words of advice were very sound because two years later Stuart won the local Open Trial with Meg. David's son Angus ran second with Charlie, the kelpie David had loaned Sarah Matheson to work. Moreover, Meg produced a great line of dogs, which were very much in demand. These dogs were part of the legacy Angus Campbell bequeathed to his family.

Chapter Seventeen

Catriona wrote regularly to Dougal during his sojourn at university in the United States. Dougal, however, wrote infrequently and his letters were usually brief and penned hastily because most of his time was spent studying or visiting horse studs. When he finished his course he didn't come back to Australia but spent six months at a leading horse clinic. From there he travelled to Britain, and by invitation spent another six months at a large animal practice in Wales. There followed trips to Ireland to inspect some of the United Kingdom's leading thoroughbred sires and finally, a trip to Deauville in France.

Dougal MacLeod had become not only a top vet but a walking encyclopaedia on thoroughbreds, thanks to his remarkable retentive memory. He had studied all the major breeding theories, from Bruce Lowe to Colonel Jean-Joseph Vuillier. The Lowe system was largely old hat now, but had once influenced some thoroughbred authorities. Vuillier sought to determine the relative importance of the blood of Eclipse and Herod. Some studs, such as the Aga Khan's, were influenced by the work of Vuillier. Under the Vuillier system there is an arithmetical formula for working out the 'dosage' of blood of any offspring.

The 'average' thoroughbred breeder would never study genetics at the level Dougal achieved, but the real cranks certainly did and the percentage of blood of certain horses was considered of great importance. It was the study of thoroughbred genetics that consumed Dougal's spare time. Dougal was a smart fellow and he realised that to be accepted as a top vet in Australia he had to know as much – or more – about thorough-bred genetics as his clients.

The passing of Angus Campbell coincided with the return of his prodigal grandson. Dougal arrived back at High Peaks without any fanfare, driving a new four-wheel-drive Toyota. He parked outside the old homestead and found Anne in her garden. Anne's first thought was that Andy had returned to her, Dougal was so much like him.

'Dougal, you're back,' she said, as Dougal embraced her. 'It's so wonderful to see you – Catriona didn't say a word!'

'I didn't tell anyone,' he said. 'I thought I'd surprise you all.'

'No doubt you will,' Anne said. 'Are you back for good?'

Dougal nodded. 'I may go overseas from time to

time but I've returned home to work here, Nanna.' He could see that his grandmother had aged since he left for the States, and it was good to see her again. But when she offered him a cup of tea he said that he had better pass for this time and go on down to see his parents. He would come again and have a meal with her.

Catriona was just as surprised to see him as Anne had been. 'Naughty, naughty, not letting us know you were coming, Dougal.' She, too, was struck by his resemblance to Andy.

'Where's Dad?' he asked, after their long hug. Dougal was thinking how trim and terrific his mother still looked for her age.

'With clients at Glen Morrison, Dougal. Are you home now? For good?' Catriona couldn't resist asking.

'I am,' he said.

'Have you any idea what you're going to do?' she asked.

'I'm thinking of opening a practice in Scone. I'm sure the horse capital of Australia could support a specialist horse vet. I've earned as good a lot of credentials as any vet in the country, and I understand thoroughbred genetics as well as anyone.'

'Scone isn't far away so that would be wonderful,' Catriona said. 'I'm so very proud of you, Dougal. Do you need some money to start up?' Catriona wanted to get the money business discussed before David came home. Yet although Dougal's defection still rankled, David was quite proud of what his son had achieved.

Catriona used to read him their son's letters and she noticed that he always seemed to listen intently. However, Catriona had doubts whether he would be a party to giving or lending Dougal money.

'I will need some financial assistance, Mum. I can probably get a decent loan from a bank,' Dougal said thoughtfully.

'Let me know what you need, Dougal,' Catriona answered.

'I'll be looking for a house with a few acres that I can use for horses. I'll have to build a surgery and stalls. There should be something suitable around Scone.'

They talked about his sojourn overseas and Catriona brought him up to date with the latest developments at home.

'Do you have a girlfriend, Dougal?' Catriona asked.

'I have no time for girls, Mum. I put all my time into studying. I didn't go overseas to have fun.'

'I realise that, but I thought you might have met someone special,' Catriona said, smiling.

'Well, I didn't. Plenty of time for ladies after I get set up here,' Dougal said. 'But speaking of new wives, how do you like Sue-Ellen, Mum?'

Catriona had sent Dougal the money for him to fly back for his brother's wedding but he hadn't stayed long and Angus and Sue-Ellen had left the night of their wedding.

'Sue-Ellen is strong and capable, and probably the best possible girl Angus could have, Dougal. She has great commonsense and is so very very practical. Angus

431

was fortunate to find her. Of course, he has settled down very well since he came back from Longreach. Angus and David are working well together. David is very pleased with Angus.'

'Where's Moira?' he asked.

'With David, Dougal.'

He nodded. It seemed nothing much had changed there. 'Does she have a boyfriend?' he asked.

'Not a one. There are plenty of would-be boyfriends but they look pipsqueaks after David,' Catriona said, and sighed. 'Your father has acquired a new property in New England called Glenview. We'll have to take you up there, Dougal – it's such a pretty place.'

Dougal wasn't greatly interested in properties, but he was impressed by the fact that his father now had eight of them.

'I thought you might like to come over to Scone with me, Mum. We can have a look around at what's on offer in the property line,' Dougal suggested.

'I'd enjoy that, Dougal,' Catriona said enthusiastically. 'When do you plan on going?'

'Oh, in the next day or two – no point wasting time. I've spent umpteen years studying and it's time to start making a living!' Dougal said.

Catriona thought silently that David would second that. He reckoned that Dougal should have begun working after he finished at university, but Dougal had had other ideas.

'You look great, Mum,' Dougal said by way of an afterthought.

'Thank you,' she said. Catriona liked to be told that she looked well. She didn't work out quite so strenuously these days and as a consequence had put on just a smidgin of weight. She considered that as David had withstood Sarah Matheson's appeal and her avowed love for him, she had very little to worry about now. She was currently a much happier and more relaxed woman.

'And how is Dad?' Dougal asked. He and his father had never really been matey but Dougal had enormous respect for what his father had achieved. He had great respect too for his father's ability and acumen where horses were concerned. Dougal knew that from a practical point of view his father could lose him. A case in point was the way that his father had looked after Western Star. For a man professing only a small interest in and knowledge of thoroughbreds, his handling of the stallion had been masterly. He had not pushed the horse into early racing, instead judging in some undefined fashion that Western Star needed time to mature. He had ridden Star until he was four and then raced him only lightly that year. At five the stallion carried all before him. There was no doubt about it, his father had a great talent with animals.

'Busy, as you would expect of a man with eight properties. We are short-handed but Angus is really pulling his weight, which is a big load off David's mind. Sue-Ellen has been the making of Angus. She and David both knew there was a lot of good in Angus even though he behaved like a clown at times,' Catriona said with a smile.

Dougal, who had never in his life behaved like a clown, nodded sagely. Angus had inherited their father's instinct for working with animals.

'I suppose that now you're back for good, you'll be looking for a nice young woman,' Catriona suggested with a smile.

'Slow down, Mum. I want to get my practice set up before I even think about marriage,' Dougal said.

He sat talking with his mother and drinking tea until his father and sister came home. Moira hugged him and his father shook hands with him, which was par for the course when the two men met.

The one regret Catriona had out of her marriage was that her husband and eldest child weren't close. Dougal had always been reserved in nature – even 'prickly' – and now, like a lot of vets, he had an air about him akin to arrogance. Knowledge sat on Dougal like a crown. For a young vet his technical knowledge of horses was awesome. There was probably no other vet of his age who knew more about equine problems than he did.

'In the US it's the age of the specialist vet,' he told them after dinner that evening. 'There's a joke over there that there's specialists for right and left eyes,' he said with the glimmer of a smile.

'And what is your speciality, Dougal?' Moira asked.

'Horses generally, and reproductive problems specifically,' he said firmly. 'Some mares have as many problems getting in foal as some women do getting pregnant. Sometimes it's just a simple problem and sometimes it's complex. If it should be the case with a valuable mare then it's worth spending a fair bit of money to get her right.'

Although Dougal didn't spell it out, they all knew he was probably referring to Starana, who had never produced a foal. At current prices, a Starana yearling would be worth a mint.

'There should be enough problem mares in this area to test your mettle. They call Scone the horse capital of Australia and I suppose there's justification for the reputation. There's horses of every kind in the general area of Scone. Some of the thoroughbred investments are staggering. That's even without what the Arabs have spent,' David said.

'That's what I reckon,' Dougal agreed, pleased to have this sign of support from his father.

'Well, you've got your first account, Dougal. There's a mare down at Strath Fillan that we haven't been able to get in foal. You had better have a look at her,' David said with a grin.

Dougal examined the mare and three months later she was in foal. He told his father that the mare had had an infection. He had cleared up the infection, let her go for one heat period and mated her the next. David was impressed, but Dougal told him that it had been a simple procedure.

With a bank loan and money from his mother, Dougal purchased a small property on the outskirts of Scone. There was a quite presentable house, some horse yards and a good water supply. Catriona assisted with some changes to the house and left Dougal to do all the rest. There was an office, a surgery, an operating theatre, recovery rooms and outside stables. This all cost a lot of money, but inside three years Dougal paid off the bank and his mother. Word of his skill spread throughout the district and beyond, and breeders were bringing him problem mares even from Queensland.

Emily Matheson considered that because of her friendship with Catriona and David's help over the years, she was honour-bound to use Dougal for her veterinary work at Glengarry. The first time he came was to sew up a mare that had cut herself on a loose sheet of iron on the corner of a shed. The second time was for a difficult foaling. This visit was memorable for two quite different reasons. The first was that Dougal recognised Starana in a paddock beside the house. The second was that he met Sarah Matheson again.

Sarah had tried working at different things since leaving High Peaks. She had been a governess, a shop assistant and a stud groom in turn, but never for very long. Being a stud groom was the closest she came to the life she had had at High Peaks, but when the manager mauled her she hit him with the handle of a pitchfork and left. She was advised she could sue the manager for damages but Sarah didn't want everyone to know what had happened.

Because she was at a loose end and because she was so good with horses, Dougal offered Sarah a job. She was to be his secretary. Sarah said she'd think about it.

Dougal hadn't made a good impression on her when she was at Strath Fillan, and Sarah considered him 'snooty' and arrogant. There was also the fact that he was David's son. Even now when she thought about David she was close to tears, although she hadn't spoken to him since she left High Peaks, and had only seen him at funerals.

Sarah pondered Dougal's offer for a week or so before deciding to accept it. She needed money and it seemed the best and most interesting job in sight. To get in on the ground floor of a new enterprise offered some kind of challenge.

It was a shrewd move on Dougal's part to employ Sarah Matheson. Before very long all the many young men who were nuts about horses knew that the new vet had a slashing good sort for a secretary. One way to meet her was to give the vet some business. Which they did. Consequently, Sarah met quite a number of young men, some from very good families. None of them, however, made a lasting impression on her because they just didn't stack up when compared with David MacLeod.

Sarah liked the job well enough and she was full of admiration for Dougal's skill as a vet. On the personal side, he lacked warmth and rarely offered praise and encouragement. David had often complimented her on a job well done. He had occasionally chipped her for doing something silly as he was entitled to but on these rare occasions it was done in such a manner that she took it in good part.

'I'd like to talk to your mother on Sunday morning, Sarah,' Dougal told her when she was about to leave the office one Friday afternoon. 'Will you ask her if about ten would be convenient?'

'I'll ask her,' Sarah said.

Dougal was almost always punctual. It took something quite extraordinary to make him late. 'I want to talk to you about Starana, Mrs Matheson,' Dougal began, without preamble.

'Oh, yes. But surely there isn't much to talk about, is there? Starana is an old mare now. She's our pet,' Emily said.

'I thought she was once *my* pet,' Dougal said. 'Dad let her go against my wishes.'

'Dougal, I'm sorry – I had no idea,' Emily said.

'It's past history now, Mrs Matheson. What I want to know is how hard did you try to get Starana in foal?'

'Does it matter? Starana is an old mare now, Dougal,' Emily said.

'It matters,' Dougal said patiently. 'You did try to get her in foal, didn't you?'

'Yes, of course. I didn't have much money to spend on service fees but we tried. I had less money for vets and it would have cost a lot to treat her. I got a quote and I just didn't have that kind of money, Dougal. I had to bring the girls home from boarding school after my husband's death, as you know.'

'I understand that it was a difficult time for you, Mrs Matheson, and you did the best you could to keep both your family and the property going under the circumstances. I suppose you realised that a Starana foal would have helped solve your financial problems,' Dougal said.

'There was certainly that glimmer of hope, but I thought that if David and Catriona weren't prepared to spend money to try and get her in foal, I'd be a fool to take the risk. I didn't have the money, anyway,' she said.

'Will you let me try and fix her?' Dougal asked.

'What, now? The mare is getting on in years and has never had a foal. For me to spend money on a mare of her age would be crazy,' Emily replied.

'You wouldn't have to spend money, Mrs Matheson. I'd be prepared to treat her for a third share of any progeny Starana might have,' Dougal offered.

Emily looked at him in amazement. 'Do you really think she could have a foal, even now?' she asked.

'It's possible. If the problem is what I think it could be, I can fix it. Then we can mate her and see what happens. If the stallion I'd mate her with is too expensive for you, I'll help you financially. We'd need a written agreement on the business,' Dougal said.

'I'll think about it and let you know, Dougal,' Emily said. She wouldn't make a decision until she had talked to David. David had given her the mare and he should be consulted. She decided not to say a word to Catriona this time because it would get back to Dougal that she had consulted his father.

Emily managed to get David on his own and outlined Dougal's proposition. 'What do you think I should do, David?' she asked.

439

David shrugged. 'What do you have to lose, Emily? Equine reproduction is Dougal's field and he just might be able to work a miracle with Starana. The odds are against it, but you never know. If he does get you a foal it could be worth a lot of money. Would you be happy to give Dougal a third share of that foal and any other foal she might produce? If this worries you, why not simply pay Dougal to treat her?'

'It could be a lot of money down the drain that I really can't afford, David.'

'I'll lend you the money, Emily,' David said.

'I couldn't accept money from you, David. It's very kind of you to offer but if we don't get a foal, I'd be worse off than I am now,' Emily said.

'Then accept Dougal's offer – you have nothing to lose. If by chance he can get Starana to produce a foal you'd have two-thirds ownership and that's two-thirds more than you have now. A foal from Starana could be worth half-a-million in today's market. Quite apart from what she did on the racetrack, Starana is a full sister to Western Star and he is one of the boom sires now. Their mother was a great mare so you've got a blend of the Ajana and Star Kingdom families in Starana,' David encouraged.

'The money would come in very handy, but I wouldn't feel right about taking two-thirds, David. You gave me the mare when I was at the lowest of tough times. If the miracle happens and we get a foal – or foals – you deserve a third of the share,' Emily said.

'Nonsense, Emily. If Starana had foaled after you got

her, there was no agreement we were to get anything. You've looked after her all these years so anything you get, and sadly it's odds-on you won't, is yours. You make your arrangements with Dougal and leave us right out of it,' David said firmly.

'You've been very good to us, David. I don't want you to think I'm ungrateful for all you've done. A share of a Starana foal would be some recompense,' she said.

'First get your foal. I appreciate your thanks but we don't need the money, Emily. Besides, I know how much you and Sarah want to breed top racehorses. Everybody needs a break. Maybe this will be the break that makes all the difference.'

Emily could quite understand why Sarah loved this big, generous man. Catriona had been fortunate to have him for her husband. If only, she thought. 'Well, thank you, David,' was all Emily could say.

'No thanks needed, Emily. Dougal fixed one of my mares. Maybe he'll be able to fix Starana. It's a long shot, but veterinary science has come a long way.'

From the way David spoke Emily sensed he didn't really have much conviction about a positive result. It would take a miracle to get a mare that had been barren for so long in foal. Emily felt much the same way but Dougal was supposed to be a veterinary genius and if he felt there was a chance, what did she have to lose?

When Emily told Dougal she was prepared to go ahead he nodded and handed her some papers to sign. He had had them drawn up by a solicitor because he felt they would be required. Emily read through the papers carefully and signed them. It was an agreement that in the event of Starana producing a live foal – or foals – Dougal James MacLeod was entitled to a third share of proceeds of sale(s) of such horses and/or a third share of race winnings, should the horse(s) be raced. In the event of said horses being raced he was to provide one third of the costs.

'There's one more thing, but I haven't put it into writing,' he said.

'What is it, Dougal?' Emily asked.

'If I get Starana in foal I want you to keep quiet about it. I don't want anyone to know about it, including Dad and Mum, until there's a live foal on the ground,' he said.

'If Catriona comes here, and she does visit, she'll know if Starana is in foal,' Emily said.

'Then hide Starana and tell Mum we're still trying,' Dougal said.

'I'll do my best, but first we have to get the foal,' Emily said.

'There's generally only so many problems that can prevent a mare going in foal. Some mares have what is called "silent heat", which can go unobserved for years but can be treated by "tracking" the mare's cycles. Alternatively, when a mare comes in heat regularly but doesn't get in foal there may be an infection, which can be treated with penicillin. Another possibility, although rare, is that a mare may have blocked oviducts, perhaps caused by an infection early in her life. The vet examines the uterus with a scope, finds the entrances to both oviducts and blows them out with compressed air to re-establish a pathway for the sperm to reach the egg. A pregnancy occurs in the oviduct, and the fertilised egg then rolls down into the uterus.' Dougal added that he had seen only one such case, which was in Kentucky.

'So what do you think it is in Starana's case?' Emily asked.

'I think she has blocked oviducts,' he said. '*If* we can open them up, she should go in foal, even now.'

Emily looked at him admiringly. 'I'm starting to believe you're some vet.'

Dougal smiled thinly. 'It's taken a lot of years, Mrs Matheson, and my father has never forgiven me for clearing out on him. This is one way I can prove myself to him. He gave up on Starana, but I never did.'

So that's what's really behind it, Emily thought. A son trying to justify himself to his father. This was the one field where Dougal outshone his sire and he was hell-bent on proving it.

They took Starana into Dougal's hospital and, just as he anticipated, he found both oviducts blocked. He cleared them and the next time Starana came on season, they bred her to a son of Sir Tristram. She got in foal immediately and Emily hugged Dougal when he gave her the news. Dougal insructed her to take the mare back home and put her in a paddock on her own, but where she could see other horses over the fence.

When either David or Catriona asked Dougal or Emily if they had made any progress with Starana they replied that they were still trying. David thought they'd be trying for a long time. In his opinion, a mare that had been barren for so long couldn't miraculously go in foal. But for all his great livestock knowledge, David MacLeod didn't know everything. Equine reproduction was a field for the specialist.

Meanwhile, to help get his son on his feet, David gave him as much veterinary work as he could. Although he was a horse specialist Dougal was a top vet, period. He did the sheep insemination and the embryo transplantation for his father's stud sheep and cattle while the horse work picked up. All of this work on the MacLeod stud sheep was carried out at Glen Morrison.

Dougal was all business. There was never any levity such as had been the case when Kate and Greg and Sarah had worked with David at Glen Morrison. Dougal was closer in nature to his grandfather than to his father. As David said to Catriona after one veterinary session with Dougal, 'if he smiled his face would crack'. It was all so serious that sometimes it was an ordeal to work with his elder son, which was such a contrast to working with Angus. There was always a degree of humour when young Angus worked with him because he told outrageous jokes and picked up bush gossip seemingly out of the air. Angus had become the most popular young man in the district. David wondered how a warm, sweet young woman like Sarah could put up with Dougal. He was brilliant, no doubt about that, but there was no empathy between himself and Dougal.

Anne, who was always perceptive from afar in these matters, and who had a soft spot for Dougal, said that the root cause of his lack of humour was his determination to justify himself to his father. Dougal understood very well that his father believed he had let him down; that all the work and worry associated with acquiring land for his children had not been justified in his case.

Of course, Anne was right. Dougal *did* want to justify himself to his father and he wanted to do it not only by demonstrating his professional skill but by using this skill to become a wealthy man like his father. Starana represented Dougal's first opportunity to put himself in possession of some real money. He could have treated the old mare for a substantial fee but that would have been chickenfeed to the financial rewards he could earn from the share of even one Starana foal. Dougal knew that Emily and Sarah were short of money and he also appreciated how much they wanted to breed top-class racehorses. He had no doubt that Emily would have consulted his father before agreeing to allow him to treat the mare. Dougal MacLeod was a shrewd fellow.

Some time later Emily Matheson rang Catriona and invited her and David for lunch. This happened a couple of times a year and Emily came to High Peaks on similar visits. Sarah was never present when David and Catriona went to visit Emily. On this occasion, Dougal was with Emily. After lunch Emily said that she had something to show them. They all walked down to the big shed Emily had long ago converted into a set of stables. One end of the shed had been set aside for a foaling room and was fitted with strip lighting. Emily opened the door into this brightly lit room and then stood to one side with Dougal. There in the middle of the room was Starana, and beside her there was a dark, spindly-legged foal, busy pushing under the old mare's belly.

David and Catriona looked from the foal to Emily and then to Dougal. It was impossible not to distinguish the look of triumph in his eyes. Starana had been his special horse and he had wanted his father to have her treated. Instead, David had let her go against his son's wishes. It had taken years but he had proved his point; he had won.

David, being the man he was, offered his hand to his son. 'Congratulations, Dougal. I didn't think it could be done.'

Dougal nodded. He didn't have to say anything. The proof of his skill was there in front of them.

'Emily,' Catriona said, as she embraced her long-time friend. She didn't have to say much either, because Emily would understand how pleased Catriona was for her. Starana's foal would make all the difference to Emily and Sarah. And if the mare could have this foal maybe she could have another one or two. This was a filly and its breeding value was stupendous. Filly or colt, it didn't matter. Starana had been a speed machine like her great dam and her brilliant full brother.

'Why on earth didn't you let on?' David asked later. He wasn't happy about being kept in the dark.

'There was always the risk that Starana would abort after being barren for so long,' Dougal answered. 'I didn't want to raise false hopes until there was a foal on the ground. I asked Mrs Matheson not to say anything.'

David nodded. That made sense. 'What was the mare's problem, Dougal?'

So Dougal explained about the blocked oviducts and how he had cleared them. He had taken a significant risk expending so much money on a service by the Sir Tristram horse but if there was only one Starana foal it had to be as well-bred as possible. The difference in the value of this filly and one by a cheaper sire was incalculable.

It was at that moment that David recognised Dougal had been right in his decision to become a vet. It had been a disappointment to David and he was still disappointed that his elder son had made a separate career, but he was a clever and gifted fellow, and he would undoubtedly build a great career in the veterinary field. If there had been a couple more sons Dougal's defection would not have affected him so badly, but to try and run eight properties with one son was a tall order.

A few weeks after showing his parents the product of his skill, Dougal asked Sarah Matheson to marry him. In typical Dougal fashion he didn't take her to dinner to pop the question but put it to her after she had finished work one evening. There had been no previous intimation of any affection for her on Dougal's part.

'Marry you, Dougal?' answered Sarah, stupefied.

'Yes, marry me, Sarah,' Dougal said calmly.

'Do you love me, Dougal?' Sarah asked.

'I like you, Sarah. You're very good with animals and we get on well. You're the only woman I've met I feel I could live with. I can offer you a satisfying, comfortable life, Sarah.'

'I couldn't give you an answer right now, Dougal,' Sarah said. She needed time to think about his proposition. Her first thought was that it was impossible. Dougal was a brilliant vet, but a fairly humourless man – too serious, and a bit too arrogant for her liking. Then there was the fact that as much as she tried to put it from her mind, she was still in love with Dougal's father. It was crazy, but there it was. How could she marry the son of the man she loved?

Driving home, Sarah tried to consider her options. Apart from loving David, her greatest passion was horses. She, like her mother, was imbued with the desire to produce great racehorses. If her father had lived and had continued to finance their dream, they would have done it, too. Instead, they had had to budget to survive on the property. And unlike her sister, Sarah couldn't face living anywhere but on a property. Now that they had a Starana foal, and perhaps another one or two in the future, there was every prospect that she and her mother would realise their dream of owning a horse that could win classic races.

Did she really need a man?

No, she decided she didn't. Not any man. Dougal was a good-living, clever vet and he would be a good provider, but what kind of marriage would it be? She had always been shy of men until she met David MacLeod. David was so much more man than any other male she had ever met that no one measured up to the standards he set. Even now she felt queer inside when she thought of David. But would she ever meet anyone like him? Would she meet anyone better than Dougal?

Catriona and Moira went to Sydney on one of their annual shopping expeditions, during which Catriona met up with some of her old school friends. Sarah knew this because her mother and Catriona talked on the phone virtually every week.

David took the call one evening and was surprised to hear it was Sarah.

'I need to talk to you, Mr Mac,' she said.

'Have you got a problem, Sarah?' he asked.

'Not exactly a problem, Mr Mac. I need some advice. Can I come and see you on Saturday afternoon?' Dougal had asked her to work the Saturday morning so she would get a sandwich and drive straight to High Peaks.

'All right, Sarah. I'll be here at two.'

He hoped his mother wouldn't ask him about Sarah but she was usually having a sleep after lunch. And it wasn't unusual to have visitors on a Saturday afternoon, anyway.

Sarah arrived a few minutes late, apologising. They sat on the front verandah where she had first asked him for a job those years ago. She was wearing a skirt and blouse rather than the jeans she had usually worn when she worked for him, and there was no doubt that she was a fine-looking young woman.

'You must think I've got a lot of cheek coming to you like this, but you're the only person who can help me, Mr Mac,' Sarah began.

'Surely not. You must have admirers galore, Sarah. Couldn't Dougal have helped you? He's a clever fellow,' David said.

Sarah tilted her head and smiled. 'Dougal has asked me to marry him, Mr Mac.'

'Good heavens, has he? Well, he could hardly do better than you, Sarah. I'd say he's made a very good choice.' But the thought of this sweet, warm young woman being married to his dour son filled him with foreboding. Dougal wasn't the man for Sarah.

Sarah got up and walked to the edge of the verandah. From there she had a view of the country below Yellow Rock and the mountain itself.

'I need to know something, Mr Mac. You know I love you. I still love you and I don't love Dougal. If there was no Catriona, would you marry me?'

Her question almost took his breath away. He realised it must have taken a lot of courage to ask it. And he knew he would have to answer it with equal candour.

'Why do you ask such a question, Sarah?'

'I don't know much about men and have never wanted to. I never liked a man until I met you. I used to see you watching me and I thought perhaps you liked me a bit more ... a bit more than as someone who simply worked for you. There was something in your eyes but maybe I was foolish thinking that because I knew how happily married you were, and are. But I have to know. One way or another, I have to know,' she said.

'What did you tell Dougal when he asked you to marry him?' he asked, without answering her question.

'I said I would have to think about it,' she said.

'You don't love him?'

'No, I don't love him. Dougal is a clever man, he has high principles and he'd be a good provider. A girl has to ask herself if she could do better,' she said with a wry smile.

'Dougal isn't the man for you, Sarah. He's my son and I agree with you that he is a clever vet and a good-living man but he isn't the right man for you. He's too full of himself and a little arrogant and cold. I would hate to think of all your warmth wasted on Dougal. You're great with animals and Dougal appreciates that. It sounds more like a business arrangement than a marriage. If you came for my advice, there you have it,' he said.

Sarah's eyes were wide and fixed on him. 'You haven't answered my question, Mr Mac,' she said.

'No, I haven't. I love Cat, and I've always loved her. Next to Cat you're the sweetest woman I've known, Sarah. I hated it when you left here and I've missed you every day since. But Cat is my wife, and there is no place for you in my future. This is as far as it goes, Sarah. I've answered your question but I would never cheat on Cat.'

She looked up at him through eyes wet with tears. 'I wouldn't expect you to,' she said. 'I've heard what I wanted to hear.'

'You surprise me, Sarah. I never imagined you would need my help to make up your mind over something like this. You had definite ideas and weren't backward in expressing them – that was one of the things I liked about you. It would be you that has to live with Dougal,' he said.

'Things aren't always simple, Mr Mac. It's a tough world for a woman on her own. Some day I'd like to have a child or two and it's not easy to do that on your own. I look at Dougal and I ask whether I could do better. He doesn't drink, doesn't smoke and works hard. He isn't . . . well, he isn't –'

'A bundle of laughs?' David suggested.

'That will do, Mr Mac. Dougal isn't a bundle of laughs but he's a good man. Then there's the fact that he's your son, which raises a different set of problems.'

'I understand what you're trying to say,' David said. 'Look here, Sarah, I'm not an expert where women are concerned but it seems to me that you're asking yourself whether you can live with Dougal even though you don't love him and he doesn't actually love you. What I think you have to ask yourself is whether you would prefer to live without him. I don't know how many times you can fall in love, but I'm willing to bet that you'll find another man you'll love with all your heart and he won't be a man twice as old as you like David MacLeod.'

'Perhaps,' she said, 'although I haven't much time for men generally – they don't impress me. I prefer horses.'

'Then stick to horses, Sarah. Now that you and Emily have a Starana filly, you'll have something really worthwhile to work on and a promising future.'

'I've dreamed of owning a horse that could win big races,' she said.

'That's fine. Everyone needs a dream. I once dreamt of winning the National sheepdog trials for my father. That dream became a reality when I won the trial. Yours could too, Sarah. Keep dreaming because life is a damned hard place without a few dreams.'

'The trouble is that you are in most of my dreams, Mr Mac,' she said.

David shook his head. 'You have to focus on something else, Sarah, or you'll mess up your life. I've been honest with you and you're a great girl, Sarah. I mean that sincerely. Any man who can claim your hand can consider himself very, very fortunate. But don't throw yourself away on someone who doesn't love you as much as you should be loved.'

He saw that she was close to tears again and wished to blazes that there was a simple solution to her problem.

'I knew I was right to come to you,' she said.

'So what will you do, Sarah?' he asked.

'Not marry Dougal,' she said.

'A very wise decision. A disloyal sentiment considering the subject in question is my son but with the regard I have for you, I can say nothing else,' he said.

'It is what I expected from you, Mr Mac. You are the most honest person I know. I had better leave now. I would so much like to call and see your mother but under the circumstances it would be better if I didn't. She might let it slip to Mrs Mac that I was here and that could cause trouble for you,' she said.

'I'll tell her anyway,' David said.

'You amaze me,' Sarah said. 'Will you tell her everything?'

'Not everything, but I'll certainly tell Cat that you came here for advice. I wouldn't want her to think I had tried to conceal the fact that you came here. We've always trusted each other and that's the way it has to be in a marriage,' he said.

She kissed his cheek. 'Thank you, thank you for everything,' she said.

'Good luck, Sarah. Good luck with whatever you do,' he replied, warmly. He watched her walk down the steps to her vehicle, and noted that she didn't turn back. Her old white utility had been exchanged for a newer model. He wished to blazes she was still working for him. It had been great working with her. Why did she have to fall in love with him and spoil everything? He wondered how differently he would have treated Sarah if he didn't have Cat.

News reached David a few weeks later that Sarah had left Dougal's employ and had accepted a position at a horse stud in Britain. Emily told him that she was working there to gain experience – as good an explanation for her departure as any, David reflected.

Catriona and Moira arrived back from Sydney with a couple of cases of new clothes and accessories and full of accounts of the 'new' Sydney. For his part David couldn't care if he never saw Sydney again, or any capital city for that matter. Cities were tiresome, cold places and he confined his visits to Royal Show times and wool sales.

'Did you have many visitors, darling?' Catriona asked.

'Yes, any interesting ones, Dad?' Moira added.

They were having dessert on their first night back and catching up on the local news and gossip. 'A couple of reps, two ram buyers, a bull client and the fuel fellow. Oh, yes, and Sarah Matheson,' he said casually.

Catriona sat up straight and Moira's eyes became bright.

'Sarah Matheson. Sarah hasn't been here since she resigned,' Catriona said. She might as well have come straight out and said what she was thinking. Why did

Sarah come here while David was on his own? She would have known he was on his own because Emily knew that she and Moira were going to Sydney.

David knew precisely what his wife was thinking. 'Sarah came to me for some advice,' he said.

'What kind of advice, darling?' Catriona asked. The old alarm bells were ringing again.

'Dougal asked Sarah to marry him,' he said bluntly.

The two women looked at him in astonishment. This wasn't the answer they were expecting, and it had them stunned.

'Dougal asked Sarah to marry him?' Catriona repeated.

'That's right,' David said, and went on eating his dessert while the others watched him.

'What advice did Sarah want from you?' Catriona asked.

'Whether or not she should,' he said through the peaches and custard.

'What did you tell her?' Catriona asked.

'Well, Dougal doesn't actually love her and she doesn't love him so it would be a marriage of convenience rather than love. Dougal regards Sarah as an asset to his business and Sarah wonders if she would ever do any better than Dougal. She recognises that he's not a bundle of laughs but he's a good-living fellow who would be a good provider. She also wants a child or two later in life, and is wary of doing this on her own. I told her that the big question wasn't so much whether she could live with Dougal as whether she wanted to live without him,' he said.

'Good heavens,' Catriona said. Her husband's answer stunned her. Not because she found fault with it but because it was so sound.

'So what is Sarah going to do, Dad?' Moira asked.

'I have no idea, Moy,' he said. Sarah had told him that she wouldn't marry Dougal but at that stage he didn't know she had handed in her resignation and was going to the UK. He knew that Catriona would ring Emily posthaste to try and learn more.

'It's strange that Dougal didn't say anything to me,' Catriona said. She thought he might have let her know what he had in mind.

'Ah, well, that's our Dougal, isn't it?' David said with a wry smile.

'Do you approve of Dougal's offer, David?' Catriona asked.

'It's not for me to approve or disapprove, Cat,' David said in a side-stepping answer to her question. If he had been a totally one-eyed parent he would have responded by saying that he did because he reckoned that Dougal would never find a better woman than Sarah Matheson. But he reckoned that Sarah could find a more convivial partner than his son.

This was not the answer Catriona wanted and she let him know it. 'You must have an opinion one way or another. You aren't usually reticent on such matters – or any matter if it comes to that,' she said.

'I doubt that Dougal could do much better in a wife than Sarah Matheson, Cat,' he said.

'Hear, hear,' Moira said.

This was a very clever answer for a fellow who was supposed to be a dyed-in-the-wool bushie, and it left Catriona high and dry. She couldn't find a way to extract more than this from her husband, but she was far from satisfied that he had given her his honest opinion.

Catriona's view was reinforced a fortnight later when she learnt that Sarah had resigned from her son's practice and was off to the UK. She would have given anything to know just what advice or opinion David had tendered Sarah but whatever it was, she had turned Dougal down. Catriona's private view was that David had advised Sarah against marrying their son. It was the straight-from-the-shoulder kind of thing David would do. He was never less than honest and sometimes honest to the point of bluntness.

Nor was Dougal much help to her because he didn't mention his proposal to Sarah, and Catriona couldn't very well bring it up without revealing how she knew of it. If she let on that Sarah had talked to David about the proposal this would only lead to more bitterness on Dougal's part. He would blame David for Sarah turning him down. So she and Moira agreed that it was better to say nothing. David, they knew, would certainly not refer to the matter. Catriona wasn't sure whether she should be happy or relieved. While it would be a relief to see Dougal happily married like his younger brother, whether Sarah was the best possible choice was another matter. Although Sarah was the daughter of one of Catriona's oldest friends, there wasn't much behind her in the way of property, which meant wealth. Like her parents, Catriona was of the view that a man as clever as her son could find better prospects for a partner than Sarah Matheson. More important was the fact that Catriona knew that Sarah had been in love with her husband and could still be in love with him for all she knew. If so, she wasn't the right woman for Dougal. But the inkling persisted that David had suggested to Sarah that Dougal wasn't the right man for her. That was a totally different kettle of fish.

By the time Sarah came home, Starana had foaled a second filly and was in foal again. Her mother had already refused a big offer for the first foal, which was being trained to race. This was the forerunner to a return to prosperity for Emily Matheson.

Over at High Peaks it wasn't horses that were a concern right now, but kelpies.

Chapter Eighteen

It could easily be assumed that with eight properties to run and a business to oversee, David MacLeod had no time at all for his kelpies. But this wasn't so. David continued to trial locally for some years until his stud stock and property interests became so demanding that he was unable to devote enough time to training his dogs. But with so much mountain country, dogs were an essential part of station life – sheep were just as difficult to muster as they had always been – and while David didn't attend trials as often as he once did, his dogs were still a big part of his life. David also kept Greg Robertson supplied with dogs, although in comparison to the hill-country properties, Molonga and Wirrewarra were relatively easy to muster.

David's kelpies were still full of the blood of Nap, Clancy and Belle. At Inverlochy David and Stuart had started a line of dogs with Meg, the imported collie Angus Campbell had purchased before he died. David recognised that you couldn't breed dogs too close and he liked the go of the collie bitch so much that he reckoned she was worth using as an outcross. He wanted to see what the progeny of this cross were like before he decided to use them.

The dogs were never neglected and David had built new pens to house them. When Kate had retired from Glen Morrison she asked if she could look after the dogs for him and she did this very well until not long before her death. When Moira came home from school she too looked after the dogs and their pups, and Catriona would also help at times.

David tried earnestly to keep abreast of developments in the sheepdog field. He noted the increase in popularity of yard-dog and utility trials while at the same time good three-sheep kelpies seemed to be on the decline. David knew that some of his current dogs had the potential to win three-sheep trials and it irked him that he hadn't sufficient time to do them justice. He had always tried to work at least one dog at the local trial to 'keep his hand in'. He didn't work a dog the year Angus Campbell won the Open with Rob Roy and he hadn't worked since then. Young Angus was working some of the dogs from High Peaks and he was a very good handler, but the old yearning was still there. When both Angus and Stuart Campbell told David that some handlers were saying he was finished, he was determined to have one final lash at the Merriwa Trial. It so happened that some of the locals decided to up the prize money and run a championship trial to coincide with Merriwa's annual wool promotion, the Festival of the Fleeces.

David had a female line going back to the great bitch Belle, and from a bitch of this line he had bred a black-and-tan dog he called Rip. The venerable but still fanatical breeder, Bruce McClymont, had tried to buy Rip when he saw him work. The dog was then not much above a year old but had so much natural ability Bruce fell in love with him and compared his work to Clancy's. David declined Bruce's offer for Rip because he felt that this was probably the best male dog he had owned for a long time – for one thing Rip had wonderful distance off his sheep, a rare and priceless trait in a trial dog. Most kelpies, and certainly most current kelpies, wanted to come onto sheep too quickly, which was devastating for three-sheep trial work; Rip could adjust his distance to suit the pace of sheep.

David knew that if he could find the time to educate Rip he was capable of winning any trial with him. He put fresh wethers into the old training paddock above the house and devoted time to working Rip either early in the morning or late in the evening. It was as if the years had peeled away and he was back training Clancy and Needle. Rip didn't have Clancy's rare hypnotic power over sheep but he did have his beautiful hold-and-drive footwork. Rip wouldn't move an inch more than he had to because he had the anticipation of the old MacLeod dogs and was always in position.

Further criticism of David came via Stuart Camp-bell, who told David people were saying he was one-eyed and out of date because of his attitude towards yard trials. Infuriated, David resolved to knock the damning rumours on the head quick smart. He had a brother to Rip that lacked his class but was a very useful dog. Spike had less eye than Rip and he would push up on a mob fairly well.

David got hold of a couple of videos of yard trials and studied how the top dogs and handlers worked, and how these trials were scored. Using these videos as his training aids, he began training Spike as a yard dog. Spike soon took to running over sheep and he had just enough eye to hold sheep in the bigger yards. When Bruce McClymont drove up to make another attempt to buy Rip he saw Spike and said he was a dog David would have no trouble selling for a tasty sum if he wanted to let him go. David reckoned that in the light of the sheep he had to handle, Spike was probably too useful to let go. He would be just about perfect for Greg Robertson, too.

Rip and Spike were coming along well, and David was pleased with their work. But on the land it's not uncommon for disaster to loom when things are looking good. However, that this should involve Moira took David completely by surprise because he believed his daughter was just about perfect. And whether 'disaster' is an accurate description for what almost happened to her could be disputed. Certainly David treated the matter as if it were an imminent catastrophe.

This near disaster involved Catriona's longtime best friend, Susan Cartwright, who became Susan Hunter when she married. Susan had finally had a child –

a daughter she named Karen. Karen was several years younger than Moira, and the apple of Susan's eye. But Susan's marriage was an unhappy one. She continued to play a lot of tennis, which helped to make up for what was lacking at home. Michael had put on weight because he drank too much, and intimacy had disappeared from their marriage long ago. When Michael found out Susan had been having an affair their marriage finally came to an end. Susan went to live in Tamworth and Karen went to school there.

Susan and Catriona's friendship had cooled over the years, but Susan came to tell Catriona that she and Michael had parted and that she was going to live in Tamworth, at least while Karen finished her schooling. Catriona shook her head because the mere thought of parting from David sent cold shivers through her bones.

'It's all right for you, Catriona. You've got a lovely man. If I had married David, things would have been different.' After all these years, Susan still spoke bitterly of lost opportunities with David.

'That was never on, Susan. David would never have married you. You wouldn't have changed, not even for David. You married Michael because you couldn't get David and you've never done the right thing by him. Half the time you've been away playing tennis. Did you have to be unfaithful to him?'

Susan stood and glared down at her old friend. 'I never thought I would hear you say such things, Catriona. Everything always fell into place for you, didn't it? You were always just that much prettier than me, just that much smarter, and David fell into your lap because you were neighbours. I'll bet you seduced him into bed to make sure you got him,' Susan said in a cold fury.

'I never did, and that's a rotten thing to say,' Catriona said.

'Don't deny that you offered to,' Susan countered.

Catriona had been about to deny that she had, but remembered that she had even offered to become pregnant so that she and David could be married. 'I was desperate to marry David. I admit that, but I loved him, Susan. David was the only man I ever wanted.'

'And you still have a great sex life. Michael started drinking and put on weight and he wouldn't touch me. I wasn't going to do without sex for the rest of my life. I'm far better off now – I'm my own boss. If Michael doesn't keep paying me I'll take half of what he has. He knows that. He wouldn't like to lose half his precious property,' Susan spat.

'You're not the girl I used to know,' Catriona said. 'If you had taken more interest in Michael's cattle and the property generally, maybe he wouldn't have started drinking, maybe he wouldn't have put on weight and maybe you wouldn't have had to sleep around to get what you want,' Catriona said.

'So it's all been my fault. That's what you're saying, isn't it? Typical!' Susan said, the pitch of her voice increasing by octaves.

'I'm not suggesting it's all been your fault but it seems to me that you have to shoulder a lot of the blame. The only thing you've got out of your marriage is Karen. If you don't set her some sort of example, heaven knows how she'll end up.' Catriona warned.

That was the final straw. 'You look after your family and I'll look after Karen,' Susan said, and stormed out of the house in a high temper. Her car almost side-swiped David's utility as she rounded the bend towards Inverlochy.

'What happened between you and Susan?' David asked his wife when he came into the house.

Catriona gave him a precis of their conversation and he whistled. 'You weren't very sympathetic,' he said.

'No, I wasn't. Susan keeps telling me that her life would have been so different if she had married you and not Michael. That's nonsense. Susan is Susan, and a leopard can't change its spots. Susan is rather self-centred. I'll amend that – Susan is extremely self-centred. Karen is the only person she has ever really cared about. Oh, she probably liked you well enough, David. The thing is that if she is playing about with men what kind of example is that for Karen? I have no patience with Susan these days. And after that flu I was feeling in no mood to listen to her,' Catriona said.

Life moved on for Susan in Tamworth. Still playing fine tennis, she met Gary Trainor, a handsome and very good doubles partner. Gary was a wool representative for one of the leading wool and stock firms and he had recently been posted to Tamworth. Susan was much older than Gary, but the pair quickly developed a part-nership in the bedroom as well as on the court. Susan was, in fact, in seventh heaven. She had her income, her tennis and a satisfying sex life with a man many years her junior.

Life for Susan was wonderful until Gary got an eyeful of Susan's eighteen-year-old daughter, Karen. Gary's big weakness was women – he simply couldn't resist them. And Karen, young, naive and yearning for romance, fell head over heels in love with Gary Trainor. When Karen threw herself at him, he took what she offered him without any thought of the consequences – let alone marriage.

In the course of his duties as wool rep Gary made his way to High Peaks to meet David MacLeod. David was at the top of his company's list of clients in the northern area. The previous wool rep had retired after a lifetime at the job, and David had got on with him very well. But Gary Trainor didn't appeal to David one little bit. He was, to use one of Anne's words, too 'smarmy'. A great-looking fellow and he dressed well, but full of bullshit. Granted he seemed to know what he was about, but that was only ever half the story with David MacLeod. If he didn't like a man, he didn't like him and that was that. He liked Gary Trainor even less when he saw the fox's eyes wander over his daughter.

In his pleasure at the way Moira had fitted into his life since coming home from boarding school, David had overlooked the fact that Moira was a woman, and she might one day behave like a woman and want more than he could offer her at High Peaks. And despite David's conviction to the contrary, Moira wasn't perfect. She was a fine judge of sheep and cattle, but underneath all of that Moira was a woman, with a woman's feelings and desires. She had been looked at, admired, many times, but never by a man as handsome as Gary Trainor.

Moira had her own vehicle and it wasn't long before she was driving to Tamworth to play tennis with Gary. Gary was clever with women, and quite the charmer. But his shenanigans could last only so long. He hadn't managed to seduce Moira to bed, which was his intention. Meanwhile, both Susan and Karen stood willing in the wings. Karen, a virgin until she threw herself at Gary, became pregnant. This news stunned Susan, and she demanded to know the name of the man who had put her daughter into this state. Karen told her it was Gary Trainor.

Susan looked at her in disbelief. 'You don't mean it?' she gasped. She was still involved with Gary and the thought that he had been going behind her back with her daughter was monstrous.

'Yes, I mean it, Mum,' Karen sobbed.

Susan was lost for words. She didn't know how to handle this problem. Her first thought was that Gary would have to marry Karen. But on reflection she knew that such a course posed problems. Gary obviously played about. He wasn't the kind of man she wanted to marry her only daughter.

Susan confronted Gary in a blazing row, which had as much effect as the proverbial water on a duck's back. For Gary, women were objects to be enjoyed, and he had enjoyed a lot of women. Susan got nowhere with him and she sensed that he was mocking her. One way or another she had to fix him. Meanwhile, she had a pregnant eighteen-year-old daughter who wanted to keep her baby.

It was the sight of Gary Trainor playing tennis with Moira MacLeod that provided the answer to Susan's dilemma. If Gary was dating Moira then it was odds on that he was either sleeping with her, or intended doing so. Susan reckoned that if David MacLeod knew what kind of man Gary really was, he would tear him to pieces. Susan was still furious with Catriona, but not so with David. The problem was how to get to him without Catriona being aware of it. The solution seemed to be to drive to Glen Morrison and to get Shaun Covers to ring David for her. The old chap was still there and she was sure he would oblige.

Susan's plan worked, and David met her in the bull shed at Glen Morrison, which might have seemed an inappropriate place to meet and to discuss personal matters, but that didn't matter. There, with red-and-white bulls chewing their cuds all about her, Susan poured out her story. And it seemed to her that she could feel David's anger building as she told it. He had not liked Gary Trainor from day one, but this sordid tale was worse than he had ever anticipated. If the bastard had so much as touched Moira, he vowed he would belt the tripe out of him. Trainor was a scoundrel and he deserved whatever he got. But first David needed to get more evidence to back up his case.

'Right, you leave Trainor to me, Susan. I'll deal with the mongrel. How can I help you? Are you short of money?' he asked.

David's compassion really broke Susan up. It was so David-like that even faced with a personal crisis he should try to help someone else. This was the David a lot of people didn't know. He was always spoken of as being tough and hard yet he had been helping people all his life. She still remembered how he had fought Stanley Masters and Wade Missen when they were at the little primary school at the foot of the Range.

'I'm all right, David. I don't know what Karen is going to do. She says she's going to keep the baby. I know being pregnant outside of marriage isn't the disgrace it used to be, but she hasn't begun to live and there she is with a baby inside her. Catriona was right, I've been a poor example for Karen,' Susan said.

David went back to High Peaks and put in a call from his mother's phone. He reckoned there was no point worrying Cat until he had all the facts. First of all David rang Lew Hooper and asked him to use his old police contacts to advise him on the best private detective agency in Sydney. Lew, an old man now but still sharp up top, called back in under an hour. David then wasted no time in calling the detective agency.

'I want you to give me a full rundown on a chap by the name of Gary Trainor, who is currently a wool representative with Premier Wool and Stock Pty Ltd in Tamworth. I understand he was based in Goulburn and that he is a very good tennis player. Can you do that?'

David listened while the voice at the other end told him details about the fees. 'If you can do it inside two days I'll double that fee,' he said. 'I want you to fax the details to my solicitors in Tamworth.' David then had a cup of tea with his mother and gave her the full story.

In two days he had all the background he needed on Gary Trainor. From his solicitors in Tamworth David rang Rohan Bridges, who was general manager of Premier Wool and Stock. Premier sold most of his wool and a big percentage of his stud stock – not to mention cast for age flock sheep.

'Rohan, this is David MacLeod,' David began.

Rohan Bridges sat up straight. He hadn't had more than a couple of phone calls from David MacLeod since he became general manager. Thanks to a tip from MacLeod he had once won a lot of money on Western Star. MacLeod was one of their most important clients.

'What can I do for you, David?' Bridges asked.

David didn't beat about the bush. 'You've got a wool rep in Tamworth by the name of Gary Trainor. He's no good, Rohan. Morally, he's no good. I want you to shift him right out of New South Wales, preferably move him to Western Australia. You'd be better off sacking the mongrel, but that's up to you.'

'What's he done, David?' Bridges asked.

'There is a detailed report on him from a detective agency and it's available from my solicitors in Tamworth. If you don't want to take my word, they'll send you this report. I've added a few things. Rohan, I want this man recalled immediately. If you don't do it you'll lose all my business . . . the wool clips, stud stock and the commercial sheep.'

Bridges was silent momentarily. While the company wouldn't go down the gurgler if it lost the MacLeod business it was the flow-on effect that was the greater concern. If David MacLeod removed all his business from Premier the perception would be that he was dissatisfied with their handling of his wool and stock. MacLeod was an icon with a large following – the impact of his withdrawal of business could be devastating.

'You had better send me that report, David,' Bridges said.

The report was faxed immediately and that same afternoon Gary Trainor was instructed to report to head office in Sydney the following day.

David drove home feeling little satisfaction. He had to face Moira and that was going to be far from pleasant. He found her at work on the computer. She was entering station accounts, and smiled up at him as he came and stood beside her. He put his hand on her shoulder as he spoke. 'Leave that for the moment, Moira. I need to talk to you.'

She followed him out to the front verandah where her mother was already seated in her usual cane chair. Moira took the chair beside her and David pulled up another chair so that he faced her.

'The first thing I want to say is that you won't be seeing Gary Trainor again,' he announced.

Moira's eyes immediately flashed fire. 'You can't really stop me, Dad,' she said.

'He's not worth a hair on your head, Moy,' he said, using his pet name for her.

'As far as you're concerned no man will ever be good enough for me. You simply want me here with you,' Moira answered, angry.

'That's nonsense, Moira. If the right fellow came along I'd give you both my blessing. The fact is that Gary Trainor is a scoundrel – a moral delinquent. I didn't like him the first day I met him and I was right. He's good-looking and he's a smooth talker, and that's how he charms women. You weren't the first he fooled, and you won't be the last.'

Catriona sensed that her husband was building up to something. He had something on Gary Trainor and he was going to reveal it. Moira was in for a shock.

'What do you mean fooled? I didn't sleep with him, if that's what you think,' Moira said forcefully.

'Thank heavens for that,' David said with real relief in his voice. 'Because Gary has been having an affair with Susan Hunter and, while carrying this on, has made her daughter, Karen, pregnant.'

He heard Catriona's sudden intake of breath and saw the shock that spread across Moira's face. 'He was sleeping with both of them. Not that either of them knew that. It seems that Karen threw herself at him because she developed a crush on him, and Susan was his doubles partner and turned to him for sex.'

'Poor Susan, and poor, poor Karen,' Catriona said softly.

'That's not all. Trainor is married. He's got a wife in the eastern suburbs of Sydney. Seems she's something of a free spirit too. Trainor goes back to see her every so often.'

Moira's face had turned white. Presently she got up and left them. They heard her close the door of her bedroom. Catriona looked at her husband and gave silent thanks for him. 'What else is there?'

'I should think Trainor will be recalled to Sydney immediately. I told Rohan Bridges that if he wasn't sent out of New South Wales they would lose all our business.'

'How did you find out about him?' Catriona asked.

'Susan met with me. She saw Trainor playing tennis with Moira and wanted to warn me about him. I employed a detective agency to check him out. Sure enough it turns out Trainor is a womaniser from way back. He got another girl into trouble and it was hushed up.'

'Susan met with you?'

'That's what I said, Cat. Susan is very upset, and I think you ought to contact her. Here's her number,' he said, and took a small scrap of paper from his shirt pocket and gave it to her. 'If she hadn't come to me, Moira might have ended up in the same boat as Karen.'

'Thank God for Susan's warning,' Catriona said.

'Amen,' David replied.

It took Moira a week before she could bring herself to talk to her father. She was so ashamed of herself for doubting his motives when he gave vent to his opinion of Gary Trainor that she wondered if things would ever be the same between them again. He didn't push her into a reconciliation but left her to her own devices.

It was Sunday after lunch when she finally came to him. He was reading the *Land* newspaper in his big chair in the lounge room and Moira sat herself on one arm and took the paper from him. He put out one great arm and she fell into his lap. She kissed his cheek and he returned her kiss.

'I'll never doubt you again, Dad,' she said softly. 'And thank you.'

'That's what fathers are for, Moy,' he said.

'How am I ever to find a husband like you?' she asked.

'I'm sure they're about, sweetheart – you just haven't crossed the right path yet. But don't be taken in by a fellow's looks. It's what he is that matters. By the way, one thing you said about me was true. I don't want to lose you. I'd be less than honest not to tell you that. After Cat, you've been the biggest thing in my life. I mean that. But I'd give you up for the right fellow. Of course, I'd prefer him to be part of the show here,' he said.

'For a tough, hard man you can be a real softie, Dad. Now, am I forgiven?' she asked.

'Nothing to forgive. You made a mistake, Moy, and

we all make mistakes. Nobody is perfect – nobody in the whole wide world. You wanted someone to love and you wanted to be loved. I'd forgotten that you're a woman. I tried to make you like a son and I was wrong,' he said.

'Can we do anything for Susan and Karen?' she asked.

'Susan asked me if I would speak to Roger Cartwright about them going back there. There's an overseer's cottage going to waste and it could be done up for them. Roger's opinion of his sister is less than flattering, but Susan is entitled to go back home and take Karen with her. It seems Karen wants to keep the baby, though why she would want any part of Gary Trainor beats me,' he said.

Moira shivered. It could have been me too, she thought. What an idiot to go for a fellow like that with a father like David. Gary was nothing like him. Nothing at all.

Catriona came in and found her daughter on her husband's lap. She had a momentary pang of something approaching jealousy that always assailed her when another woman seemed to be usurping her place.

'Friends again?' she asked brightly.

'Lovers,' Moira said, as the words of the TV commercial flashed into her mind. She laughed and threw both arms about her father's neck. He laughed too, and then picked her up and put her on her feet. She felt the strength of the man and blessed him for it. She knew what lengths her father would go to to protect her. It made her feel good to know that.

She simply wants love and affection, Catriona thought. Beneath the mannish clothes there is a woman who wants to be loved. She remembered how it had been for her when she wanted David so badly. There had been years when she wanted him to hold her and tell her he loved her. And she had had to wait for him while he pursued his dream of winning the National Sheepdog Trials for his father. Of course, it had been worth the wait, but frustrating at the time. Unfortunately there was nobody like David out there for Moira. There were young men, but they couldn't hold a candle to David. Just as other good women throughout the centuries had been attracted to rotten men, so Moira had turned to Gary Trainor – and it could have ruined her life.

Subsequently, it seemed to Catriona that the Gary Trainor episode drew Moira even closer to her father. Of all men on earth Moira knew that he was the most trustworthy and loved her most. Catriona often watched her husband and daughter walking hand-in-hand through the orchard up to the dogs or to saddle horses. They would ride away together to muster so perfectly content in each other's company that they could have been lovers.

It was Moira who was first to congratulate her father when he won the Maiden Yard Trial with Spike. This win silenced the critics who had labelled David MacLeod as one-eyed. David didn't consider the win of great importance because most of his attention was focused on the three-sheep trial with Rip the next day. He had won a Maiden Trial with Rip at a small event the previous month so the dog went straight into the Open.

In the first run of the Open the judge took a point off Rip for smelling the ground, where a bitch in season had urinated earlier in the morning. Bitches in season weren't permitted to work at the trial but sometimes a worker would have one there anyway. The long and short of it was that Rip scored ninety-nine and if he hadn't smelt the ground he would have scored the perfect 100. This equalled the score David had put up with Belle thirty years earlier.

Before the final of the Open David rubbed eucalyptus oil around Rip's nostrils. Rip didn't smell the ground this time. He ran an absolutely perfect round to score 100 points from the judges. Rip had dropped only one point over the two rounds. It was the best performance ever recorded at the Merriwa trials, and was never surpassed. That was the last time David MacLeod worked a dog at a sheepdog trial.

The first person David rang that night was Bruce McClymont. The old kelpie breeder was elated when David gave him the news of Rip's success. 'I'll bet that win silenced a few of your criticis,' Bruce said gleefully. 'And you won the Maiden Yard Trial, too. What a lark!'

In Bruce McClymont's world one man stood out on his own: that man was David MacLeod. If he hadn't met David his life wouldn't have been the same.

'And you won't sell him to me, David?' Bruce persisted.

'No, I won't, Bruce. Rip is too valuable for me to let go. But bring a couple of bitches up to him. You can have a couple of services to Rip,' David said.

'I'll take you up on that,' Bruce said. He knew that this was a concession on David's part as he didn't take outside bitches to his stud dogs. So he would be the only breeder to have litters by Rip, which was quite a coup.

Catriona and Moira knew that David had pushed himself hard to find time to get Rip and Spike in shape for the trial. He really didn't have time to trial dogs any more. There were too many other things for him to attend to and, like everyone else on the land, David was short-handed. He was here, there and everywhere – today, meeting ram or bull buyers; tomorrow, off to help Greg Robertson at Molonga or Wirrewarra. Angus and Sue-Ellen ran the horse side of things very efficiently but David went to Strath Fillan to help at shearing and crutching times.

Glenview didn't take up a lot of David's time, as the young chap who looked after it could do the drenching. David went up there at shearing time because he kept a close eye on the wool. It was the wool from Glenview that made the big money and added gloss to his sheep stud.

Glen Morrison and its management was David's major concern. Shaun Covers had hung on there well past retirement age and was now ready to leave. Glen Morrison was David's shop-window property and required a full-time manager. There were bulls, rams and steers in feed continuously, and a constant stream of buyers.

David didn't have a lot of options when it came to finding a replacement for Shaun Covers. He could move Angus and Sue-Ellen up to Glen Morrison, but if he did that he would need someone else to look after Strath Fillan and the mares that came to be serviced by Western Star. This was an important and profitable part of the overall MacLeod operation, and Angus and Sue-Ellen were doing a great job. Alternatively, he could bring Greg back to the high country and give him the manager's job at Glen Morrison. This would mean putting on an outsider to manage Molonga and Wirrewarra. In the long term David had plans for Tim Barden in that job, but for the time being Tim was at college.

David had discussed the matter with Catriona who then discussed it with Moira. Moira decided it was now up to her to relieve her father of some of the responsibility of running the eight properties. Kate had looked after Glen Morrison and so could she. Kate had been a role model for Moira.

'Dad,' she said to her father over dinner, 'what about letting me look after Glen Morrison for you? It's time I got out from under your feet here.

'You mean live there on your own?' David asked in surprise.

Moira nodded. 'Kate did, so why couldn't I? You're there nearly every day and Lew isn't far away. There are clients there all the time, so it's never lonely.'

'Except at night,' David said. 'A young woman alone at night. Is that what you want?'

'I wouldn't be frightened, Dad. And it seems to me that it's about time I really pulled my weight and took some of the responsibility off your shoulders. You can't go on forever looking after everything, and I'm the obvious choice. I've looked after the place when Shaun has been on holidays so it isn't as if I can't handle it,' Moira said.

David knew that what his daughter said made sense. If she had married he would have lost her. This way he would still see her virtually every day and he knew she would do a great job – Moira knew stud sheep and cattle as well as any man, and his clients would love her.

'You've got the job,' he said.

'Thank you, Dad.' She knew it would be a wrench to leave High Peaks, but it was her place to do it. It was as simple as that. Dougal had his profession and his own life and she was next in line. Her father had trained her to be a judge of sheep and cattle and managing Glen Morrison was the way she could help him most. If a suitable knight in shining armour came along, well and good. If he didn't, too bad.

So Shaun Covers retired and Moira took his place.

The large photograph of Aunt Kate in the lounge room of the homestead, which Shaun had never removed, reminded Moira that she was the second woman to look after the sweeping property. Kate held a special place in everyone's memory – particularly her father's – but now Kate was gone Moira had to prove that she could do the job.

For his part, David had no doubt that his daughter could manage Glen Morrison. She wasn't yet the stockperson Kate had been but she was a better judge of stud stock. Kate, in her lifetime, could rise to every challenge on the property. She could shoe a horse as well as anyone, and was unrivalled looking after ewes and cows in trouble birthing. Moira hadn't shown any great willingness to put her arm up a cow's backside, but of course Kate had been a theatre sister before she moved to Merriwa, so that sort of thing was second nature to her.

What appealed to David was that Moira was so keen to shoulder some of the responsibility for running High Peaks Pastoral Company. If the properties were to be retained in future it would be up to Moira and Angus to look after them. That was why he had to let her manage Glen Morrison – to prepare her for what tomorrow held. Life was short and in twenty or so years, if he lived that long, his useful life would be as good as over. He wondered sometimes if it was worthwhile carrying on given all the problems, natural and man-made, that one had to worry about. It was the love of the land and good stock that motivated him to carry on. He knew that some would advise that it would be better sense to sell up everything and invest the lot. But what would he do? And where would that leave Moira and Angus? His father had worked himself into an early grave to build a future on the land for him. To throw it all away now would be an act of pure bastardry. David couldn't do it. He couldn't deny, though, that he hadn't thought about it, because he had had a gutful of useless politicians who had no vision and who thought only of what they could do to keep themselves in power at the next election. And then he told himself that he was foolish because he had a great operation all up and it was still paying its way.

Secretly, Catriona was pleased that Moira had moved to Glen Morrison because it meant she had David to herself now, and together they had privacy. Moira was old enough to look after herself, and she would manage quite well in the big Glen Morrison homestead. It was David who was her main concern, and in the years left to her she wanted as much of him as she could get. The young people had their own lives to live. It was time they took over so she and David could enjoy more holidays and maybe another trip overseas. She would like to visit the place where her father had died and go to Iona, the place that had affected him so deeply. A life didn't take long to pass. David had amassed enough to pass on to his family, and it was time he eased up. Or so she thought.

David always reckoned that when things were going smoothly, sure as blazes trouble of some kind would be lurking. That was life on the land, and you had to accept the rough with the smooth. It would never be any different – not while there was such variation in the seasons and livestock to care for. So, after a period relatively free from major problems, it was only to be expected that trouble was just around the corner. It came to the MacLeods in the form of a phone call.

Catriona could tell from David's facial expression that it was bad news. Or unpleasant news. She could also tell from the questions he asked the caller that it involved sheep.

'Is it bad news, darling?' she asked. She always tried to involve herself in just about everything they did.

'The news was bad enough, but what it might lead to could be disastrous. It could be the end of our merino stud,' David replied gravely.

'David, no,' she said, 'you can't be serious.'

'It's this Ovine Johne's Disease thing. If a stud tests for it and gets even one reactor, you can't go on selling rams. That was Jim Lawler on the phone. He's had a couple of reactors. When I was starting off I bought a big ram from Jim.'

'How precisely does this affect us, darling?' Catriona asked.

'If we test for OJD and get any reactors, even one, we're finished as a stud. I can refrain from testing and go on selling rams but it would be a reasonable bet that most buyers would want to know if the sheep have been tested. It's a marketing plus to have an OJD-free flock,' he replied.

'How does this OJD thing affect sheep?' Catriona asked.

'It's a wasting disease caused by an organism in the gut. Every country in the world that runs sheep appears to have the disease. There's some vets that support eradication of an entire flock, which can wipe out generations of breeding, and there are other control measures. It seems that there isn't a really reliable test but you have to go with what there is.'

'Can you do anything to prevent it?' she asked.

'There's vaccines in use overseas and I believe there's a limited amount here. I don't know much about the business but the vaccine would seem to be the way to go. I'll talk to Dougal and see what he says. Meanwhile, I'll have to decide what to do about testing for OJD.'

'How much would it affect us if we got a positive test for OJD?' Catriona asked.

'It wouldn't destroy us, or anything like that, but it would mean the end of selling rams and the income that brings in. It would be a blow after the money we've invested.'

'And of course, you wouldn't be able to show sheep?' she said.

'That's exactly right, Cat. We wouldn't be able to sell stud sheep and we wouldn't be able to show them,' he said.

'Then you had better talk to Dougal,' she agreed.

Dougal hadn't had much experience with Ovine Johne's Disease and had only a sketchy knowledge of the problem. But he promised to talk to some of his colleagues and to come back to his father with a better appreciation of how to handle the matter.

Sure enough, Dougal was as good as his word. He was impressed that his father had consulted him on the matter and he threw himself into a total understanding of the disease. Inside a week he had absorbed virtually every item of technical information available on Ovine Johne's Disease and was informed and comfortable about discussing the problem with his father.

They sat in the lounge over morning smoko and discussed the matter calmly and logically. It was Sunday morning, so Dougal for once had some time to spend with his parents. 'Have you noticed a tail in your older ewes? I mean, are there any sheep that don't seem to be doing as well as the others?'

'Can't say that I've noticed any, Dougal. I haven't seen all the ewes at Molonga and Wirrewarra for a little while but there are no bad doers in the stud ewes at Glen Morrison,' David said firmly.

Dougal nodded. 'So far so good. The situation is that Ovine Johne's Disease is a notifiable disease. If you've got it in your sheep, you're supposed to notify the Department of Agriculture. I can arrange for your sheep to be bloodtested and if there are no reactors you get placed on the category MN1. That is, you've monitored negative at first testing. You can proceed to MN2 and MN3 after further testing. The rub is that if you test and there's a reactor or reactors, then you'll be defined as an infected flock and you won't be able to sell stud sheep,' Dougal said.

'So what would you advise, Dougal?' David asked.

'I suppose you could go on selling sheep for the time being, but more and more of your clients will probably want some assurance that your sheep are clean. Some may demand it and if you can't give them such an assurance they would probably buy rams elsewhere,' Dougal said. 'Conversely, there's probably some who regard this Ovine Johne's Disease as a heap of bullshit, as just another sheep problem, and would buy rams from you whether you tested or not.'

'What are the chances of the disease being here, Dougal?' David asked.

'There is less chance of it being here than in some other districts, Dad. Have you bought any sheep from the south lately.'

'I bought a ram from Jim Lawler. He's had a couple of reactors. That's why I called you, Dougal.'

'How long ago?' Dougal asked his father.

'Close to five years?' David answered.

'The disease has a long incubation period but if you had it, you'd see it in some of your older sheep by now,' Dougal said.

'So what do you suggest?'

'It's up to you, Dad. If you test and your sheep are clean, it's a plus. If you test and you get a reactor

487

or reactors, you're in trouble. It will be the end of your merino stud and I have some idea what that would mean to you. You can hold off and wait for a vaccine. They're using one in New Zealand but it's only being used under very controlled conditions here so far. That's the safe approach but it leaves a question mark over your status and some of your clients might not like that,' Dougal said.

'I'll have to think about it,' David said.

Dougal nodded. 'Do that, Dad.'

Later, after Dougal had left them, Catriona came and sat beside him. 'So what are you going to do about this Ovine Johne's thing, darling?' she asked.

He looked at her for a few moments before answering. 'I think I'm going to test them,' he said.

'I would have bet that you would,' she said.

'You know me that well?'

'I think I do, darling,' she said and took his hand.

'If we win, we'll win well. If we lose, then we'll be out of the stud sheep game. I think that it's one of those situations where you can't be half-pregnant, to use a term I once heard from Kate. We'll do the right thing by our ram clients and it will remove any uncertainty. We might be back in the flock sheep business but what the heck. We can always start again,' he said.

So Dougal arranged for all the stud sheep on Glen Morrison, Molonga and Wirrewarra to be tested for Ovine Johne's Disease. It took three days with travelling, and was quite an operation for the High Peaks

Pastoral Company. David prowled about like a great panther while the testing was being done. Although he had tried to assure Catriona that the outcome wasn't too important, he was very much on edge about it. The merino stud had become an important part of his life and of the total High Peaks operation. Moreover, it was an important part of his plan to promote Moira and Angus as top merino breeders and judges. It would be a huge setback to lose the stud.

Catriona was not at all taken in by her husband's professed indifference to the outcome of the testing. She knew what he had put into the merino stud over and above the financial investment. For the days leading up to the results of the testing, she was even more loving than usual. As she was always very loving where her husband was concerned, this meant that she went to great lengths to please him and to keep his mind off the possibility that the testing would reveal reactors.

When Dougal rang one lunchtime Catriona could see the lines of tension on David's face. Then, almost miraculously, they disappeared. He nodded a couple of times before putting the phone down. Catriona looked at him expectantly.

'They're all clear. Not a reactor,' he said.

'Darling, how wonderful,' she said as she went to him. His great arms wrapped her to him and she felt his hard body pressed tightly against hers. 'Thank you for helping me get through this, I don't know what

I'd do without you. Now I'm going to ring Jim Lawler.'

Catriona listened while David gave Jim Lawler the news. He was clearly delighted to be able to relay the cleared results.

'Jim, you need any help to get started again, you come to me,' he said, before putting the phone down.

'So it's business as usual?' Catriona asked, smiling.

He looked at here and then bent and lifted her into his arms. 'Not for a little while, darling.'

'David, what if someone should come in?' she said.

'I can clearly recall one occasion when you didn't care about that in the slightest,' he said. 'Are your squibbing? That's not like you, Cat.'

'I thought you might have had enough of me after the past few days,' she said.

David put her down on the edge of the big bed and laughed softly.

'Enough of you? I hope there'll never be a time when I can say I've had enough of you, Cat,' he said.

Any concern Catriona may have had of someone walking in on them simply melted away. Later, resting on one elbow and looking down at the man who had been the light of her life she teased, 'I'll have to find another problem like Ovine Johne's if it will mean that I'm going to be loved so well.'

'Don't even joke about it, sweetheart. And this is my thanks for what you did for me. Now I'll have to go and do some work.'

She stretched out and sighed. 'I don't know how

you can think about work after that. On second thoughts, yes, I do. I know you. If you'll wait while I have a shower, I'll come with you.'

'Race you to it, darling.'

She smiled as she watched her very large, very naked husband run for the bathroom. It was almost as if the good news on the testing for Ovine Johne's had made him a young man again. Thank God, she breathed.

Chapter Nineteen

It wasn't her coming birthday that excited Anne, because birthdays only reminded her of her age and that was anything but exciting. Age might bring respect and some degree of wisdom but she found her physical limitations irksome to the extreme. What did excite Anne was the birth of her first great-grandchild. And when Sue-Ellen put the wee baby boy into her arms Anne regarded the occasion as one of the most significant moments of her long life. This baby, Andrew James, put a special imprint on her marriage to Andrew MacLeod. She had helped to perpetuate the ancient name of MacLeod through her son, David, and his son, Angus. Now, the lineage would continue through this baby.

'He is lovely, Sue-Ellen,' Anne said, as she held Andrew James. 'What does Angus think of him?'

'I believe Angus is quite proud of him. He can't quite believe Andrew is his,' Sue-Ellen said with a smile.

'Such a name, and such a man to live up to. It is a lot to put on a little baby.'

'David did it, so it can be done, Sue-Ellen,' Anne said gently. She could have said that David had surpassed his father but there was no need to. Sue-Ellen was full of admiration for what David had achieved and had told Anne so.

'Are you happy with Angus, Sue-Ellen?' Anne asked. She was the matriarch of the family and could ask such a question. Sue-Ellen, for all her strong views, had often gone to Anne for advice.

As Sue-Ellen considered this question her eyes dwelt on Anne. Anne MacLeod was the most respected, and perhaps most loved, woman in the district. Once, Anne had been quite beautiful – the best-looking young woman in the Merriwa district. She had been wife to the toughest man in the high country and mother of the most successful. Now, the lustrous dark hair was grey verging on white, and the once active body occasionally relied on a stick for support. Yet Anne still cooked most of her meals and still pottered in her garden.

'Oh yes, Nanna. Angus is the kind of man I hoped he would become. He behaved like a goat in his younger days and I told him if he wanted me as his wife he would have to grow up – fast. Angus is very clever, and very talented with animals. I'm sure he loves me and he's very thoughtful. That means a lot. And, of course, he has a wonderful, supportive family, which also means so much. David couldn't have been nicer to me from day one. There aren't many David MacLeods, are there?'

'I refuse to answer that because I would be seen to be biased,' Anne said with a smile.

'Then there is Moira, who is just a lovely, warm person. We have lots of chinwags,' Sue-Ellen said.

'And how are you getting on with Catriona these days?' Anne asked.

'Oh, all right, Nanna. But there's no secret that David seems to be her main interest. I suppose you can't blame her because David is a very special kind of man. I wouldn't say Catriona is snooty, but I can't talk to her like I can to you,' Sue-Ellen confided.

'Don't sell Catriona short, Sue-Ellen. She may have a superior air about her but she would have defied her parents and all they stood for to marry David. He is the light of Catriona's life. There are some women who regard their husbands as such, and Catriona is one of them,' Anne said.

'Dougal is a lot like Catriona. In attitude, I mean,' Sue-Ellen continued.

'Yes, you're right. Dougal resembles Andrew in appearance but he has that aloofness that some people call arrogance. David believes it's part of being a vet – they get carried away with their own importance. Dougal is very clever and he knows it. I have chipped him about his attitude on more than one occasion, Sue-Ellen. Old ladies, especially old grandmothers, can do that sort of thing. But I have a soft spot for Dougal that I developed when he was quite young, because he was different. Dougal was nothing like his father who put a lot of grey hairs on my head because of his escapades with horses. Angus is more like David, except that David always had a greater sense of responsibility as a teenager. Angus needed a strong woman to take him in hand, and you've been the woman, Sue-Ellen. You've been the making of Angus. He'll be fine now.'

'I think he will, Nanna. Men can be great, or utter bastards. If you manage to catch a good one, you can thank your lucky stars. I've got strong views about the place of women in society but I wouldn't want to go through life on my own. Angus, and now junior here, make life very worthwhile,' Sue-Ellen said.

'Very laudable, Sue-Ellen. When all is said and done, it's one's family and friends that make life most worthwhile. Now, if you want to get on the right side of Catriona, get her to talk to you about the young David. Catriona will really open up about those early days. What a lovely child she was. She used to ride up here on her grey pony, Princess. I always wanted Catriona for David. Andrew used to say I was silly as she would marry a silvertail, but I disagreed. Funny how things work out, Sue-Ellen. I've said that family is important, but it's especially important on the land. Andrew realised that, and David after him. You need a supportive family to survive on the land. What is so sad now is that properties can't support the number of people they used to and many young people have to move away. David realised that if he wanted to keep his sons on the land, he would have to acquire more property. His biggest disappointment was Dougal's decision to be a vet. That really threw David. Of course, David wanted more sons but Catriona didn't want to have more than three children,' Anne said.

'She didn't? Why ever not, Nana?' Sue-Ellen asked, intrigued.

'It's her secret, Sue-Ellen,' Anne said. 'But between you and me I believe her decision was to do with her appearance.'

'Good heavens. I don't know what she has to worry about. If I look as well as Catriona does at her age, I'll be very happy,' Sue-Ellen said.

'A massive amount of effort has gone into keeping Catriona that way. Most women simply wouldn't bother. David is Catriona's soft spot, Sue-Ellen. If you wish to get close to her, get her to talk about him,' Anne advised.

'I was going there anyway, Nanna. Angus said he'd get his own lunch if I wanted to have mine here,' Sue-Ellen said.

'You'd be very welcome to have lunch here but I'm sure Catriona would like to see you, too. You have a powerful ally in Andrew James,' Anne said with a laugh.

'Who I will have to feed very soon.' Sue-Ellen said. 'I was determined to breastfeed this fellow just so I know what it's like and from all that I have read lately it's the best way to go,' Sue-Ellen said.

'Why else would we have been given breasts, Sue-Ellen? I'm sure it was for the perpetuation of the species and not simply for men to admire,' Anne said.

'That's an enjoyable by-product,' Sue-Ellen said, and they both laughed.

Sue-Ellen found her mother-in-law busy at her correspondence. There were letters to old school friends overseas and to friends she and David had made on their trip with her parents.

'Sue-Ellen, how nice to see you,' Catriona said with some enthusiasm. 'And how is the young man today?'

'Hungry. I'll have to feed him, Catriona.' Catriona had asked Sue-Ellen to call her by her first name in preference to anything else.

'Feed away. Can you stay for lunch?' Catriona asked.

Sue-Ellen nodded. 'That would be lovely. Angus said he'd get his own lunch if I wanted to have mine here or with Nanna Anne.'

'Anne would have enjoyed seeing you and young Andrew. She is so clucky over babies. Her main regret in life was that she could only have one. I believe she would have had a dozen for Andrew if she had been able. He and David wanted lots of sons with a daughter or two thrown in,' Catriona said.

'And you felt differently?' Sue-Ellen asked rather boldly. She felt that as the conversation had opened so providentially she should strike at the heart of the matter immediately.

'I did my duty and had three children, Sue-Ellen. Three is more than enough to look after. David wanted more because he wanted sons for his properties and the way things have turned out, perhaps I was selfish not having more children. But David has never reproached me for stopping at three. I did offer to have another child if Angus had turned out to be a girl. Now that I want David to ease up it would be a great advantage to have a couple more boys. Dougal leaving to become a vet was a big disappointment for David; perhaps the biggest disappointment of his life, other than his father's early death. Of course, he is very proud of what Dougal has achieved for himself but that doesn't do us much good here.'

'Yes, but from what I understand Dougal never had his heart in the land, and you need to love it to put up with all the problems ownership of property imposes. But, as Anne says, everyone is an individual and you can't make people what they aren't,' Sue-Ellen added.

'You're right, Sue-Ellen, but it's tough on Moira who has had to be more son than daughter. Maybe she'll never marry. She had one bad scare over a man and David rescued her from that situation. She's talked about having a baby or two artificially – to me, not to David – so there's something for her to love and maybe carry on here. But you can't count on that, can you?'

This was interesting but not really the road Sue-Ellen wanted to travel. 'I would very much like to know what David was like as a boy. Apart from Anne, you're probably the only person who knew him at all well. You went to school with him, didn't you?'

'Up to sixth class, and then I went away to boarding school. David went to school in Merriwa. Andrew and Anne didn't want him to go away and David certainly didn't want to go. I doubt they could have afforded to send him to boarding school, anyway. And even if they did, as Anne has said, David was such a free spirit he might have run away!' she said, and laughed. 'David without his dogs and horses would have been like the proverbial fish out of water. Not having been to boarding school was one of the things my parents seized on when I told them I wanted to marry David. There was never anyone else for me although he kept me dangling for a long time,' Catriona said with a faraway look in her eye.

'What was he really like, Catriona? I know he won a sheepdog trial when he was only ten so he must have been a remarkable boy with animals, but what was he really like?' Sue-Ellen asked.

'He was something of a loner because he didn't have any close mates. All he wanted to do was muster sheep and ride horses in the hills. He thought I was a little pest and if he knew I was coming he would clear out up into the hills. That's how I came to go over the side of Yellow Rock: I wanted to show him that I could ride that mountain on my grey pony. I went to meet him and that was nearly the end of me.'

And so for nearly two hours Catriona talked about the young David. Sue-Ellen could see, as Anne had told her, that it was a subject dear to her heart.

'Of course, my parents knew they had been wrong about David,' Catriona said. 'He put together much more property than Daddy had and surpassed his success with sheep and cattle. Daddy was big enough to acknowledge I had been right and he and Mummy had been wrong. But I would have married him if he hadn't a penny to his name. The big question was whether or not he would have asked me. David was a man, a real man. He was one of the only men who ever stood up to my father. But when David and I went to Canberra for the National Trials and Daddy heard that David had two dogs in the final, he and Mummy came down to see him win it with Clancy. David and Daddy became very good friends, which pleased me very much. They helped each other in many ways. Daddy got David started with his Hereford stud and David put in a lot of time showing Daddy how to handle a sheepdog. Things worked out very well in the end,' Catriona said, with misty eyes.

'But was he a tough little boy?' Sue-Ellen asked.

'Tough? I suppose he was tough to the extent that he was very strong for his age, and because Tim Sparkes had taught him how to box. And he adopted a tough exterior to be like his father and some of the other hill fellows who used to work dogs and compete at drafts,' Catriona said.

'He did fight for you, didn't he?' Sue-Ellen pressed.

'Twice, Sue-Ellen. The first time was in our last year at primary school. There were two perfectly horrid brothers, Bill and Wade Missen, and they had a mate by the name of Stanley Masters. Stanley and Wade came down to where Susan and I were sitting under a screen and trees. Stanley put his hand down my front and I screamed. David came out of nowhere and belted him.

Years later the same three fellows – all heavy drinkers – tried to rape me the night of the Debutantes' Ball. David took on all three of them,' Cariona said, and shuddered.

'What happened to them?' Sue-Ellen asked.

'They all went to prison and they're all dead. Bill and Wade started a big bushfire on Poitrel and the police chased them that same day. The Missen boys hit a tree on the Bunnan Road and they were both killed. Stanley Masters was knifed while still in prison.'

'Whew, that's some story. David must have been a tough young man. You couldn't have had a better protector, Catriona,' Sue-Ellen said.

Catriona nodded her agreement. 'If David hadn't followed those boys the night they tried to rape me, I don't know what would have transpired. My life might have been very different.'

'I was just saying to Nanna Anne that if you get a good man, you're very lucky. The women in this family seem to have married good men,' Sue-Ellen observed.

'Andrew's father, that was Grandfather James, wasn't crash hot, Sue-Ellen. He had a good war record but socially he was a high flier and he and Andrew didn't get on well at all. Andrew blamed his father for his mother's death, which happened on that bridge into High Peaks. After that Andrew hardly spoke to his father and he blamed him for the property being so heavily in debt. By all accounts Andrew's mother was something special and Andrew thought the world of her. David was worried for a time there that Angus might have taken after his grandfather. Thankfully, he hasn't. You can take a lot of credit for that, Sue-Ellen,' Catriona said with a smile.

'Oh, Catriona, surely having good parents counts for the most,' Sue-Ellen protested. 'Angus was basically decent, just a wee bit wild! Once he focused his attentions on me, he forgot about all that silly business. Men can be so childish at times – they do foolish things to try and impress their mates, and seem to take longer to grow up. If Angus hadn't had supportive parents and a place to come back to, maybe he would have made a mess of his life,' Sue-Ellen said.

'You could well be right, Sue-Ellen,' Catriona said. 'There is just that one negative factor in the line and Anne says it could have come in through James and his mother. The rest of it is nearly pure Scot, including my mother's family. They were all very careful, hard-working people committed to building up property and doing the right thing by the community. Some would say they were a bit dour and lacking in colour. The same thing has been said about me because I don't mix readily. I'm not that kind of person. I have David and my family and some old friends and I'm happy. I don't need lots of people around me. But David and I have helped quite a few causes in this district. David isn't as openly public-spirited as Daddy was, who was head of just about everything, but he's probably donated more money than Daddy ever did. It's just that David is a different kind of person and he works in a different kind of way. Oh, dear, how did we get to talk about David?' Catriona said with a laugh.

'You still love him, don't you?' Sue-Ellen asked. 'After all these years, you're still very much in love.'

'I still love him, Sue-Ellen. David has been my life since I was a small girl. Although I can assure you that for several years I rated much lower in David's eyes than his dogs and horses. At one stage I became so desperate I offered to get pregnant so we could be married. I was stunned when he refused and told me I didn't understand him at all. I didn't, either. David would never have chosen that route to marry me,' Catriona said.

'Catriona,' Sue-Ellen said with her eyes wide and with a new appreciation of her mother-in-law, 'you must have been desperately in love and terribly frustrated.'

'All that, Sue-Ellen. And my parents pushing me to marry from a heap of well-bred young men. There wasn't one of them that meant a thing to me. They didn't rate with David. My parents couldn't understand why I wanted him because at that stage the MacLeods were still battling. Some of those same young men who wouldn't have anything to do with David in those days, now chase after him. Funny how money changes things, isn't it?'

'I understand what you mean, Catriona. I think it is really awesome to be able to say that you still love a man after years of marriage. I mean, really *love* him. So many marriages don't last the distance these days,' Sue-Ellen said.

'I couldn't imagine life without David, Sue-Ellen. I really couldn't. There wouldn't be any purpose in it.

I suppose that sounds silly when one has three children, but it's the way I feel. David and I have been through so much together from such an early age, shared so many experiences, that it would be simply awful not to be with him. I don't know how Anne got through those years when Andrew was away shearing. And then to lose him. I have always felt terribly sorry for Anne. She was my ally right from the very beginning and in some ways I have been closer to her than I was to my own mother. Anne is such a very understanding and commonsense person,' Catriona said.

Sue-Ellen looked at her mother-in-law and wondered how she managed to stay looking so young. Her body still looked great and her skin was fresh and virtually wrinkle-free. Maybe her gaze wandered a shade long because Catriona caught it and raised her long eyebrows. 'What is it, Sue-Ellen?' she asked.

'I'm amazed how well you look, Catriona. If I'm in the same shape at your age I shall be very happy,' Sue-Ellen said.

'Good cosmetics and plenty of exercise, Sue-Ellen. You have to work at looking good. I should hate to have David regard me as a frump,' she said, and laughed.

'Not much danger of that, Catriona,' Sue-Ellen said and laughed with her.

'Besides, I like to be fit and well for David. He never stops working and I have a job to get him to take a holiday. He doesn't have time for sheepdog trials or campdrafts any more. I'm his only relaxation, if you know what I mean,' Catriona said with a hint of wickedness.

'I know what you mean,' Sue-Ellen said and laughed again. 'I should imagine that going to bed with the young David would have been quite an experience,' she said.

'It's still an experience, Sue-Ellen,' Catriona said.

Sue-Ellen returned to Strath Fillan with increased respect and admiration for her mother-in-law. It seemed to her that in the last couple of hours she had come closer to her than at any time since she came to the high country to live.

'How were things up at High Peaks?' Angus asked her that night as they sat over dinner.

'Very fair. I saw Nanna Anne and had lunch with your mother. What remarkable women they both are. Anne is just a lovely person but up until today I hadn't got really close to your mother. Catriona opened up a little this afternoon and I found her a much warmer person. Maybe Andrew James made the difference. And maybe it was getting her to talk about your father as a boy. Anne suggested I do that, and it worked a treat. When your mother talks about David she's a different person. She still loves him to distraction,' Sue-Ellen said.

'I worked out long ago that I – well, me, Dougal and Moy – rated second to Dad where Mum was concerned,' Angus said. 'It was one of the reasons I ran off the rails a bit. I reckoned Mum didn't really love me and Dad expected far too much from me. It seemed Dougal had let him down and Moira was a girl so I was the big hope. I couldn't say that we were ever neglected except that we had a nurse so Mum could spend more time with Dad. Mum wanted us away at school for the same reason. Mum's still crazy about Dad. She must spend a whack of money keeping herself looking the way she does. Mum's always been dead scared some other woman – a young woman – would take him from her. Bit pathetic, really.'

'Not if you love someone the way your mother does,' Sue-Ellen said sharply.

'Dad would never touch another woman. He had plenty of opportunity when Sarah Matheson worked for him. If Dad could withstand Sarah's charms, he could withstand any woman. Mum has never had any cause to worry that Dad would play around elsewhere. Mind you, I think she keeps him well occupied. Moira lived with Dad and Mum for years and knows more than she lets on. She says Mum does some way-out things to keep Dad interested in her,' Angus said, and grinned.

'Why are you looking like that, Angus? Aren't I way-out enough for you?' Sue-Ellen asked.

'Nothing like that, sweetheart. It just seems a bit silly a woman Mum's age working so hard to stay looking good for her husband when we all know he has never thought about anyone but her,' Angus said.

'I think it's really sweet – a lot of women don't bother. I must say that my admiration for your mother has increased enormously, Angus.'

'Oh, she's some woman all right, sweetheart. There's

a lot more to Mum than what you see, and what you see is pretty good,' Angus said.

Catriona went up to see Anne and took with her one of the presents she had bought for her mother-in-law's birthday. It was a dark green woollen pants-suit she had purchased on her last visit to Sydney. Anne had been wearing slacks suits for some years chiefly, so she told people, because her legs weren't what they had been.

'It's lovely, Catriona. So soft. Thank you very much,' Anne said. She realised the suit would have cost a lot of money because Catriona never skimped on clothes. She went out of the lounge room and when she returned she was carrying two thick leather-bound diaries.

'This is the record of my life on High Peaks, Catriona. These diaries also contain all that I have been able to find out about my own and the MacLeod families. The diary finishes today. I want you to take over now, Catriona. My eyes are not the best and it is time for a younger person to look after the record,' Anne said.

Catriona was overwhelmed. She opened the top diary and flipped through some pages. They were all written in Anne's lovely clear script and on some pages there were newspaper cuttings of David's exploits.

'Are you sure you want me to take over the diaries now? You could go on for years yet,' Catriona suggested.

'Perhaps I could. But quite apart from my eyes, what would a woman my age have to record? All the main incidents and happenings from the past are there and although David tries to keep me up to date on what is going on, I find it hard to concentrate now. You are at the centre of things and have been for years. You had university training so you should manage the records very well. It is time, Catriona,' Anne said firmly.

When David called in to see his mother he found her in her garden watering plants. She sat down on a garden seat beneath a large grevillea and he sat down beside her.

'I'm wondering what you would like for your birthday,' he began.

She looked at him and marvelled again that she had produced so remarkable a man; the boy who had become a millionaire grazier yet whose essential character had never changed.

'Nothing material, dear,' she said and smiled at him. 'If I were able, I should very much like to ride up Yellow Rock with you and Catriona and to stand on the top for one last time.'

David smiled. 'Is that what you want, to stand on top of Yellow Rock?' he asked.

'If I were able,' she said.

There was virtually nothing he wouldn't do for her so if she wanted to stand on Yellow Rock, that was what he would give her.

'That shouldn't be a problem,' he said. 'I will hire a helicopter to take us there.'

She looked at him with surprise in her eyes. 'Do you mean that?' she asked.

'I wouldn't joke about anything to do with you, Mum,' he answered.

She touched his arm and then put her hand over his. 'No, I don't suppose you would. Well, I have a special reason for wanting to be there one last time,' she said.

'Leave it to me, Mum,' he replied.

'I'd like to have lunch up there,' she said.

'I'll get Catriona to lay on lunch,' he said.

'And boil the billy.'

'That too,' he said. He got up and looked down at her. 'Anything else?'

'Nothing else.'

'Right. I'll book it for two days hence. The weather forecast looks okay. You can go back to your watering,' he said.

When David returned from the old homestead Catriona sensed he had a mission.

'Mum wants to have lunch with us on top of Yellow Rock in a couple of days, Cat. I asked her what she wanted for her birthday, and that's what she asked for. Can you lay on a good lunch and pack a billy?' he announced.

'How on earth are you going to get your mother up Yellow Rock, David?' Catriona asked.

'Hire a helicopter. Mum didn't turn a hair when I said I would do that. I'm just going in to organise it. Manny Thompson owes me a few favours so I reckon he won't mind taking us up there,' he said. Manny Thompson was an American who owned one property in Merriwa and another in North Queensland. He had come to Australia on a visit, and liked the country and

Australians so much that he stayed. He now bred Angus cattle on his Merriwa property and Brahman-cross cattle further north. It hadn't taken Manny long to hear about David MacLeod and he had come to him for advice on several occasions. The two men got on famously, which was helped by the fact that both were keen horsemen.

'Am I included in this aerial shivoo?' Catriona asked.

'Of course. Mum asked for you too.'

Two days later Manny Thompson picked them up from a paddock by the old High Peaks homestead.

'Got everything?' the grazier pilot asked.

David nodded. 'Down to the last item.'

The helicopter lifted off in a shower of dust and twigs. In no time at all they were rising well above High Peaks in the direction of Yellow Rock. Anne, Catriona and David were all treated to views of the High Peaks hill country they had never before experienced. But the flight ended all too quickly.

David looked at his watch and then up at Manny. 'Would you pick us up at three, Manny?'

'Will do, David.'

Once they had landed David assembled the three collapsible chairs and sat his mother in one before starting to gather wood for the fire.

Anne stood up and looked out over the surrounding countryside. 'Oh, this air, isn't it incredible?'

'It always seems that way,' David agreed. He got a fire going while Catriona laid out food and plates on a small table. His mother didn't eat big meals and he had

510

brought the pick of their fillet steak. It was from a steer fed in their own feedlot and its taste and succulence could hardly be bettered.

'This is where Andy proposed to me,' Anne said nostalgically when she had finished the meal. David thought she had enjoyed it. She was talking now between sips of tea made in the much-loved blackened billy. 'Of course, I had been hoping he would propose to me for months. He hadn't even kissed me, which was surprising, but it seemed his mother had told him not to rush a girl. When he did kiss me – twice actually – it was rather wonderful. I suppose I could say that our life together really started up here that day. Something inside me turned over the first time I saw Andy at a dance in Merriwa and I had been going riding with him for months. I knew he was the man for me but I wasn't sure he thought I was the woman for him. When he asked me to marry him that day we were here, it was a big relief,' Anne said with a brief smile.

'The MacLeod men seem to choose odd places for their proposals,' Catriona said. 'David proposed to me across there, in the big cave on Wallaby Rocks. I waited a great deal longer than you did, Anne. It was a huge relief, too. And Sue-Ellen told me that Angus proposed to her initially in a sheep yard at Longreach. Not very romantic sites for committing oneself to a man, Anne.'

'I couldn't think of a more perfect place for a proposal than Yellow Rock. Look out there. Could you find anything more wonderful?' Anne asked, and pointed to where the creek threaded its way like a silver snake towards Merriwa. 'This is a world beyond the world. Everything was so wonderful that day. And then we were married and I had my own house – and not too long after I had you, David. Andy did so much want more children but he never by word or deed indicated his disappointment. You gave him so much pleasure, David. Yes, it all really began up here.'

'Oh, look there. It's a black rabbit. I've never seen one before,' Catriona exclaimed with delight, and pointed through the fence to where the all-black animal sat beside a splintered rock.

'That's the first black rabbit I've seen here since I was a boy. Dad and I saw one when we were up here mustering,' David said.

As he spoke there was a rush of mighty wings from behind them and a shadow passed them by. 'Oh, he's after the black rabbit,' Catriona screamed in David's ear.

'No, he's not. There's a rabbit beyond the black one. It's in the open,' he said. The great bird banked slightly and fell like a stone with claws extended and picked up the second rabbit, which screamed pitifully. The eagle lifted like their helicopter and soared away into the vault of blue sky.

'Nothing has changed up here since I first came to Yellow Rock,' Anne observed. 'The eagles were taking rabbits then and they're still taking them now. But at long last I've seen a black rabbit in the wild. He's gone now but I'll remember seeing him.'

'I was told that the trappers caught quite a few just after the war. They got a quarter of a million rabbits off one place in six months. There were gingers and blacks and even an odd pure white. The whites don't last long as they're too easily seen,' David told them. 'Had enough tea, Mum?'

'I've had an elegant sufficiency of everything. It was lovely, and lovely of you to get me up here, David. When I told you I wanted to be here for one last time I didn't dream you would actually be able to arrange it,' Anne said.

'David has a way of making things happen, Anne. If you mention that you'd like something, you'll find it on your lap, so to speak. This wasn't a hard wish to grant,' Catriona said.

'Well it's just lovely – you can't imagine what this day has meant to me. And if I had my time over I would do it all again. Maybe I wouldn't want Andy to go away shearing to help us buy Poitrel, but Wilf wanted us to have it so there you are,' Anne said.

'Speaking of Poitrel, it's going to be unoccupied for a while,' David said.

'Why is that, David?' Anne asked.

'Jean and Julian can't cope any longer. They're too old to look after the house and garden at Poitrel and have decided to move to Merriwa. So after all these years, we will need a new occupant. I must say I will miss Jean, in particular, enormously, because she has been a terrific help and a very sweet person. There is no doubt that old age is a pain in the butt,' David said.

'What will you do, David?' Anne asked.

'I don't know right now, Mum. Moira is going to

feed the animals for a while but we'll need someone there. You can't leave a property unoccupied these days – there are too many vandals and stock thieves on the go. Lew keeps his eyes open but he's an old man now and hardly the tough police officer he used to be,' David said.

'The old order changeth,' Anne mused.

'I'm afraid it does. There's just not the honesty there used to be. The politicians are giving the land a tough time, too. Men used to dream about owning land in Australia and it was land and what it produced – wool, initially – that made Australia. Now they're even telling us how much rainfall we can store on our properties. Damned ridiculous,' David said fiercely.

'Steady, darling,' Catriona said. David had become increasingly bitter about what was happening to the land and its people. He hadn't spared himself from the time they had decided to purchase Poitrel yet the returns on all the properties were very low. Costs were beating the rural industries.

'There's over twelve million dollars tied up in properties and stock and it's returning us about half of what you could get from a bank investment. Except that I'm a land and animal person I would be better off selling up everything. Then I think of High Peaks owned by strangers and I know I couldn't let it go. And there's Moira and Angus to consider,' David said. 'Maybe Dougal was right to make his own way. He'll earn a good living without the government on his back. Why are politicians so lacking in vision? The world wants our produce because it's generally cleaner than anywhere else but costs and damned regulations are killing us. They really are,' David said. He got up and proceeded to douse the fire. 'Take a good look, Mum. One of these days this may all be national park. Who can say? I don't have anything against national parks and if we can't make a profit from wool and beef in this country, that might be the only option.'

Any further discussion on the matter was interrupted by the beat-beat sound of the helicopter.

'Thank you, David. It has been lovely to come here again,' Anne said and kissed her son.

'It was no big deal, Mum,' David said gruffly.

'It is for me, David,' Anne said, with tears in her eyes.

As the helicopter settled he picked his mother up in his arms as if she weighed no more than a feather, and carried her across to the craft. 'There she is, Manny,' he said, as he handed her up to his friend.

David helped Catriona up into the helicopter and then whispered in Manny's ear before taking his seat. Manny nodded, and the big bird lifted and banked towards Wallaby Rocks. For the next few minutes Anne was given a panoramic view of the four MacLeod properties. At the end of this tour Manny did two slow circuits of the area between Poitrel homestead and the Strath Fillan boundary fence. David seemed particularly interested in what lay beneath them. 'Okay, Manny, back to High Peaks,' he said at last.

It was as Lew Hooper had told him; cattle had been stolen from Poitrel.

Chapter Twenty

It was Lew Hooper who first twigged that the two men in the truck with the dark-green cattle crate were up to no good. The ex–police officer was getting on in years but his ingrained watchfulness had never left him. Lew knew all the local trucks and this wasn't one of them. Many trucks visited Strath Fillan to deposit and pick up brood mares, so this in itself wasn't suspicious. But this particular truck stopped beyond the Poitrel homestead and while one man urinated beside the truck, the other walked to the fence and looked up the hill. Through his binoculars Lew could see the man inspecting the fence. The truck then turned about and went back towards Inverlochy. It was before dawn the next day that the truck returned. Lew didn't rise as early these days and the truck was just leaving when he walked out the back door. There were cattle in the crate but he couldn't tell how many. Lew walked back into the house and rang David, who was having an early breakfast.

'I think you've just lost a few head of cattle, David. There were two fellows in a truck behaving suspiciously yesterday evening. When I got up the truck was just leaving. I think they took cattle from Poitrel,' Lew said.

'Thanks for the info, Lew. Stuart says he's lost cattle lately. Maybe we can grab them next time,' David said. He hated thieves of any description but right now with the high prices for cattle, stock was being stolen across a huge area of country. The police Stock Squad was pitifully inadequate for the job it was required to do. It was undermanned, and had no chance of countering determined stock thieves. Ten good steers could nett thieves $5000, which was a lucrative return for a night's work. Both sheep and cattle were being stolen. Wool could be shorn and lost through the wool selling system and there were butchers willing to acquire and slaughter cattle. David reckoned that if they had got away with taking his cattle once, they would try again, and if it was their practice to load at first light, he could circumvent them.

'What is it, David?' Catriona asked, as David came back from speaking to Lew. There was a grimness about him she had not observed for a long time.

'That was Lew Hooper, Cat. He thinks two men just took cattle from Poitrel. It tallies with what Stuart told me. There's others that have had cattle stolen too. Well, we shall have to do something about it, won't we?'

Catriona knew that when David spoke in that manner he would certainly do something about it. Trucks with dark-green stock crates weren't all that plentiful so a watch had to be kept for just such a truck. Lew Hooper alerted police to a description of the truck. David told Catriona, Moira and Angus that he proposed to sleep at Poitrel for the next few weeks and to get up early each morning. 'Then I'll stay there too,' Catriona announced.

'I'll move over there too,' Moira added.

'There's no need for you to be involved, Moira,' David told her.

'I want to be involved, Dad. I'm part of this outfit, aren't I?' Moira said with some heat.

'Of course you are, but these fellows may never come here again. And if they do, it could get rough. I'm not going to let them get away,' David said.

'I've always got my shotgun under the seat of the ute so I'll back you up,' Moira said with a tight smile.

David looked at Angus and shrugged. 'If they come, ring me straight off and I'll race up to give you a hand,' Angus said eagerly.

'First thing we do is block their exit. They can't get out via Strath Fillan so they'd have to head for town. We put vehicles across the road and that will box them in. You agree, Lew?' David asked.

'Absolutely, David. If they come I'll run my old truck out to the road to help you block it. Then I'll ring the boys and tell them to get here real quick,' Hooper said.

'There's not much more we can do, Lew. If they're going to pinch more cattle they have to use the Poitrel road or they can't utilise a truck,' David said.

It was over two weeks before the cattle poachers came again. David had been up at four a.m. each morning to watch the road. Nerves were beginning to become a little ragged because it seemed that their precautions were going to be unnecessary. And then through the darkness of a Sunday morning, the lights came up the road from Inverlochy. The truck was travelling very slowly and not making much noise. David quickly rang Angus and then Lew Hooper and gave them slightly differing messages. 'This could be it. There's a truck just going past us. Lew, don't move until you see our two vehicles leave here and then put your vehicle across the road.' And to Angus: 'They're here, Angus. Get yourself up to the last corner while it's dark and Moira will call you when we make our move.'

David stood at the window and watched the truck creep up the road while Catriona and Moira got dressed. As darkness faded he saw that the two men had rigged up a small yard with collapsible steel panels and were bringing down a small bunch of Hereford steers. There was a dog behind the cattle and they seemed to be giving no trouble. They baulked at the makeshift yard and finally went in. Then they were forced up the ramp, which was closed quickly behind them. The yard was dismantled and strapped into place at the rear of the stock crate. The dog was jumped into a small crate and then the two men ran for the front of the truck.

'Go, Moira,' David yelled and ran for the utility outside. Both vehicles roared down the track and out onto the road. David knew it would be a near thing but he wanted the evidence on the back of the truck before he moved. Out of the corner of one eye he saw Lew Hooper's old red truck come out onto the road as he slammed the utility across it with Moira right on his tail.

For a few seconds he thought the truck was going to try and crash through their vehicle blockade but when Lew Hooper added his truck to their vehicles the driver must have realised that he couldn't get through that way and risk smashing his vehicle. The truck stopped and two men got out and sized up their opposition. The two women were judged of no account and the big old man hardly a bother. It was the man walking down the road towards them that they knew was the real opposition. And as David drew nearer to them there was something about one of the men – the dark-haired man on the passenger side of the truck – that stirred dormant memories. This man knew from what he had been told about David MacLeod that there was no point getting into a fight with him because MacLeod would slaughter him. When twenty metres separated David from the truck, the dark-haired man reached into the truck and came up with a shotgun. 'This is for Stanley, you big bastard.'

'No, Reggie,' his partner yelled as the shotgun went off.

The blast hit David in the right shoulder and stopped him.

'*David!*' Catriona screamed.

Moira grabbed her shotgun as the man called Reggie

paused to evaluate what damage his first shot had done. David swayed and looked down at the blood draining from his shoulder. He felt a cold rage sweeping through him and steeled himself to walk on. The fellow with the shotgun drew it to his shoulder as Moira triggered her gun. This time the cartridge missed David because the man called Reggie had collapsed on the ground. Angus, who had materialised while this drama was being enacted, kicked the man's shotgun away and joined Lew Hooper beside the driver of the truck. Lew reached into the truck and pulled out the keys.

'I'm making a citizen's arrest. Get into the truck and stay there.'

'I didn't want any shooting,' the man said.

'Then you shouldn't have teamed up with him,' Hooper said, and jerked his finger at the other side of the truck.

'Is he all right?'

'I should say he is far from all right but we'll see what we can do for him until the ambulance gets here. Angus, you watch this fellow while I see how David is,' Hooper said.

Catriona and Moira had David on the seat of his utility. They had taken off his shirt and Catriona had wrapped her blouse about his shoulder. It was already blood-soaked so Moira followed her mother's example and removed her own blouse.

'We'll have to get him up to the house, Lew. There's sheets there we can rip up,' Catriona said with a catch in her voice. 'Hang in there, darling.'

'How's the shooter?' David asked.

'Lew is looking at him now. Is it hurting?'

'You could say that, sweetheart. I think that fellow is related to Stanley Masters.'

A cold wave of revulsion approaching nausea swept through Catriona. 'Oh, God. Not after all these years,' she muttered.

'I think so. Just before he shot me he said that it was for Stanley. I thought he resembled someone I had known in the past,' David said.

'The ambulance and police are on their way,' Lew said. 'The shooter needs help. There was a towel in the truck. I've used that but he's losing a lot of blood.'

'I had to shoot him, Lew. If I hadn't he would have shot Dad again,' Moira said.

'Of course you did. If you hadn't, I would have thought I might not have been in time,' Lew told her. 'If he lives he'll be facing an attempted murder charge.'

'We're taking David up to the house, Lew. If you follow us up I'll find some sheets and bandages for that fellow,' Catriona said.

'Lew had better stay here with Angus, Mum. I'll get the sheets and bring them back,' Moira said.

Catriona looked down at herself and then at her daughter. 'Just as well we're wearing bras or we'd be a sight,' she said with a nervous giggle. Shock was getting to her now with the realisation that David had come close to being killed. Moira had probably saved his life. Even so, he had lost a lot of blood and his shoulder was a mess. What damage had been done to it would not be known until the doctors had attended to him.

They got David up to the Poitrel homestead and made up a pad from a sheet and pinned it into place. Catriona silently thanked Jean for the first-aid chest she had kept constantly stocked. 'I wish you were here, Jean,' she breathed.

'When you're better, we are going for a long holiday, David,' Catriona said.

'Are we?' he said.

'Yes, we are. Just you and I. That shoulder won't be right for ages,' she said.

'Right now I'm more worried about Moira than my shoulder or going for any holiday. They could charge her,' David said.

'Surely not. If she hadn't shot that fellow, you could be dead, darling,' Catriona said with undeniable logic.

'I'm well aware of that but the courts frown on people taking the law into their own hands. Lew will be a help, but we'll have to see what transpires before there's any thought of a holiday. If that fellow dies, it could be worse for Moira,' he said.

'Are we never to have any peace from that frightful Masters family? Imagine one of them surfacing after all these years,' Catriona said.

'We don't know that he is a Masters. He certainly resembles Stanley but he could be a fellow Stanley knew inside or outside of prison. Maybe he was a friend Stanley told about us. We'll have to wait and see,' he said.

Reggie Masters – for he was Stanley's younger brother,

born after his father left the district – was in a bad way when the ambulance arrived just ahead of the police car. For two days it was touch and go whether he lived or died. He did however pull through, and was charged with attempted murder. With four witnesses who testified that they heard him say he was shooting for his brother, Reggie Masters didn't have a leg to stand on and was put away for a tidy sentence. His accomplice was jailed for stock stealing and received a much shorter sentence.

The ambulance had taken David into Merriwa Hospital and from there Manny Thompson, contacted by Catriona and accompanied by an ambulance officer, had flown David to Newcastle Hospital. Catriona had driven down to be close by her husband and stayed there until he was taken back to Merriwa. Once installed there, he was visited by a veritable host of people. Some of these came at odd hours and unknown to Catriona.

Catriona usually brought Anne with her because David's mother had to be assured that he was recovering satisfactorily. Linda Barden was one of his first non-family visitors. Linda didn't have to sneak in at night like Susan Cartwright, who was still averse to meeting up with Catriona. Susan came hard on Catriona's departure one evening and David reckoned she must have been waiting for her to leave.

'Susan,' he said as she bent and kissed him. 'Long time no see.'

'You can blame Catriona for that,' she said. 'Why did you have to get yourself shot?'

'I didn't have any say in the matter,' he said. 'The fellow pulled a shotgun out of the front of the truck and let fly. His second shot went wide because Moira got him just in time.'

'You could have been killed, David. How is the shoulder?' she asked.

'Still stiff, but healing okay. I'll need physio for a while. How are you, Susan?' David asked. He hated talking about himself and especially about matters of a personal nature.

'I'm all right, David. I'm still playing good tennis,' she said.

David looked at her and tried to remember when it was he had first seen her. He thought it must have been when she first came to the school near Inverlochy. She would have been five or six and a pretty, dark-haired charmer. Catriona was blonde and her best friend. They had gone away to school together and both had wanted him.

'That's good,' he said.

'Well, it's not as good as it could be but it would be worse if I didn't have tennis,' she said. She knew him well enough to know that he would never criticise her for making a mess of her life. David wasn't like that. He was always doing positive things.

'If I had married you, my life would have been very different,' she said.

'You think so?'

'Yes, I *know* so,' she said.

'It would never have worked, Susan. I wouldn't have wanted a wife who was away playing tennis all the time,' he said.

'I wouldn't have wanted to play tennis all the time if I had been married to you,' she said.

'That's easy to say now, Susan. I never at any time thought we'd hit it off. I had my doubts about Catriona too, but she scored a lot of points standing up to her parents about me. She was prepared to leave home to marry me,' he said.

'I would have left the country to marry you,' she said.

'You weren't keen enough on the bush and animals, Susan. It wouldn't have worked.'

'I'd have tried real hard, David,' she said.

'Like you tried with Michael?' he said.

'That was a mistake, David. I married him when Catriona finally got you. Michael isn't worth your little finger. He's just not enough man.'

'These things happen, Susan. How is Karen?'

'I suppose you had to ask that out of politeness. It wouldn't have been to remind me of my foolish behaviour,' she said.

'No, it wouldn't, Susan. You know me better than that,' he said.

'I think I do. Karen is well. She has a daughter, in case you didn't know,' she said.

'I didn't. I hope it works out okay for you, Susan.'

She sighed and got up. 'I shall never forget the day you fought Stanley Masters. What a very formidable little boy you were. And what are you now? A million-aire grazier. You made Angus Campbell eat his words,' she said.

'Angus was all right, Susan. He was snobby but his heart was in the right place. He helped me a lot,' he said.

She bent and kissed him again. 'Look after yourself, David.'

'You should try and make it up with Catriona,' he said. 'You were friends a long time and life is too short to be uptight about a few words.'

'Catriona owes me an apology for what she said to me,' Susan said firmly.

'Was it untrue?' he asked.

'No, it wasn't untrue, but what one looks for from one's best friend is support, not criticism. We aren't all as fortunate in our choice of husbands as Catriona. There are other girls who were with us at school who are divorced. Anyway, what's done is done, David. You won't tell Catriona I was here, will you?' she asked.

'Not if you don't want me to,' he said.

She raised her dark eyebrows and smiled at him. 'You really are too much, David,' she said and walked out of the room.

A couple of nights later David had another nocturnal visitor. Emily Matheson had relayed the news of the shooting to Sarah and via Emily's phone calls to Anne and Catriona, Sarah was aware when David was brought back to Merriwa.

Sarah Matheson stood at the doorway of his room and looked intently at the man on the bed before almost running towards him. She kissed him much more passionately than Susan had done and held her face against his briefly before standing up and looking down at him. 'You silly man. You could have been killed,' she said by way of greeting.

'Hello, Sarah, nice to see you. Look, I didn't have any option. I didn't know the mongrel had a shotgun in the truck.' He was getting tired of repeating this story. 'You look young and wonderful,' he said in an attempt to change the subject.

'I would hardly come to see you looking frumpy,' she said.

'You could never look frumpy, not even with mud and blood and manure over your clobber,' he said.

'If you keep saying things like that, you'll make me cry, Mr Mac,' she said.

David looked into Sarah's shining eyes. They told him that what she felt for him was still much more than mere friendship. But it was no good Sarah fretting over him. She was the kind of young woman the bush needed to raise children who would be prepared to tackle its problems. Sarah would smile or laugh her way through any difficulty. And now David would have to be cruel to be kind. He would have to tell her that she should stop thinking about him and make her own life.

'You asked me once whether I felt anything for you, Sarah. I think you're a terrific young woman and I have a lot of time for you – you know that. But I'm a very happily married man and even if I weren't, I'd be too old for you. You're only the same age as Moira. You should have a nice young man, Sarah,' he said.

She sat down on the hospital chair and looked at him. 'Is that what you really think?'

'Why would I lie to you, Sarah?'

'Yes, why would you, Mr Mac?' she asked. 'To stop me thinking about you?'

'You should stop thinking about me, Sarah. It will only make you unhappy.'

There was a pause before he spoke again. 'I believe you're back home with Emily,' he said. He reckoned he needed to change the subject.

'We're in the money again, Mr Mac. Tristar has won us a fortune so Mum asked me to come home and help her. You should be pleased because Dougal gets a third of her winnings,' Sarah said.

'Oh, yes, I am pleased for him,' he said. Dougal had come to see him and told him what he had won so far. It was so far in excess of what his veterinary fees would have been as to be positively indecent. He couldn't say that Dougal gloated but he had a dig about all the years that had been wasted because he, David, hadn't had Starana treated instead of letting her go to Emily Matheson.

'Where to from here?' Sarah asked.

'I have a lot of physiotherapy ahead of me. When I am finished with that Cat says that we are to have a long overseas holiday. There are things in her father's diary that she wants to check on ... where he died and the man who found him. Then there is Iona,' he told her.

'Who or what is Iona?' she asked.

'I don't know a lot about it. Not as much as Cat does. It's a small island off the west coast of Scotland next to a larger island called Mull. Cat tells me it has been the burial place of Scottish kings. It is the holiest place in Scotland because one of the saints went there in the sixth century and began a monastery. Cat says it's the cradle of Celtic Christianity. Missionaries were trained there and took Christianity throughout the British Isles and to Europe. Angus Campbell had wanted to go there all his life. According to what he wrote in his diary, he had some kind of vision of something there. If that sounds incredible, I should point out that Angus wasn't the kind of man who made things up. We didn't get to Iona on our last trip and Cat very much wants to go there,' he said.

'How wonderful,' she breathed and for a brief moment tried to imagine what it would be like to take a trip like that with David. It was mind-blowing.

'Yes, it could be very interesting. I would also like to meet the man who sold Angus his last border collie. She's a bitch called Meg, and I think she's just about the best border collie bitch I've ever seen. She isn't a typical border collie at all. According to the pedigree that Stuart received, she wasn't bred by the man who sold her to Angus but came from a fair way north of him. I'm wondering if she was related, even remotely, to the original collies that came from the Rutherfords,' he said.

'Goodness, it will be an interesting trip,' Sarah said, envious.

'Oh, Cat has a lot more planned than that. It's hush hush, but Cat is working on a novel based on the MacLeod family. You're the first person I've let into her secret so keep mum about it. What it means is that we're going to be visiting Dunvegan Castle and a lot of other MacLeod landmarks so Cat can absorb the atmosphere,' he said.

'You'll be very proud of Catriona if she gets her novel published,' Sarah said.

'Mum handed over her diary to Cat so a lot of MacLeod stuff is in that. Cat had a good education and has an Arts degree and she writes very well, which is more than I can say for myself. I suppose a novel is another matter, but I'm all in favour of her having a bash at it. Living in the bush and with a bushie like me can't have been the most exciting life a woman could have had,' he said.

'I'm sure Catriona has never regretted marrying you, David,' she said. The name sounded easier on her tongue each time she spoke it. Life couldn't offer anything more beautiful than for her to take Catriona's place.

'So she has told me,' he said dryly. 'Cat wants to have me wholly and solely on this trip which is why she insists it will be only the two of us. There'll be no phones going at all hours, no ram and bull clients and no dog people intruding into our lives. Her words, not mine, Sarah.'

'I can understand that,' she said as she stood up. 'You need to sleep, David. It's been wonderful to see you again. Mum won't tell Catriona that I came to see you,' she said.

He sighed and settled back in the hospital bed which was not long enough to accommodate him adequately. He wondered if he should tell Cat that Sarah had been to see him. Either way, he couldn't win. If he didn't tell her and she found out, she would say that he was keeping things from her; if he told her, he probably wouldn't score any points for honesty.

There were many others who came to see David, but Catriona and Moira came most frequently. Moira had been shaken by the fracas but she told her father that she had no regrets for what she had done.

'For what it's worth, you have my thanks and gratitude, Moy. I don't want to depart this life just yet and if that mongrel had hit me with a second shot that might have happened. I'm very sorry you had to be involved like that, but you acted with commendable speed and I'm proud of you. When someone opts to shoot at you, they deserve what they get. If he hadn't been stealing our cattle, he wouldn't have got himself shot. Years ago in the old Wild West they used to hang stock thieves when they caught them,' he told her.

'I'd do it again too, Dad,' Moira said fiercely. 'I'm

not sorry for shooting him. He was trying to shoot you and he got what he deserved.'

He really was very proud of her. Not just because she had shot a man to save her father but because his daughter was such a damned great woman. She was running Glen Morrison like an old hand and was never averse to chipping in to help them when there were other jobs to be done. A fellow had no right to expect a daughter to do what Moira was doing. He hadn't expected that she would still be with him, assuming that by now she'd be married and elsewhere. That she was still with him was a colossal bonus.

There weren't many people who had earned high praise from David MacLeod. Moira glowed. Was there ever such a father? She had clashed with him only once and that was over Gary Trainor. Her father had been right and she had been wrong. He had stopped her from making a fool of herself – and worse – for which she was very thankful. Gary Trainor hadn't been worth her father's little finger. She could see that now. But she wasn't the first woman to make an error of judgement where a handsome man was concerned.

Moira was initially charged with manslaughter but the charge was later withdrawn. David brought in one of the best QCs in the country to defend her from the outset. When it was all over he persuaded Manny Thompson's wife, Cheryl, take Moira to the US for a look at the country. Manny kidded that it suited him fine because he wanted to go barramundi fishing in the Kimberley, and Cheryl hated fishing.

David had to make a few changes in management so he brought Tim Barden down to Glen Morrison to look after the stud sheep and cattle in Moira's absence. On her return Tim would live at Poitrel. Tim's brother, Bobbie, who was every bit as keen on the bush and animals as Tim and who had been helping Greg Robertson, was now employed to look after the New England property. With all her children grown up and working at different localities, Linda Barden was now on her own in the big house at Molonga. After discussing the matter with his mother, David proposed that Linda be offered the job of looking after his mother. She would have the cottage Greg Robertson and Sarah had lived in. She would also have the job of looking after David's dogs, because he could see that Catriona was serious about he and her taking a holiday overseas. Linda would be close to Tim and she could see him quite often. Linda agreed to this offer because she was at a loose end and was the kind of woman who hated inactivity. She had a big soft spot for David MacLeod and not just because he had employed two of her sons – he had given her a rent-free home for years and couldn't have treated her better. David MacLeod was the best man Linda had ever known. Looking after his mother was going to be a pleasure. Indeed, just being part of the MacLeod 'empire' was a pleasure.

David had months of physiotherapy after his shoulder healed though it was never quite the same for the rest of his life. News of his shooting had spread far and wide and there was hardly a day that did not see at least one visitor call on him. One of the first to High Peaks was Bruce McClymont, who came all the way from the Riverina to see him. Although he was an old man now and white-haired, he was still a sheepdog man through and through as he would be while he could stand up.

With his beloved Mona in a nursing home with Alzheimer's disease, Bruce was now looked after by his daughter, Marilyn, who was divorced. Her son, Ian, had thrown up his job in Melbourne to come back to the property and was, according to Bruce, 'dog-mad' and keen on station life generally. 'He'll be the one to carry on with the dogs, David,' Bruce said with great pride.

'That's wonderful, Bruce. It would be a blow if all your efforts to build a top kelpie stud went down the drain,' David said.

'It's a great relief, but the whole rural scene is a worry. As if costs and bad seasons weren't bad enough, we've now got the worry of the Family Court. There's places that are having to be sold because of marriage settlements through the Family Court. I know of properties that have been in the same family for generations and they've gone down the gurgler. Divorce used to be too damned hard but it's too easy now,' Bruce said.

'I couldn't agree more, Bruce. I was only saying to Mum that except for the fact that I love the life, it would make good economic sense for me to sell everything and invest the money. I'd have over twelve million dollars in assets. But selling up would put several people out of work and leave me at a loose end. I mean, what would I do?'

'Handle kelpies and win a lot of trials,' Bruce suggested.

'Maybe I could. Then there's the fact that High Peaks is rather special to me. Dad is buried there and Mum will be one day. Kate is there beside Dad and my grandmother is there too. When my time comes I want to lay my head to rest at High Peaks. It wouldn't seem right to have the property in anyone else's hands. Then there's Angus and Moira who are stockpersons through and through. Dad spent his life working to make things better for me – to give it all up now just doesn't seem right. We're doing something really worthwhile but we're not making much money out of it. Where would all our towns be if we all gave up? There's enough of them in decline as it is.'

'You're not wrong there, David,' chipped in Bruce.

'I reckon I'll keep going for a few more years and then assess the situation. It could be the wrong way to go as property values may decline if things get worse. It could be that one day we'll sell everything and just keep High Peaks. I'll sit out here where we are today and swap yarns about the days when things were better,' David said.

'Well I want you to know that knowing you has made a big difference to my life, David,' McClymont said earnestly. 'I would have liked to know your father better because from what I could tell he was a real man. His word was his bond and he was a great dog and horse handler. It was a damned shame he died at such a young age. And getting Nap on loan put me years ahead with the dogs. The best dogs I've got go back to him. What a dog he was, David.'

'Yes, Nap had an extra dimension to him, Bruce. Clancy was the better trial dog because he was a freak on three sheep but Nap thought like a human. He was the most complete dog of all the dogs we've had here. I've always regretted sending him away but if anyone had to have him, I'm very glad it was you, Bruce. You did the right thing by me and by Nap and I'll never forget that, Bruce. You brought Nap back three years to the day and you know me well enough to understand that keeping one's word rates very highly with me,' David said with evident feeling.

'That's the way I was brought up, David. The old man was a bit of an autocrat like Angus Campbell but he was straight as a pine tree. Only way to live, he told me,' McClymont said.

'Dad was just the same,' David agreed. 'Some people said he was too hard and tough but he helped a lot of people in one way or another. He'd crutch or shear sheep for people he knew and wait months to get paid for it. He always knew he would eventually be paid. Dad had no time for slackers and welshers and it was these people who said he was hard. If the local minister told him that someone in town was having a bad time he'd send in a side of mutton or some beef to help them out. Not many people knew that side of Dad. Sure, he was a tough man but he was a very fair man. His father was a playboy of sorts and Dad had to make up for his deficiencies. I've never forgotten him for one day, Bruce.'

'Life is too damned short, David. Oh well, I have had a pretty full, happy life. If you get a good wife, that's the big thing. Mona was just right for me. I've bred a few decent kelpies and they led me to you. That day Clancy won the National was, next to my wedding, the greatest day of my life,' Bruce said with emotion.

'It was great for Dad, Bruce. I was so damned pleased I could give him that. Dad won a lot of trials but I reckon that Clancy's win topped anything he had done. It put the MacLeod name up in lights and that's what I wanted for him. Dad would be tickled pink at me owning all these properties as he had the old Highland love of land in him. Dad liked land and sheep. If he was alive now nothing would give him greater pleasure than to walk through the ram shed at Glen Morrison so he could inspect the wool on those rams. When I was very small he used to point to certain of our sheep and tell me that it would shear well or not so well. It's good to remember those things now,' David said.

'Bruce, I'll wager that you two are talking sheep-dogs,' Catriona said as she appeared on the front verandah with a tray of smoko. 'And I'll also wager that I haven't had a mention.'

'Now, now, Catriona, that isn't fair. David doesn't have to mention you for me to know how he feels about you,' Bruce said with a smile. 'We could be discussing worse things than sheepdogs. You wouldn't like us to be discussing women, would you?'

'I don't know about *your* women, Bruce, but I know of several who wanted David. A couple would still have him, bung shoulder and all,' Catriona said, as she rested one hand on her husband's sound shoulder.

'I'll bet he's never given them two glances,' Bruce said. 'The way I heard it, he wouldn't even look at you for a long time so David could hardly be described as a ladies' man.'

'It's true – I'd almost given up on him. When his shoulder is right again I'm going to take him away, Bruce. David can look at some sheepdogs in Scotland. Moira and Angus can steer the ship here for a few months,' Catriona said, as she sat down beside her husband.

Bruce McClymont regarded her with affection and admiration. Catriona was still a great-looking woman and she was a woman still unashamedly in love with her husband. 'My forebears came from over there but I've never been there,' he said. 'Mona and I talked about taking a trip one day but it's always been hard to leave the place and the dogs. Ian used to come back for some of his holidays but it wasn't long enough for us to get away. Don't reckon I'll go now. Be a bit much for me. If I go anywhere it will be into hospital to get my hip fixed up. Now that Ian's with me I can manage that,' Bruce said. 'I don't reckon I'll get up here again, David. The drive is too much for me now. I have to keep stopping or I fall asleep.'

'I think it's about time we paid you a visit, Bruce. I'll make it a top priority as soon as we get back from overseas,' David said.

'That would be great, David, but don't leave it too long. I get awfully tired these days. I don't reckon I'll handle many more young dogs. Have to teach the young fellow to do that before I shuffle off,' McClymont said.

'Life is pretty damned short,' David said pensively. 'Especially when you view it against the age of something like that,' and he pointed up towards Yellow Rock. 'It seems only a short time ago that I was following Dad up that mountain and here I am a grandfather.'

'That's right. Life is damned short and a fellow shouldn't waste the time he has. You haven't wasted your life, David. I suppose I could have done more with mine but sheep and the dogs always kept me busy. I made enough money to satisfy me and I've had a good life with a fine wife. A fellow can't ask for much more than that.'

'Whatever I am, Bruce, I owe to Dad. He taught me how to work a dog and it was his dogs that gave me my start. And it was learning how to handle

stragglers in this hill country that illustrated the importance of class dogs as distinct from hool-em-ups. At
ten years of age I was bringing straggler wethers down
from the high country. You need class dogs for that
job, Bruce. I've got to tell you that I loved it. I came
alive when I got up amongst the hills of this here high
country on a good pony with a dog running behind. I
used to get into trouble at school because I was forever
gazing out the window at our hills. Other boys played
cricket and footy and they thought I was odd for not
wanting to join in. I never minded hard work, either.
Dad and I used to go up in the hills to ring green
timber and I had a slightly smaller axe than him. I was
a tough little boy, Bruce.'

'So Catriona has told me,' McClymont said dryly.

'Just as well for her I was, Bruce. Oh well, that
was then and this is now. A fellow shouldn't dwell
on the past, but the trouble is that the past has a way
of coming back to haunt you,' David said.

'You mean this Masters fellow?'

David nodded. 'He came right out of the past. We
knew nothing about him.'

'I should think he'll be out of circulation for quite
some time, David.'

'You can't count on that any more, Bruce. The law
seems to be getting easier on creeps,' David said harshly.

'You and Catriona go off and enjoy your holiday,
David. I'll think of you standing on some hillside
watching border collies work their trials and I'll be
wishing I was there with you.'

'I doubt Catriona will want me to be watching too many trials. She has other things in mind,' he said with a grin.

'I'll be looking forward to hearing if you see any more collies like Meg,' McClymont said. 'Maybe you could send me a card after you visit the fellow who sold her to Angus Campbell.'

'I'll do that, Bruce,' David said.

Next morning he and Catriona stood at their front gate to farewell Bruce McClymont. The old chap seemed almost reluctant to leave. He walked up and down beside his utility before finally gripping David's left hand.

'Look after yourself, David. Thanks for everything – for the dogs and for your friendship. I can't put into words what it's meant to me.'

'It's been a pleasure, Bruce. There's nobody I hold in higher esteem than yourself. For what it's worth, in my opinion you've been one of the men responsible for keeping the kelpie where it is today,' David said.

'For you to say that means a lot to me, David,' McClymont said with a catch in this throat. He turned to Catriona and she put her arms around his neck and kissed him.

'Look after yourself, Bruce. We'll come down and see you when we get back from overseas,' she said.

'Thank you for looking after me, Catriona. If I were younger and fitter I'd like to be going to Scotland with you but from what I heard you want David to yourself this time.

Catriona looked at her husband and smiled. 'I do, Bruce. David and I have things to do together.'

'If things go wrong and I don't see you again I want you to know that I regard David as the best man it has ever been my privilege and pleasure to know,' he said, before he turned and got in the utility. After going through the ramp the vehicle stopped beside the dog yards and they saw McClymont get out and stand looking at the dogs.

'What is he doing, darling?' Catriona asked.

'Bruce is saying goodbye to the MacLeod kelpies, Cat. He'll never come here again,' David said thickly.

After a few moments the white utility pulled away and was lost to sight.

Catriona took her husband's left hand in hers and together they walked back up the path and into the house. 'Off with your shirt, buster,' Catriona said, and began unbuttoning his shirt. 'The quicker we get that shoulder mobile, the quicker we can get away,' she added. Between the physiotherapy treatments at the hospital, Catriona was rubbing David with goanna liniment and giving him lamp sessions.

'Remind me never to get shot again,' he said as she pointed to the bed.

When she had finished rubbing him and he had his shirt on again, he turned and faced her. 'Cat, there's one thing I'd like you to do before we go away,' he said.

'What's that, darling?' she asked.

'I'd like you to make it up with Susan,' he said.

'Why?' she asked.

'You were friends for a long time; for as long as I've known you. I think you were too hard on Susan. Sure, she's made something of a mess of her life but it's when things go wrong that people most need their friends. I would much prefer to know that you stood by her. A lot of women make errors of judgement where men are concerned. If Susan had got herself a different husband, things might have turned out much better for her,' he said gently.

'You mean if she had got you instead of Michael,' Catriona said harshly.

'No, I don't mean that at all,' he said. 'I was never interested in Susan and you know it. I'd like to think that my wife is too big a person to allow a quarrel to spoil what was a very long friendship.'

'You think that I was in the wrong and that I'm a small person?' Catriona said, with tears forming in her eyes.

'I don't know or care who was in the wrong and I don't consider you a small person. I simply want to think that you are bigger than to let a few words destroy a friendship. I'd like this quarrel between you and Susan settled before we go overseas. If you aren't disposed to settle it, so be it. Now, I'm going to have a cup of tea,' he said.

He walked out to the kitchen and began filling the jug. Catriona came up behind him and took it from him. 'I'll get the tea,' she said. He nodded and withdrew to the front verandah. The *Land* newspaper beckoned and he sat down and began to read it. Presently, Catriona joined him with tea and biscuits. She took the paper from him and seated herself on the arm of his big chair.

'You've made me feel inadequate and petty, David,' she said.

'That wasn't my intention, Cat,' he said.

'Well, you have. Turning my back on Susan when she needed me most was a pretty miserable thing to do,' she said.

'Mmm,' he murmured.

'Does that mean you agree with me?' she asked.

'I agree with you. It was a pretty miserable thing to do, Cat,' he said.

'So I'm not perfect. So I'm not up to you in a lot of ways. So I make mistakes,' she said.

'Just like Susan,' he said. 'None of us is perfect, Cat. I don't expect you to be perfect just as I'm sure you don't expect me to be perfect. One thing I feel strongly about is standing by one's friends when things get tough. So Susan has made some poor decisions, but basically she's still the same Susan Cartwright who was your friend. I don't know much about women but from what I've read and heard, women commit infidelities because they're searching for something they've never really had. I think Mum got it right when she said that Susan's problem is that she has never had a man love her well and truly. If she had, things might have turned out much more satisfactorily,' he said.

'You amaze me, David,' she said. 'For a dog and horse man, you amaze me. I'm the one with the education but you make me seem a first-class drip. If it means so much to you, I'll try and make it up with Susan.'

'Thank you,' he said.

Chapter Twenty-one

Catriona and Susan had a tearful reconciliation at the Cartwright property, which Susan's brother, Roger, now managed. When she drove away Catriona felt very much better. She had not admitted it to David, but the truth of the matter was that she had felt bad about her part in the quarrel. David had been right to ask her to settle it. She had not told him where she was going – only that she would be away for the morning. He had nodded, looking at her for a few moments, and then walked out of the house to see his mother.

That evening, after they had had dinner and were washing up, Catriona told him where she had been that day. 'I met with Susan this morning,' she said abruptly.

'How did it go?' he asked.

'Tearfully,' she said.

'What are a few tears between friends,' he replied, kissing her cheek softly.

'We both admitted we had behaved stupidly, had

morning tea and talked about our trip. Susan said she had been very unhappy when she met Gary Trainor. He was so good-looking and so charismatic on court, she thought he was the answer to her prayers. The fact that he might be married never occurred to her. Susan had no idea he had seduced Karen until Karen told her she was pregnant. You know the rest,' Catriona said.

'Feel better?' he asked her.

'Much,' she admitted.

'Good. Sorry I picked you up on it but I thought it should be settled before we left Australia. We haven't had many differences of opinion but that quarrel was worrying me. Susan has her faults, but her heart is in the right place, Cat,' he said.

'Susan's heart has been in too many places, darling,' Catriona said, with an attempt at humour.

'Good one, Cat. I hope you will invite her here,' he said.

'I have. Susan wants to come and see us before we go away,' Catriona said.

It was several months before they could leave, what with the trial of Reggie Masters and David's shoulder. They had planned to leave in May, but the trip was put back to June and then early July. It was mid-summer in Scotland so July was still a good time to go. There were so many arrangements to be made, both domestically and internationally, that they were relieved it would be early July and not May after all. Moira and Angus assured David that he shouldn't worry as they were perfectly capable of looking after everything.

David worried even more about his mother. 'I don't like leaving you, Mum. Catriona wants this trip and she's got her heart set on writing this damned novel. I feel I owe it to her to make this trip. There are things in her father's diary she wants to check on that are important to her, too. I feel that if she can get her novel published she'll feel really fulfilled,' he said.

'Don't worry, David. I shall be all right. Linda is here and if I have the slightest problem with my health, she will look after me. You are to go away and not worry. You deserve this trip and I agree with everything you have said where Catriona is concerned. She had a good education and apart from managing your book-work, she hasn't utilised it. Give her as much time as she needs, David. Thorough research is crucial if one wants to come across well in a novel. Let Catriona absorb the atmosphere of MacLeod country and don't rush her away to take in a sheepdog trial,' Anne said with a smile. She was perhaps the only living person who could speak to him in such terms.

'I understand all that, Mum,' he said.

He sought out Linda Barden and told her that he would ring frequently to check that his mother was all right. He also told her that if she had the slightest concern about Anne's health, she was to put her in hospital no matter how much she protested. His mother, he said, always cracked hardy.

'Don't worry, David. I'll watch her like a cat,' Linda assured him.

'Well, she is an old lady and very precious to me,' he

said. 'The last time I went on a honeymoon' – Catriona was referring to the trip as their second honeymoon – 'I lost my father. I don't want to lose my mother while I'm away on this one. I realise she has to go some time but I don't want it to be while I'm away. I was with Kate when she went and I want to be with Mum, too.'

'I understand, David. I really do. Your mother wants you to have this trip and she doesn't want it to be spoilt by you worrying about her,' Linda said firmly.

'It's a hell of a thing when you have to choose between your wife and your mother, if you know what I mean, Linda,' he said.

'I know what you mean, David,' Linda said, and patted his arm. She had idolised this man almost from the very beginning – he was her guardian angel. No man could have done more for her and her family.

'You must see that she eats well, too. Mum is inclined to pick at her food now,' he said.

'Don't be an old hen, David. I had five children and a couple of them were fussy eaters. I'll look after your mother very well,' Linda said.

'I've got to say that it's a great relief to have you here, Linda. You're one of my favourite ladies,' he said a mite sheepishly.

'Be off with you! Go and enjoy yourselves.'

So they left, he with misgivings and Catriona with joy in her heart that she at last had David to herself. She and David would do everything together and they had so much to look forward to.

They flew to London and spent a few days there while Catriona delved into matters genealogical and David looked at campervans. From London they drove in leisurely fashion to Edinburgh, where Catriona spent more time with a genealogical society while David explored the city by foot and purchased tartan cloth for his 'ladies'. Moira and Sue-Ellen had both requested lengths of the yellow, black and red MacLeod tartan.

After two colourful days in Edinburgh they left to drive to Inverness via Perth, Braemar and Grantown. Catriona wanted extensive photographs of Culloden Moor, site of the Jacobite rebellion, which they had seen briefly and from a distance on their previous trip with Angus and Jane Campbell. This time Catriona was determined to walk the moor. Though not timid, she declined to actually camp on the moor because of the men who had died there. Instead, they camped at a burn not far distant.

'Can you imagine what it must have been like here?' she asked, as they sat at their dinner table in the long twilight of a lovely summer's day. She gazed across at the moor and described to him the order of battle as Bonnie Prince Charlie's clans, very much outnumbered, faced up to the English redcoats and dragoons. This time the English were determined there would be no more Jacobite rebellions. No mercy was given to the wounded and they were dispatched by ball and bayonet where they lay. The ringleaders were hanged or sent into slavery overseas. The prince and a handful of his supporters fled through the mountains, he with a huge price on his head, until with the help of Flora Mac-Donald, he escaped to France. The dwelling places of Highland supporters were burned to the ground and their stock killed or run off. Leaders of the rebellion who were not captured were proscribed and survived precariously until the Act of Indemnity was proclaimed.

'No, Cat – I can't imagine what it would have been like fighting in such a bloody battle. It gives me a queer feeling to know that it happened here. I can imagine some of it, like men fleeing through the hills with the horse soldiers tailing them. I have trouble coming to grips with the fact that wounded men were killed where they lay but if you say that is what happened, I believe you,' he said.

'It happened,' she said. 'The clans were smashed. It was forbidden to wear the tartan and some of the High-landers who survived Culloden went to France and served in the French army.'

'Men of those two armies probably passed over this very spot,' he observed.

'Very likely,' she agreed. 'It's incredibly cold here in winter – I wouldn't like to be here then.'

'I wouldn't like to be in any of these cold northern places in winter,' he agreed. 'Beats me how they live here in that cold. Or how they lived here before there was any decent heating. They must have been tough people.'

David and Catriona found plenty of hospitality wherever they went. They were invited to visit one Scot-tish farm carrying several thousand sheep and there, for the first time since he was shot, David shore a sheep. He sailed through the job with little effort considering the twinges he still occasionally experienced. They drove west and spent two weeks on Skye, Lewis and Raasay, all of which was MacLeod country. Dunvegan Castle on the west coast of Skye was the hereditary seat of the clan.

During these two weeks David learnt more about his ancestors, descended originally from 'son of Leod', than he had thought possible. He learnt that there had been two branches of the MacLeod clan, though both descended from Leod. There were the MacLeods of Lewis (or of Torquil) and the MacLeods of Harris. There had been earlier, much earlier, David MacLeods. It was from the MacLeods of Harris that David descended. William MacLeod had left Scotland and its troubles and migrated to Canada. He then moved to the United States where, because of his knowledge of cattle, he was offered a position. Later, he took up land of his own and the MacLeods still own this ranch today. One of William's grandsons, Angus MacLeod, migrated to Australia about the time of the big gold strikes. Angus struck it lucky and subsequently purchased land along the Lachlan River. Periodic floods drove him off this selection and he moved to country between Glen Innes and Armidale. There were many Scottish families in this area of country that became known as New England.

Angus MacLeod fathered six sons and three daughters. One son, Tormid (an ancient name), went as an officer to the Boer War. After returning from South Africa, Tormid purchased a large property in the Hunter River district of New South Wales. Tormid married an actress of some repute and their only son, James, was Andrew's father and David's grandfather. When the few huge original properties around Quirindi, Willow Tree and Merriwa were subdivided into smaller properties, Tormid MacLeod purchased a hill property very cheaply. Tormid established James on this property but he left it to join the Second AIF in 1939.

Anne had a complete history of the MacLeods in Australia and Catriona was bolstering this record by research into William MacLeod's background. It was all very interesting except that bookwork of any kind, setting aside bush poetry particularly, and some other poetry to a lesser degree, was not David MacLeod's cup of tea. What he preferred to do was talk with Scottish farmers and hear their problems. And because he had never had time to fish, he wanted to try his hand at fishing. Catriona had no time for fishing. She was seasick twice off Skye and thereafter would only tolerate David fishing if it was in protected waters.

And so by slow degrees they moved down the west coast of Scotland. Once back on land Catriona's appetite was restored to normal. Sometimes they stayed in inns and sometimes in the van. It depended on the weather, which could change very quickly from sunshine to rain. It was when they started out on Angus Campbell's route that David noticed a new intensity about Catriona. She referred to her father's diary constantly, sometimes reading out extracts for her husband to absorb. It was in the western Highlands, the country of his Campbell ancestors and of the Camerons and the MacDonalds, that Angus had spent his last days on earth. In effect, he had come back to the land of his fathers to die.

What Catriona deduced as she read through the last pages of her father's diary was that although he was experiencing pains in his chest and knew that his heart was playing up, it didn't seem to concern him very much, if at all. He hadn't taken the option of having a heart operation and didn't seem to care whether he lived or died. What seemed to be clear was that Angus Campbell had been quite happy to die in Campbell country.

Catriona knew that she would never forget the bliss she experienced as she and her husband drove down the west coast of Scotland towards the places that were the *raison d'être* for their trip. There were so many things that made this pilgrimage an almost magical experience. There was the changing nature of the landscape with the high country to the east and the island-dotted sea to the west. There were tiny hamlets and larger villages and there were people everywhere who wanted to talk about Australia. Sometimes they would eat at an inn, or stay at an inn, but in good weather they stayed close to the campervan.

Despite the grandeur of most of the places they visited, Catriona knew her husband well enough to realise that his heart was not fully in their trip. His heart and mind were always preoccupied with his interests at home and with his mother. In their lovemaking Catriona gave herself to him with such exuberance that he had no cause to complain about that aspect of their journey.

It wasn't until the evening before they were to reach Loch Etive that David seemed to relax. It was at Loch Etive that they were to visit Willie Cameron, who had sent Meg out to Australia for Angus Campbell. The prospect of meeting this good handler and inspecting his dogs brought about David's lightness of mood. Catriona sighed as she watched him set out plates and knives and forks for their evening meal. There was still the same smooth unhurried way of doing things that she had first noticed in the early days of their relationship. She knew that deep down, setting everything else to one side, David's great interest was sheepdogs. He liked horses, and indeed all livestock, but he had been a boy wonder with sheepdogs and they still held his heart. No matter that what they had seen was wonderful, it couldn't hold a candle to the prospect of seeing sheepdogs in action.

They had come down by Portnacroish and Loch Creran, crossed Loch Etive at Connel and camped the night on the shore of the loch. From here it was only a short drive to Willie Cameron's farm. Catriona had written to Cameron from Australia advising him that she and her husband, who was a sheepdog icon in Australia, would be making the trip and that they would like to visit him. Catriona had explained the circumstances of her father's death after leaving Cameron and that she was Angus Campbell's daughter. Willie Cameron had written back telling them that he would be happy to meet the daughter and son-in-law of so grand a gentleman as Angus Campbell. They had rung Cameron two days previously (there was now a phone at the farm) and told him that they hoped to see him in a couple of days. Catriona had also, through officialdom in Canberra and police headquarters in Inveraray, been in touch with veterinarian Alisdair Grant who had found her father in his campervan.

There had been a sharp shower just on dark but the next morning dawned bright and clear with a cool breeze coming down the lake from the west. The land that swept before them was part of the first country settled by Irish people in the days when Scotland was known as Dalriada. It was the country of legend and folklore and song; the country of Campbells, Camerons and MacDonalds, among several other clans.

The road to the Cameron farm led through some of the most typically Highland country they had seen. There were small unnamed streams running away towards Ben Cruachan (Cruachan was the war cry of the Campbells of Argyll and Breadalbane) before they came to the small hamlet of Glennoe by Glen Noe. Willie Cameron's farm was close by and, as Willie explained later, behind him were the real Highlands with Beinn Eunaich at the head of Glen Liver and Glen Noe.

From the moment they met, David instinctively liked Willie Cameron who was, he reckoned, a real dog man. There was now a wee Willie Cameron so Jean Cameron stayed inside the farmhouse and Catriona felt that she should stay there too. Catriona would have preferred to be with her husband but good manners dictated otherwise.

Of course, David wanted to see Willie's dogs in action so after he had had a look at them, he asked if he could see them work. Willie didn't seem reluctant to show them off and was obviously very proud of Glen, the dog Angus had seen when he visited Willie. There were Cheviot-cross sheep that Glen cast around and handled beautifully. The dog did everything he was told. There was a whistle command for every voice command and these sent the dog either way in what Australians called the side commands and Americans referred to as flanking commands. At long distances the smallest variation in whistle was enough to move Glen one way or the other or to drop him. It was impressive control and no doubt needed for the kind of trials the Scottish used. The dog didn't have to think for itself as most of its work was done by its handler. There was a young bitch Willie had not long started and she was under good control too. But there was no bitch like Meg.

'Have you nothing by Meg's sire to show me?' David asked.

'I didna keep anything, Mr MacLeod. They were a wee bit fresh for the trials,' Willie answered. 'And how would Meg be going?'

'Meg is a really good bitch for our conditions. Look, call me David please, Willie – I'm not one for Mister. Meg, now. She has a lot of things in her that I like and she works more like a kelpie than a border collie. We mated her with a kelpie and got some cracking good dogs. My brother-in-law, that's my wife's brother, has her. Stuart's place is next to mine. I was hoping to have a look at more dogs by her sire,' David told him.

'There's plenty to be seen but they're away away up north. I used the dog because I wanted to try something that didna have Wilson blood, you ken. The Wilson dogs had a grand name and everyone used them so much that it's a mite hard to find a top dog that doesna have the blood. Ross has such a name up north I took my old bitch up to him,' Willie said.

'Are there many collies that look like Meg up there?' David asked.

'Losh, man, there's plenty. There's dogs almost all black and red-and-whites and an odd lemon-and-white and there's greys and grey-and-whites. But they're not just up north. You can find them anywhere. A lemon-and-white ran for Wales one year. There could be more of the black ones up beyond Ullapool and I've heard that some of them have island blood in them. It doesna matter what colour they are; it's the work that counts,' Willie said sagely.

David nodded. 'My sentiments entirely, Willie.'

They walked down to the house where Willie announced it was lunchtime and asked them would they stay for a wee bite. Over the mutton and potatoes they talked about farming matters and farming problems and David learnt that Willie ran eight hundred sheep and about a hundred head of cattle. It didn't seem enough for a decent living but of course livestock returns were much higher in the United Kingdom. Willie also grew potatoes.

'And what would you run out in Australia?' Willie asked.

'About twelve thousand wethers on the hill-country places and about seven thousand breeding ewes on the other three. There's about five hundred stud ewes in them. We breed rams from them. Then there's about four hundred head of commercial cattle and about two hundred stud Hereford cows for bull breeding. We have a small lot feeding set-up where we test our steers,' David said.

'You couldna look after all that yourself?' Willie said in amazement.

'Goodness, no. I have a son and daughter who run a place each and help otherwise, and there are other people too. We stand a thoroughbred stallion and my son and his wife look after that side of things,' David said.

'You'd no get time to work dogs?' Willie said.

'I don't these days. My son Angus is a good handler and has won trials. Sadly, my trial days are in the past,' David said.

'David won the National with a kelpie,' Catriona told them. 'He scored the possible hundred points in the final.'

'You dinna say,' Willie said. He was still trying to come to terms with how a man could manage so many sheep and cattle.

When they went out to the van to leave, David extracted two bottles of top-quality whisky he had purchased on the trip. 'I'd like you to have these for your hospitality, Willie. Maybe when you and Jean are having a nip on a cold night you'll remember the Australians who came to see you. I'll certainly remember you both and this place.'

'Well, that's generous of you, David – thank you.'

'By the way, what did Angus pay for Meg, if it isn't a rude question?' David hoped the gift of the whisky would soften Willie's reaction to the question.

'Mr Campbell gave me ten thousand dollars for her, David. It wasna what I asked for her. I would have asked two thousand pounds for her but he offered me the ten. I told him she wasna ready to take but he wanted her. There's dogs that have made that amount of money, mostly to Americans, but trained dogs. Meg wasna finished, you ken?'

So Angus had really handed over ten grand for Meg. It was the last great gesture of his life and David reckoned the old chap had been right about his selection. Angus had learnt a hell of a lot.

'I took her down to London and sent her from there,' Willie explained.

'Maybe I'll come back and see you again one of these days, Willie. I've a notion to travel up north so I can have a look at the dogs you talk about.'

One day they would need to use another outcross and maybe there were dogs in northern Scotland that would do the job. When he retired it might be good to go up north and just poke about. Maybe look for the descendants of the Rutherfords and see what records they had.

David and Catriona travelled back to the main road by the side of Loch Etive and left it where the road turned south-west to join the A85. This road took them through the Pass of Brander before they stopped to boil the billy and so Catriona could photograph Lochawe, one of the legendary homes of the Clan Campbell. They left the A85 shortly after leaving Loch Awe, the picturesque lake nearby, and drove down towards Inveraray on the A819. They camped beside a lovely waterfall rather than travel any later. Next morning they picked up mail in Inveraray and then met up with Alisdair Grant who was to show them where he had found Angus Campbell.

Alisdair Grant was a fine upstanding man with the eyes of a lynx. Grant had made some enquiries after being contacted by Catriona and had discovered that the MacLeods were people of real substance. Scottish officialdom had done a check on David's interests which they said were 'extensive'.

'We don't like taking you away from your clients, Mr Grant, and we're quite prepared to pay for your time,' David said on meeting the veterinarian.

'You'll do na such thing,' Grant said firmly. 'One

day soon I'll likely go to Australia to look at things and you might be able to do something for me.'

'Name it,' David said. 'We do embryo transplantation of stud sheep and cattle and you'd no doubt find that interesting.'

Grant beamed. 'And you'd use artificial insemination for your stud sheep?'

'Oh, yes. We inseminate hundreds of ewes to the top rams.'

'The very thing. I've been wanting to see your merinos since I was a vet student,' Grant said.

He took them out in his station wagon and they left the van at his surgery. They drove out on the A83, which skirted Loch Fyne, and Grant entertained them with tales of local history. The Clan Campbell was the most powerful of the Scottish clans in this area. The chieftain of the Campbells of Argyll was referred to as MacCailean Mhor. The castle of Argyll to which Angus Campbell had been headed was not a great distance out on the A83 but Angus hadn't made it. He had died beside a small stream perhaps three-quarters of the way to the castle.

Grant turned off the road and pulled up beside this stream. 'This is where I found your father, Mrs MacLeod,' he said.

'Catriona,' she said and flashed him a quick smile. Few people had ever been able to withstand Catriona's smile and her brown eyes.

'Well, Catriona, let me say that it was no a bad place for your father and a Campbell to die. Up beyond

Argyll there's Clachan and Rob Roy's house on the Brannie Burn. You could say that he had come home,' Grant said.

'Now that we know the spot could you take us back and we'll bring the van out here? We'd like to spend a night here, Alisdair,' Catriona explained. She and David had discussed this previously. Although Catriona had declined to camp on Culloden she had no such fears about camping where her father had died.

After stocking up with a few provisions, Catriona and David returned to the place of Angus's death. It was while David was sitting at the camp table that he remembered the mail they had picked up in Inveraray earlier in the day. They had arranged with Moira that she should send mail to Inveraray and then to Edinburgh.

'There's a card from Moira,' he said as he flipped through the mail. He read it first and Catriona saw his face harden. 'What is it, darling?' Catriona asked.

'Bruce McClymont is dead,' he said. 'He died a fortnight ago. Moira went to his funeral.'

This had been one of the arrangements he had made with Moira. She was to represent him if Bruce passed away. He had not rung home for over a fortnight because Moira had told him he was not to be a fusspot as everything was going well.

'I did as I promised and attended Bruce's funeral,' he read. 'It was at Deniliquin and it was very big. I read your eulogy and Bruce's grandson read another. Ian is gorgeous – and *unmarried*.

'PS. I think Ian *liked* me. I sure liked him. M.MacL.'

Catriona looked at her husband and shook her head. She could see David's hand in this development. He and Bruce had had their heads together a lot on Bruce's last trip. Bruce had told them that his grandson was shy of girls, was like a fish out of water in Melbourne and had wanted to be back at the station for years. Bruce wanted his dogs carried on and Ian was supposed to be 'dog-mad'. David wanted somebody special for Moira and Ian McClymont just might be that person. The two men had so much respect for each other that a marriage between the two families couldn't be bettered. It would give David the extra son he had so much wanted.

Catriona could see by the faint smile that came and went on her husband's face that these possibilities were in his head. They softened the fact that Bruce McClymont was no more.

'I can see you've been plotting a bit, David,' she said.

'I simply asked Moira to attend Bruce's funeral if he died while we were away,' he replied.

'Simplicity has nothing to do with it, David. If I know you, and I think I do, you and Bruce would have discussed the possibility of getting Moira and Ian together. If this hadn't happened I'll bet that Bruce would have sent Ian up to you to show him how to work dogs. That way he could meet Moira,' she said.

'Now you mention it, Bruce did say something along those lines,' David teased.

'Ha! I thought so,' Catriona said triumphantly. 'You're matchmaking, David.'

The big man leant back so far in his camp chair it threatened to give way. 'What if I am? What if they sell Jimbawarra and invest the money and Ian comes up to me? That way we keep Moira and we get another son,' he said.

'I thought that was your plan of campaign. You're very devious for "just a bushie", David. You really are,' she scolded.

'I wouldn't call it devious, Cat. It's simply good planning. Do you want me to do the spuds?'

'You're changing the subject, David. Yes, you can do the spuds. How long do you think it will be before Ian comes up to see us?' Catriona asked.

'Not very long, Cat. If he's lost his heart, maybe a week after we get back,' David said with a grin.

'God, I put up with a lot,' Catriona said. 'And I only lived next door to you.'

'Don't let's go over that again,' he said. 'These long evenings are great, aren't they?'

'There you go changing the subject again, David. Do you want steak or chops?'

'What about a bit of both?' he answered.

Later, after they had eaten, they lay together on a rug and looked out across the deepening purple of the Highlands. 'Do you think Daddy had time to appreciate this place?' she asked.

'I doubt it, Cat. Alisdair said he probably ran the vehicle in off the road when the big pain hit him. He may have died at that time or else he stayed in the van until a bit later,' he said.

'What do we do now? Head for Iona?' she asked.

'I think so, Cat. That is, if you're sure you can handle the boat trip?'

'It's not the open sea, David. The islands are well protected, aren't they?' Catriona asked.

'I believe they can be rough at times, but we won't go in rough weather. That's the beauty of having the van. It's only a small trip from Oban to Iona but there'll be some swell from the ocean,' he said.

Catriona groaned. She had experienced the effects of the Atlantic swell and they were still fresh in her memory. But if they had to go by boat to reach Iona, so be it. Iona, of all places mentioned in her father's diary, was the most important to her.

It was an eerie feeling to be camped in the spot where her father had taken his last breaths. Catriona couldn't get to sleep for some time as she thought of her father and what it must have been like for him in those last few conscious moments. Did he regret being away from his family? It didn't seem so. Certainly if he had entertained any doubts about the wisdom of taking this last trip they had not come through in his diary. Conversely, he had seemed very pleased he had made the effort. Iona, and what he had witnessed there, seemed to have made everything worthwhile.

Catriona was still asleep when David called her for breakfast. He, as usual, was up early and had been for a walk up the road towards Argyll Castle. 'You mean thing. You might have called me,' she told him.

'You were sleeping like a log, Cat,' he said between

mouthfuls of bacon and eggs. 'It's a top morning. We'll drive up to the castle so you can get your photographs and then head back to the coast. I'll make a few phone-calls in Inveraray. Do you want to meet your relations at the castle?'

Catriona shook her head. 'Not on this trip, David. I'd like to get to Iona while this good weather lasts. If we go in, they might ask us to stay and I wouldn't like to refuse,' she said.

David nodded his understanding. The aristocracy didn't intimidate him but he had no special desire to meet Angus Campbell's relations. What he wanted most of all was to get back home as soon as possible. Yet he didn't want to spoil Catriona's happiness. It was quite apparent that she was enjoying every moment (on land, at least) of their trip.

Later, in Inveraray, they rang Anne, Moira and Angus and found that everything was going well at home. Anne told him he was a fusspot to worry about her and not to hurry back. Finally, he rang the Riverina and spoke with Bruce McClymont's daughter, Marilyn.

'I'm ringing from Inveraray in Scotland, Marilyn. We didn't know about Bruce until yesterday evening when we picked up Moira's card at the post office. We've been in the west of Scotland for the past three weeks. Cat and I want to say how very sorry we are to know that Bruce has gone. He was one of my very best friends and a man for whom I had the utmost respect. I would have gone through fire and flood to be at Bruce's funeral, Marilyn. I'm pleased Moira could stand in for me. We made that arrangement before Cat and I left.

'As soon as you feel up to it, Cat and I want you and Ian to come up and see us. Will you do that? Bruce was anxious for me to meet Ian and to help him with some handling tips. You will come? Splendid. We'll be home within the fortnight, Marilyn. I'll ring from High Peaks,' he said, and put the phone down.

Catriona, who had been standing next to him as he talked to Marilyn Taylor, patted his arm. 'Will they come?' she asked.

'They'll come.'

'I don't know why I ever let you get away with calling me Cat, David. I cut people dead for doing that,' Catriona said.

'What brought that up?' he asked as he started the van.

'Calling me Cat to people I've never met. They must wonder who you're talking about,' she said. 'It's not as if Catriona isn't a nice name. Next to Flora it must be the most celebrated name in Scottish literature. Robert Louis Stevenson wouldn't have referred to his heroine as Cat.'

'I wouldn't know about that. Catriona always seemed a mouthful of a name for a little blonde girl. As to why you allow me to call you Cat, the fact of the matter was that you wanted me so much you would have allowed me to call you almost anything,' he teased.

'Ha,' she said as she dug him in the ribs.

'We won't get to Iona if you keep doing that to the

driver,' he said. 'How far is it to that place with the unpronounceable name?'

Their destination was Oban, where Angus Campbell had taken a boat for Mull, but they had opted for a longer drive down Loch Fyne rather than go back via the A819. They agreed that it would be preferable to see new country than to look at country they had already traversed. The place David referred to was Lochgilphead, which was not far from where the southern road joined the Inveraray road. It was near where Loch Fyne joined a smaller loch close by the island of Eilean Mor.

Alisdair Grant had given them the name of a fisher-man who lived in Oban and who was known to supplement his income by ferrying tourists to Mull and Iona. This man was a kinsman by name of Hector Grant. They could probably have picked up a boat lower down the coast than Oban but Catriona preferred to follow as closely as possible in her father's footsteps.

'It's only a hop, step and a jump by Australian standards,' Catriona answered.

'Then there's a fair haul to Oban.'

The boat trip from Oban to Iona occupied a little less than three hours and was a summer-only excursion for tourists. Winter gales made the trip too hazardous for small craft. You could get to Iona by slipping up the Sound of Mull (which separates the island from the Scottish mainland) to Tobermory and then after rounding the tip of the island, heading south between a string of small islands that included Staffa, which inspired Mendelssohn to write *Fingal's Cave*. This trip took something under four hours and although full of interest, it exposed travellers to a greater stretch of sea than the southern route. David considered the latter was by far the best bet for a wife who turned green in any kind of swell. Catriona was hardly ever sick but she very soon became ill in a boat. David, who had never been in a boat of any kind before this trip, was unaffected by chop or swell.

They passed through Lochgilphead and drove on to Kilmartin where they had lunch by the cairns. From there it was a leisurely drive to Oban, and from Kiltraw on the Barbreck River they were more or less in sight of the sea until they reached the northern extremity of Loch Melfort at Melfort.

'How can Loch Melfort be a loch?' Catriona asked. 'I thought a loch was a lake surrounded by country. This loch runs into the sea.'

'It isn't the only one, Cat. Some of the other lochs run into the sea, including the Linnhe Loch that splits the country. But there are plenty of drowned lakes that don't run into the sea. They're replenished each spring by melting snow. Some of them are beautiful.'

'There's a distinctive sort of wild beauty about a lot of Scotland,' Catriona said. 'There's so much . . . there's so much that is picturesque, particularly on this coast, but there's a wildness never far away. There are gales and snow that one has to live with all winter. Gales come out of the Atlantic with very little warning. I couldn't live on some of these islands – how would you get off them in bad weather?'

'I dare say the locals are well used to such conditions, Cat. They're a hardy breed, these islanders. They've lived here for a long time, and some wouldn't live anywhere else,' David reflected.

They camped that night by Loch Feochan, got up early next morning and hunted up Hector Grant, who lived in a small cottage not far from the Oban waterfront. Hector was ready for them because they planned to be back at Oban that evening. Everything depended on the weather because even in mid-summer a storm could spring up from anywhere and this could mean staying on Iona for the night. Against this possibility, David rolled up a swag of blankets in plastic and Catriona packed food into a backpack emblazoned with the word 'Australia'. They took enough food for Hector Grant but the fisherman told them he always carried his own.

It was shortly after seven and a bright clear morning when they slipped down the Sound of Kerrera and out into the Firth of Lorn. Here there was a gentle swell that increased slightly as they came out from behind the protection of Mull. David looked anxiously at Catriona who gave him a quick smile. Following her seasickness at Skye she had purchased pills to ward off the malady and had taken the first before they left Oban. So far, so good, he thought. It was important that Catriona remain well because this excursion to Iona was perhaps the highlight of the whole trip for her.

He thought the best thing he could do for his wife

was keep her mind off the sea and occupied with other matters. To this end he had a big map of the Hebrides spread out on his knee and was following every aspect of their sea trip with keen interest. The hills and mountains of Mull some distance to their right were always in sight until the boat swung away to clear Sgeir Dhoirbh at the southern extremity of the Torran Rocks.

'Whew, just imagine hitting them at night,' David said, and pointed to the rocks.

'It was no a rare thing in the old days,' Hector Grant said from the wheel.

Once clear of the rocks the skipper turned the boat northwards towards the channel known as the Sound of Iona that separated the small island from the most easterly point of Mull. The swell was greater here before subsiding marginally as the boat slipped into the protection afforded by the island. Catriona took her husband's hand and squeezed it. He felt it damp on his palm and knew she was pent-up with anticipation about what she might find on Iona.

Presently, the boat came abreast of Baile Mor on the eastern shore of Iona. Grant anchored the boat and put the dinghy in the water. It was a short row to the shore where, before they did anything else, David said he had to have smoko.

'Smoko?' Grant said with a look of bemusement on his face.

'It's Australian for morning tea or something to eat. Not lunch, something between breakfast and lunch,' Catriona explained.

'I ken you now,' Grant said. He looked at her husband's tall figure and nodded. 'Your man would take some filling.'

'You can say that again,' Catriona said, and laughed. She had picked up cake and shortbread when they bought their bread and other provisions in Inveraray.

'Will you be all right here until we get back, skipper?' David asked.

'As right as could be,' Grant said. His English was remarkably clear for a west-coast Scot. 'They're long evenings but I'd like to be awa' by four. That would put us back in Oban about seven.'

David nodded. That gave them five hours. The island was about three and a half miles long and the abbey was only a mile or so to the north of Baile Mor. 'We'll be back here at four, skipper.'

Encumbered only by his backpack they set out for the abbey. They passed by a nunnery and then came across the first of the several crosses they were to see that day. They inspected a shell-littered beach, watched over by mewing gulls. Before long they reached the renovated cathedral. Here, close by the site of the monastery St Columba had established in AD 563, a new Dominican abbey had been built in AD 1203. Some relics of this building still remain.

They went into the cathedral and knelt while Catriona almost inaudibly whispered a short prayer for her father. Outside again they walked to the old cemetery where the remains of half a hundred or so Scottish kings are buried, together with the remains of kings of

Europe. This island was considered not only the holiest place in all Scotland but one of the holiest places in the world.

On a rocky rise they paused in their wanderings to have lunch. With their faces to the west they were looking out towards the Atlantic. David, the map across his knees, pointed out to sea. 'Why this place, Cat? Why of all the islands in the western Hebrides did St Columba choose Iona? Look here. If he sailed from Ireland he'd have passed Islay and Colonsay before he got to this rocky little place,' he said.

'Maybe he was meant to come here and not some more salubrious place,' Catriona said. 'Maybe it was uninhabited because it was so unattractive for settlement in comparison with the bigger islands. And remember, darling, there was no Christianity here until St Columba brought it. Would Christian missionaries have been received with open arms on this wild coastline?'

'I don't know, Cat. All I know is that it would have been a damned tough place to live on. There would have been fish but you have to catch them and in winter that wouldn't have been easy. I suppose you could grow spuds and a few other things here because it rains a lot. No doubt they brought food of some kind with them to keep them going but there was no refrigeration. I reckon they were pretty marvellous fellows to exist here. It wouldn't be the easiest place to live today, let alone in the sixth century. But why this island was the chosen one beats me,' he said.

Catriona leant her head against his chest and he put

his arms around her. 'It's a very long way from High Peaks,' she murmured.

'A very, very long way,' he whispered in her ear.

'You're homesick?' she said.

'I can't help that, Cat. High Peaks is my country. I know it all so well. And I'm worried about Mum,' he said.

'Moira said she was all right.'

'Mum would tell Moira she was all right no matter what. She wouldn't say anything to bring us home one day earlier,' he said.

He had been thinking a lot about his mother lately. He had taken her too much for granted. His father had been his inspiration but his mother had been the rock he had built his life on. He hadn't told her that for a long time and now it seemed important that he should.

Catriona felt him stiffen and leant back and looked up at him. It was their intimacy in moments like these, on days like these, that thrilled her. The whole trip had been wonderful and had indeed been a second honeymoon as she had intended.

'Look up there, Cat,' he said, and pulled her to her feet with him.

She followed his finger and saw it. It was a line of white clouds that seemed suspended in mid-sky. A golden ray of light shone clean through the cloud and danced upon the waves. All at once it seemed that there was absolute silence; the wind was still, no gulls cried above them and there was no sound from anywhere. Neither could speak or even whisper. Then in seconds the golden rod of light was gone and overhead the gulls were screaming.

'Do you think that it was something like that Daddy saw?' Catriona said at last.

'That, or something more, or maybe he imagined more than he saw, Cat. If there is a God, He would be just as likely to appear here as anywhere. This *is* the most sacred place in Scotland. Whatever Angus saw, he went to his death in peace and that's more than a lot have done.'

Catriona looked out over the sea – the endless, rolling sea that stretched all the way to North America. 'Just up there is Staffa,' she said. 'It's even smaller than Iona. The first thing I shall do when we got home is buy Mendelssohn's *Hebrides Overture*. I shall shut my eyes and remember this place. It would be nice to see the cave on Staffa that inspired it but I'm ready to go home now, darling,' she said.

'Then let's go home, Cat,' he agreed.

Hand in hand they walked back to Baile Mor where Hector Grant awaited them. 'You'll na doubt be ready for afternoon smoko,' he said with a poorly concealed grin.

'Now that you mention it, skipper, I could do with a drink of tea and spot of cake before that trip back,' David said. 'There might be just enough tea in the last thermos to eke out three cups.'

'And I'll take some more pills. I don't want to spoil this day by being sick on the way back to Oban,' Catriona said.

The freshening wind from the great ocean to their west seemed to speed their way back to the mainland. It was just after seven when they docked, and the day held another two hours of daylight at least. David paid Grant and gave him a handsome bonus into the bargain.

'What do you say, Cat, shall we hit the road for a couple of hours and see where night finds us?' he asked.

'Let's,' she agreed.

'It will be two hours nearer to home,' he said with a smile.

On the boat trip back from Iona Catriona, to keep her mind off the swell, had been tossing up whether to suggest they take in the border country before flying out from Edinburgh. It was the place of legends, and of both family and border feuds. It seemed a shame not to learn what she could while she was so close. Yet it could be the reason for another trip. Against this curiosity she had to balance the enthusiasm she had to begin work on the novel. David's remark settled the matter. She had always known that he would have preferred not to make this trip but he had agreed because he realised she wanted it so badly. And David had been simply wonderful the whole time. Now he wanted to go home; home to High Peaks, home to his mother and to Moira and Angus, his dogs, his horses and the whole operation.

'Do you think we could stay at an inn tonight, David? I'm sticky from salt water and I feel filthy,' she said.

'If we can find a decent one, Cat,' he said. 'You don't look filthy.'

'Thank you,' she said, and smiled at him gratefully. 'I assure you I feel it.'

They drove through Connel and Taynuilt and down the A85 to where the full sweep of Loch Awe lay golden in the westerly sun. Up past the legendary Lochawe of the Campbell dynasty and through Dalmally and still there was daylight. Catriona could hardly stay awake and as hard as she fought against losing concentration, her eyes kept closing. And then by the crossroads where the A85 joined the A82 they came to Crianlarich.

'Crianlarich, Cat. This is far enough for tonight.'

It was definitely far enough, Catriona thought. Any longer and I'll be asleep.

'Strath Fillan is close by, David. The real Strath Fillan.'

'What is so remarkable about Strath Fillan, Cat?' he asked.

'It's mentioned in Scott's *A Legend of Montrose*, darling. Montrose says, "Oh, for a guide through the skirts of Strath Fillan" or words to that effect.'

'Who was Montrose?' he asked.

'He was ... I'll tell you about him when I'm not so sleepy. But our Strath Fillan would have been named after this place,' she said.

'Undoubtedly,' he agreed. 'We must find out who owned the place originally.'

A hot bath soothed the weary Catriona, and although she was still too sleepy to do justice to a late supper, she hung in there while David polished off a solid meal. She was asleep within five minutes of getting into bed.

It was nearly seven when she woke and she found David had bathed and shaved and even been for a walk. She was disappointed to find the bed empty because she had wanted David to make love to her this last morning in the Highlands. He, meanwhile, had probably imagined she simply wanted to sleep.

They drove to Edinburgh by Stirling and Catriona took pictures of the castle where so many grim deeds had taken place over the centuries. 'What brutes we were,' she murmured. 'Perhaps some of your forebears ended their days here.'

'Perhaps they did,' he agreed. 'But not all of them, thank goodness.'

They reached Edinburgh in the late afternoon and flew back to Australia the next day, eager to feast upon the hills and high-country air of High Peaks.

Moira drove down to pick them up at Mascot International Airport. She told them on the phone that she was quite up to coping with the traffic. David thought that she looked exceptionally lovely and he attributed the glow in his daughter's eyes to her delight in having them back home. Catriona, far more perceptive in such matters than her husband, realised almost immediately that there was another reason for Moira's radiance. Moira was in love, and Catriona had no doubt that a certain young man from the Riverina was responsible.

'You look great, Moy. Haven't had too much to do?'

'I've had a fair bit to do, Daddy, but not too much,' Moira replied.

Later, after they had cleared the Sydney traffic, Moira gave the wheel to her father and got in the back seat. 'How was the trip?' she asked to neither parent in particular.

'Cat has it all written down. She'll give you a full account of the whole business,' David told her.

'It was wonderful, Moira,' Catriona said. 'The only sour note was that I kept getting seasick around the islands. It was all right after I took some pills but not so good before that.'

Moira filled them in on the state of things on the various properties but seemed pent-up with excitement about something.

'Is that all?' David asked.

'Oh yes, and Marilyn Taylor wants to know if it would be all right for her and Ian to come up for a visit,' Moira said.

'What did you tell them?' David asked without a change of expression in his voice.

'I told them I would ask you and Mum when you got back,' she said.

'There's no need to defer to us, Moy. You can have anyone you like at Glen Morrison. You aren't a little girl any longer. You want to have guests, you have them,' he said.

'I know that, Dad. It's just that I know how close you and Bruce McClymont were and I thought you would want to have them with you. You did invite them before you left. I thought it might seem like second-best if they stayed with me,' Moira said.

What a girl, he thought. He was trying to think of a suitable response but Catriona beat him to it.

'That was very thoughful of you, Moira. It would be much better if Marilyn and Ian stayed with us. Both David and I held Bruce in very high regard and he would want his family to be with us.'

'That's what I thought,' Moira said.

Nothing he had seen overseas looked half as good as the bridge across the creek below their old homestead. It told him that he was within a bull's roar of home. Home meant his mother, and all she signified.

Anne had been having afternoon tea on the front verandah. Linda had brought it to her with a rug to place over her knees. Anne liked to have her tea there on nice afternoons. It was lovely to watch the different colours of Yellow Rock and to think of the past. Coming to Merriwa had changed her life. She often wondered what her life would have been like if she had not met Andrew MacLeod. And how different it would have been if she had not produced a son like David.

A white car came up the slope and crossed the ramp into High Peaks. It pulled up in a swirl of dust just outside her front gate and almost before it had stopped a front door burst open and the tall figure of her son came round the car and then through the front gate. He came up the steps two at a time as she rose to meet him.

'Mum,' he said.

'David,' she said, and fell into his arms. He picked her up and kissed her and then carried her down the steps to greet Catriona coming through the open gate. Linda Barden watched him from the verandah.

'I'm not a child, David. I don't have to be carried about,' she half-scolded him. 'I can still walk on my own two legs.'

He put her down on the path and Catriona hugged her. 'Anne, it is *so* good to see you,' Catriona said. 'And David worried about you the whole time.'

'He had no need to, Catriona. I am quite well and Linda looks after me splendidly,' Anne told her. She looked beyond her son and daughter-in-law to where Moira stood. Moira gave a very slight shake of her head and Anne knew then that she had not told them about Ian Taylor's phonecalls. She and Moira had talked about Ian. Moira had asked her how a girl knew if she was really and truly in love.

'I'm sure you're ready for a cup of tea and Linda has made a cake and biscuits,' Anne said.

'We're ready,' David answered enthusiastically.

'You've never not been ready for cake, David,' Anne said with a smile.

They went into the old homestead where Linda Barden had the smoko laid out on the big table in the lounge. Above the fireplace were the photographs and trophies David remembered so well.

'Linda,' he said, and she kissed him her greeting. 'How are you? And how are the boys?'

'I'm well and the boys are fine. And Moira and Angus have done a great job.'

'I'm sure they have. I can hardly wait to get changed and to get stuck into things again,' he said.

He was relieved to find his mother looking so well. His secret fear right through the trip was that he would lose her as he had lost his father. He had tried not to show his anxiety and hoped he had succeeded.

'Was it a good trip, Catriona?' Anne asked.

'It was wonderful, Anne. I did a lot of research on the MacLeods and took a lot of photographs of MacLeod country. It's a pity they lived on islands because I got dreadfully seasick. I'll tell you more about that some other time. David didn't turn a hair, which was remarkable for a landlubber,' Catriona said with a wry smile.

'Did you achieve all you wanted to achieve?' Anne asked.

'Very much so, Anne.' She had followed her father's footsteps to the very end and she had had David to herself.

'Did Iona reveal anything to you?' Anne asked.

Catriona looked across to her husband before answering. 'We're not sure, Anne. It could have, and then again it might not have. It's certainly a very special place.'

They talked on until David stood up. 'I reckon it's time to go, Mum. What's the score with the dogs, Linda? Have we got plenty of dog tucker?'

'Yes, and you don't have to feed them tonight. I'll

do it. You and Catriona go on down and get unpacked. I stocked the fridge with food for you,' Linda said.

'That was very sweet of you, Linda,' Catriona said gratefully. 'Moira, are you coming with us?'

'Do you want me to?' Moira asked.

'Moira, why wouldn't we?'

'I thought you might like to be alone the first night back,' Moira said.

Catriona shook her head. 'We've been alone a lot, Moira. David's talked about you all the way home. I'm sure you've got a lot to tell him.'

They drove down to the home David had built for Catriona to come back to after their honeymoon at Yeppoon. The native trees and shrubs looked to have grown a lot while they were away though they really hadn't. As they walked up the path to the house David stopped in his tracks.

'What is it, David?' Catriona asked.

Without replying he lifted her in his arms and carried her up the steps and into the house. She looked into his eyes before she kissed him. 'You great brute,' she said, '. . . but I love you.'

Moira looked on with interest. At least half the parents of her old school friends were divorced or living apart so it was rather wonderful that her own parents were still so close. She felt that she would hate to have a broken marriage. It would be so unfair for the children. Of course, her mother doted on her husband. Moira knew how hard she had exercised to stay slim and youthful for him. But her father was worth it. He was the most wonderful man she knew. How could she leave him? Even for Ian?

'Moira, dear, would you ring and see if Angus and Sue-Ellen would like to come up for dinner?' Catriona said. 'And you might ring Dougal and tell him we're back.'

'Will do, Mum,' Moira said.

'Has he been ringing often, Moira?' Catriona asked.

'Who, Mum?'

'Ian Taylor, of course.'

'How did you know?' Moira asked.

'Mothers know quite a lot, Moira,' Catriona said with a smile.

'Yes, he has been ringing a lot. Does it show?'

'It shows. We'll talk more later. Goodness, it didn't take David long to change,' she said.

He came into the lounge wearing gaberdine trousers and a blue check shirt.

'That's more like it. I'll walk up and have a look at the dogs, Cat.'

'I thought you might,' she said, and smiled at him.

David walked up the road and over the grid to the orchard and dog yards. It felt good to be treading his own soil. A couple of the dogs barked tentatively until he spoke and then they wagged their tails in response. He sat down on the big hollow log that would always be referred to as 'Nap's log' and looked at them. He had seen some great border collies on the trip, some beautifully schooled dogs, but he wouldn't swap his kelpies for any of them. He knew what these dogs could do and for everyday work they didn't require a lot of training to do the job. Working at the UK International was a different matter. What it came down to was that it was horses for courses. He would have liked to track down Meg's relations but Catriona was bitten with the writing bug and he had let her have her head. Some day he might go back to see what he could dig up in the dog line in those northern hills.

He thought the dogs were in great shape. Linda had done a fine job looking after them. Children or dogs, it didn't matter, Linda was tops. He thought a lot of Linda Barden. Years ago, when he was a tough little rooster and anxious to prove himself with dogs and horses, he hadn't thought much of girls or of females generally, his mother and Kate Gilmour being the exceptions. What he had found since then was that the bush would be a much tougher place without its great-hearted women. His own life would have been different entirely if he had not had Catriona. Then there had been Kate who had been like a second mother to him, not to mention Sarah Matheson and Linda Barden. And Moira. Moira gave him more pleasure than he had ever expected to receive from a daughter. To top it off there was Sue-Ellen, who had pulled Angus into shape and made him the man David had always hoped he would be. Without all of these women his life wouldn't have been anywhere near as full or rewarding. 'Ah well, even tough little roosters grow up,' he muttered to himself.

He turned and walked back down the track and, as always, his attention was focused on Yellow Rock. It seemed such a long time since he had first ridden up the mountain on a led pony. Yellow Rock had been part of his life and it would be there long after he was gone and forgotten. It was not as grand or impressive as some of the Scottish mountains but it was *his* mountain, and that made all the difference. So many things had happened on Yellow Rock that it was never far from his thoughts and his heart. It was as if the mountain made the man. The man and the mountain.

Chapter Twenty-two

Ian Taylor and his mother, Marilyn, came to High Peaks about three weeks after David and Catriona's return from overseas. Marilyn was a handsome woman with dark, wavy hair and a lot of personality and intelligence. David's first thought on meeting her was why any man would want to part from her. But, as Catriona said to him later, maybe her husband wasn't worth staying with and it was Marilyn who walked away from the marriage.

Ian Taylor was a very nice-looking man, taller than his grandfather Bruce, but very reserved. On better acquaintance he proved to possess a dry, quick sense of humour. His mother told them that he was shy of girls, especially forward girls, but he never for a moment took his eyes off Moira. David resolved to discover whether the young man had anything in him and, much to Moira's horror, carted him off on his own. He discovered that Ian Taylor couldn't ride because there were no horses on Jimbawarra and that he couldn't shear because he had never had to. Ian was very keen on dogs and would talk dogs until the cows came home. He had some knowledge of merino sheep and was trying to come to grips with micron measurement. He couldn't tell a good bull from a bad one and didn't know anything about cattle, period. Despite these inadequacies David liked the fellow. He discovered that Ian had a degree in law and commerce and some kind of diploma or degree in computer science.

'How did you come to do that sort of thing? I would have thought that with a McClymont mother, you would have stayed on the land,' David commented.

'I wanted to jackeroo, but Dad insisted I do law. He's a barrister in Melbourne. After Dad and Mum split up I resigned and went with her to Jimbawarra. I was glad I did because it meant that I learnt a fair bit from Grandad before he died,' Ian told him.

'What now?' David asked.

'I don't rightly know, Mr MacLeod. Mum's other sisters want their share of the estate and that means selling the property. They don't want to keep it and their husbands are all in good jobs. It would break Grandad's heart, and then there's the dogs. They're willed to me and I want to keep them going. Grandad loved his dogs, and I'm fond of them too. I'd like to learn how to handle them and maybe work in trials later on. If we sell the place, Mum's share wouldn't be sufficient to allow us to buy another property to eke a living from. It would be enough for her to invest and live on. I could always go back to Melbourne except my heart's not in it,' Ian said.

He talks well but what has he got in him? was David's thought. He would soon find out. 'Look, I have to go and look at cattle. Do you want a riding lesson?'

'Crikey, yes,' Ian said enthusiastically. It was the greatest response David had seen from him since he arrived.

'Right. I'll put you up on one of Catriona's old mares. She's foolproof, so you should be able to manage her,' David assured him.

David called in at the house and told Catriona that he and Ian were going off to look at cattle and would be back for lunch.

'Riding?' she asked.

'Riding,' he said.

'Ian can't ride. He told me he couldn't,' she said.

'He wants to learn. I'll put him on Clover,' David replied.

Moira came back from feeding at Glen Morrison to discover that her father and Ian had gone off somewhere on horses. Moira wasn't happy – she knew very well that Ian had come up to see her and the very first morning her father had gone off with him alone. But knowing her father as she did, she knew he would have done it for some very good reason.

After they had ridden for some time and looked at the cattle on the lower country, David saw Ian begin to shift in the saddle. 'Bottom getting a bit sore?' he asked.

'A bit.'

'We'll head back for the creek and put on the billy,' David said.

'We don't have a billy,' Ian replied.

'There's one at the creek. In fact there's a billy at several places, Ian. When you're run in a bit, I'll take you up to Wallaby Rocks and show you the big cave where I sheltered with the dogs and some sheep during the big fire.'

'I read about that in Grandad's scrapbook,' Ian said. 'You had Nap and Clancy with you.'

'That's right. It was also where I proposed to Catriona. It's some cave.'

He took the saddles off the horses and spread the saddlecloths on the ground.

'Stretch out there for a while, and I'll boil the billy,' he said.

Ian eased himself onto the saddlecloths and sighed with relief. 'I'm stiffer than I thought I'd be.'

'Most people are the first time. You should talk to my mother. Dad brought her out here and she felt very stiff that first time. She had a hot bath and felt better after that. Next time she was better and in no time she was riding everywhere,' David told him. He handed him an enamel mug and a couple of Anzac biscuits.

'Where did these come from?' Ian asked.

'From my saddlebag. I put them there this morning,' David said.

After Ian had drunk his tea and consumed the biscuits which, David noted, he did with relish, he looked much brighter.

'You know what you should do, Ian,' David said.

'No, what, Mr MacLeod?'

'You should take your clothes off and have a splash around in the creek. Best thing out for stiffness and soreness,' David suggested.

Ian looked up and down the creek. 'It would be pretty cold, wouldn't it? And I don't have a towel.'

'Cold is the shot. What do they do for footballers when something goes wrong? Whack on ice. You can use the top side of your saddlecloth to dry yourself. And there's nobody here to look at you.'

Only you, Ian thought. And if there is a more formidable man anywhere I haven't met him. Nevertheless, it would look wimpish not to do as his host suggested and he *was* very stiff. And there was still the ride home.

'Good heavens,' Catriona squealed as she watched the two men by the creek. The powerful glasses brought them into sharp focus.

'What is it, Mum?'

'Ian is going into the creek. He's in the altogether. Want a look?' Catriona said playfully.

Moira reached for the glasses and laid them beside her. 'No, I don't want to spy on him.'

'No doubt about your father, Moira. David will try him out,' Catriona said, with a shake of her head.

'I'll kill him,' Moira said.

But she was as sweet as apple pie when her father and Ian arrived back for lunch. As soon as lunch was over Moira took Ian by the hand and led him out of the room. 'Ian wants to have a look at our rams, Dad. We'll see you later,' she said sweetly.

David had been going to give Ian a shearing lesson, after which he intended working a dog, but Moira had beaten him to the punch. He decided to go and see how Marilyn was getting on with his mother and Linda. Anne had asked her there for lunch. He told Catriona he was going to the woolshed, and he did go there later but he went to his mother's first.

It seemed that the three women were getting on just fine. They were all intensely practical, commonsense women so why wouldn't they get on, he thought. He went back to the woolshed and pressed a couple of bales of wool before going back to Catriona.

'You smell of sheep or wool,' she said.

'Well, I'm not getting changed before evening,' he said firmly. 'Marilyn is getting on well with Mum and Linda,' he said.

'Did you expect her not to?'

'No, but one never knows with people,' he said. 'I might have a drink of tea and then run down to Strath Fillan.'

'Very well. I'll put the kettle on,' she sighed.

'What is it, Cat? Are you not feeling well?' he asked.

'I'm having some problems setting out the book, David. There are too many interruptions for one thing. You lay things out and then you have to leave them for something or other,' she said.

'I can get the tea,' he said.

'I have a lot of work ahead of me and perhaps you'll

594

think I'm neglecting you. I won't neglect you, David. I would never neglect you. I promise,' she said.

'Go your hardest, Cat.' He reckoned she would be distracted until she got the book written. He could see that it was something she felt compelled to do.

'Thank you,' she said, and put her arms around his neck and kissed him. 'And thank you for being so wonderful on the trip. I meant to tell you before now but we have been rather busy. It was even better than the first honeymoon. I hope you got something out of it,' she said.

'I got quite a lot out of it and you know that damned well,' he said and grinned. Catriona blushed and turned away. 'I hope you're not going to put any of those episodes in your book, Cat,' he added.

'Of course not. The Scottish part will be about a different period,' she said.

'That's a relief. Do you think it's a goer with Moira and Ian?'

'There's something there, darling. Why don't we just wait and see?' Catriona said.

'I suppose so. Ian might make something. He needs knocking into shape for this game,' David said. 'It seems he's a computer expert as well as a lawyer and that could be a plus,' he added.

'It will be Moira's decision, not ours, darling. I know you don't want to lose her but she must have a life of her own. I think Ian is rather sweet,' she said.

'Sweet? What do you mean *sweet*?' he asked with a frown.

'Ian is somewhat unusual for a man, dear. He's a little shy but there's quite a bit to him below the surface. I understand he's very clever. He doesn't smoke and he doesn't drink. I think he would make a very understanding husband,' Catriona said.

The Riverina visitors stayed a fortnight, during which time David and Moira staged a battle of wits for Ian Taylor's company. David mostly won because Moira was disadvantaged by living at Glen Morrison. When David didn't have Ian on a horse or on a handpiece they were away working dogs. Moira was furious with her father, but realised there was more to his behaviour than he was letting on.

A month after Marilyn and Ian left for the Riverina Ian came back. He told them that they were putting Jimbawarra on the market because if they didn't do it willingly, there would be legal proceedings against his mother. He had advised her to sell the place. It was a blow, but there it was.

David sensed that there was more Ian wanted to say so he took him up to the woolshed where they sat side by side on wool bales.

'Get it off your chest, Ian,' David told him.

'Get what off my chest?' Ian asked.

'Whatever it is that's bothering you.'

'I want to marry Moira,' Ian said.

'What does she have to say?' David asked.

'She hasn't said yes or no. I think she wants to talk to you,' Ian said. 'I think she wants to know what you think about it. About me,' he added hastily.

'Good heavens. It's her life and her decision, Ian.'

'I understand that, but I get the impression that if you don't like the idea of having me for your son-in-law that might influence her decision,' Ian said.

There was no doubt that women took the cake, David thought. Once Moira was all set to throw herself away on a mongrel like Gary Trainor yet she was baulking at a decent fellow like Ian Taylor. He had no doubt that Ian would make something of himself wherever he was. But if he married Moira, David wanted him here.

'I don't have a lot of money, Mr MacLeod. Not by your standards. Mum would give me something from the sale of the place and I have some money saved up. I could earn good money if I went back to Melbourne but Moira wouldn't want to do that,' he said.

'Do you love Moira?' David asked.

'Oh, yes. I love her all right. Moira is the first girl I feel I really connect with, Mr MacLeod.'

'We'll talk more after I talk to Moira,' David said.

Moira and David talked down in the ram shed next morning. They sat on bales of lucerne hay and while he chewed a straw his daughter told him that Ian had asked her to marry him.

'So?'

'I haven't said yes and I haven't said no,' she said.

'Why? Don't you love Ian?'

'I nearly made one bad mistake and you got me out of it. I realise I was carried away by Gary's charisma and that I didn't really love him at all. I don't want to make the same mistake again. It's terribly important to me that you like the man I marry,' she said.

'Gary Trainor isn't fit to be in the same country as Ian Taylor,' David replied. He saw her face lighten and pressed on. 'Do you love Ian?'

'I think I do ... quite a lot,' she said.

'What else, Moy?' he asked.

'I don't want to leave you, Dad. Not even for Ian. My life is here.'

'Then you don't love Ian enough to marry him,' David replied. 'If you love him you will go wherever he wants to go. That's a wife's duty. Cat would have left home to marry me. No, you can't love Ian enough or you wouldn't hesitate.'

'It isn't a black-and-white thing, Dad. I'm scared. The mothers of half my girlfriends are divorced or separated. Marilyn is a warm, generous lady and she's separated from her husband. Ian seems to be a good man, but what if he's not? Love has messed up the lives of countless women. You're the only man I trust implicitly. I can stay here and not risk anything,' Moira said.

'Most girls can't leave their parents quick enough to do their own thing, Moy. Don't you want a family?' he asked.

'Yes, I want a family, but you don't have to be married to have children. There are clinics where you can go to get pregnant,' she said.

'I wouldn't be in favour of you doing that sort of

thing, Moy. No way. Look, I don't want to lose you from the operation here. You've been for me the son I expected Dougal would be, and more. That's a big thing to say about a girl. But I'd be the worst kind of father if I put my interests before yours. So where do we stand? Are you going to say yes or no?' he asked.

'I'll marry Ian if you can find a place for him here, Dad,' she said softly.

David found it hard to conceal his jubilation. He had had to make her say those words. It had to be her decision.

'So you want to have your cake and eat it too?' he asked.

'That's what I want, Dad. If anything goes wrong I want to have you behind me,' she said.

His daughter had just paid him one of the greatest compliments he had ever received. Being a good dog handler, even a legendary handler, and a good stock-man, was all right, but being a good parent was something else.

'Ah well, between the two of us, we ought to be able to knock Ian into shape, Moy,' he said with a grin.

She put her arms around his neck and kissed him. 'Thank you, Dad.'

'Dixon's place adjoining Glen Morrison is on the market. I might try and buy it. We'll need a bit more land here if Ian is going to come aboard. I could farm a fair bit of Dixon's and grow more grain for our own use. Ian could become the farmer of the outfit.' He didn't tell her that he had already taken an option on Dixon's. He hadn't been going to buy any more property because by any standards he had sufficient but having a son-in-law made a difference. If Ian came good it would be almost as good as having an extra son. 'I had better go and put Ian out of his misery and you had better talk to your mother, Moy.'

David found Ian talking to Catriona about computer programs. He winked at Catriona and then told Ian that he wanted to show him something.

The two men walked up the track to the dog yards where they sat down on Nap's log. There were magpies carolling in the trees overhead and from up in Jimmy's Paddock they could hear crows cawing raucously. 'This is the drill, Ian. Moira will marry you if she can stay here. She's asked me to find a place for you. I can do that but it's up to you whether you want to accept Moira on those terms. I put it to her that it seemed as if she wanted to have her cake and eat it too. I said that it was a wife's duty to go wherever her husband wants to go and that if she loves you, that's what she should do. But the thing is that Moira had a near miss with a fellow who wasn't worth your little finger. There's also the fact that, like it or not, your parents are separated – as are at least half of the parents of Moira's school friends. Moira is just a wee bit scared about what might happen if she's made a mistake about you. She wants to be here because she trusts me and knows that I'll always be here for her,' David said.

'I can understand that, Mr MacLeod. I'm not too happy about my parents being separated. I appreciate that things are different now to what they used to be but I would sincerely hope that Moira and I never want to separate. Moira is the best thing that has ever happened to me.'

'There's another aspect to consider. Would you have any problem working with me? I'm not the easiest man to work with, as you've probably decided. If I think you're making a mess of something I'll damn soon tell you. If you can wear what I dish out, I'll make something of you,' David said.

'Grandad told me you were the best and fairest man he knew, Mr MacLeod. I know I've got a lot to learn. I'm not lazy and I think I'll be able to handle what you dish out,' Ian said with a smile.

'That's the spirit,' David said, and clapped Ian on the shoulder.

'I'll have Moira on any terms, Mr MacLeod. Now, can you really find a place for me here?' Ian asked a mite anxiously.

'I'm looking to buy the place next to Glen Morrison, Ian. I have actually put a down payment on it but I didn't tell Moira. I thought it might do for a kind of, well, wedding present. It's a decent place with a good house on it. The people who own it are too old to work it properly. I think it could be farmed a bit more. I use a lot of grain and it would be handy to grow our own.'

'In that case I'd be happier if you'd allow me to

provide some of the money to purchase this place. Mum is going to give me some money when she sells Grandad's place, probably a couple of hundred thousand. I know it wouldn't get near what you probably have to fork out but it would make me feel I have contributed something in my own right. I don't want to come here entirely dependent on you, Mr MacLeod. I've heard of men who married their way into money and property and I don't want you to think I'm one of that breed. I'd like to feel that I've made a financial commitment to your grazing empire. It wouldn't be a lot when compared with the money you've got tied up in property and stock, but it would still make me feel better,' Ian said, and gave David a sheepish grin. 'I think Moira would approve too,' he added.

'I appreciate your point of view, Ian. If that's what you want to do, I'll go along with it. I'll talk to my legal eagles about whether I can put Dixon's place in your and Moira's name. You'll own it and maybe I can lease it back so that the stock and grain off the place can be worked in with the overall operation. You'll have to discuss with Moira where you want to live. Glen Morrison is the better house and you can live there if you prefer it. If your mother would like to say in the bush she might like to live at Dixon's. You should talk that over with Moira as the mother-in-law thing sometimes worries new brides.'

'You seem to have thought of everything, Mr MacLeod. And Mum and Moira appear to get on very well,' Ian said. 'Mum hasn't said what she wants to do after we sell the property. There's a lot of things to do to tidy up everything. Once we decide where Moira and I are going to live I want to build a decent set of dog pens so I can bring Grandad's dogs up here. Crikey, I've got a lot to learn.'

'Knowing that you've got a lot to learn is the first step, Ian. Between Moira, myself and the rest of us we'll soon have you firing. You'll be competing at our local sheepdog trials in a year or two. And you couldn't have a much better judge of sheep and cattle than Moira. She's better than most men. Angus is good too, and he's an excellent dog handler. You get on well with him, don't you?'

'Extra good, Mr MacLeod. He and Sue-Ellen have been great. Dougal worries me a little as he's a bit overpowering. I feel very inadequate alongside him.'

'You shouldn't. I'm told that you're a very smart fellow in your own field. Some vets have a very inflated view of their own importance. There's others that haven't and are very down-to-earth fellows. Dougal is a brilliant fellow but he's a pain in the neck at times. Dougal and I don't hit it off as well as we should. I suppose I'm a lot to blame for that because I had built my hopes on him coming back here after he left school. There's more to it than that but enough said for now. Dougal is well on his way to being a very wealthy fellow so he's better off financially than Angus or Moira. They get a salary out of the total proceeds but it's nothing like the money

Dougal earns. Of course, he did years of study to get where he is now.'

'What is your candid opinion of the state of agriculture?' Ian asked. 'You've got a hell of a lot of money invested in land and stock so you must be concerned with its profitability?'

'Candidly, you'd probably earn more money at your caper than you will here. I'm not getting a very good return for the money I've got outlaid in property and stock. The wiseacre economists tell us that we have to look at farming as a business rather than a way of life. There's some sense in that notion but if we adhered strictly to it there would be a massive exodus of people from the land. In strictly financial terms, I would be far better off if I sold everything and invested the money. But what would I do? And where would that leave Angus and Moira and the people who have worked for me for years? Where would the bush be if all the people who know and love it pulled out because they aren't making much money?

'The way I look at it is that if I can get some return from the properties and have a good life while I'm doing it, I'll carry on. Farming is a very worthwhile occupation, Ian. It can be damned hard too because no season is the same, and Australian costs have gone through the roof. But understanding how to produce top-quality merino wool is just as much a science as any form of science. Right now the emphasis is on fine wool and we've got to try and produce it while maintaining fleece weight. We need to produce softer wool so the prickle factor is important. We've got these things well in hand here but it's taken years to do it.

'Sure, there are problems and the politicians aren't helping us. In many cases they're simply an impediment to progress, Ian. They talk about what they're doing for farmers but in many cases they've been responsible for some of the problems they're now trying to fix. The biggest problem of all is that there is no long-term plan for Australian agriculture. Some of the grower organisations have been less than impressive, too. The wool industry is just one example and then there's the grain mess and the dairy deregulation which is going to put hundreds of dairy farmers out of business. It took us two hundred years to get a grading system for beef and whether it's the right one is a matter for argument. I could go on and on. Basically, a lot of our problems stem from government decisions.

'The thing is that I don't know any other game,' David continued. 'And I like livestock. I also like working stock with good dogs and good horses. It's a more satisfying life for me than being stuck in an office and driving to work in city traffic. Maybe I'm a dinosaur, but I'll stay with the land for the time I have left to me. I've put together a fair whack of property and I'm keeping several families. On top of that I'm contributing in a fairly big way to quite a few businesses that need farmers to survive. The long and short of it is that you have to want to do it, Ian.

If you're lukewarm about the land, or lazy, you shouldn't take it on. Now, you had better go and collect Moira so you can bring her up to the house to give Catriona the news. I'll go and tell my mother.'

David left his future son-in-law and walked to the old homestead. He was whistling as he climbed up the steps, which always indicated that he was feeling very happy about something. His mother and Linda were in the kitchen, making some concoction together.

'You sound jaunty,' Anne said to him as he burst into the room.

'You haven't heard it but there is going to be a wedding in the not-too-distant future. Moira will want to break the news to you so please play dumb. I shouldn't let on but I reckon you'll be pleased, Mum.'

'And of course it's Ian?' Anne said.

'It is Ian,' he said.

'Oh, how splendid! Ian is such a nice young man. If only Bruce were here to hear this news,' she said, with warmth in her voice.

'And Moira will be staying here too,' he said, and helped himself to what was left of the morning smoko. He sat down and ate a piece of cake and watched the Mixmaster whirr into action. Catriona was a beaut woman but she couldn't get near his mother when it came to making cakes. Presently he got up and walked to the door.

'Must go, Mum. Lots to do. For your ears only, Bruce did have a hand in this romance,' he said as he hurried out the door. He was whistling as he skipped down the steps and continued past the dog yard.

Anne looked at Linda with a glimmer in her eye. 'No wonder David is so pleased with himself – he is going to acquire the extra son he always wanted while also keeping Moira here.'

'I'm very pleased for him,' Linda said. 'David has been so very good to us.'

'He has been a wonderful son, Linda. If he had not been so special I would have missed not having a daughter even more. You were so fortunate to have five children, Linda.'

'I didn't think so when I was left to rear them, Anne. It was tough raising them on my own. I was fortunate that Tim and then Kitty were such a big help with the younger ones. They were such a lively bunch when they were younger. But when one sees the problems some parents have, one has to be thankful for five normal, healthy children,' Linda said.

Ian and Moira drove down the track just as David reached his front gate. He waited for them to get out and then followed them up the path to the homestead.

'Moira has something to tell you, Cat,' David said as they walked into the lounge.

'Mum, Ian and I are engaged,' Moira said in a rush of words.

'Well, that is good news,' Catriona said and kissed them both.

'And we'll be living here. I believe Dad is giving us Dixon's as a wedding present.'

'Less a couple of hundred thousand, which Ian is going to contribute to its purchase,' David said. 'So you'll have a wedding to organise, Cat. That and the book ought to keep you busy.'

'And I suppose your only contribution will be to act the role of the proud father on the day,' Catriona mocked.

'I'll be contributing a bit more than that, sweetheart,' he said, and thought about what Dixon's was going to cost him. The house would have to be renovated and painted on top of that, and then there was the cost of the wedding. But there was only one daughter so he had to make a job of the wedding. He hoped Moira wouldn't want it in Sydney because if she did a lot of their friends probably wouldn't go. Some couldn't afford to go.

'We had better have a little preliminary talk about how you want it done, Moira. Put the jug on would you please, David,' Catriona said. She flashed him the smile she had perfected over the years. It implied a lot and usually signified that she was very well pleased with something he had done.

'Isn't it a bit early for that?' Moira asked.

'I suppose it is, but I'd like to have a general idea of what you would like. We need to think about booking a church and reception place,' Catriona replied.

'I'll talk to Ian and see if he has any ideas,' Moira said, and gave him a quick smile.

'Traditionally the planning of a wedding has very little to do with the bridegroom, darling. We have to do the organising. You can talk to Ian about where you spend your honeymoon – that's his responsibility. Of course, you could always go to the house at Yeppoon, but Ian may have grander ideas. Does Ian know about the house we have there?' Catriona asked.

'As a matter of fact, he doesn't. There have been too many other things to discuss. I didn't get around to mentioning it,' Moira said.

'I'd like to take Moira somewhere really special,' Ian said. 'I'm sure the Yeppoon house is very nice but I'd like to go to some place she hasn't been to before.'

Catriona thought of her own honeymoon at the Yeppoon house. She had waited years for David and to finally have him to herself had been sheer bliss. He had surprised her with his loving and his attentiveness those early heavenly weeks of their marriage. She had told him so at the close of their second week at Yeppoon. 'You're a surprise packet, David MacLeod,' she had said, resting on one elbow and looking down at him.

'How so?' he asked sleepily.

'I didn't think you would be so, so . . .'

'So what, Cat?'

'Well, so loving. It doesn't go with your tough bushy image.'

David had laughed and pulled her down to him. 'Funny you should say that, Cat. Three people told me I had to forget about everything but you. They all told me, in different ways mind you, how I should treat you. As if they needed to tell me.'

'Who told you, David?'

'Dad, Mum and Kate, sweetheart. Who else? Mum and Kate gave me the drill from your side of things and Dad added a few extra details. He had never spoken to me about that sort of thing – Mum did all that. The first time was after I had the fight with Stanley Masters and before Jane gave me that party.'

Catriona dragged herself back to the present. 'I had a lovely honeymoon at the Yeppoon house. It was wonderful, wasn't it, David?'

'Fantastic, sweetheart. And then we went over to Aberfeldy and cut out cattle for a few days. I suppose you could say that I had the rough and the smooth of things,' he said with a broad grin.

'David,' Catriona protested.

'Dad, that was naughty of you,' Moira added.

Ian appeared lost for words.

'I can recommend the Yeppoon house, Ian. Cat and I were very happy there and it won't cost you a red cent into the bargain. If Cat and Moira are going to talk wedding, you and I can push off. I want to talk to you about those dog pens you want to build. If you're going to live at Dixon's, you can put them up there. But if you're going to live at Glen Morrison, they'll have to be built well away from the other buildings.'

He put down his cup and stood up. 'Let's hit the track, Ian.'

The two women watched them walk down the path. 'Ian will get jolly tired of hearing David's "let's hit the track",' Catriona said.

'Oh, I don't know. The others all stood up to it fairly well. Even Sarah.'

'Sarah would have tolerated anything David said ... or did. Poor Sarah. They'll all have to come to the reception, Moira. Let's start on a list. I'll put down who I think should come and you can add the people you want.'

'Very well, Mum,' Moira said patiently, glowing from the events of the day.

Chapter Twenty-three

Catriona had assumed that her own vision for Moira's wedding would be approved by her daughter without much argument. She soon discovered, however, that when it came to nailing down the essential details Moira had very firm ideas from which she could not be budged.

Mother and daughter had completely different views about where the wedding should be held. Catriona wanted the actual ceremony held in Sydney, which Moira vetoed immediately. She had spoken to her father and his view on the matter matched her own – the wedding should be held in the country. If St David's in Merriwa wasn't large enough to accommodate the number of people likely to attend, then they could hold the ceremony in Scone. Like David, Moira was concerned that a lot of people who would like to see her married wouldn't be able to afford a weekend in Sydney. Well, they might be able to afford it but it was likely to be an extravagance they'd prefer to avoid. There was

Greg and Liz and Shaun and the Barden boys, but most of all there was Anne. A trip to Sydney would be too trying for Nanna. Catriona argued her case but lost. The wedding would be in Scone.

Catriona thought that the reception should be held in a hall in either Merriwa or Scone. Moira, however, wanted it held in a marquee at home. Where exactly, she hadn't decided, but definitely at home. Large marquees were available, some of them lined with silk and designed especially for wedding receptions, and these were commodious enough to accommodate the number of guests they planned to invite, as well as a band and a dance floor.

David said that although High Peaks had the most sentimental appeal for siting a marquee, there wasn't enough flat ground to peg it out. The reception would have to be held at either Poitrel or Glen Morrison, and David favoured the latter. It had the grandest homestead and there was a large area of well-grassed flat ground alongside it that was perfect for a marquee. It had plenty of parking space into the bargain. These were sound reasons, but one reason David didn't give for hosting the reception at Glen Morrison was that there would be a number of guests from interstate who hadn't seen his prized stud bulls and rams. These were housed only a couple of hundred metres from the Glen Morrison homestead, and David reckoned it was a safe bet that some of the keener land people would end up in the sheds looking at his livestock. This could mean a sale or two.

It wasn't that he was money-mad, but the fact was that as things were on the land now, you couldn't afford to neglect the chance of making a sale. Stud breeding was a very competitive business and you had to be on the job all the time.

The only issue Catriona and Moira agreed upon was *the dress*. Unlike some of her friends who had opted for off-the-shoulder wedding dresses, Moira had her heart set on an older-style gown along the lines of her mother's. She had dressed up in her mother's wedding gown on more than one occasion and had a very good idea how she would look in a similar dress. The heavy satin gown with its opalescent overtones had become slightly discoloured and lost its lusture so she couldn't use her mother's original dress, but was determined to model her own dress on its style.

Catriona and Moira looked at wedding dresses from Muswellbrook to Newcastle only to return to High Peaks without one. Catriona had been much luckier. Her mother-of-the-bride outfit was a cinnamon–gold lace dress with matching accessories. David expressed enough interest in it to ask if he could have a preview, but Catriona told him he would have to wait until the day of the wedding.

The two women went back to Newcastle and looked at shops in new suburbs and old without finding the kind of dress Moira had set her heart on. After several fruitless hours they walked down a small arcade in search of a place to have a cup of tea and a sandwich before making the return drive to Merriwa. Right at the end of the arcade they found a boutique they hadn't previously visited. Both women pulled up dead at what they saw in the window. A single dress was spotlighted in the shop's foreground falling to the floor in perfect folds. The dress's satin body lining was overlaid by a shimmering, transparent, gossamer-like organza. Tiny pearls covered the almost butterfly, puff sleeves, which came to just above the elbow. Clear organza adorned by a delicate swirl of lace flowers extended from below the elbow and tapered to the wrist. The bodice was nipped at the waist and billowed out to a full skirt and long wide train. Semi-circular trails of lacy organza flowers were featured at intervals on back and front to the hemline. Transparent organza joined the small lace collar to the bust line.

'Crikey, what a dress,' Moira said. 'Do you think it's my size?'

Moira was five feet nine inches on the old scale and she had a bust to equal her mother's. If the dress fitted her, she had the figure to carry off the ornate gown.

'It might need some alterations but we won't know until you've tried it on,' Catriona told her.

There was one big snag – the shop was closed. A small card taped to the inside of the glass door informed prospective clients of the boutique that the shop would be closed until ten-thirty the following Monday.

'Blast,' Moira said. It was a word she had picked up from her father who sometimes used it very forcefully, and it caused her mother to frown. Moira's speech, in Catriona's opinion, occasionally lapsed into an earthiness that belied her boarding-school education.

'Don't fret, Moira. We've got the name of this boutique. We can track down the owners through Telstra and get them to hold the dress until we can get back here next Monday.'

Both women were mesmerised by the gown. Catriona was certain that Grandma Jane's milk opal brooch, which Catriona had worn at her own wedding, would look perfect pinned to the transparent neckline. They debated together whether a long or short veil would be preferable and, like most brides-to-be, Moira was getting well and truly caught up in her coming wedding.

'Exciting, isn't it, darling?' Catriona said.

Moira nodded. 'To think that everyone will be looking at me!'

'You will be a lovely bride, Moira, and David will be the proudest man in the country when he escorts you down the aisle. Dougal is very clever and Angus is very talented but you are David's crowning achievement. The fact that you want to stay here, to be with him, puts the icing on the cake for your father. That was why he reacted so strongly to your flirtation with Gary Trainor. It was something like waving a red rag at a bull, Moira.'

Moira wrinkled her pretty nose and grimaced. 'Don't remind me of that episode.'

'There's also the special fact that Anne is still here to be at your wedding. That will put a lot of gloss on the day for David, and will mean the world to your grandmother. You couldn't have had a better father, Moira. And you're so like him in so many ways.'

'And not like you, Mum?'

'Not much like me, dear. Except in figure.'

'I've been lucky in that department – unless I can't squeeze into that dress,' Moira said, and laughed.

'We'll cross that hurdle when we come to it, Moira,' Catriona replied, sensing her daughter's anxiety.

Catriona tracked down the owner of the boutique who assured her that the dress would be held for her if she could be sure she would be back at the shop on Monday morning. So Catriona and Moira drove back to Newcastle and Moira tried on the dress. It was too tight on her but Dell Cousins, the owner of the boutique, told her that it could be altered. As Catriona expected, the gown was very expensive. She paid a substantial deposit and made plans to return in a fortnight.

By the time they returned, the dress fitted perfectly. It was wrapped in tissue and boxed, and they took it back to High Peaks. Moira was enormously relieved that she had her dress and began to look at other matters relating to the wedding. Her bridesmaids were to be two special girlfriends from boarding-school days, Charlotte Bowers and Felicity McDonald. Charlotte had married early and Moira had been one of her bridesmaids. Felicity had spent some time overseas but was now with an advertising agency in North Sydney. Charlotte had a three-year old daughter, Kara, who was the obvious choice for flower girl. Charlotte would be matron of honour and Felicity her other bridesmaid. As both Charlotte and her daughter had auburn hair and Felicity was a brunette, certain colours were taboo. After conferring with her mother and both Charlotte and Felicity, Moira settled on aqua blue. Kara would wear a white organza frock with puffed sleeves and an aqua satin sash. David resolutely refused to consider wearing anything grander than a black dinner suit and Ian was easy on the matter of clothes, so that point was settled without fuss.

The catering again came up for discussion with suggestions that it be done by a professional catering company in Scone. Moira and David resisted strongly. David, with his pro-bush sentiments, wanted Merriwa people to do the catering. He suggested that rather than giving the job to one organisation, such as the RSL, the work be divided among the RSL, the bowling club and a small catering business run by a local woman. If any one of the three didn't agree, they didn't have to be involved. David wasn't going to have it said that he ignored the locals. It would be a big reception, big enough for the three organisations to get something out of it, and that was the way he wanted it. Of course, he got his way and nobody had cause to complain about the quality of the food. The reception would be held in a grand, silk-lined marquee and there would be a covered walkway connecting it to Glen Morrison homestead – a precautionary measure in case of rain. The marquee and coolroom were supplied by a Tamworth company.

There were a few extra details such as the hire of limousines to bring the bridal party back from Scone to Glen Morrison, and a band to play music for the dancing. David and Catriona didn't stint on anything because this would be their only opportunity to stage a wedding and they wanted it to be an unforgettable day for all who attended.

There were a great many other things to attend to – not the least of which was where relations were going to stay. Ian's best man was Greg Roper who had been with him at school, and his other groomsman was Lisle Weston who had been through law school with him. They were all going to stay at a Scone motel. David booked out the Merriwa motel for two nights because even with all the homesteads he had, there would not be enough accommodation for everyone without it. Ian's mother, Marilyn, and his sister Lynn, would be staying with David and Catriona, along with Charlotte and Felicity. On the Friday Moira and Catriona drove to Tamworth to pick them up from the airport and had their hair done while in the city.

It was a clear, almost cloudless spring day when the morning of Moira's wedding finally arrived. Catriona and Dougal arrived at the church some minutes before the bridal cars and, before entering the church on the arm of her eldest son, Catriona fussed over her daughter, ensuring Moira's train fanned behind her perfectly. Almost as soon as Catriona had slipped into the front pew beside Anne, Angus and Sue-Ellen, the organ burst forth triumphantly with the wedding march. Everyone in the church craned their necks for a first view of the wedding party, but more specifically the bride.

Almost bursting with the importance of her role, the little flower girl played her part like a professional, leading the bridesmaids up the aisle like a fairy. Charlotte and Felicity followed, each carrying a magnificent bouquet of Cécile Brünner roses. Eyes were misty as they turned to gaze on Ms Moira MacLeod and her handsome father. A shaft of light from the stained-glass windows high up in the church fell obliquely across the aisle as Moira, on her father's arm, glided forward, smiling and nodding at the admiring guests.

Moira was a vision of exquisite beauty. As tall as she was, her father topped her by several inches. Catriona's eyes shifted from her daughter to her husband, the love of her life. David looked so splendid even with the grey hair now thick at his temples. Her heart beat a little faster as she watched him pass her. She felt Anne's hand in hers and gave it a little squeeze, knowing her mother-in-law was filled with as much pride as she was.

Ian Taylor was full of pride and happiness as he turned to gaze at his lovely bride. It was almost like a fairytale, he thought for one fleeting moment. His grandfather had talked incessantly of David MacLeod and the MacLeods generally, and now, almost unbelievably, he was to marry David's only daughter. Moreover, he was to make his home not in Melbourne practising law, but in the high country as a member of the MacLeod family, with a stake in the High Peaks Pastoral Company. From when he was just a small boy he had wanted to be on the land, but had been forced to study law by his father. Now he was to be part of High Peaks and would learn how to work kelpies and the land, under David MacLeod's tutelage. He was to be brother-in-law to Dougal and Angus and a genuine member of the MacLeod family. He could hardly believe that Moira MacLeod, so beautiful and talented, was actually going to be his wife.

Others in the church had different thoughts. Anne was overwhelmed with pride as she watched her son and grand-daughter walk down the aisle. If Anne hadn't come to Merriwa all those years ago and not married Andy, they would not be here today. Andy would have been so proud of Moira. There was so much of Andy in David and Moira – in their height, their colouring and their bearing, but also in their character.

Moira paused ever so slightly when she reached the front pew, and her eyes dropped to meet her grand-mother's. She nodded almost imperceptibly before passing on to take her place beside Ian. It was a gen-erous gesture full of love, and Anne felt tears forming in her eyes.

Dougal MacLeod, the man who resembled his grandfather most of all, albeit only in looks, reckoned that his father had got what he had always wanted even if he had had to wait twenty-odd years longer than he had expected. In Ian Taylor his father had acquired his extra son. Dougal didn't mind because he was doing what he wanted to do and making good money. For Dougal, the outlook couldn't be brighter.

Angus and Sue-Ellen had been anxiously trying to keep young Andrew amused as Moira made her entrance. Sue-Ellen's own wedding had been a small affair when compared against Ian and Moira's, but she wasn't at all jealous of David and Catriona's extravaganza. She had her man and she had a lovely little boy who carried a name revered in the MacLeod family. Indeed, she was very pleased for Moira who had been a good friend to her from the first day she came to High Peaks. As for Angus, he reckoned that Ian Taylor was a very decent sort of fellow. He had to be for his father to agree to the marriage because every man and his dog knew how much David MacLeod thought of his only daughter. At last there would be another fellow to absorb the flak when things didn't go as well as his father thought they should.

A couple of rows further back two women had mixed feelings as they watched the bridal party ascend up the aisle. Susan Hunter (nee Cartwright) realised once again how very different her life would have been if she had married David MacLeod. He was still the most splendid man she had ever met and Catriona was so very fortunate to have him as her husband.

Sarah Matheson, the only young woman in the church who rivalled Moira in looks and figure, had one quick glance at Moira and then focused all her attention on David. David was the only man she had ever loved, and he had spoilt her for any other man. But she was full of happiness for Moira because Ian Taylor seemed a very nice man. Knowing David as she did, she couldn't believe that he would have sanctioned the wedding if he had any doubts about Ian. She wondered, though, how a lawyer would shape up at High Peaks.

For Moira and Ian, the ceremony itself passed in a blur. They made their vows to one another and Moira's hand trembled as Ian slipped the gold band over her finger – a symbol of their eternal love. As the newlyweds made their way down the aisle, with frequent stops to receive greetings of congratulations, the first low notes of bagpipes sounded. Two pipers, dressed in the yellow, black and red tartan of Clan MacLeod, took their cue from the minister who reached the porch just before Ian and Moira. The pipes burst forth triumphantly – the traditional piping of the newlyweds into their new life.

Outside the church the lovers were showered with rose petals and kisses as cameras flashed. The bridal limousines led the way back to Glen Morrison for the luncheon reception, followed by a great string of other vehicles.

It was a celebration the guests would remember for a long, long time. They first caught sight of the beautiful marquee as they made their way up the long, winding driveway. Appetisers and pre-dinner drinks were served on the wide verandah of the Glen Morrison homestead and the surrounding lawns, the nearby hills creating the perfect backdrop. But guests weren't officially greeted by David and Catriona until they made their way to the marquee for lunch.

The marquee looked like something from another world. White linen tablecloths dressed the large, long tables, and the finest silver and glassware made them sparkle. The walls were lined with tall jardinières of peach blossoms and other blooms, filling the marquee with perfume. More flowers graced the tables. The wedding cake had been proudly placed on a small table close to where the bridal party was to sit. There had been no need to go far afield for the cake – the Merriwa Show was testament to the culinary talents of the local ladies. It was a traditional three-tiered white cake decorated with delicate lacework in icing and fresh flowers.

Prawns, asparagus and oysters were served for entrees, followed by large roasted turkeys, baked hams and roast beef from a Glen Morrison steer, accompanied by a selection of salads and specially baked dinner loaves of brown and white bread. Then there were the desserts, if anyone had any space left for them – three kinds of ice creams to add to the fruit salad, pavlovas and strawberries. There was an amazing variety of drinks on offer, ranging from mineral water to Scotch, including a fine selection of Australian wines and several brands of beer. Being a bushie himself, David insisted that there be an ample supply of tea available, knowing how most country people liked to finish with a cuppa.

A happier afternoon could not have been possible, and both Moira and Ian were beaming from the arrival of the first guest till their own departure from the festivities. After many joyous speeches, the six-piece band roused guests to the dance floor. Both Susan and Sarah got to dance with David, but it was Catriona's arms he truly longed for.

As soon as he released Sarah, David made his way to

his wife who, as usual, looked stunning. The gold lace dress so became her that she took David's breath away.

'It was a very good thing that Anne and Kate insisted that you learn to dance,' she told him, as he piloted her about the floor.

'I agree now, but I didn't then,' he confessed, laughing. 'I didn't envisage that one day I would be dancing with a gorgeous lady in a gold lace dress,' he said.

Catriona laughed. 'You see how farsighted we women are, David,' she said.

'Hmmm.' His hand felt the silk lining beneath Catriona's lace gown. 'By the way, you feel terrific in that dress, Cat.'

'Thank you, darling.' David had told her that she not only looked gorgeous but also felt terrific. It was the kind of compliment that made her glow inside. It didn't matter what anyone else told her; it was what David said that mattered.

Later, after the newlyweds had left and the dancing and merriment had died down and a few amongst the crowd had slipped away, as David had predicted they would, to look at the MacLeod bulls and rams, David and Catriona left the others and took Anne and Linda back to the old High Peaks homestead that had been her home since her marriage.

'It has been such a magical day,' Anne said. 'You should both be congratulated. You gave Ian and Moira a lovely wedding.'

'Yes, a beautiful wedding,' Linda agreed. 'Moira

looked absolutely divine, and everyone could see how proud both of you were of her. I never saw a prouder father make his way down an aisle.'

'I'd say David has come out of it very well,' Catriona said.

'What do you mean, Catriona?' Anne asked.

'Moira is going to stay here and Ian is the extra son David always wanted. Furthermore he's got another dog crank to maintain Bruce McClymont's kelpies and his own. If that wasn't enough, he's just sold a bull for enough money to nearly cover the cost of the wedding,' Catriona said.

'You make it sound as if it were all planned,' Anne said, and stole a look at her son.

'Well of *course* it was planned. David and Bruce dreamed it up on Bruce's last trip. Bruce brought Ian to Jimbawarra with the object of introducing him to Moira. I'm yet to determine which one of them actually initiated the idea, though I'm inclined to favour David. What a pair of plotters. Well, their scheming worked, though it's sad it wasn't until Bruce's funeral that Ian and Moira met. David is so pleased with himself – he'll be hard to live with in future.'

After David and Catriona had left, Anne told Linda the real story. 'It was me, Linda, who suggested to Bruce that he try and introduce Ian to Moira. Bruce told me that Ian was fed-up with living in Melbourne and wanted to come back to Jimbawarra. Bruce thought it was a great idea and put it up to David, who agreed wholeheartedly.'

'So you were the initial matchmaker?' Linda said with a smile.

'Yes, I was. Bruce McClymont was a very nice man, Linda. A very honourable man. Bruce told me all about Ian and how keen he was on the dogs and that his father had more or less forced him to do law. It was a shame, as Catriona said, that Moira had to meet Ian by way of Bruce's funeral but look what came out of it. Bruce would be chuckling now. Once Ian begins to know the ropes, David may be able to ease up a little. I don't want him working forever. Work killed Andy, and I don't want it to kill David. Perhaps being responsible for getting Ian here may prove to be the last thing I can do for my son,' Anne said.

'So now there's only Dougal to get settled,' Linda said.

'I'm not at all worried about Dougal. He has his vocation and thanks to his skill and Starana, Dougal is well on the way to becoming a wealthy man. Dougal will be all right, Linda. I could wish that he and his father were closer, but they will always be very different men. Ian may make up for the loss of Dougal. Well – not quite, but almost.'

'Ian wants to learn and that makes the difference,' Linda encouraged. 'He couldn't have a better teacher than David.'

'If Ian can stand up to David, he'll be all right, Linda. David has his faults. I have never been blind to them. He is intolerant of people who don't come up to his high standards. David is still living largely by

Andy's standards. Marriage softened him a little, but he is still a wee bit hard at times. He isn't perfect, Linda.

'David has been a lovely son in many ways and he has given me a great deal of joy but he is now so busy he hardly has time for anything but the properties. He used to love to trial his dogs but he has no time for that now. There are eight properties now because David wants to leave a legacy for his children. I would be far happier if he sold most of them, invested his money and did a bit of trialling. I might as well talk to the man on the moon as to David because he won't listen to me.'

'David is very kind and very generous, and has been very good to my family,' Linda said.

'I worry David has become too big, Linda. He has a lot of money invested in properties and stock and it's a big responsibility. The land was never easy and it's not easy now. Bad times are a way of life in Australia and there needs to be a better recognition of that. But I've talked too much and now I must go and have a little lie-down,' Anne said.

She lay down for an hour or so, made a cup of tea and took it out to the front verandah. From here she could see much of her garden. The native plants had brought birds galore and the garden was usually full of birdsong. Away in the distance Yellow Rock towered above the countryside. It was all very familiar and very comforting. Clouds draped the mountain and there was a forecast of rain for the next day. It wouldn't matter now that the wedding was over, and they usually needed rain.

A man walked up the track and Anne felt her heart beat faster. It looked like Andy.

'Hello, Nanna. How are you after your big day?' Dougal asked.

So it wasn't Andy. It would be Andy next time.

David had changed into working clothes after leaving his mother and Linda. Before feeding his dogs he made his way to the tree-shrouded knoll where his father, grandmother and Kate were buried. He had erected a substantial seat made of bush timber in keeping with the nature of the place. It faced the three headstones that were inscribed with the modest details of the three people buried on the knoll. From here David saw Dougal's Land Cruiser come up the road and stop outside his mother's house. He turned back to his father's grave and looked down at it.

'Well, it all went off all right, Dad. We've got a lawyer in the family now. He doesn't know much about the bush but I think he's a trier and he's keen on the dogs. I reckon that between Moira and me we'll make something of him. You'd have been real proud of Moira today, Dad. If she's like me, as everyone says, then she's a lot like you too. She's a great judge of stock and she'll be judging a Royal Show any day now.

'Ian is a computer whizz too, Dad. I don't understand computers, but they make record-keeping a lot easier. You wouldn't realise how big our show is now, Dad. There's eight properties. They would have kept you busy, because they're keeping me busy. But it's time for me to feed the dogs, Dad. They're still okay. I'll talk to you again soon.'

He came down off the knoll and walked up the track to feed his dogs. He was a millionaire but he still liked to take the time to feed his dogs when he could and to sit on Nap's log and watch them eat. As he sat there he reckoned that his father's spirit had never left High Peaks. It was so tangible a thing that he could almost feel his father's presence. And perhaps in death his father and Bruce McClymont were reunited and making up for the lost years. He liked to think so. If that were not so, why was there an Iona?

He stood up and looked at Yellow Rock. He wondered how Ian would handle the mountain. But that was some way down the track and he wouldn't push the boy too hard. He reckoned Ian Taylor would be all right. He had damn well better be all right because eight – and soon to be nine – properties took a lot of managing. Things were getting tougher and many farmers couldn't handle the rate of change.

As David walked back down the track he saw that Catriona was standing at the front gate waiting for him. She had changed from her lovely gold lace frock to her favourite oyster-grey stretch slacks and blouse. He knew now that Catriona and the bond they shared together was his greatest asset. He had a great mother, a fine daughter, one not-so-bad son in Angus, another son who was brilliant but difficult, and several loyal employees who were almost family. But it was Catriona who knew him best. Catriona knew that he went up onto the knoll to talk to his father and she knew that he wanted to do it alone. He knew that if he had to sell up everything he owned, which of course he didn't, and he had Catriona, he would be happy.

Catriona held out her hand to him and he took it and then put one arm around her waist. Together they walked up the path to the house. At the steps she turned and faced him. 'You've never been sorry you married me, have you, darling?' she asked.

He shook his head and smiled at her. 'Of course not. I was thinking as I walked down the track and saw you waiting by the gate that if I had to sell up everything and still had you, I would be happy.'

'For a man who once considered me a little pest, your view has certainly moderated.'

'Ah well, little pests grow up. Some of them grow into lovely creatures. Then there's always one that becomes the queen. You're my queen, Cat.'

Catriona's smile lit up the evening. 'Come inside, darling. I've got a story I'd like you to read.'

The Call of the High Country
Tony Parsons

In the heart of Australia's rugged high country, three generations of the MacLeod family battle to make a living on the land.

As a young married couple, Andrew and Anne work together to make the very best of their property, High Peaks, but at what cost to their happiness?

In time the property will pass to their son, David. Handsome and hardworking, he is determined to become the best sheepdog handler in the land. Nothing is going to stand in his way – not even the beautiful Catriona Campbell, daughter of the wealthy graziers next door.

An inspiring and heartwarming saga of a family battling through hard times, of a love that defies all odds, and of dreams that won't be broken.

'A true-blue Aussie saga of family trials and tribulations, success and sheepdogs, love and luck. Outback romance addicts will find it just right,'

Australian Women's Weekly

Jessica
Bryce Courtney

Jessica is based on the inspiring true story of a young girl's fight for justice against tremendous odds. A tomboy, Jessica is the pride of her father, as they work together on the struggling family farm. One quiet day, the peace of the bush is devastated by a terrible murder. Only Jessica is able to save the killer from the lynch mob – but will justice prevail in the courts?

Nine months later, a baby is born ... with Jessica determined to guard the secret of the father's identity. The rivalry of Jessica and her beautiful sister for the love of the same man will echo throughout their lives – until finally the truth must be told.

Set in the harsh Australian bush against the outbreak of World War I, this novel is heartbreaking in its innocence, and shattering in its brutality.

'A deserved best seller, based on fact, a story told with heartbreaking honesty.'
Australian Women's Weekly

Pieces of Blue
Kerry McGinnis

'What about it, kids? Shall we head out for the bush and a bit o' freedom?'

So starts the story of a remarkable journey.

At the age of six, Kerry McGinnis loses her mother. Her grief-stricken father, Mac, is left with four young children to raise. After a desperate attempt to manage alone, Mac gathers up his family and leaves the city to go droving.

For the next fifteen years, the McGinnis clan travels the continent, droving, horse breaking and living off the land. Schoolrooms, comfort and civilisation are a long way off as Kerry grows up in the harsh outback, where the animals are often her closest friends. Wild adventures and strange encounters colour their days, and by night their father tells tall tales around the campfire.

With the memory of her absent mother ever present, Kerry begins her difficult journey to young womanhood. In this stirring memoir, Kerry McGinnis gives us a sometimes tragic, sometimes hilarious but always passionate depiction of the ending of childhood and the beginning of adult life.

'This is a beautifully written collection of fragments, vivid but tantalising snapshots of McGinnis's life.'
Sydney Morning Herald